Helen Phifer is the #1 bestselling crime and horror novelist of the *Annie Graham* and *Lucy Harwin* series. Helen lives in a small town in Cumbria with her husband and five children surrounded by miles of coastline, and only a short drive from the beautiful Lake District. She has always loved writing and reading since the days she learnt how to in infant school. Unable to find enough of the scary stories she loves to read, she decided to write her own.

You can contact Helen on her website at www.helenphifer.com and on Facebook and Twitter: @helenphifer1.

Also by Helen Phifer

The Good Sisters

HELEN PHIFER

ONE PLACE. MANY STORIES

HQ
An imprint of HarperCollins*Publishers* Ltd
1 London Bridge Street
London SE1 9GF

This paperback edition 2019

1

First published in Great Britain by
HQ, an imprint of HarperCollins*Publishers* Ltd 2016

ISBN: 9780008348755

MIX
Paper from
responsible sources
FSC™ C007454

This book is produced from independently certified FSC™ paper
to ensure responsible forest management.

For more information visit: www.harpercollins.co.uk/green

Typeset by Palimpsest Book Production Ltd, Falkirk, Stirlingshire
Printed and bound by
CPI Group (UK) Ltd, Croydon, CR0 4YY

*I dedicate this book to all my amazing readers;
you are what makes this all worthwhile and I'm eternally
grateful for your support.*

Helen xx

Chapter 1

Kate Parker pushed her sunglasses on top of her head and stood with her hands on her slender hips, admiring the building in front of her. It was huge, old, a complete wreck – and all hers. This was going to be her home for the foreseeable future, hopefully for ever. The acre of land surrounding the building was overgrown and neglected, but there was a lot of potential. The one thing that Kate had always had since she was a child was vision. She knew that this sad, unloved building – once the work had been completed – would make an amazing boutique bed and breakfast, as well as the perfect home for her daughters.

'What do you think, Amy? Does it meet with your approval? I hope so because I'm going to be investing everything that you left to me, and every penny I get from the prick when the divorce is finalised, to turn it into our dream.'

Her voice echoed then fell flat in the clearing and she had to blink back the tears. Amy – her best friend, and the sister she'd never had – had also shared this dream with her. Ever since they'd met fifteen years ago this had been their plan. She would have loved it. They had spent two years looking for the perfect property to renovate, but had never found one that quite ticked all the boxes or was within their price range. Then came the

1

devastating news that Amy had been diagnosed with terminal cancer.

The pain in her heart always took her by surprise, the grief a sharp sting that would take her breath away. It was so ironic that now Amy was no longer here, and Kate was on her own, she had enough money to buy this property. She'd heard about it from one of the girls at the estate agent's where she used to work before her perfect life had been washed away from under her feet.

Sam had phoned her up the same day that she'd been asked to visit and make a valuation ready to put it on the market. Luckily for her, Sam hated Kate's ex-husband Martin – who owned the estate agent's – almost as much as Kate did. She had come and picked Kate up, driving her to view the property. They hadn't been able to go inside because it was boarded up at every door and window, but Kate had fallen in love with its Gothic structure, large arched windows and overgrown, neglected grounds.

Sam had handed the owners' details to Kate and told her she would give it a few days before she rang them back to double check they wanted Parker's Estate Agents to go ahead and market it. Kate had phoned the owners the minute she got back to her cramped, one-bedroomed flat and told them she was prepared to make them a cash offer, saving them the extortionate estate agent's fees, if they agreed on a private sale.

Not only did the owners agree there and then that she could buy it, they told her they would accept her offer, which was substantially lower than the three hundred thousand they had told Sam they were looking for. Six weeks later, she was now the proud owner of the house and not only had she got it for a bargain but she had also managed to swipe it from under her greedy, soon-to-be ex-husband's feet. She didn't know what was more fulfilling: getting the property before he did or the fact that she was about to make her lifelong dream come true.

The sound of tyres crunching along the gravel broke her trance and she turned to see a battered grey van that belonged to the cowboy heading towards her. Amy had nicknamed him 'the cowboy' because of his love of checked shirts, faded jeans and rigger boots. Oliver Nealee worked for Martin at the estate agent's, doing all his property maintenance, and Kate was hoping she could convince him to take over the project management for the renovations on the house. She didn't know any other builders, and he was always such a polite, funny, hard-working man. She knew she could trust him. It was probably the meanest nickname anyone could call him – the cowboy – but it just suited him.

He parked behind her, narrowly missing her pushbike, which she'd left discarded in the long grass, and she had to grab it and drag it away from the front tyres. He swung his legs out of the van and for the first time ever she caught a glimpse of his tanned, muscled calves. The denim shorts he had on were faded just like his jeans always were.

'Sorry, Kate, I didn't see your bike there.'

'My fault, I just dumped it when I got here.'

He looked at her and she hoped he wasn't thinking what a mess she was. Her blonde cropped hair was badly in need of a cut. She wasn't wearing any make-up and since she'd left Martin she hadn't bothered to keep up with the Botox and fillers – all the money she'd spent the last three years trying to look much younger than her 45 years and he'd still had an affair with the office junior who was 23.

'It's been a while. How are you? You look great.'

She began to laugh and felt her cheeks burn. 'Always such a gentleman. I'm okay, thanks. I know I've looked better, but I have no one to please now so I don't bother.'

'Well, you look lovely. I think you look better than you have in a while.'

There was a pause. She hoped he wasn't going to mention her drinking. She didn't drink as much as she used to when she was with Martin. She knew one day she would be brave enough to try and stop. In fact, she was so excited at the thought of getting her life back on track she had decided to try and cut it down once she moved into her new house. It wasn't something she was proud of and until now she hadn't had much reason to stop. Martin had taken her job, home, children and life away from her, leaving her with nothing. Who could blame her for drowning her sorrows in a bottle or two of wine every night?

'So what's all this about then? Dragging me away from unblocking a toilet for Martin?'

'I see he still has you doing all his glamorous jobs then? I wanted to know if you would help me – well, not help me, I mean work for me. I'll pay you more than what he pays you. I need someone to sort this out for me and I'd like it to be you.'

He looked around the building and the grounds then whistled. 'That's some restoration project you have there, Kate. It's going to be a big, messy job and it won't be cheap. I can tell you that without going inside and taking a look. Are you sure you want to do this?'

Kate stared at the house – her house – then turned and glanced at the gardens before looking him straight in the eye.

'I can live without modern conveniences. I already have been in the crappy flat that I'm living in now. What I can't live without is this house. I can't explain how it makes me feel. I actually tingle inside when I look at it. I've never really believed in fate, but I truly believe that this house is supposed to belong to me. I knew it the very first moment I set eyes on it. And if not driving a fancy car or having my nails manicured or my hair cut and coloured every month means that I can afford to renovate it, then those are just a few of the sacrifices that I'm willing to make. So yes, I'm sure I want to do this. Do you think it's really bad? I haven't even been inside, but I got it for a complete bargain after I fell in love with it. It's the only time I've ever felt love at first sight. Would you be able to take the board off so we can get in the front door and take a look around it?'

'If I take the board off the door the house is going to be open and insecure for anyone to get in, unless the door actually works and it's just been boarded up to keep it secure.'

'Please can you take it off – and then can you fix the door for me if it needs it? Because I need to move in, today, and I don't want it to be insecure.'

He looked at her as if she'd gone mad. 'You want to live here, on your own, when you haven't seen the inside? It might not be in a fit state to live in. How long has it been empty?'

'Twenty, maybe forty-odd years, I think. I'm not too sure, but yes, I hate it where I live at the moment. It's a cramped council flat. Last night the flat opposite mine was broken into and set on fire. The drug dealer above me had his door kicked in and seven bells of shit kicked out of him the day before, so yes living here has got to be a better option than living there.'

***

Unable to speak, Oliver shook his head, thinking that she was either insane or plain stupid for buying this house without even looking inside it. But he'd always had a soft spot for her and if he was honest with himself a bit of a schoolboy crush. He used to watch Martin treating her like a second-class citizen, openly flirting with anything in a skirt and generally being a bastard to her. If he hadn't had enough problems in his own life he would have liked to take him to one side and teach him a thing or two about how to treat a lady, but Martin paid his wages. So until the day he didn't need the money, he'd been stuck and unable to have his own opinion.

Oliver grabbed his toolbox from out of the back of the van. Opening it up and taking out his cordless drill, he began to unscrew the board off the front door. He wondered if she was still drinking as much. He wondered if the purchase of this house had been when she was in an alcohol-fuelled haze or whether

5

she had it more under control now. She was such an attractive woman; it would be a shame to watch her lose her sparkle as the alcohol dulled it until she looked like all the other alcoholics her age. It made him so angry inside to see her drowning her life away inside a bottle, when Ellen – his wife – had fought for every minute of hers.

***

Kate stood watching him with her fingers crossed behind her back. This was going to be amazing. She had such a good feeling about it and just knew that it was. As he took the last screw out and prised the board from the door frame, she let out a small whoop of delight. Behind the faded board was a big, arched stained-glass door that would have looked at home in a church. It was beautiful. The dark oak looked in good condition and pretty solid. The brass lock was rusted and he held his hands out for the keys. Kate passed them to him and watched him fiddle around with them for a few minutes. It wouldn't turn. He looked at her over his shoulder and must have seen the disappointment that was etched onto her face.

'I've got some WD-40 in the van.' He walked over to retrieve it and returned a minute later with a can of spray-on grease and two huge torches. He handed them to her then sprayed the grease in and around the lock. He tried once more and this time with a bit of twisting the key gave in and turned. He shoved his shoulder against the door, which was stuck, pushing it open to reveal the darkness inside. It smelt damp, and fusty, and it was very black inside.

For a fleeting moment Kate felt an overwhelming sense of despair wash over her, but no sooner had she questioned what was going on and it was gone, leaving her feeling excited once more. They switched on the torches and stepped inside, sweeping the beams around the entrance hall that was now covered in a thick layer of dust. It had obviously once been very grand. The walls, which were all oak-panelled, were covered in thick, grey dust. The staircase was huge and from what Kate could see underneath the dirt and debris, the floor was made up of ornately tiled mosaics.

What stood out the most was the huge crucifix draped in thick cobwebs hanging on the wall directly opposite the front door. She shivered. Church and religion had been her worst nightmare when she'd been a kid. Her mother used to make her go every Sunday without fail. She'd have to listen to Father Joe deliver the longest, most boring sermons. She looked across at Oliver's face, trying to work out if he was impressed or not.

'Well, what do you think?'

'I think that you have taken on a huge task and you're a braver person than I am, but it doesn't seem as bad in here as I thought it would. I'm surprised to be honest, although for all we know the floors could be dangerous and full of dry rot.'

He picked up a piece of discarded wood spindling, which was lying on the floor, and banged it down hard on the tiles to make sure they were safe to stand on.

'Follow me, Kate, I mean it – don't walk off on your own. This place could be a death trap for all you know.'

She squealed and grabbed his arm. 'It's beautiful though, isn't it? I mean it has so much potential. I can't wait to get it cleaned up and started.'

***

He couldn't help smiling to himself in the darkness. Her enthusiasm was catching. It did seem to be a pretty remarkable building.

They were so busy looking down at the floor, making sure it was safe to walk on, that neither of them saw the faceless, black, hooded figure hovering at the top of the stairs watching them.

Kate's torchlight caught the corner of the thick, silver crucifix that hung around its neck, making the light reflect a little. It disappeared back to where it had come from. Back into the shadows where it had dwelled for far too long.

As they walked further into the house, Oliver just hoped that Kate had the money to turn it from this into something habitable. He knew that Martin had taken everything away from her after the court case and he couldn't help wondering where she had got the money to buy it from. Maybe it was a severance gift from Martin.

***

They walked from room to room. There were a lot of broken windows, which was why it was boarded up, and there were also an awful lot of crosses on the walls. They were everywhere and Kate felt a cold draught run down her back. It was creepy to have so many in one house. Even the church didn't have so many of the damn things plastered around. Whoever lived here must have been some kind of religious nut. She made up her mind that her first job would be to take them all down when she came back with boxes, bags and a huge skip to fill with all the junk from inside.

She was also going to do some digging and find out the house's history. When she had a minute, she would go to the records office attached to the local library and see what information they had on it. She wanted to make a scrapbook about the house now and what it would be like when it was finished. Something for her girls to treasure and that guests who stopped by might find interesting. This was her house now and whoever lived here before her had left years ago. She would turn it into the kind of home she'd dreamt about since she was a teenager.

There were still a lot of pieces of furniture that had been left behind, which was a nice bonus. Most of them were covered in dirty, grey dust sheets and she lifted the corners to take a peek at what was hiding underneath. Although some of it was no good, there were some pieces that were still okay. She would put them all in the outhouse and either sell them or have a go at restoring them herself to use in the bedrooms. Once they'd been painted white or grey instead of the dark, almost black oak they would be much brighter and look a lot better.

***

Oliver and Kate cautiously made their way from room to room. The ground floor was pretty solid. There were a couple of holes in the floorboards in three of the rooms, but the other five were not too bad. The plaster was falling off some of the walls and the wiring wasn't very good. Oliver didn't think it would be a huge job to knock out walls and add en-suites to the bedrooms. Years ago, he'd owned a thriving building business which had refit offices, hotels and pubs, so this wasn't going to be anything that he couldn't do. The only reason he'd sold the business was because his wife Ellen had been diagnosed with motor neurone disease and he'd wanted to take care of her.

He felt excited at the prospect of some real work, a proper project to get his teeth into. Martin Parker was an egotistical prick, but he'd come in handy and Oliver had needed something to do to keep his mind from dwelling on Ellen's illness and her awful, drawn-out death. The odd jobs he'd done for him had kept him busy enough that it kept some normality in his life.

***

It was much colder on the first floor than downstairs and Kate found herself wishing she'd worn her jeans and not a pair of cut-off shorts and a strappy vest top. It was dark and gloomy, and there were even more of those bloody crosses. She couldn't wait to rip them all down. They came to the smaller staircase that led up to the second floor and attic. Oliver went first and she followed close behind.

It was a little lighter up here because there were a couple of gaping holes in the roof. There were fewer rooms up here, but they were huge. This floor would be perfect for her to have a large en-suite bedroom and the girls could each have a large room. Not to mention their own living quarters if they decided that's what they wanted – and if she could afford it after the work had been done on the rest of the house.

There were some crumpled boxes shoved into one corner and she pushed one open with the tip of her torch. Inside were piles of old leather Bibles and psalm books. Whoever had lived here must have been a travelling Bible salesman. The thought made her smile. Either that or some kind of religious fanatic. She wondered what the previous owner would have made of a woman buying this house all on her own. She did the same with the next box, which had an old, wooden cigar box inside it. She pulled it out to take a closer look.

Oliver was studying the holes in the roof and had dragged a wooden trunk over that he could stand on to get a better look. Kate opened the cigar box and smiled to see a thick, navy book with gold edges on the pages and the word 'Diary' stamped in gold on the front. She picked it up, wondering who it had belonged to and if whoever it was had loved this house the way that she did.

Across the room, Oliver was making lots of 'ah' noises. She stood up and walked towards him. Halfway across the huge, open space she heard the sharp sound of scratching coming from one of the darkened corners and paused. Her heart began to race. Oh God. Mice, she didn't mind, but that sounded loud. Too loud to be a mouse. She'd die if the house came with resident rats.

10

She waited and listened to see if it happened again. Relieved that it didn't, she put it down to a bird or maybe one of those nuisance grey squirrels that everyone kept saying were vermin, but that she found cute. She could cope with mice, birds and even squirrels. She wasn't even going to acknowledge that bigger things with long tails and sharp teeth could be behind the noise. That way it wouldn't be true, would it? She reached Oliver and shone her torch at the gaping hole, not really understanding what he found so fascinating about it.

'So here's the big question: what do I need to have fixed first and would you be willing to come and work for me full-time?'

He stepped down off the trunk. 'The roof. You need to make the building waterproof before you even think about doing anything else in here. As keen as you are to get started, if we don't seal these holes you might as well take your money and throw it on a bonfire.'

'Can you do it for me, or if not do you know someone who could?'

'I can do it. I've got a few jobs on for Martin, but they're only small so I can make a start. I know a couple of lads who'll labour for cash, but this isn't going to be cheap, Kate.'

'I know, don't worry. I have the money. I'll pay you a lump sum up front and the rest on completion. Can you draw me up some plans or do I need an architect?'

'It's up to you. I know a very good architect if you'd like me to give him a ring and get him to come out for a site visit. I can't really give you a proper price until it's all been taken into consideration.'

They made their way back downstairs and she breathed out a sigh of relief. She didn't like the attic as much as the rest of the house. Even though it was open in places it felt as if the air was much heavier up there. She was sure once the roof had been fixed and there was working electricity it wouldn't feel so dark and oppressive. Back on the ground floor she returned to the large room, which was off the huge room she assumed had been the lounge. It was in pretty good condition. The windows in here weren't broken and the floor had no holes in it.

'Please can you take these boards off for me now? I want to see what this room looks like in the daytime. I might have to set up camp in here until there's a room upstairs ready.'

'Kate, are you being serious? I'm sorry to be the bearer of bad news, but you really can't live here, in this house, with it in this condition.'

'Yes, I am – and why can't I? As far as I can see it only needs a couple of new windows, doors, electrics and the roof fixed. It looks structurally sound. You said so yourself. The rest is all cosmetic work.'

'I did, but it's a wreck. It hasn't been lived in for how long? There's no heating or hot water. How will you manage?'

'I have a bed, sofa, camping stove and a cool box. I'll be fine; I might look like a complete wuss, but I can assure you that I'm not. I'm not saying I'll like it, but I'm desperate to get started and I can't stop in that flat another day. If I check into some hotel while I'm waiting for a room to be ready I'm wasting money, far too much money. I can be clearing up whilst I'm here and getting on with jobs that aren't too difficult.'

'You're braver than I am. I like my home comforts too much.'

'Yes, well, so did I, but since Martin decided to take away everything I had, I've sort of got used to doing without. Except for the wine – I can't do without that. My life wouldn't be worth living if I couldn't have a glass or two to numb the pain.'

She started to laugh and he joined in, only they both knew that she meant it. Although she would never admit it to anyone, Kate knew she was an alcoholic. It had all stemmed from her teenage years of drinking every weekend down the park with her friends, then when she was old enough, nights out in the pub. It got even worse after her miserable marriage to Martin, when he

12

would tell her he was working late and she knew he was out wining and dining his latest conquest.

Then the shock of Amy's terminal cancer diagnosis had tipped her over the edge and turned her into a full-blown, can't-get-through-the-da-without-a-drink alcoholic. Maybe one day when this place was finished and her life looked as if it might get back on track, she would get some help to tackle it. For now, she would try her best not to drink too much, even cut it down to one bottle a night instead of the usual two.

'That's emotional blackmail, making me feel sorry for you – you know that, don't you? Right then, I'll take these boards off and we'll see what we can do. Where's your stuff?'

'Back at the flat. I'll have to find someone to help me bring my bed and clothes here. I don't think they'll fit on the back of my pushbike.'

'Well, let's see how bad this room is and then if you decide you're going to do this, I'll drive you in the van to see what you need and bring you back.'

'Really? Thank you so much, Oliver. I'll pay you for your time.'

'No, you won't. I'll do this because I think you're mental and also because you're a friend.'

She squeezed his arm. 'Aw, you're such a sweetie. Thank you.'

4 January 1933
Mother Superior Agnes Nicholas looked outside the window at the snow-covered garden and shivered. It was cold enough inside the convent and they had roaring fires burning in the lounge, kitchen and upstairs bedrooms. To be outside in this weather didn't bear thinking about. She hated the cold. It made her swollen, arthritic bones ache.

Sisters Mary and Edith had spent most of the morning filling up the wood baskets so they wouldn't have to go out into the garden when it got dark. Now that only the three of them lived here, the convent was far too big. Poor Sister Emily had died of pneumonia in the hospital three weeks ago, and Agnes couldn't shake the sadness that filled her entire being, every minute of every day. Emily had been far too young to die. In turn it had made Sisters Bernice and Joanna realise life was far too short to waste on God, and they had decided to leave the next week. Leaving just the three of them to it.

Agnes wouldn't be surprised if the church shut this place down and moved them somewhere else; it was far too big of a house for three women to run. Since that strange woman had turned up at their door that night, hammering on it as if the devil himself was chasing her, things hadn't been quite right. The woman, who finally told them her name was Lilith Ardat some hours after she had been inside their home, had been crying and begging for their help. All three of them had been loath to turn her away, despite Agnes's nagging feeling inside the pit of her stomach that she was bringing trouble to their door.

Edith had silently pleaded with Agnes, imploring her with those huge, blue, innocent eyes until she'd relented. Agnes had nodded her permission at Mary, who had then ushered the woman inside and down to the kitchen, wrapping her in a thick woollen blanket. She had sat her down by the crackling fire. Edith had fetched the woman a small glass of sherry and then they'd all sat down and asked her what was wrong and how they could help her.

The story the woman confided in them was one of horrific abuse, which had sent shivers down Agnes's spine, but despite the horror she was hearing and the fact that she was a nun, there was a part of Agnes that didn't like Lilith Ardat. She couldn't put her finger on it, but the sly smile that would spread across her face after she finished each sentence had something to do with it. Agnes got the impression the woman was enjoying sharing her tale of violence and woe with the three of them.

If Lilith was telling the truth, then the poor woman had been severely mistreated, but Agnes wasn't convinced that she was. Although Agnes had no idea why Lilith would turn up at the convent so late on such a cold night if it wasn't true, she couldn't shake the niggling feeling from the back of her mind that Lilith wasn't entirely what she seemed, or that she wasn't the person she was trying to portray.

Mary loved a good tale of woe and despair, however. She had been sucked in wholeheartedly, gasping and making loud noises of objection throughout the woman's tale of horror at the hands of her husband. Edith had only just said she was bored of not having anything more exciting to talk about than what Father Patrick might preach about in his Sunday sermon. She sat transfixed by the small, raven-haired woman in front of them.

Agnes had kept her distance. She didn't know whether it was her intuition or her basic mistrust of most human beings that had stepped in, but she hadn't gone too close. The woman had skin that was whiter than the driven snow, and lips that were red – blood red. There was a blue and yellow bruise beginning to form across her left eye and forehead.

She told them it was where he'd hit her, but Agnes thought it looked more like the kind of injury you got when you were in one of those motor cars and it stopped suddenly. As if the woman's head had hit the steering wheel with force; although why this woman would be out driving a motor car at this time of night in this weather God alone knew the answer. This was not the sort of weather to be out gallivanting around in. It was far too cold and dangerous with the ice that covered the roads and paths.

'She can stay in Sister Emily's room. I'll go and make up the bed myself.'

'No. I don't think that would be appropriate, Mary.'

'Why not? It's not like Emily is going to need it anytime soon is it?'

Agnes stared at Mary in horror; the girl was so insensitive at times. It didn't seem right to put her into Emily's room so soon after she had passed away.

'She can stay in Sister Bernice's room, Mary, and I'll have none of your petulant arguing. Have some thought about you.'

'Yes, Mother Superior. Sorry, I didn't mean it like that. I'll go and make the bed up.'

Edith glanced across at Agnes. She too seemed glad that they weren't about to move a complete stranger into Emily's room so soon. It wasn't right and she would tell Mary this when they were alone, but she wouldn't say anything in front of their guest. It wasn't the time or the place.

'Whilst Mary makes up your bed, would you like something to eat? A sandwich perhaps, or some toast?'

'No, thank you, I'm not hungry. I don't eat an awful lot. I have a very small appetite.'

As the woman said this she glanced across at Edith, who was the complete opposite and had a very big appetite with a fuller figure to complement it. Agnes noted the faint redness that crept along Edith's cheeks. The girl had major issues with her weight and her even larger appetite. Not that it mattered to Agnes; everyone was different. The world would be a very strange place if everyone looked the same. Lilith stood up, shrugging the blanket from her shoulders.

'Would you mind if I used your bathroom? I need to clean myself up a little. I must look a complete mess. I'm so embarrassed because I never leave the house looking like this. What on earth must you think of me?'

Edith smiled and stood up, leading the woman from the kitchen to the first-floor bathroom. Agnes couldn't help but shudder when Lilith passed close by her. The woman didn't seem to notice and she was grateful to God for that small mercy. Agnes had no idea what was wrong with her, but every single nerve in her body was screaming at her to stop the clock and make the woman leave, only she couldn't do it. How could she send such a small, slight thing out into the subzero, freezing temperatures? She would more than likely freeze to death before she reached the village; in fact, it was nothing short of a miracle that she hadn't frozen to death before she'd reached the convent, because it was so far off the beaten track that most people who were looking for the place in broad daylight couldn't even find it.

Agnes could hear the muted whisperings of the strange woman and Edith's voice as she led her along the first-floor corridor to the bedroom that had once belonged to Sister Bernice. After what felt like for ever, Mary came downstairs, followed by Edith.

'I trust you've made our guest comfortable for the night?'

Both women nodded in unison.

'Good, I'm tired so I'll be off to bed now. Make sure that you double check all the locks on the windows and doors. I don't want any more unwelcome visitors tonight. Do you hear what I'm saying? I don't care who is knocking on that door – we don't let anyone else in. Especially in case it's Lilith's angry husband. I'm too old and too ugly to be fighting drunken bullies at this time of night. Goodnight, Sisters. Let's hope we all get some sleep.'

Agnes caught the look of fear that passed between the two much younger women in front of her and was glad. They were no match for a violent bully of a man and she would rather scare them into making sure they were safe than have them opening the door for every man, woman and child. She slowly shuffled up to bed; there would be no kneeling on the cold, hard, wooden floor tonight for her to say her prayers. She'd never be able to get back up again; instead she would climb between the heavy cotton sheets and pray. Surely God wouldn't mind an old cripple seeking a bit of comfort on this cold, bitter night?

When she finished in the bathroom, Agnes went into her bedroom and for the first time in for ever she locked her door. Unable to shake the feeling that Lilith wasn't quite what she seemed, it had made her unsettled and at a loss for what to do.

Maybe a trip into the village – if the roads were clear – to speak with Father Patrick or Constable Crosby would help her decide what to do. If not, first thing in the morning, she would telephone them both and ask them to pay her a visit.

Chapter 2

Five weeks of nonstop hard work and the house was much cleaner, lighter and smelt better. Oliver and his two labourers had been in every day, working until six or sometimes later. As they opened up each room the house felt a lot better. Kate spent every hour working alongside them. By the time they went home she would make herself something to eat then sometimes carry on until ten or eleven.

When she was on her own she would open a bottle of wine, drinking it as she cleaned, sanded or painted – whatever needed doing first. She hadn't been drinking as much because she was so tired, but if she didn't have a drink at all, sleep wouldn't come until the early hours.

Tonight, she'd managed to not have one, even though her hands were beginning to shake like some old drunk's and she felt like crap. She wanted to see how bad it would feel to go without. By nine o'clock she knew she had to go to bed because the craving was so bad. Her mouth was so dry that she kept whispering 'just one sip', but she knew if she could make it through until the morning she might just be ready to go to the doctor's and get some help.

She lay there on her bed, waiting for the usual tiredness to kick in. It didn't. She'd never been so awake as she listened to the clock on the mantelpiece ticking away. Each tick sounded louder than the last and as she stared at the wall, she heard a door bang from somewhere up on the second or third floor.

Her heart was in her mouth and then she realised that Ollie – she'd shortened Oliver to Ollie because it was much easier to yell – had probably left a window open to get rid of some paint or plaster fumes. It was just a draught, nothing else. Looking at her phone because it was too dark to see the clock face, she saw it was 3 a.m. She turned on her side, closing her eyes when she heard the scratching again.

Her mouth felt even drier as she lay still, trying to figure out where it was coming from. It didn't sound like the scrabbling sound she imagined a rat would make. Did she know what a rat actually sounded like? No, she couldn't say that she did. What she did think it reminded her of was sharp fingernails. Scared to move, she waited for it to happen again.

It sounded as if it was coming from inside the wall opposite her bed, which was ridiculous as outside her room was the hallway. She sat up, leaning over to turn her bedside lamp on, and felt better as the warm glow filled the room. She got out of her bed and crossed to the wall by the door. Her heart racing, she pressed her ear against the wall and waited for it to happen again. Five minutes passed. She couldn't hear anything.

Her imagination was running wild and she imagined someone on the other side of the wall in the same position as she was, ear pressed against it listening for sounds of movement from inside her room. Her neck started to feel stiff and she stood straight, telling herself she would have to get some mouse traps tomorrow. There was no more scratching, so she got back in the bed and knew that first thing tomorrow she would ask Ollie to check for rats or squirrels.

As she lay there thinking about how much she liked having the cowboy around, she felt a warm sensation spread over her, and then she reminded herself he was married and that it was an absolute no to even think about him as anything more than a friend. She knew how much it had hurt her deep inside to see Martin openly flirting with women who were half of her age. Every time he had done it had been like a kick in the stomach – a reminder from him that she was never quite good enough for him.

Her eyes finally getting heavy, she was drifting off when a loud thud on the floor above her made her eyes fly open. It had come from the room that was almost finished. She jumped and sat up, pulling the covers over her. She was probably extra jumpy because of the lack of alcohol flowing through her veins. She waited, holding her breath, but there was nothing more until she finally lay back down. Squeezing her eyes shut she willed her brain to shut down and let her sleep. But then, from the same room, came the sound of footsteps on the wooden floorboards – not heavy or loud, but light.

Kate reached out and turned on the small bedside lamp once more, her heart racing. Someone was upstairs. She listened, not daring to breathe out, and they came again. They were definitely footsteps – walking faster this time. Her hands were shaking. She didn't know what to do. She picked up the phone to dial the police, but her finger hovered over the button. This was her house. She should really go and take a look. It didn't sound as if it was some six-foot rugby player stomping around, more like a ballet dancer moving gracefully.

She threw back her covers and stepped onto the cold, tiled floor. *Shit, it's freezing.* She didn't dare to put her too big slippers on because of the noise they made, so she picked up the torch from under her pillow and then crossed the room and grabbed the small, wooden baseball bat that she'd got on a holiday years ago. She wasn't a violent person, but if someone had broken into her house they would get a quick whack on the head for their troubles.

Creeping from her room, she left the door ajar because it creaked loudly as it closed. She made her way to the staircase. She stood at the bottom, listening for any sign of where her intruder could be. Her mobile phone felt heavy yet comforting in her pocket. There was no sound from upstairs so she made her way up, taking each stair one at a time then pausing when she reached the top.

The room above hers was seven doorways down the wide corridor. She shone the torch around and every one – except for that one – was shut. She was tempted to run outside and phone the police, but her pride wouldn't let her. She'd feel like an idiot when the nice young officer they sent did a check of the gardens and stumbled across her recycling bin. They would think she was running some kind of private drinking club with the number of empties inside it, then they would ask who lived here and she would have to say 'just me'. She could feel the look of pity they would give her, burning her soul to the core.

No, it was better for her to have a look around. If she still wasn't happy, she could phone Ollie. No doubt he would come and make sure she was okay. Although she had no idea what his wife would think about her disturbing him at such a late hour. She waited, but couldn't hear anything. Her heart pounding, she began to walk towards the open door.

Had she shut all the other doors today or had he? They had agreed to keep them all shut to cut down on the draught until the entire house had heating in. She would ask him tomorrow when he came. Tomorrow seemed so far away at this moment in time. The torch felt heavy in her hands and the beam was moving everywhere because she was shaking so much.

Before she knew it, she was standing right in front of the door she thought the footsteps had come from. The darkness inside was all-consuming. *Come on, Kate, you know the score. There could be some mad axeman waiting in there for you. How many times have you watched the film and screamed at the television for the stupid woman to phone the police or to run?* But she couldn't. She had to check inside that room and prove to herself she wasn't hallucinating. After all she'd been living here for five weeks now and had never heard anything up until tonight, and then the voice inside her head whispered: *You've never been sober before tonight. You're normally comatose by now, oblivious to the world in your wine- or vodka-induced sleep.*

Lifting the torch, she shone it directly through the door as if to prove herself wrong. She wasn't imagining this. Her heart was pumping the blood around her body so loud she could hear the fast thump, thump of it in her ears. The beam shone into the darkness. Her mouth was dry as she moved the torch around and couldn't see anything. A little braver now, she stepped forward and reached her hand around the door frame, feeling along the wall for the light switch. As her fingers found it, she pressed it and held her breath.

Light flooded the room – the empty room in which a window was still open and the piece of net curtain across it fluttered with the breeze. She smiled to herself, relieved that it was nothing, and then she turned and saw the crosses. Her feet froze to the spot and she let out a shriek. On the wall above the light switch, there were three wooden crosses all hanging in a row. She had been in here earlier and there wasn't anything on the freshly painted wall then.

How had they got up here? The very first thing she'd done the day she moved her sparse belongings here had been to go around with a cardboard box and take down every single cross and crucifix that had been dotted around the house, because they completely freaked her out. She had then taken the full box outside to the shed around the side of the house, not wanting to throw them away because it didn't seem the right thing to do. She had quite happily pushed the sellotaped box into the side of the shed and left it there.

So who the fuck had put these up on her freshly painted walls?

If they thought it was some kind of joke they could think again. She crossed the room and slammed the sash window down a little too hard. Minute pieces of wood splintered off and fell to the floor with the impact. Bugger, she needed to be more careful. A whole houseful of new windows wasn't on her list of priorities. Not until she had to anyway. The plan was to only replace the ones that wouldn't open or were broken; the rest would be taken care of when the money started to come in.

She walked over, about to pull the crosses from the wall, when she realised how dark it was outside, how late it was and how no matter how brave she felt she wasn't walking around to the shed at this time of night. Instead she walked out of the room, turning off the light and shutting the door firmly behind her with her trembling hands.

She needed a drink. Turning on the landing light now, she switched off the torch, not wanting to drain the batteries. The upstairs landing looked so much better bathed in light. She would need to have some wall lights fitted or at least a couple of side tables and lamps that were kept on all night so the guests wouldn't get freaked out by the darkness.

Kate let out a sigh. She'd never even considered anything like this. It was a much bigger project than she'd realised. It wouldn't be half as stressful if Amy was still here to help her. Hot, salty tears filled her eyes. She missed her friend so much since she'd died six months ago. She didn't think she'd ever really laughed since. Well, not like the pair of them used to – setting the world to rights over a couple of bottles of wine. Amy would say something funny and they would laugh until the tears rolled from their eyes.

Kate wondered if anyone would ever make her laugh like that again. She certainly hadn't had anything to laugh about lately. She found herself downstairs in the huge kitchen that was an empty shell apart from the fridge, microwave and a battered old pine table with three chairs. She opened the fridge and pulled out the vodka. She didn't want to sit around drinking a glass of wine. She needed an extra-large shot of something strong that would knock her out.

Grabbing a wine glass off the end of the table where what little cutlery and kitchen essentials she owned were stacked, she filled it to the top with vodka, emptying the bottle. Leaving the bottle on the table she went back to her room, sipping the vodka as she went. She didn't want to spill any and waste a single drop.

She left the lamp on. It was staying on. The thought that she should be checking the house filled her mind. She wasn't that brave. If someone wanted to break in and put up crosses on the wall, they could get on with it. There wasn't anything apart from the builder's tools worth stealing. She knew the scratching was probably mice or worse still, rats. Ollie would deal with them for her. She might have even imagined the footsteps, because Ethan or Jack had probably put the crosses on the wall before they left for some kind of joke. They weren't to know that they'd freak her out. In fact, it made perfect sense and she convinced herself that was what had happened.

Ollie could deal with those two as well as her vermin problem, and sanity would be restored to her life once more. She looked at her lonely bed. God what she'd give to have someone lying in there waiting to wrap their arms around her. She was so bloody sick of being on her own. As she sat down on the bed, she lifted the glass to her lips, closed her eyes and then drank it down. She coughed and spluttered as the neat vodka burnt its way down her throat, filling her with warmth. Her head began to feel muzzy.

Putting the glass on the bedside table she climbed back in, feeling sick as the room started spinning. She muttered to herself: *Too much, Kate. One of these days you're going to kill yourself* – and a part of her wondered if that would be such a bad thing. The last few days, she'd had fleeting moments of despair at how much work needed to be done before they could open the house for business, followed by mild anxiety attacks. She'd never been one to suffer with her nerves, but she'd go into certain rooms or parts of the house and her stomach would start to fill with butterflies for no particular reason, which was unsettling her. She'd think about the huge project that she'd taken on and brush the feelings away as anxiety.

She had no one who wanted her. Maybe dying would be the best thing for her – even though the thought of leaving her girls terrified her. Just then, her eyes closed as she finally fell asleep.

Upstairs, the footsteps that had paused continued from room to room, looking for something that had been lost a very long time ago, but Kate was oblivious to it all.

***

Ollie let himself in with the spare key that Kate had given to him. He was much earlier than usual, but he wanted to get the next room finished. He had told himself that if he managed to get two bedrooms up and running, with the bathrooms plumbed in, then maybe Kate could have her daughters over to stay with her.

Martin couldn't really say no to her now she wasn't living in that grotty council flat and it might cheer her up, because although she'd never said as much he could tell she was feeling down. If she had her kids to stop it also might mean she would drink a little less. He felt bad for checking up on her, but he counted the empty bottles every morning in the recycling.

It was none of his business what she did and he knew this, but he liked her. If he was honest with himself, there was something about her that he found very attractive and he didn't want to see her throwing her life away. She had so much to live for – plus he kind of felt responsible for her now he was seeing her every day. The poor woman was even lonelier than him and he'd thought he had it bad.

He was surprised to see the same number of bottles as yesterday and was secretly pleased, until he got to the kitchen and saw the empty vodka bottle on the table. *Bollocks.* He walked down to her room. It wasn't like her not to already be up and pottering around. Then again, he was early and it looked like she'd hit the hard stuff last night.

Lifting his hand to knock on her door, he stopped mid-air. *What are you, her father? This is none of your business, Ollie, so keep out of it.* Instead he listened at the door for any sign of life. He heard a gentle snore and the bed creak as she moved. He couldn't help but wonder what she was sleeping in and then he stepped back and walked away.

This was well and truly overstepping the mark. It was beyond their working relationship and he felt like a dirty old man for even thinking about her like that. Instead he went back to the kitchen where he began to make some toast and a pot of tea, banging around loudly and hoping she'd wake up.

As he finished setting the teapot on the table, he turned and jumped to see her standing there yawning. She was wearing a pair of mismatched pyjamas. Her hair was tousled and sticking up and she didn't have a scrap of make-up on. She looked so sexy. Mortified, he had to turn away before she noticed what a funny shade of red his face had turned.

'What time is it?'

'I'm early. It's only eight o'clock. I thought I'd get started on that second bedroom. I wanted to make a big difference today.'

'Thanks, Ollie, that's really kind of you.' Kate sat down, putting her head in her hands.

Ollie poured her a mug of tea out and passed her some toast. As he reached over he caught a whiff of her perfume. It was the same one his wife had worn. Funny how he'd never noticed that before. Then again, he'd never been in such close proximity to Kate in her pyjamas either. Normally they were both covered in plaster dust and muck. She sipped the tea and picked up a slice of toast, nibbling on the corner. She held her head up with one hand. He kept telling himself not to say it, but it came out before he could help himself.

'Heavy night?'

She looked at him and he saw the faint redness beginning to creep up her neck. He could have kicked himself. It was none of his bloody business what she did so why was he so bothered?

'Not really, I couldn't sleep. I tried my best to drift off but then I heard scratching on the wall and I thought I heard noises coming from the bedroom above mine. I had to go and investigate, but there was nothing there.'

'It's an old house, Kate. It would make lots of noises anyway as the floorboards settled once the air cooled. With the amount of work we're doing, it's bound to increase – especially at night when there's no one banging around up there and you're here on your own. I never thought to mention it to you.'

She nodded her head. 'Oh, that reminds me. Did you leave that bedroom window and door open?'

'No, I was the last one in. I'm sure of it and I could swear that I shut them both. Why?'

'They were both wide open when I went up there and it was freezing cold. And I didn't think the crosses were very funny either.'

He didn't have a clue what she was talking about. His first instinct was that she'd been drunk and didn't know either, but then it bothered him that the window was open. He distinctly remembered closing it because he'd wondered whether or not he should leave it open an inch to air the room out.

'How wide open was the window?'

She put the mug down and lifted her hands apart quite some distance.

'I didn't leave it like that. I'm positive.'

'Well, someone did. It doesn't matter now. It just gave me a bit of a fright being on my own and sober for the first time in, well, in a long time.'

'What happened, Kate?'

'Not much really, apart from me deciding that I'd not drink and then I couldn't sleep because of the scratching and noises.'

She leant forward onto her elbows, managing to knock her mug and spill tea all over the table. He jumped up to get some kitchen roll and mop it up.

'No, I mean exactly what happened that caused you to come back down and finish off almost half a bottle of vodka?'

He could have kicked himself. Now she was going to think he was some weirdo who was keeping tabs on her. This was her house and her life. What right did he have to know how much vodka she had left in the bottle or how much she'd drunk? She hesitated, and he knew that once more he'd put his size eleven foot in it and embarrassed her.

'I was lying in bed and heard noises from upstairs – footsteps to be exact – so feeling brave, I went up there to see what or who it was. All the other doors were shut except for that one; it was wide open. So I forced my shaking legs to walk down and have a look inside. That's when I saw the window open and figured the breeze had opened the door, but it doesn't explain who put those fucking awful crosses on the wall. To tell the truth, I was really pissed off about that last night. I spent ages that first afternoon going round collecting them all. Now I don't want them in my house and if it was some kind of joke, then that's enough and we can forget about it. But it was all just a bit too freaky at three o'clock in the morning. So can you tell Ethan and Jack no more, please?'

'First of all, I don't know anything about any crosses. I'll ask the lads if they do when they get here, but they left before I did. However, most importantly, why didn't you phone the police? It could have been a burglar or a tramp.'

She shrugged. 'I'm not a complete wimp, and I'm used to all sorts of people – I had no choice living in that flat. And let's be honest there's not much to steal, is there?'

'Phoning the police doesn't mean you're a wimp. You are on your own living in this huge house in the middle of nowhere. Phoning the police is the sensible thing to do. Or you could have phoned me. I would have come over.'

'I did think about it – ringing the police and you – but the police would have looked me up and seen that I'd been previously arrested for drunk driving. Then they'd have thought I'd had one too many glasses of wine and not taken me seriously anyway. I'm sure they have far more important things to do. I didn't ring you because I didn't want to disturb you so late. That is way beyond the call of duty as my project manager and builder.'

'What about my being your friend? I've known you a long time, Kate. I'd like to think that we weren't just in a business relationship.'

He wanted to kick himself. What was wrong with him this morning? He didn't know whether it was the sight of her sitting there, looking as sexy as hell, or the concerned big brother coming out in him, but he clearly wasn't thinking straight. She pushed her uneaten toast to one side and stood up.

'Thanks for my breakfast. I'd better go and get dressed.'

He watched her leave then stood up himself. He needed to get cracking, otherwise he was going to end up running after her and saying something he might regret later, when he was at home thinking about everything.

This was none of his business. Kate had made that quite clear. She didn't think of him as a close friend. If she had she would have called him last night and she hadn't, which hurt him, but he'd get over it. From now on he would keep it purely professional: no flirting, laughing or joking. At least the job would get done quicker. The harder he worked the less time he'd have to think about her and her situation – or so he hoped. He put the mugs and teapot in the sink then went out to his van.

***

Last night seemed so far away now and Kate had been dreaming about the last time she'd taken her girls shopping. Amy had come with them and they'd done the full works: Trafford Centre, Nando's for lunch. Back then, she had never imagined how shitty her life was going to turn less than three months later.

She noticed the empty vodka bottle was now in the bin. She needed to get a grip and sort her life out. Ollie was a kind, good-looking man, but he was also a married man and there was no way she was going to go there – no matter how lonely or scared she was or how much her hormones were telling her to.

5 January 1933

Sister Agnes had not slept more than a couple of hours. She had spent the whole night freezing cold and having the most horrific nightmares where she was burning in the depths of hell. The pain as the searing heat crackled and blistered her skin had almost been too much to bear, and at one point she'd woken up in a cold sweat – breathless – only to drift off and continue with the same dream.

Not only had she been there, but so had Edith and Mary. Mary had been doing the most sinful of things with a half-man half-beast creature and Agnes hadn't been able to look away because she was shackled by her arms to a rough stone wall.

As she opened her eyes and saw the murky, grey light filtering through the window she breathed out a huge sigh of relief. Never had she had such impure thoughts – and at her age, it was wrong. She would be praying extra hard for her soul at morning prayers today. She wondered why she had dreamt about such depraved filth.

After getting out of bed she washed, dressed, took her rosary beads from the dressing table and placed them around her neck. Instantly she felt better, purer, and closer to God and nature. She would sleep with them on tonight if it meant she wouldn't have such terrible dreams. The house was quiet. Everyone else must still be asleep, which was good. It gave her a chance to make a pot of tea and gather her thoughts.

It would also give her the chance to decide what to do about Lilith. The woman couldn't stay here any longer. There was something about her that was off kilter. Agnes never judged anyone on face value, but the sneaky grins and smirks whilst Lilith was relaying her tale of woe last night had stayed with her. Who in their right mind would smirk about being beaten and forced to do terrible things?

As she sipped her tea she felt a shadow fall over the kitchen door and turned to see Lilith standing there, watching her. She was so surprised that she spilt the hot liquid all over herself, scalding her arm. She hadn't heard the woman leave her bedroom or come down the stairs. Lilith rushed to the sink and picked up a dishcloth. After running it under cold water, she pressed it against Agnes's arm. Her touch made Agnes jump once more. The woman's fingers were colder than slivers of ice if that was possible.

'Have you hurt yourself badly, Sister?'

Agnes shook her head.

'Did I give you a fright? I'm sorry about that. I've always been an early riser. I hate lying in bed wasting the day when there's so much to do, although I do hate the sunlight. My skin is so fair that I can't go out in it. Don't you agree? Why don't you run your arm under the cold water? I'll clean this mess up and then make us a lovely fresh pot of tea.'

Agnes pushed herself up from the chair and crossed to the sink. Running the tap, she held her arm underneath it. The whole time she watched Lilith as she cleaned the spilt liquid from the table, then set about getting fresh teabags from the cupboard along with clean cups. How did she know where everything was? Last night she had been sitting sniffling and crying, too upset to watch them making a pot of tea. Once again, the feeling that Lilith was not what she seemed washed over Agnes.

When the teapot was on the table along with clean cups, Agnes turned the tap off and took a clean tea towel from the wooden rail to wrap around her arm, blotting it dry. She forced herself to sit back down. The back of her throat felt parched she was so thirsty. Lilith poured fresh cups of tea and passed one to her.

'Now you be careful, Sister Agnes. We don't want you burning yourself again, do we? There is nothing worse than the lingering slow burn of hot liquid on such delicate skin.'

Agnes took the teacup and blew on it. She hoped that her trembling hands wouldn't betray her and spill this one all over. She prayed even harder that Lilith wouldn't notice the trembling was in fact pure fear and would put it down to old age.

'Thank you, dear, that's very kind of you. I didn't sleep very well last night. I think I'm still half asleep.'

Lilith smiled, making the skin on the back of Agnes's neck crawl. Later on that night she would describe to Father Patrick that she thought being stared at by Lilith was how it must feel to be a fly trapped in a spider's web.

'I have to say I'm very fortunate that I stumbled across this place last night. I thought I was going to freeze to death out there – it was so cold. Thank you so much for giving me permission to come in.'

She nodded at Agnes as she spoke. Agnes's head was spinning. What was this about? Almost every sentence Lilith said seemed to have a hidden meaning to it. Or was that just her taking everything and twisting it to fit her mindset? At a loss for words, she forced herself to smile at Lilith. *Thank you for giving me permission to come in.* Agnes felt as if her brain was screaming at her, warning her, only she couldn't work out what her subconscious was trying to tell her. The sound of heavy footsteps running down the stairs broke the awkward silence between the two women as Sister Edith breezed in.

'Good morning, Mother Superior, how are you today?' She

looked down at the white linen tea towel wrapped around Agnes's arm and gasped.

'Oh my goodness, what's wrong? Have you hurt yourself?'

'It was just an accident, Edith – my own silly fault. Good morning, I trust you slept well?'

'Do you want me to take a look at it?'

Agnes shook her head. She didn't want Lilith looking at it again and giving her an excuse to get too close to her. 'No, it's fine; it's nothing honestly.'

'I did sleep well, but I had the strangest dreams. To be honest, I can't believe it's morning already. The night passed by so fast I feel as if I haven't been to bed.' Edith smiled at Lilith then busied herself making breakfast for everyone. By the time the porridge was bubbling on the stove and the thick crusty bread had been sliced ready to spread with butter and jam, Sister Mary still hadn't appeared and Agnes stood up.

'If you'll excuse me for a moment, I'll just go and see if Mary is okay. It's not like her to oversleep when you're banging around in the kitchen, Edith. I'll be back down shortly. Please don't wait for me – just tuck in.'

Agnes would normally make all three of them say prayers before they ate, but for some reason the thought of praying in front of that woman made her feel queasy. Today she would do her praying to God in private, as far away as possible from Lilith. She went upstairs and knocked on Mary's door. There was no reply.

'Mary, is everything okay? Do you need anything? Are you ill?'

There was no sound from inside the room. Agnes put her ear against the heavy wooden door to listen. There was no movement and Mary – who was a heavy sleeper and snored quite loudly, much to Edith's annoyance – wasn't making any noise whatsoever.

Cold tendrils of fear crept up Agnes's spine. She tried the door handle; it was locked. So Mary had been worried enough last night that she'd had to lock her bedroom door as well. That made two of them. She would take Edith to one side and ask her if she had done the same. Agnes lifted her hand and knocked on the door. Still there was no movement from inside the room. She knocked again, much harder this time and shouted, 'Mary!'

A hand on her shoulder made her jump and Agnes turned to see Edith standing there.

'Come on, Mary, what did you do last night after we all went to bed? Did you have a go at the cooking sherry again? Open the door and come get your breakfast.'

***

Edith smiled at Agnes, expecting Mary to tell her to bugger off any second.

The last time they hadn't been able to rouse Mary, she had finished off half a bottle of whisky Father Patrick had left behind. Oh, it had been funny to watch Mary walking around with her head in her hands and being sick every time someone mentioned food the day after. Agnes didn't like them to be mean to each other, but it was only a bit of a laugh. Edith knocked much harder than the older woman ever could. She stopped briefly then began to hammer on the door with her fist.

Agnes reached out her hand to stop her. 'Something's wrong. We need to get into that room. Have you got a spare key?'

Edith shook her head. 'No, sorry. I should have told you when it happened. I misplaced the key ring you gave me last year with all the spares on and seeing as how we don't normally lock our doors, I didn't think it really mattered that much.'

'Edith, what are you like? How are we going to get in there now? I'll have to phone Father Patrick or Constable Crosby to come and break the door open.'

***

35

Agnes turned to see Lilith standing at the top of the stairs watching them and she shivered.

'Is everything all right, ladies? What's the matter with Sister Mary?'

Agnes ignored her and squeezed past her to go downstairs. As she did a faint whiff of something gone off filled her nostrils. Where was that smell coming from? It smelt like meat that had been left too long and was on the turn. She left Edith knocking on Mary's door and Lilith standing watching. She picked up the phone and dialled Constable Crosby. The relief when he answered the phone almost made her cry.

'It's Sister Agnes from the convent. Please can you come as quickly as possible? We can't get into Sister Mary's room and she isn't answering anyone. We've knocked ever so hard and shouted very loudly. I'm afraid she's taken ill.'

'I'm on my way, Agnes.'

She put the heavy receiver down. It really was most unlike Mary to lock her door. She went back upstairs to see Lilith seated on the top step picking at her long, deep red painted fingernails.

'Is there anything you want me to do?'

Leave! screamed a voice inside Agnes's mind, although she would never say that. She was far too polite and that wouldn't be a very charitable thing to do. She knew that Father Patrick would be disappointed in her lack of empathy for a fellow human being.

'No, thank you, I don't believe there is. Can I ask how long will you be staying here, Lilith? Do you have family or friends you can stop with?'

The words came out before she could stop herself. A loud knock on the front door broke the interaction between the two women. Agnes went downstairs to let a rather red-faced Constable Crosby inside.

'By heck, it's cold out there, Agnes. I didn't think the patrol car was going to start. Have you woken Mary up yet?'

'No, we haven't. There's no answer. I can't even hear her snoring and trust me, Crosby, she has on occasion snored so loud that it's kept me awake all night.'

Crosby chuckled at the thought of a nun snoring. 'Right then, you'd better show me which one is her bedroom. I have to say I never thought I'd get to see the day I saw the inside of a nun's bedroom.'

He winked at Agnes who shook her head. He was a loud, brash and sometimes funny man who was also very good at his job. He was a big help whenever they had cause to ask him for any. She led him upstairs. Lilith was now standing across the hall from Mary's bedroom with Edith. Her slender arms were crossed and she smiled at Crosby, who looked at her and smiled right back.

'A new recruit into God's army, Agnes?'

Lilith giggled. 'I'm afraid not, Constable. I don't think he would let me join. I'm not a very good girl.'

She winked at him and Agnes noted the faint redness creeping up his neck. She pointed to Mary's room and he strode across and hammered on the door with his fist. It was so loud it echoed around the hall; in fact, it was so loud Agnes was sure it would wake a deaf person.

Constable Crosby stopped to listen at the door. Silence greeted him. Agnes felt the tiny hairs on the back of her neck stand on end. They didn't need a policeman to tell them something was wrong. He lifted his foot and kicked the door. It moved a little, not much. So he stepped back then barged the door using his shoulder and putting his substantial weight behind it. The door splintered and cracked. He looked over his shoulder at Agnes. They both knew the noise he was making was loud enough to wake the dead, so why hadn't Mary opened the door?

As he launched himself at the door once more, it gave with a loud splintering sound and he stumbled forwards. He seemed to be trying to take in the sight before him, but his eyes would not or could not register what he was seeing. Agnes motioned with her hand for Edith and Lilith to wait there. She stepped in behind Crosby and, just as he had, she looked around trying to understand what it was she was seeing. The normally white walls were covered in splatters of red. The smell hit them both at the same time, making them gag. Agnes lifted her hand and made the sign of the cross. Crosby uttered one word: 'Fuck.'

***

It had taken hours before the police had taken Mary's body away. Father Patrick had taken them all into the front room where they'd prayed for Mary's soul. There was no way she had killed herself and it couldn't be murder either, could it? Constable Crosby had needed to break the door down himself. The windows were shut and locked from the inside.

Agnes's first thought had been that somehow Lilith's husband had gained entry into the house, looking for his wife, and killed Mary by mistake. Then she realised it had been her who had unlocked the front door to let the constable inside and all the locks and bolts had still been fastened. It didn't make any sense and throughout everything Lilith had kept very quiet. She hadn't suggested it was her husband and she had taken to her room, locking herself inside.

Agnes had spent over an hour with Crosby and Father Patrick, talking them over what had happened since Lilith had knocked on the convent door. Father Patrick had done his best to reassure both women that it wasn't their fault. Yes, it was very strange, but they would find out what had happened. Edith, who hadn't stopped crying for hours, had started to panic when Father Patrick had told them he was going back to the vicarage and he'd had to promise her he would go home, get a change of clothes and then come back and spend the night.

38

By this time Lilith had come out of her room and was loitering in the doorway of the front room. She kept smiling at the priest and Agnes didn't like it one little bit. Agnes had asked Patrick if they could tell the woman to leave when they had been alone in the kitchen, but he'd shaken his head.

'Agnes, I admit it's all a very strange and sad coincidence, but that's all it is. We can't really tell her to leave when she has nowhere to stay that's safe. The church has always been a safe place, a haven. How many times have we offered sanctuary for those in desperate need? Over the centuries, it's been too many to count. Lilith needs our compassion and our help. We will let her stay here until she has somewhere safe she can go to.'

'Very well, Father. There's something about her that I can't put my finger on though. She makes me feel uneasy.'

'Agnes, if I didn't help the people who made me uneasy I'd never be able to do my job. It will be fine. The poor woman must be terrified, escaping a violent husband then waking up to this. We must be patient with her and show her more kindness than before.'

'Very well, Father, whatever you wish.'

Agnes wasn't happy at the thought of Lilith still being a guest inside the house. Father Patrick had offered to bring someone in from the village to clean up the mess in Mary's room and Agnes had declined. She thought it was the least she could do and she wanted to see what had happened, now that Mary had been taken away to the undertaker's, the various parts of her body all wrapped up in a sheet.

Crosby had told her before he left that they could clean up the mess if they wanted to either tonight or tomorrow. As tempting as it had been to leave it until tomorrow, Agnes wasn't a fool and knew that the room smelt horrendous already. To leave it another day before trying to clean up the blood and mess would make it unbearable.

Edith was in the kitchen with Lilith and Father Patrick, so

Agnes went to the cupboard under the stairs where they kept the disinfectant and mop buckets. She took a big bottle of bleach, a box of rags and the mop bucket. Locking the door behind her, she went upstairs. Mary's room was the seventh one along the landing. The door wasn't shut properly because of Crosby's attempts to kick it in.

Agnes's mouth felt dry and her hands were trembling at the thought of going inside it on her own, but she needed to do this. She was in charge of running this convent and the responsibility weighed heavy on her shoulders. Mary's family would be coming tomorrow and might want to stop here. It was the least they could do and she wouldn't have them going into their daughter's room if it was still stained with her blood.

Agnes was only a small woman, but she was strong. The corridor seemed to her as if it had increased in size because Mary's bedroom door looked so far away from where she was standing at the top of the stairs. As she forced her feet to walk forwards, she began to pray under her breath. She prayed for Mary and for the rest of them because she couldn't shake the feeling that what had happened to Sister Mary was just the beginning of something terrible.

The smell hit her as she got halfway along the landing and her empty stomach lurched. She crossed herself. How had this happened to Mary? What had happened? It didn't make any sense to her whatsoever. They had all been fine last night.

Agnes thought she heard the sound of heavy footsteps coming from Mary's room and she paused to listen. The police, doctor and undertakers had all left. There should be no one here. She waited, her heart racing. *Stop it, woman, you're scaring yourself.* Holding herself straight, she walked the last few steps and listened at the door, pressing her head against the wood to make sure there was no one still in there. She was greeted by silence.

She pushed the door open and gasped once more; the sight in front of her eyes was horrendous. Earlier had been bad enough, although the shock had numbed some of it. The blood was everywhere. It was as if someone had taken a paintbrush and splashed it all around the white walls. The bed had the white outline of where Mary had fallen, but surrounding it and bleeding into it were dark, almost black congealing pools of blood.

The stench was how Agnes imagined an abattoir would smell. That was it. Mary had been butchered to pieces in her own bedroom and not one of them had heard a sound. How had that been possible? Her eyes fell onto the book on Mary's bedside table: Mary Shelley's *Frankenstein*. Something bothered Agnes about that book, but she didn't know what. Why had Mary been reading that? Mary and Edith had been to the picture house in the town to watch it and both of them had come back scared of their own shadows for days. So what was it that had compelled her to go out and buy the book?

Agnes stepped forward and reached out for the soft, leather-bound book. As she flicked open the front page, her eyes began to stream and her nostrils flared at the strong smell that was emanating from it. It smelt like embalming fluid, but what on earth would that be doing on the pages of a book? Agnes had helped out at the undertaker's a few times back in her younger days and although it was hard to describe exactly what it smelt of, it always had the same effect on her. Dropping the book back, she stepped away. Something strange was happening in this house and she didn't have any idea what it was.

Agnes started to blot, wipe, scrub and wash every trace of blood away that she could find. Every couple of minutes she would twist her head from one side to the other to look behind her. She couldn't shake the feeling that she was being watched. Mary's room was huge, but so were all the others. It was a massive house, which had obviously been designed for a wealthy family. Not a small group of women who had given up their everyday lives to serve God.

She was kneeling on the floor, scrubbing at a particularly stubborn bloodstain, when she felt the skin on the back of her neck prickle as a cold gust of air rushed against her. She pulled herself from her knees, which made two loud clicks that echoed around the room as they straightened up. Agnes half expected that woman, Lilith, to be standing in the doorway watching her. She turned around. There was no one there.

The room was beginning to smell much better. The harsh, coppery stench of the blood was being wiped away by the strong-smelling ammonia. There was another smell coming from the corner of the room where Agnes felt as if someone was standing. It smelt like electricity. Agnes would describe it to Father Patrick as the smell in the air when there was about to be a thunderstorm. She waved her hand in front of her, expecting the air to crackle and fizz, but it didn't.

She hummed to herself, one of her favourite hymns. She was too old to believe what her mind was trying to say. It was being ridiculous. She was being silly. For whatever reason, Mary had done that to herself. Agnes didn't know why or even want to know how, but there was no evidence that suggested any other explanation.

She turned back to the floor and felt her heart miss a beat to see the book that had been on the bedside table moments ago now on the floor, next to her mop bucket. How? There had been no noise, no draught. Agnes knew that she hadn't knocked it over herself; with a hand that was shaking so much she found it hard to get her fingers to pick the book up, she gripped it as tight as she could. The icy-cold leather stuck to her fingers and she shook them, almost dropping it with revulsion.

She started to read the words in front of her and the room began to spin. Frankenstein's monster had just killed Victor's new wife Elizabeth. Tucking the book into her pocket she left the room, unsure of what or who was watching her, but certain that someone was. She went to the bathroom to clean herself up. Her clothes were ruined and smelt terrible. She turned on the taps and began running herself a bath. As she undressed, she looked into the mirror, asking herself: *'Are you going mad, woman?'*

She didn't feel as if she was. Her face didn't look much different. Well, apart from the few new wrinkles that had appeared around her eyes and forehead overnight. Once more the feeling she was being watched made her shiver. She turned around to check the door was still locked. Then she slowly bent to look through the keyhole and make sure that there wasn't anyone peering through it; although what anyone would want watching a 60-year-old naked woman was beyond her.

She squinted; all she could see through the tiny lock was the landing outside the door. Wondering where Lilith was, Agnes straightened up and walked across to step into the bath. This wouldn't be a quick in and out like usual. She would be spending as long in here she could. She needed to soak away the smell of dear Mary's blood, not to mention her aches and pains from being scrunched up on the floor scrubbing.

As she sunk into the steaming water she wondered what had happened to change the dynamics of this house of God, and try as she might the only conclusion that she could come up with was the arrival of Lilith Ardat. Why did she feel such revulsion towards the woman? Agnes didn't dislike many people; it wasn't in her nature. Why had they let her in? What was it that she had said to Agnes earlier? *'Thank you for giving me permission to come in.'*

Agnes had her own horror book tucked away in her bedside table drawer. She had read Bram Stoker's *Dracula* many years ago. Her copy had been a gift from her sister – just before she'd died – so even though Agnes hadn't particularly enjoyed the story, the fact that the book was more sentimental to her meant that she kept it close to her. Agnes had been terrified of the vampire

Count Dracula and his wicked, evil ways when she'd read it, but she knew it was only a story. All this talk of not having a reflection and needing to ask permission to enter someone's house was plain ridiculous. Or was it?

Chapter 3

The house no longer smelt old, damp and empty. It now smelt of plaster, wood filler and paint. There were two bedrooms finished and the en-suite bathrooms were plumbed in so that Kate could have a hot shower after a hard day's graft. She had begun reading the old diary that she'd found on the very first day and had to stop because it was terrifying her. She'd discovered that the house had been a convent at one time, which explained the crosses when she'd moved in.

The first few pages had been written beautifully. Then the writing had changed as if the writer, Agnes, had been in a hurry to document what was going on. Kate read about a nun who had died here, in her house. She shuddered as a strange feeling washed over her. She had a great-great-aunt called Agnes who had been a nun. What if this book belonged to her? She pushed the thought away. Agnes was probably a popular name back then. It was just a coincidence.

The death of the poor woman sounded so violent. After she finished reading, Kate had then gone upstairs. She had gone into each bedroom, studying the floorboards for bloodstains. Unable to distinguish any from the paint splatters and dust, she'd given up after Ethan had asked what she was looking for. Kate had laughed and gone back down to put the small diary away because it had terrified her. She was just relieved that all of this had happened such a long time ago.

To take her mind away from the terror in that small book, she had spent hours poring over the magazines that her friend Sam had dropped off for her. Kate was trying to decide on a practical yet perfect kitchen. She didn't want to spend a huge amount of money. Because of the size of the room, it was going to be expensive – even if she picked a cheap one.

Ollie had been a godsend. She didn't know what she would have done without him these last few weeks. He always stayed later than Jack and Ethan – the lads who worked for him. Kate often wondered what his wife thought about the amount of time he was spending here, but it wasn't any of her business. For all she knew, they could be on the brink of a divorce and his wife was glad to see the back of him. She wished she knew because the more time she spent with Ollie the more she liked him.

Kate sat down on the top step, an overwhelming feeling of tiredness taking over her. As exciting as this project was, it was taking it out of her. Today she hadn't been able to shake the headache that she'd woken up with. She decided she needed strong painkillers washed down with a mouthful of vodka. She crept down to the kitchen for a shot of the ice-cold alcohol that was in the freezer compartment. After glugging down the tablets she went straight to the bathroom and brushed her teeth. Ollie was hardly going to find a 45-year-old alcoholic attractive, was he? And she still felt embarrassed by the need to use alcohol to get her through the day, although she wasn't drinking as much now. She was making a conscious effort to reduce her intake.

As she patted her mouth dry, she looked into the mirror. Her life had gone almost full circle and she was lucky it didn't show on her face. The wrinkles she had feared so much in her thirties hadn't put in much of an appearance, except for the laughter lines around her eyes – although the last twelve months she hadn't really had much to laugh about. Maybe they were crying wrinkles because she'd spent a whole lot more time crying than she'd done laughing.

The air, which was normally full of minute particles of plaster dust, smelt different. As Kate turned around to open the bathroom door, she inhaled again. What was that smell? It smelt like old leather, burnt skin and garlic all mixed together and it was rank. She looked around the bathroom then opened the door out onto the corridor. It was stronger out here.

The lads had all gone into town for their dinner – even Ollie had gone with them and he normally ate a packed lunch, but all they'd been talking about during the morning had been meat and potato pies and cream cakes from the bakery. She stood and listened to the house. It was so silent and still without the workmen banging around and singing.

Kate wondered if it was some kind of chemical that they'd used and walked along the hall to the room they had all been working in. The door was shut. She was sure it had been open when she'd passed it to go to the toilet. She heard her name being called and stood still. Was she hearing things? It sounded like Amy's voice calling for her, but that was ridiculous. She waited, her head turned to the side.

'Katie, where are you?'

It was so faint, but there was no mistaking it was Amy's voice and Kate smiled briefly. 'Amy, where are you? I'm here.'

Even though it was broad daylight, her heart raced as she thought about her dead friend calling out to her from the same room where the crosses had appeared on the wall with no explanation. Both Jack and Ethan had strongly denied having anything to do with them when Ollie had questioned the pair of them.

She walked towards the room. Pressing her ear to the heavy wooden door, she listened to see if there was anyone inside or if it was her imagination. Call it instinct or whatever, but her mind was screaming at her not to open the door whilst she was alone in the house. There was a loud thump from inside as if something heavy had been dropped from quite a height. It made her jump away from the door as her hands began to shake. What was that?

She pulled her phone from her pocket and pressed 999, her finger poised above the green call button, ready to ring for the police. If it was Amy inside there, she wouldn't scare her. Placing her head back against the door, she heard the sound of something heavy moving towards her. It was too big and clumsy to be her friend, who had been a tiny little thing. It sounded as though it had to drag itself towards the door.

Kate pulled back, terrified. She wanted to know what was in her house, but she wasn't brave enough to open the door and see. She opened her mouth to shout that she was calling the police. Nothing came out. Instead she heard a loud thud as whatever it was caught the ladders on the other side of the door and they crashed to the floor. Which meant it was at the door and it would be coming through it very soon.

She forced herself to turn and run as fast as she could down the stairs and to the front door, where she slammed full force into Ollie. He was carrying a white paper bag with meat and potato pies inside. He dropped the pies to hold his hands out to catch her, but she was coming that fast she managed to knock them both to the floor in a heap.

'Get out, we have to get out.'

***

'What's the matter, Kate? Have you hurt yourself?'

Ollie wanted to sound like a gentleman, but she couldn't have really hurt herself when she was lying on top of him. He was slightly winded, but it was the pies that had sustained the most damage. One of them had exploded all over the inside of the bag and there was meat and potato filling seeping out all over the floor. She pulled herself off him and turned to look behind her. There wasn't anything there.

'Something was coming. There's something in the bedroom. I don't know what the fuck it was, but it knew my name. We need to get out and call the police.'

He stood up and held his hand out to pull her up from the floor where she was kneeling, her face whiter than the paint he had all over his hands.

'Whoa, what do you mean? What's coming?'

She shook her head and grabbed his hand, tugging him back out of the front door. He looked down at the mess that was his dinner on the floor, then followed her outside. She didn't stop until she reached his van and clambered inside, slamming the door shut.

***

'All right, Kate, what's up with you? You look as white as a sheet.'

Ollie opened the door. He shrugged at Jack and Ethan, who were both sat in the back seat eating their pies.

'Do you want to tell me what happened? Why you almost gave me a heart attack and crushed my dinner that I've been dreaming about eating all morning at the same time?'

Feeling stupid, Kate felt her cheeks begin to flush as she realised she sounded like a lunatic.

'I smelt something weird in the bathroom. When I came out it was stronger on the landing and then I heard my friend Amy call my name. Only it couldn't have been her because she's dead. I followed the voice and the smell to the room you were working on less than half an hour ago.'

All three men were leaning forward, obviously wondering what she was going to say next.

'I sound stupid, don't I?'

49

Ollie shook his head. 'No, not at all. You heard your name called, something smelt weird and then what happened?'

'I couldn't open the door. I was too scared so I listened and I heard the sound of something heavy. It was cumbersome and it was slowly moving towards the door. Well, I knew you lot had gone to get some dinner and it scared me. There's someone or something inside the house and I don't know who or what it is!'

'You wait here. Me and the masked avengers will go inside and investigate.'

'Shouldn't we just phone the police?'

'I'm pretty sure whatever or whoever it is won't want to mess us three around. We'll be fine, won't we, lads?'

'Speak for yourself, boss. If something scared Kate then who are we to doubt that?'

'I don't bloody believe it, you wimps. What's wrong with you?'

Ethan got out of the van. 'I'm not a wimp, but Jack is a complete wuss. Aren't you, Jack?'

Jack gave Ethan the finger. 'I'll wait here with Kate, make sure she's okay.'

Kate could feel her hands shaking and she clasped them together. She felt so cold even though it was a warm autumn day. She watched as the two men went inside her house and felt as though she'd just sent them in to their deaths, the feeling of dread in the pit of her stomach was so intense.

'I can't stay here and wait. I have to go with them.' She jumped out and ran to the door, closely followed by Jack who was muttering underneath his breath. She ran into the entrance hall, stepping over the crushed pies on the floor and saw Ollie and Ethan almost on the top stair. She ran as quietly as she could until she was on the step behind them. Ollie pointed to the bedroom that they'd been working in and she nodded. Ethan looked at Ollie who was now standing with his hand on the doorknob. He twisted it then threw the door open.

Kate, whose legs had turned to jelly, saw that the room was

empty. There was no huge man in there with an axe waiting to kill them all, and no ghost of Amy. Ollie stepped inside followed by Ethan. They checked the en-suite, but the door hadn't been hung yet so they could see straight inside it from where they stood. All of them let out a huge sigh of relief except for Kate. She knew that she'd heard something inside there. She could also detect a very faint odour, the same as before, but it was residual and not as strong.

***

Ollie didn't say anything. He was wondering if she'd been on the vodka again whilst they'd been gone. Alcohol could play strange games with a person. He stole a glance at her to see if she was a bit worse for wear, but she didn't look like she was. What she looked was scared and he wanted to pull her close and hold her more than anything.

'I'll go and check the attic. Ethan, you and Kate can check the rest of the rooms on this floor. Jack, you go and check the ground floor. I'll also do the cellar. Is that okay with everyone?'

They all nodded and Kate muttered, 'I swear to God I'm not going mad. There was someone inside this room.'

No one spoke. They just went their separate ways and checked every room, nook and cranny in the whole house. After ten minutes they all met up again in the kitchen. Kate had picked Ollie's crushed pies up, which were still steaming hot, and put them onto a plate for him. He took one look at them and began to laugh. In fact, he laughed so hard that tears fell from his eyes.

'That's the funniest thing I've ever seen. One of them was yours, by the way, so I should divide that mess onto another plate.'

***

Kate smiled. Ollie had the nicest laugh she'd ever heard. Martin's was such a loud, false guffaw, but this was a proper belly laugh.

'No, thank you, I've done enough damage. I don't want to deprive you.'

'I already had one in the car on the way back. I swear I'm not eating that on my own. I'll only eat half if you have the other. I'm not being rude, Kate, but you never eat. Even a pie in that state will do you a world of good.'

'If you don't mind sharing then that would be great. I'm actually starving. It's the smell that's making my mouth water. If I don't look at the mess on the plate, I'll be able to eat it.'

Ollie turned to take a plate from the cupboard and a knife from the drawer. After scraping half of it onto the other plate, he passed it to her. She picked up a fork from the draining board and began to eat, hoping it would stop the sick feeling in her stomach and stop her hands from shaking so much.

Ethan and Jack left them to it and went back upstairs to finish painting the walls of the room that had caused all the fuss. Ollie dead-eyed the pair of them, clearly warning them not to start gossiping about Kate when they got up there. He waited until they were out of sight and she'd finished eating.

'So do you want to tell me what exactly you thought was going on, Kate? I'm worried about you. This is a huge house for one person to live in on their own. You're bound to get a bit spooked. I know that I certainly would.'

'I'm not hallucinating or drunk if that's what you think. We both know that I drink, but I don't drink through the day and I've been trying to cut down of an evening as well.'

She thought about the swig of vodka she'd downed her tablets with, but that didn't count, did it?

'I didn't say that. I don't like the fact that you've heard things. And what about those crosses? We haven't got to the bottom of how that happened, have we? Does Martin know about this place?

52

Because I'm worried he has something to do with it and is trying to scare you half to death so you'll leave.'

'I don't know, Ollie. I didn't think about that. You know, I wouldn't put it past him. He's such a sneaky bastard. If he thought I was doing well for myself he'd jump straight in and try to rip it all away from me.'

'Do you think we should get some basic CCTV cameras that cover the outside of the building and the drive? That way, if anyone is sneaking around you'll be able to see them and ring the police. I know it's an extra expense, but it would make me feel a whole lot better and you would feel a bit safer. I hate leaving you each night on your own.'

Kate felt her heart skip a beat at his last words. Had he really just said that or was she making a much bigger thing out of it than was completely necessary? Why the hell were all the nice men spoken for? He was such a gentleman and she hoped his wife appreciated just how lucky she was. If she was married to Ollie she wouldn't ever want to let him out of her sight because he was too bloody perfect.

'Do you mean that? I mean, do you think cameras would make it better?'

'It wouldn't hurt. If you wanted I could have them fed through to my laptop at home as well, and then both of us could keep an eye on the place. Plus if we catch Martin or one of his cronies on camera you can give it to the police and they won't be able to deny it. I have to say, though, you are the bravest, craziest woman I've ever met. Not to mention stubborn. Most people would have run off by now and booked into a hotel.'

'Do you know anyone who could fit some cameras for me?'

'I do. I'll give him a ring now.'

He wandered off, pulling out his mobile phone, and she put the plates in the sink, filling it with hot, soapy water. She had no idea what had been upstairs, but she knew something had been and she didn't think it was Amy. When she had a chance she

53

would Google what the hell that smell had been. Funny how it had all but dissipated when the men had come back. She didn't believe in spooky stuff as a rule, but the footsteps, crosses and now this were making her wonder exactly what was going on.

This house had once been a convent, a holy place of residence, and women had lived here all alone then. The number of crosses and crucifixes around the building had been unreal. She would have to pluck up the courage to read the rest of the diary to see what exactly had happened here. She could also do some research to find out more about the history of this place as well. When had it stopped being a convent and who had last lived in here?

Ollie had been right about one thing: she was stubborn. She always had been since she was a little girl. This was what she and Amy had dreamt about so there was no way she would turn her back on it just because she'd had a bit of a fright. When this place was open and she was a respectable businesswoman who was earning her own money, she would be able to take Martin to court and fight for custody of her girls.

She missed them so much. It was like a huge, gaping hole in her heart that couldn't be filled. It ached and ached. She missed tucking them in at night and reading them bedtime stories. The smell of their freshly washed hair, as she kissed their heads good-night, filled her nostrils. The pain that followed was so intense it was as if someone had taken a knife and pushed it right through the middle of her heart. Coupled with the loss of Amy, it was no wonder she'd unravelled as much as she had.

Kate felt as if she couldn't breathe. She pulled on her jacket and walked to the front door. She needed some air, some space away from the house. She walked outside.

***

Ollie, who had been speaking on the phone to his friend about how many cameras were needed, watched her from the landing

54

window. He wanted to run after her, walk with her, look after her. What was happening to him? He'd sworn that he'd never look at another woman after Ellen's death but here he was, attracted to a woman who wasn't remotely interested in him. He was so angry with himself because he felt as if he was being unfaithful to Ellen even thinking about Kate in this way, but he couldn't help it.

For the last five years he'd watched Ellen get sicker and sicker. It had taken away every feeling except despair from him. He'd forgotten how it felt to have every nerve ending in your body on fire just being close to someone you found attractive on every level. Not to mention the embarrassment of the erection he'd got when she'd knocked him to the floor earlier and almost straddled him. He'd had to push her off so she didn't think he was some kind of pervert.

He watched Kate heading towards the stream and the woods, and wondered if he should run after her, take some time out to walk with her. Then his phone rang and he answered it, to confirm they would need at least four cameras to cover the building. When he looked up she was gone, and his heart ached for her just a little, enough for him to realise that he was in big trouble and falling for her whether he wanted to or not. He hadn't been able to save Ellen, but if he tried maybe he could save Kate from throwing her life away and make her realise that he was there for her.

Chapter 4

Kate found a narrow, overgrown path that led to a stream, which was bubbling away with the recent rainfall. There were some stepping stones across the stream that were covered in green moss. She had no idea how she'd known this, she just had. As she cautiously stepped onto the first one, she expected her feet to go from under her and land arse first in the freezing-cold water, but she managed to keep her footing. Only four more to go.

She stepped onto the next, then the next until she reached the other side and jumped the last bit. Landing on the slippery banking, she almost fell. After windmilling her arms, she managed to catch her balance and let out a sigh of relief. This side of the river was much darker than the open ground she'd just crossed. There were lots of trees and she could just make out where the narrow path continued. Having no idea where it led – but now intrigued – she followed it, enjoying the silence of the woods around her.

Whoever had lived in the house must have used this path quite a lot. After ten minutes she saw a clearing in the trees and the tall spire of St Mark's church came into view. She carried on walking and smiled to see the clearing open onto a worn, wooden gate. It was like the book she'd read when she was a girl: *The*

Secret Garden. The gate didn't look as if it had been used in a long time. The black, cast-iron latch was rusty. Still, Kate had to try. She needed to know where it led. She felt as if she'd been brought here or even as if she'd been here before – a very long time ago.

After jiggling it around, it gave enough so that she could lift it. The gate was stiff, swollen with years of rainwater, and she had to tug it with both hands. It opened a tiny bit – just enough for her to get both hands through the gap. She wrapped them around it and pulled as hard as she could. It didn't open all the way, but it opened just enough for her slender figure to squeeze through. As she did, she turned around and was surprised to see she was in the vegetable garden of another large house. A long overgrown, neglected vegetable garden. It looked as if the current owner didn't have a lot of time or love for tending his garden.

This house was almost as big as the one she lived in. It had the same Gothic, arched, tall windows and was built of the same red brick. Whoever had built her house had also built this one. She felt a cold shiver run down the length of her spine and wondered if she should even be here. Was she trespassing? Probably, but she wanted to go and ask the owner if they knew about the house and its history. There was obviously some kind of connection between them.

Taking the least overgrown route to the house, she fought her way through the dense blackberry and gooseberry bushes. Their sharp thorns snagged her jacket and caught the soft skin on her hands more than once. By the time she'd reached the back door of the house she was out of breath and itchy. She didn't dare to knock on the back door – that seemed so rude – but she couldn't see a way to get to the front door.

There was a padlock on the gate and she wasn't about to start climbing over the garden wall. Someone might call the police and think she was a burglar. That was all she needed. Martin would have a field day. She'd come this far. It seemed stupid not to at least give it a knock and speak to whoever owned it. She walked up the three steps and banged on the back door twice, then she stepped away. It didn't seem as if there was anyone in. She couldn't hear any noise and the curtains were drawn.

Kate was ashamed to say that she didn't even know who any of the locals were. They changed almost as often as Martin changed his girlfriends. She lifted her hand to knock again when the key turned in the lock and an extremely good-looking young man opened the door. His expression was one of mild confusion as to how someone was knocking on the back door when the gate was clearly padlocked.

'Can I help you?'

'I'm really sorry to be so rude. I wondered if I could speak with the owner. Is he in?'

'He is. Why don't you come inside? Can I ask you, though, how on earth you got here?'

Kate felt her cheeks begin to burn. *Answer that without sounding like a complete weirdo, you idiot.*

'I erm, I followed a path from my house through the woods and it led to the gate at the very back of the garden.'

'Is there a gate out there? I never even knew that. The day I moved in I took one look at that garden and walked straight back inside the house. Gardening has never been my thing. I much prefer playing *Call of Duty* when I get a minute. Terrible, I know, and not very healthy, but we all have our vices.'

He started laughing and Kate joined in.

'Sorry, I didn't even introduce myself. I was so shocked to hear someone banging on the back door I thought I was hearing things. Tell me, did you fight your way through all those brambles? That must have taken some doing.'

'I did and I'm sorry. I bet you think I'm a right weirdo but honestly, I'm not. I'm Kate Parker and I live in the big old house on the other side of the woods.'

She held out her hand, which he took and shook firmly.

'I'm Father Joseph, but you can call me Joe. I don't really do all the formalities unless I have to. It's nice to meet you, Kate from the other side of the woods. Now what can I do for you, because there must be some reason you decided to break and enter into the jungle of my back garden?'

Mortified to realise the man was a vicar, Kate was about to splutter an apology when he laughed again.

'Gotcha, I don't care. If you're brave enough to enter the back of beyond there must be a good reason.'

'I just wanted to know if anyone knew the history of that house I've bought? It looks very similar to this one, only bigger. I'm in the process of renovating it. I'm turning it into a bed and breakfast, but there have been a couple of strange incidents and it just made me wonder who lived there before. Well, I know it was empty for at least twenty years and I know it was a convent in the 1930s, but I don't know anything else.'

'Ah I think I know the place you're talking about, although I've never seen it myself. I've only been living in the vicarage three months and I'm still getting my bearings. It's a shame Father Anthony wasn't here; he would know. He was the parish priest here for a very long time – over thirty years. Would you believe that he took over from Father Patrick – who was here even longer? I'm sure Father Anthony would know all about your house, but he's not been very well. He's in the retirement home.'

'Oh, that's a shame, bless him.'

'If you like I can make some enquiries. I'm going to visit him tomorrow. If he's well enough I'll ask him if there's anyone you can talk to. Have you tried the records office at the library?'

'No, not yet and that would be brilliant, thank you. I'll go into town when I have a minute. I'm up to my neck in renovations. The builders are knocking the house to bits.'

'Ah I see. When you say strange things have happened, what exactly do you mean?'

Kate didn't want to say that she thought someone who smelt

of old leather, burning flesh and garlic was in her house, and that they were possibly putting up crosses on her freshly painted walls like they were going out of fashion, in case he thought she was completely off her head. She wanted to tell him something, however. He had the kind of face that made you want to confess your sins without setting foot inside a church.

'Earlier on I thought I heard my friend calling my name when there was only me in the house, only she died three months ago. When I'm on my own at night, after the builders have gone, I hear footsteps on the floor above me, but whenever I go and check there's no one there.' She stared at him, waiting to see if he would start to laugh at her, thinking she was mad. He nodded his head.

'Would you like a cup of tea?'

'Yes, please.'

'Sit down. I'll make us a strong pot of tea and then we'll talk.'

She sat down on the hard wooden chair and watched as he poured boiling water into the teapot. It was very relaxing watching someone else take over for a change. He put a cup and saucer in front of her and took a packet of chocolate biscuits out of the cupboard, shook half of the packet onto a plate and put it on the table.

'My mum would be so proud if she could see me now.' He winked at Kate, who laughed. For a priest, he was a funny guy.

'So, Kate from the other side of the woods, it's time to talk serious. Do you believe in ghosts? Spirits? Zombies? The undead?'

'I suppose so. I can't say I've ever really thought about it. What has that got to do with my house?'

'For want of a better word, I've always been fascinated with anything that wasn't quite normal. I wouldn't usually disclose that to someone who I've only just had the pleasure of meeting; however, I get the impression that you need my help so I'd be grateful if you could keep this between us. I loved reading and hearing about ghost stories when I was a kid, then as a teenager

I used to go on ghost hunts with my friends. Granted, most of the time we were pissed and wouldn't have heard a ghost if it had been screaming in our faces, but we did it. You name an abandoned building and we would go, in the dark with a crappy old camcorder and a torch. Any old hospital, church, cemetery, you name it we went there.'

'I don't understand. How do you go from being a ghost hunter to becoming a priest?'

'Because, Kate, this is where it gets serious. I saw some scary stuff that I couldn't deny existed and if that exists then so must God. In fact, I scared myself so much I couldn't stand to be on my own. So I figured the best way to get over it was to become a priest – plus you get a free house and it's not the worst job in the world.'

He laughed that infectious laugh. 'I can't believe I'm telling you my deepest, darkest secrets when we've only just met, but there's something about you, Kate. You remind me of myself a little. What I'm trying to say in the most ridiculous way ever is that sometimes things that go bump in the night can't be explained in a rational way. Of course, we should always, always look for ways to debunk stuff – that's a given – but when things can't be explained then we need to look for other explanations. These incidents you've told me about, I find a little worrying.'

'So you think my house is haunted then?'

'No, I'm not saying that. What I'm saying is just because it doesn't sound rational don't discount it. You're doing a lot of renovating by the sounds of it so it could just be the house settling at night or it could be that all this work you're doing has disturbed something that had once been at peace. However, there are different types of haunting. There are your benign spirits who just want to stay where they were the happiest, or they might not even realise they're dead. I look at it this way: they are still living their life in a different time frame to you and I. Sometimes we get caught up in each other's worlds, usually only for the briefest of moments, but it does happen. And then there are the real, scary, serious hauntings of either a person, place or even an object. I don't want to scare you, but if there is something in your house calling your name and mimicking your friend; well then, you need to be very careful because this isn't a residual haunting. It's intelligent.'

Kate shuddered. The thought that she might have spent her money on a haunted house was not an attractive one. She sipped her tea, wondering if she'd made a mistake coming here or whether she'd been led here by someone who was looking after her. Her first thought would be Amy; her friend wouldn't want her putting herself in any danger, be it spiritual or conventional.

'I can see by your face you're not impressed with me, Kate, and I'm sorry. I just believe in being honest. I don't want you to spend months hoping it will go away if there's another reason for it.'

'No, it's not that at all. I just never expected my walk in the fresh air to clear my head to end this way. It's all a bit bizarre.'

'Maybe you were meant to find me. After all, that took some determination to cross the jungle out the back. Why don't I give you a lift home – save you ripping what skin you have left on your hands to bits – and I can take a look at the house for you? I'll make some enquiries and be back in touch as soon as I find something out. How does that sound?'

'Bloody marvellous. Thank you so much, Joe.'

He nodded and stood up. 'To be honest, I was stuck and was just about to lose my life, so maybe you were sent to save me from that bloody game that has taken over everything.'

He picked up his keys from the dresser in the hall and she followed him to the front door. An old VW camper van painted pale blue and cream was parked outside.

'Wow, I'm impressed. You don't see many priests driving one of those.'

'Thank you; to be honest, you don't see many priests like me.

I like to be different and besides she's been on many a ghost hunt with me. She knows how things work.'

He opened the door for Kate and she climbed in, wondering what exactly Ollie would think when he saw her getting dropped off in this by a man half her age who wasn't wearing anything that remotely resembled a vicar's outfit. Joe jumped in and started the engine, which sounded like a tank.

'She's a bit noisy, but you soon get used to it.'

Kate nodded. Her hands were stinging now. She needed to go home and wash the scratches before they got infected. She just wanted to put her pyjamas on and drink a bottle of wine to blot today out. Clear her mind of what happened earlier, of thoughts of her ever-growing crush on Ollie and of her newfound, slightly crazy friend. Could today get any stranger? She hoped not. She didn't think she'd be able to cope with it.

As she directed Joe to the drive of her house, she saw Ollie hanging out of the first-floor window shouting up at Ethan who was hanging out of the one above. Her heart lurched. Good job health and safety didn't visit often. She watched as Ollie turned to see who was driving the camper van. He lifted his hand to cover his eyes and squinted. As they got nearer, the surprise on his face when he realised she was in the passenger seat made her heart beat faster. *Stop it now, woman.*

'I see what you mean. This house does look a lot like the vicarage. I didn't even realise it was here. There's certainly some connection. Don't you think?'

'Yes, now that I've seen it I think there is. Are you coming inside?'

She looked at his face, which had lost all the ruddiness from earlier; there was a fine film of perspiration on his forehead as they drove nearer to the front door.

'No, I can't. Not this time. I'll just drop you off if you don't mind. I'll be in touch as soon as I find something out about the history of the house. Is that okay with you?'

Puzzled, she nodded her head. Why wouldn't it be okay? She barely knew the man; he didn't owe her anything. He stopped the van to let her get out, some distance from the entrance.

'Thanks again for the lift and erm, I'm sorry about the trespassing.'

He smiled at her then began to reverse, not even answering. Strange young man, she thought to herself. Then again you didn't get many men his age wanting to become priests, did you? She stood watching as he drove away in a plume of black exhaust fumes.

The sun was beginning to set in the sky and she wondered how late Ollie would stay tonight. She wished he would stay here all night. How nice would it be to know he was there? Hell, she wanted him to stay in her bed. She wanted to make love to him then lie next to him, just knowing that he was there. It had been so long since she'd had anyone to snuggle up with. Martin had never been the snuggling type.

Christ, she needed to stop comparing him with the useless idiot who was her soon-to-be ex-husband. Ollie was nothing like him. There was no comparing the pair of them. She let out a loud sigh. Instead she would spend tonight on her own, trying not to think of what Joe had been talking about, scaring her half to death. She would lock herself in her room with her earphones in listening to music or watching a nice, romantic film until she fell asleep and couldn't hear any footsteps or smell old leather or burning flesh. Then she would wake up in the morning, ready to start the day again. Groundhog Day had nothing on the way her life was going at the moment.

5 January 1933

Agnes towel-dried herself, relieved to be rid of the coppery smell of Mary's blood. Her hands still smelt faintly of bleach. She didn't mind that smell so much – at least it was clean. She thought about going to church to pray for Mary. It was dark outside now

64

and the ground was treacherous with black ice. She would never make it across the river. The stepping stones would be like walking on ice. Instead she decided to go the prayer room downstairs and spend the next hour praying for Mary's soul. By the time she'd done that her appetite might have returned and Father Patrick should be back.

Agnes had managed almost her whole life without a man to take care of her, but tonight it was what she needed, what they all needed. A strong male presence might be enough to deter Lilith from whatever her plans were; she just hoped that Patrick would see through the woman's sob story. The more she thought about it the more she was convinced Lilith wasn't who she seemed. The woman scared her, but Agnes wouldn't let her see that. She wasn't stupid.

Dressed in a warm jumper and slacks, she went downstairs to find Edith and see if she wanted to come and pray with her. After checking the kitchen, front room, library and dining room she finally found her huddled by the fire in the parlour, her head bent close to Lilith's. They were talking in hushed tones and didn't notice her walk into the room. She coughed and Edith jumped away from Lilith as if she'd been caught doing something she shouldn't.

'Sister Edith, I think you and I should go to the prayer room and pray for Sister Mary's soul.'

Edith stood up, her cheeks burning. 'Of course, Mother Superior.'

Edith scurried out of the room, but not before turning to look at Lilith and smile. Agnes felt every hair on the back of her neck stand on end. What had they been whispering about and why the secrecy? If Agnes wasn't wrong, Edith's cheeks were flushed as if she'd been caught doing something forbidden. Agnes led the way to the prayer room and opened the door for Edith, who darted inside.

'Is everything okay, Edith? You looked a little perturbed back there when I walked in. Is there anything you would like to tell me?'

'Yes, Agnes; no, I mean. Everything's fine. We were just discussing Lilith's ex-husband. We didn't want to upset you any further than you already are. He's a terrible man – so violent and so sadistic towards poor Lilith. I can't believe she's not dead because of him.'

'You do know you can talk to me about anything, don't you? I might look old and past it, but I did have a relatively normal life until it kicked me to the gutter and I turned to God. I'm not just a frail, old maid.'

'Of course I do, Agnes, and I don't think that at all. Thank you. I will if I need to.'

But Agnes couldn't push it out of her mind. Edith was the most impressionable of them all, and she wanted to know what that woman had been whispering to her about – more than ever.

***

Edith could feel her cheeks burning because Lilith had been talking about sex – something that she could never in a million years discuss with Agnes. Something that she'd never discussed with anyone. Lilith led such an exciting life. She had been telling Edith how it felt to kiss another woman and Edith had been enthralled. It had made her skin tingle just thinking about it. The whole reason she had joined the convent was because of her fascination with women.

Of course, she'd never acted on her feelings. Her parents would never have forgiven her if she had. She would love to know how it felt to kiss and do immoral things with another woman. She had pretty much managed to stop thinking about it the last twelve months, but Lilith had stirred something in her tonight and she had a warm, tingly feeling between her legs. She wondered what it would be like if Lilith – with her small, slender hands and long, red painted nails – was to touch her between there.

'Edith.'

Edith jumped and looked to see Agnes's outstretched hand. She couldn't concentrate. This was terrible. She tried to think about poor Mary and her body, which had been ripped into pieces, but she couldn't get past the thought of Lilith's small, perfectly formed mouth. How would it would feel just once to press her lips against it and push her tongue inside?

'Sorry, I just can't concentrate. I feel so bad about poor Mary and I can't settle.'

'Very well, you can go and do what you like. Maybe you should go to bed, have an early night. I'll pray for us both and Mary.'

'Thank you, Mother Superior, I think I'll do just that.'

Edith turned to leave and as her fingers reached the doorknob, Agnes turned to look at her.

'Oh, and Edith… I wouldn't get too close to Lilith. I don't trust her and I don't know why she's still here. Surely she has family or friends she can go and stay with? Has she mentioned anyone to you?'

Edith shook her head. She couldn't tell Agnes what she'd been thinking. That she wanted to do nothing more than get close to Lilith. Her cheeks flamed bright red at the thought and she rushed from the room. Her head down, she ran up the stairs and along the hall to the very last door at the end of the long corridor where her bedroom and sanctuary was. She didn't know what was wrong with her. Breathless, she opened the door and slammed it shut, then turned the key in the lock.

She gasped as she turned around to see Lilith lying on her bed, completely naked. Edith wanted to look away, but she couldn't. Instead she crossed the room, shedding her own clothes until she was as naked as Lilith, who patted the empty side of the bed next to her. Edith climbed in. Her last thought before she touched Lilith's pale, white skin was *God forgive me for being weak. I'm so sorry.*

***

Agnes prayed long and hard. She heard the front door slam as Patrick came in, but still carried on praying. Edith was acting strange. She had no idea where that *woman* was – probably in her room, or so Agnes hoped. It seemed that everyone had taken to meek and mild Lilith and fallen under her spell, except for her. Agnes felt repulsion fill her entire body every time she looked at her.

When she finally finished she stood up and kissed the cross around her neck, then she went to the kitchen where she found Patrick removing the emergency bottle of brandy from the back of the cupboard. She sat down, crossing her hands on her lap. He put the bottle and two glasses down onto the table. She watched as he poured both himself and her a drink. She liked Patrick. He didn't expect anyone to wait on him hand and foot like the last vicar who'd rarely made the effort to visit the nuns. When he'd finished he sat down and smiled at her.

'Agnes, can I be frank with you?'

She nodded.

'You look tired; today has been a very long day. How are you?'

She thought about saying the usual: 'Oh I'm fine, Father. I'll be right as rain tomorrow,' only she couldn't. Her shoulders felt so heavy with the physical weight of sorrow for Mary that she didn't know where to start. Her eyes were stinging with unshed tears that were threatening to spill: tears of sorrow, pain and loss. Not to mention horror at what had happened.

'The truth, Patrick, is I don't know. I feel as if something has changed in this house and I know I sound like a crazy old woman, but I'm not. I'm still the same as I was before I went to bed last night. I haven't lost my mind even though I feel as if I have.

Something is wrong. I can feel it in the air and I know how ridiculous I sound because I have no idea what it is or what to do.'

'What do you mean something has changed in the house?'

She leant in close to him. 'The atmosphere, can you not feel it?'

He shook his head. Agnes felt a wave of anger wash over her. This was no good. He didn't see or feel anything wrong. She could. It felt to her as if the house had come alive, as if it were some giant, slumbering beast that had slowly woken up after a very long time. If she strained her ears she was convinced she could hear its heartbeat, very faint, but it was there: a steady thud, thud, thud, which seemed to reverberate throughout the entire house.

'Today has been a very long one. We've all had a huge shock. What happened to Mary? Well, I have no idea, God rest her soul. I'm sure he's taken her into his arms and she's at peace now. I think perhaps you should take yourself to bed and get some rest, Agnes. I'm here. I'll sleep in the lounge. Don't worry, I'll listen out and if you need anything then shout and I'll be there.'

'Yes, Father, thank you.'

She pushed her brandy away. The sick feeling in the pit of her stomach made it churn at the thought of drinking any more of the sweet liquid. As she stood, she saw Mary's reflection staring back at her from the kitchen window. Her head hung limply to one side and her arm was missing. Blood was dripping from her mouth and the front of her nightdress was covered in the bright red liquid.

The room began to swim and Agnes heard the sound of a chair being scraped back against the parquet floor. A strong pair of arms caught hold of her before she fell to the ground. Patrick scooped her up and carried her upstairs to her bedroom as if she were no heavier than a feather. He laid her on the bed and stepped back.

'Agnes, should I phone for the doctor?'

'No, thank you; I think you're right, Patrick. I'm very tired and I haven't eaten much today. I'm sure I'll feel better in the morning.'

She watched him leave, closing the door behind him. As soon as her legs felt strong enough to carry her weight she would lock it, then drag her heavy chest of drawers across to put in front of it. What good that would do was beyond her, but it would make her feel better. A voice whispered in her ear: *It didn't help poor Mary, did it? She's still here, stuck in this house with nowhere to go.* Agnes could no longer keep her eyes open and she closed them, sinking down into a deep sleep. So deep that she didn't make it off the bed to lock her door.

Chapter 5

Kate watched Ethan and Jack drive away in Ethan's battered Corsa. Ollie was still working upstairs and she was so glad. She had been unsettled all day. It had felt as if someone was watching her and she'd kept turning around every few minutes to be greeted by empty space. As she'd crossed the hall she saw a dark shadow at the top of the stairs. Fear had filled her mind and she opened her mouth to scream, but it had disappeared leaving her questioning herself.

She had no idea what was going on. She was blaming Joe and his talk of all things spooky. Going back into the kitchen, she filled a pan with water and put it on the hob to boil. She would make some pasta that was quick and easy. After chopping bacon, garlic, chillies and tomatoes, she sautéed them ready to add to the cooked pasta. Pour over an M&S shop-bought pasta sauce and bake a garlic baguette and – hey presto! – she would look like a gourmet cook. She wouldn't have to admit to anyone she'd cheated. She took the bottle of Pinot Grigio from the fridge and poured herself a small glass. As she took a sip she felt it begin to work its magic. Her whole body started to relax. Ollie walked in and sniffed the air.

'Something smells very nice.'

Kate laughed. 'It's just some pasta and garlic bread. Would you like some? I mean it's the least I can offer after crushing your pie at lunchtime.'

He chuckled. 'It still tasted pretty good though. I don't want to put you out, Kate. Have you got enough?'

She turned around so he couldn't see her cheeks flare red. 'I most definitely have enough for the both of us, but do you need to get home?'

She wanted to ask if Mrs Nealee would have already cooked his tea and be waiting for him to go home, but she didn't. He was old enough to decide where he wanted to eat and who with. Maybe they weren't getting on after all.

He shook his head. 'No, not much to go home to really; not now I'm on my own and besides I will only dream about eating some of your pasta and garlic bread when I get there. So you might as well feed me and put me out of my misery.'

'I'm sorry, I didn't realise that you and your wife had split up.'

He smiled at her with such sadness in his eyes it made her heart ache for him.

'I think it would be easier to accept if Ellen had left me for someone else; only she didn't leave because she wanted to. She passed away last December.'

The shock almost rendered Kate speechless. She'd had no idea. So consumed in her own grief and crappy life, she hadn't read the newspapers or kept in touch with anyone.

'I'm so, so sorry to hear that, Ollie. I had no idea.'

'Don't be daft; you weren't to know. It's not something I'm comfortable talking about openly. It still hurts too much, but I guess you know how that feels – losing Amy. You two were very close, weren't you?'

She nodded. Her eyes misting up, she turned away as he sat down on one of the chairs and watched while she cooked. 'Would you like a glass of wine to go with it?'

'You know I think I would. It's been a long time since I've

had a meal cooked for me by a beautiful woman, or a glass of wine.'

He winked at her and she wondered if he was flirting with her. Or was she so obsessed with him that she was taking every single word and twisting it to fit what she wanted it to? She took out another glass and poured him one. Passing it over to him, her fingers brushed his. She jolted back her hand. It felt as if she'd got an electric shock. It must have been static. It was like a small charge of lightning rushing through her veins.

The food was ready so she plated it up and served it, slicing the garlic bread and placing it in the middle of the table. She sat opposite him so she could watch his chiselled, tanned, good-looking face. He was so attractive and she would very much like to get to know him better. He was grieving though, and it was obvious he was still hurting. There was no way she would make the first move. If he wanted her as much as she wanted him then it was down to him. When he was ready, she'd be here. It wasn't as if she had anywhere else to go. In the meantime, it was nice just to have a friend to lean on again.

He talked about how much better the house looked and what needed doing. Before long they were chatting, eating and drinking. He was funny. He made her laugh a lot and she felt so much better with him here. She wondered if he would stay the night. Ollie finished his pasta, mopping up the sauce with the last piece of garlic bread.

'That was wonderful; thank you, Kate.'

'You're welcome. It's the least I can do. I can't believe how hard you've been working on this place. It really looks so much better. I like that it's lighter now. It was so dark before. Even though we've kept as much of the oak panelling and woodwork as possible, I think the white and pale grey really lighten it up.'

'Yes, you have good taste. It's so much easier when the client knows exactly what it is they want the finished project to look like. Well, it is for me; it makes my job easier anyway.' He finished his wine and stood up. 'I suppose I'd better get going. I need a soak in a hot bath. My bones are aching a lot more than they did twenty years ago.'

Kate felt her heart sink. She smiled and didn't let her disappointment show. She wouldn't let him see how desperate she was, but the thought of being on her own tonight wasn't one she relished. She walked him to the front door so she could lock up behind him. As they walked through the house to the front hall she smelt a faint whiff of the odour from this morning and sniffed. What was that smell? She'd used garlic to cook with. She'd had the kitchen window open and the extractor fan blasting. It shouldn't be lingering at the bottom of the stairs.

'Can you smell that funny smell?'

Ollie looked around and sniffed a few times, then shook his head. 'The only thing I can smell is fresh plaster, paint and that pasta you made. What can you smell?'

'I don't know. It's like a faint whiff of garlic and burning flesh all rolled into one.'

'Nice. Nope – I don't really know what burning flesh smells like to be honest, though.'

She started to laugh, not wanting him to think she was drunk and delusional. 'It must be the garlic bread. I did burn it a little.'

He opened the front door and turned to kiss her on the cheek. 'Thank you again. It was nice eating a meal like a civilised person. I could get used to it. I'll see you tomorrow and if you need me for anything before the morning don't hesitate to ring. I mean it, Kate, if you get worried or hear noises phone the police then ring me. Promise?'

'I promise; thanks, Ollie. See you tomorrow.'

She shut the door and turned the lock, afraid that if she watched him drive away she would be too scared to go back inside on her own. His engine started and she heard the sound of his tyres on the gravel as he drove away. *Fuck, fuck, fuck.* Forcing herself to be brave, she decided to check the entire house just to make sure there was no one in it before she locked herself into her makeshift bedroom for the night.

Kate walked back to the kitchen and the drawer where she kept the huge torch Ollie had left there for her in case of a power cut; then she locked the back door and made her way into each room, checking they were secure. She got to the very last room downstairs and opened the door. When she flicked the light switch there was a bang as the bulb exploded and she swore to herself. Turning on the torch, she shone it around the empty room. Satisfied there was no one in there, she pulled the door shut.

As she made her way upstairs she could still smell whatever the odour was from before. She forced herself to carry on. She was tired and sad that Ollie had actually driven away. Maybe she should have asked him to stop. Feeling tetchy and more than a little bit angry she ran to the top of the stairs to check each room upstairs. The first two were fine and so was the third but as she got to the fourth one a feeling of dread began to settle over her. *Man up, Kate, it's just a big, old, empty house. That's it, nothing more. You're spooking yourself. This is your dream house, so check the rooms, then you can get to bed, on your own once again.*

She tutted out loud. Sometimes she wished she could turn off the internal voices in her head. Grabbing the handle she twisted the knob and threw the door open. Flicking on the light switch she grinned to herself. The room was empty. It smelt of fresh paint and the window was open a small gap. She crossed the room to pull it shut. She didn't want the wind to pick up in the night and cause any draughts or banging doors.

As she was trying to tug down the heavy wooden frame, she didn't see the figure dressed in a nun's habit watching her from the doorway. She did, however, get a creeping sensation on the back of her neck that someone was behind her and her heart raced. Kate whipped her head around, but the doorway was empty. She managed to slam the window down so loudly the noise echoed around the room. Then she turned and walked back out, switching off the light and closing the door behind her.

As she walked out onto the landing a cold chill went right through her entire body, as if she'd just walked through a cold spot. She shook her head. *No, it felt like you walked through a ghost.* She shuddered. The rest of the bedroom doors were closed. Suddenly she didn't feel so brave. Her anger at Ollie for leaving her and the strange feeling of being watched unsettled her. She was torn. Did she finish checking the rooms or did she go down to the safety of her bedroom where she felt comfortable, cocooned in her own little world and surrounded by the few things she owned that meant something to her?

A muffled thud echoed around the hall, making her jump. As she turned in the direction where it came from, a vision of a beautiful, petite, dark-haired woman flashed through her mind. She was staring straight at her. The woman smiled and whispered, 'Hello, Kate, welcome to my world.' Then she was gone and Kate knew that her name was Lilith. The word filled her mind, silently screaming a warning to her. The door from the room where she'd heard the noises earlier and where that smell had come from was ajar. How had that happened? Or more importantly who had opened it? Because it had been shut seconds ago.

Kate wasn't a fool or particularly brave, but she wanted to know what was going on. This was her house. Every penny she had was being ploughed into renovating it. If it was something to do with Martin, as Ollie suspected, then she wanted to know. If only she had cameras. She would ask Ollie tomorrow if they could hurry them up somehow.

Can you really go downstairs, knowing that someone is up here? Are you going to sleep soundly when anyone could be prowling around? She knew that she would, but only in an alcohol-induced haze and she didn't want that. She wanted to get her life back together without relying on alcohol. Her feet made the decision for her and began striding towards the door. She held the torch up to use as a weapon in case she needed to defend herself.

'I've phoned the police so whoever you are, you might as well come out and show yourself. Then you can tell me what the fuck you are doing in my house because I've had enough.'

Her voice trembled a little, but she was quite impressed with herself. As she reached the door and heard no reply, she kicked it as hard as she could with her right foot. It slammed open against the wall inside and she shone the beam around. The room was empty. Reaching in she flicked the light switch down.

As light banished the shadows she saw the outline of a huge black figure with glowing red eyes and she screamed. Horror filled her soul, and she heard a voice whisper in her ear, 'Get out, demon, you're not welcome.' The black figure vanished and she turned to see who was standing behind her. She was shocked to see nobody there. Out of the corner of her eye she could have sworn she saw the ghostly figure of a nun disappear at the top of the staircase.

Her legs shaking so much she could barely stand, she stumbled towards the stairs. Where did the nun go? As she stared down she felt a sharp push in the small of her back and lurched forwards, wondering if this was how she was going to die. As she fell forwards, another pair of hands broke her fall. They pushed against her chest, stopping her from going any further.

Kate managed to catch her balance, saving herself from falling down. She whispered 'thank you' under her breath. She knew in that moment that there was something evil in this house. The nun had saved her, but from what: a small, pretty woman called Lilith or a monster? Her hands shaking, she went into the kitchen where she pulled a bottle of wine out of the fridge and struggled to pour some into a glass without spilling it everywhere. As she leant against the sink she wondered if that had really happened or whether it had been a culmination of today's events making her mind play tricks on her.

Overwhelmed with fear and exhaustion, she picked up the almost empty bottle of Pinot and hurried to her room. She was unsure if she should phone the police. Did they attend haunted houses? She gulped down the wine, needing it to work its magic and spread its warmth through her cold, weary body.

Opening her bedroom door she took a deep breath. She liked the feeling in here. No matter what time of day it was or who was banging around upstairs, whenever she came in here it felt peaceful, uncontaminated. Where did that come from? This house wasn't contaminated – or was it and by what?

When the rooms were all finished and the attic had been turned into a self-contained apartment for her and the girls, she would keep this room as her office and library. There was something about it that made her want to keep it all for herself, her sacred haven from the outside world. Closing the door behind her she put the bottle and glass down on her bedside table then dragged a chair over to wedge under the doorknob. If anyone or anything was still in the house they wouldn't be able to get in without waking her up. If she needed to, she could escape through one of the windows. She had it all planned out.

Too tired to shower, she undressed and put her pyjamas on. Then, plugging her phone in to charge, she sat down on the bed, cross-legged, and poured herself a large glass of wine. The first one she drank as fast as she could, then tipping the rest into the glass, she turned the radio onto Smooth FM. Her eyes already felt heavy. The wine had begun to warm her insides enough to make her start to finally unwind. She wanted to fall asleep, not have any bad dreams or think about Ollie – just sink into oblivion until her alarm vibrated in the morning.

***

As the clock reached 3 a.m. the scratching began again. This time it was more insistent as it tried to gain Kate's attention. The house filled with shadows that moved from one room to the next and the beast that had waited a long time for someone to move into this sad, unloved building felt its presence getting stronger. The crosses the nun had put up were crushed on the floor of the room she'd tried to keep sacred. The nun was strong and stubborn, it would give her that, but she wasn't a match for it and never would be.

The black, winged shape stood outside Kate's door, listening. Its long, sharp talons began to scratch the door harder. It wanted the woman to wake up and hear it. It wanted to terrify her and control her. It wanted to crush her like it had the nuns.

***

Kate thrashed around in her bed. In her dream there was something watching her and it had red, glowing eyes. She tried to wake herself up and couldn't because whatever it was she'd seen earlier was now inside her bedroom, pinning her to the bed. It was strong and she was trying her best to throw it off her and scream, but she couldn't move. She was held down, breathing in the fetid stench of decay and gagging on it. Her mouth was open, but no sound was coming from it because her vocal cords were frozen.

The harder she fought against it the less she could move. She knew she was dreaming and tried to summon up the image of Ollie, the safe image of the man she wanted to come and save her more than she wanted anything. The weight was so heavy on her chest her entire body was aching from it and she began to pray the only prayer she knew: Kate Parker's version of the Lord's Prayer. She closed her eyes so she didn't have to look at the thing sitting on her chest and repeated the prayer over and over again. She felt the weight shift and carried on, then it was gone as fast as it had appeared and her eyes flew open. She took in huge gulps of cold air to ease the burning in her suffocating lungs.

She was so terrified that she couldn't move a muscle. She lay there taking deep breaths and feeling dazed. What was that? Had she just had the worst nightmare of her entire life or had it really happened? She was so scared she wanted to pull her legs up and curl into a ball under the covers, spending the rest of the night praying to God to protect her from the horror that had just happened. *It was just a dream, it was a dream,* she kept repeating over and over until she felt brave enough to try and move.

Her hand snaked out from underneath the duvet as she pressed the switch on the small bedside lamp; she felt the warm glow from the light, but couldn't open her eyes in case that thing was still there watching her. After some time, when her breathing had almost returned to normal and her sixth sense told her she could open her eyes, she did. She looked around her room and then lay her head back on her pillow.

She felt violated. This was her space and she'd come to bed relieved that she had her own sanctuary to protect her from the outside world, and it had been taken over by something dark and evil. Forcing herself to sit up, she looked to see the chair was still in the same position. *It was a nightmare, Kate – a bad dream and nothing else.* But no matter how many times she repeated it she couldn't shake the feeling that it had been real and that she was in serious trouble.

***

Ollie woke up early. He'd taken ages to fall asleep because all he kept thinking about was Kate. He should have plucked up the courage and kissed her. He thought that she liked him or he hoped that he did. She looked so desperately sad when he'd said goodbye – or was that just his overinflated ego telling him this? He looked at the empty side of his bed. It had been three years since Ellen had slept next to him. Three long years since he'd felt the warmth of someone close to him, even if it was just to hold her.

80

Once she'd got too ill to climb the stairs he'd turned the front room into her bedroom. He missed her so much, but Kate had made him realise that he didn't want to spend the rest of his life alone. He didn't want to ever forget how wonderful the years of his marriage were before Ellen got ill. He also didn't want to throw away the rest of his life. He wanted to go on holidays, but it wasn't the same on your own.

Before Ellen got ill, they'd gone to New York and he'd loved every single minute of it. Ellen had hated it with a passion; it was too busy and loud for her, but he'd enjoyed the hustle and bustle. He wondered if Kate had ever been and what it would be like to whisk her away for a long weekend to the city that never slept. He also wished there was something he could do to help her with the drinking, although she wasn't a complete mess and a stinking drunk like his dad had been.

If she continued like she was it was very likely it would happen eventually and he couldn't bear the thought of her throwing away the gift of the life that she'd been given. He'd been watching her since the day he'd first been to look at the house and had found himself in awe of her stubborn ways. He loved the fact that despite everything she'd been through she still had her fighting spirit, not to mention the fact that she was brave living in that huge house all alone. She wasn't a damsel in distress; she was quite capable of fighting her own battles and he admired that about her because it was so different to what he'd expected her to be like.

What would be terrible was if she found the bottle more appealing than living her life and began to give it all up. He wanted to offer to help her, but he didn't know if it was his place to do that or not. Was he overstepping the mark? He pulled up outside the front of her house, taking the brown paper bag with the freshly baked bagels and two lattes. He tried to open the front door with his key whilst balancing the coffees and bagels in one hand. It wouldn't turn. Kate must have left the catch on or she was still in bed.

After knocking on the front door, he waited, but couldn't hear anything from inside. This time he hammered with his fist, mild panic beginning to form in his chest as he wondered if he should have left her alone last night. Still no noise from inside. He walked around to her room and tried to peer through the crack in the curtains. The bedside light was on but it was hard to make anything out and he felt a bit of a pervert. He stepped back and banged on the window.

A few seconds later the curtain was drawn back and a tousled Kate, still in her pyjamas, was staring back at him, her eyes screwed up against the bright light. She pointed in the direction of the kitchen door and he grinned, relieved to see she was okay. By the time he'd walked around she was standing there in her bare feet with her arms wrapped around her trying to keep some warmth in. Although the sun was shining it was cold. She stepped to one side and mumbled, 'Morning.' Her voice was hoarse.

He followed her in, closing the door behind him and handed her a coffee. 'Rough night?'

As soon as he'd said it, he regretted it. Why did he always sound as if he was interrogating her?

She didn't seem to notice and shook her head. 'You could say that – well, not once I'd fallen asleep it wasn't. At least until I had the scariest dream ever. Thank you for the coffee, that's really kind of you.'

'I also brought food. I thought you might fancy a warm bagel for breakfast.'

She looked into the brown paper bag. 'You thought well. They look and smell delicious. I'm starving.'

He went to the cupboard and took two plates out, then picked up two knives from the draining board. He passed her a plate and she took out one of the huge bagels and began slicing it in half. They ate in silence and Ollie found it hard not to stare at her. There were dark bruises on her shoulders and he wondered how on earth she'd got them. He wanted to ask her about them

82

but couldn't. He didn't know why he was acting like this, but he couldn't stop himself and found that he had to force himself to look away from her.

***

'Oh, do you think you could ask your friend about the cameras? I'm willing to pay extra if he can sort something out today for me.'

'Already sorted. I felt bad leaving you on your own last night, so I rang him as soon as I got home. He'll be here by eleven and will put up as many as he can.'

'Phew, that's brilliant. I think I'll feel a lot better when I can keep an eye on the place and see who's coming and going.' She didn't add 'and see if they're human or not'.

'Was everything all right when I left?' -

Kate wanted to tell him that 'no, it bloody wasn't', but she couldn't. What if she was hallucinating or having some kind of alcohol-related episode? She didn't want him to think she was a raving lunatic. Instead she nodded and smiled at him but she didn't look him in the eyes because she couldn't lie to him. She liked him too much.

There was a loud knock on the front door and Ollie jumped up. 'I'll get it.' He went to the front door where Jack and Ethan were waiting to be let in. They went straight upstairs, the smell of McDonald's lingering on their clothes. He went back to the kitchen to get his coffee.

Before he could say anything, they heard Ethan shout at Jack. 'You're a wanker. Why did you do that? It took me ages painting those doors yesterday. It's not even funny.'

Kate stood up, her face burning. 'Shit, that's my fault. I forgot about it. I better go and apologise.'

She ran off to go and find Ethan. Ollie, who obviously had no idea what she was talking about, followed her.

'Ethan, I'm so sorry; it was me who made the mess of the doors.'

Ollie looked at the door Ethan was standing next to with his hands on his hips, looking all defensive.

'Oh, that's okay then. I thought it was Jack being a dick.'

'No, it's not okay. I didn't mean to and I'm really sorry for causing you more work.'

Kate looked up at Ethan and it was then that she noticed the cross on the door and she felt as if the air had been sucked out of her lungs. It definitely hadn't been there last night. 'Who put that there?'

All three of them shook their heads.

'It's not funny. I'm sick of this. I don't even bloody like the damn things yet someone keeps putting them up. It has to stop. Do you hear me? I don't know if you think it's funny or not. This is my house and if I wanted crosses all over it, I'd put them there myself.'

***

She stormed off, leaving all three men with open mouths and more than a little bit puzzled by her outburst. Ollie looked at the footmarks then the cross. He pulled at it, but it was stuck. It must have been put there when the paint was still wet. Which meant it had happened around the same time that for whatever reason Kate had decided to kick the door open. Jack went inside the room and shouted.

'You'd better come in here, boss. I don't know what's going on, but she's going to freak when she sees this lot.'

Ollie walked into the room and felt a chill run down his spine. The entire wall opposite the window was covered in crosses and crucifixes. Every single one that Kate had collected on that very first day and put into the cardboard box outside in the shed was now back in the house and on that wall – except for three crushed and broken ones on the floor.

Ethan pointed to the footprint on the bathroom door. He lowered his voice and whispered, 'Do you think she's losing the plot? What's she doing kicking doors? Why did she put these up if she hates them so much then try and blame us?' He held his finger to his head, turning it round in circles. 'I mean she likes a drink or four, doesn't she? When we've left, she gets hammered and maybe that's when she starts doing weird stuff. You know like an attention-seeking thing.'

Ollie crossed the room and shut the door so Kate couldn't hear their conversation. 'No, I don't think she does and don't ever let me hear you talk about her that way again. Have a bit of respect, Ethan; in case you've forgotten she's paying you cash in hand for your time and effort. I don't know what's happening, but we owe it to Kate to try and find out. Have either of you got a phone with a camera on?'

They both nodded and rolled their eyes.

'Take photos of the door and this wall, but don't show them to Kate. I'm going to go and talk to her. Stay up here and get cracking on the big room at the end of the corridor. Shut this door. I'll ask her what we should do about the crosses; actually, before you start work I want you to both go outside and check all the outbuildings to make sure no one is sleeping rough in there. I watched Kate put the box of crosses into the stone building and I can't see her going out in the night to retrieve it. Something's not right.'

'Should she not be calling the cops? I mean if there's something weird going on or someone's breaking and entering should we even be looking for whoever it is? They might be dangerous.'

'Man up; there's two of you. If Kate wants the police involved then we'll bring them in. For now get yourselves outside and check there's no one there or there's no place that anyone could hide.'

Ollie didn't miss the look Ethan gave Jack and if it wasn't so absurd he would have burst out laughing. Give them three pints of Stella and they'd take on the world, but the thought of looking through the sheds and outhouses in broad daylight was freaking them out. He turned around and left them to it so he could go and talk to Kate.

The front door was open and Kate was sitting on the top step with her dark sunglasses covering her eyes, her coffee cradled in her hands. He wanted to go to her but something held him back. The sound of tyres on the gravel drive got nearer and he went to look out of the living room window. He recognised the big navy Range Rover. *Bollocks.* He'd told him he was taking a couple of weeks off work. He'd be fuming when he saw that he was still working here. Martin was parking his car right next to his van.

Kate, who had dressed in her tight faded jeans and a big baggy grey hooded sweatshirt, stood up, pushing her sunglasses on the top of her head. Her hands were on her hips. Ollie thought she looked as if she was about to do battle. The rear doors opened and there was a loud screech as two girls, not yet teenagers but not far off, jumped down and ran towards Kate, who stood there with her arms wide open. They hit her with so much force she almost fell over. She just managed to stand her ground and Ollie couldn't help but smile at the wonderful sight of Kate cuddling her girls.

***

Kate covered her daughters with kisses and hugged them as tight as she could without squeezing the life out of them. 'I've missed you both so much. You look so grown up, the pair of you. How did that happen?'

Both girls giggled and kept hold of her. Martin got out and walked across to where Kate was standing. Even he smiled to see his daughters so happy, which made a change. Kate had to look twice at his mouth to see what was going on. His smile, which had never been anything to shout about, was now brilliant white and his once crooked teeth were now straight. He looked Kate up and down.

'Not sure what look you have going on there, Kate, but it doesn't really do you much justice, does it? Look at the state of you, of your clothes. Are you actually doing the work on this monstrosity yourself?'

Kate kept hold of her daughters and pushed her glasses back down on her eyes. She lifted a finger and pointed to his teeth.

'Good God, Martin, step out of the sunlight. Your teeth are blinding me. Where on earth did you get them from? Some poor horse must be missing them. You should really give them back.'

She giggled at her own joke. Ollie, who was still inside watching, had to stifle his laughter. *Kate one, Martin nil.*

'How dare you! I came here to make a truce and this is how you repay me.'

'Don't play the martyr with me; you gave the first insult, remember? What have you come for anyway? You didn't bother coming to visit when I was at the flat.'

Not wanting the girls to get tangled up in any arguments, she bent down and whispered to them, 'Why don't you go and have a look around our new house. Go and pick which rooms you'd like for bedrooms and I'll have the builders get them ready just for you.'

Her daughters laughed and ran off into the house.

'Don't get mucky. We have to go to Tamara's in five minutes and I don't want you both looking like your mother.'

'Ouch, what's wrong with looking like me? You're such a prick. So what do you want? Because this isn't a social visit.'

'Nothing. I heard you'd bought this place and thought I'd call and see if you were still a stinking drunk or whether you might be getting your act together.'

Kate crossed the short distance to him and slapped him across the face with her right hand as hard as she could. The sound echoed around the garden it was so loud.

'You're a fucking bitch, Kate, always have been. I should have known better. Summer, Autumn, come on – we have to go. Say goodbye to your mother.'

He spat the word 'mother' out and Kate wanted to kick him in the balls, but she didn't. She waited to kiss and hug each of her girls before they left. It might only have been the shortest visit in the history of the world, but at least she'd been able to hold, kiss and smell them, which meant more to her than anything. She bent down and whispered close to their ears, 'As soon as this place is finished I'm going to try my best to get you both here with me. In the meantime, be good for Daddy. I know it's hard because I find it hard, but it won't be long before we're back together.'

Her daughters kissed and hugged her again then ran off towards the waiting car where Martin was revving the engine. They climbed in, slamming the doors, which made Kate smile. He hated it when anyone slammed his precious car doors and she saw his shoulders tense at the noise. He turned the car and drove away. Looking at her one final time. he shook his head. She couldn't help herself and gave him the finger. The bastard could go and fuck himself. As soon as this place was habitable she would fight him tooth and nail for custody of her girls.

A battered van passed Martin's shiny monstrosity on the drive and she prayed this was her camera man because she'd feel a whole lot better if she knew no one was sneaking around outside her house once it was dark. If he had any spare she would get him to put one on each floor so she could monitor the bedrooms to see exactly who or what was going to and from them once the house was quiet.

Ollie came outside. He placed his hand on her arm, gently turning her to face him.

'Are you okay, Kate? I wasn't listening, but it's hard not to with his loud mouth. What a prick he is. Honestly, I can't believe the way he treats you, but you did really good. In fact, you did great.

It must be so hard for you not being able to see your daughters and knowing they're living with him. You're a pretty amazing lady, Kate.'

She smiled, even though her heart was breaking in two for her daughters. She could cope because once this place was up and running she would be back on track and she had the hope of getting them back to cling on to. Earning a living, she would be able to provide a safe place for them all to live. As long as she could find out what the strange smell was and who was playing games with her.

She wondered how Martin had found out about this place because she hadn't told him. It definitely wouldn't surprise her if it was him or he was paying someone to try and scare her to death because that would be just the sort of underhand, sneaky thing he would do. Especially if he thought she'd come into money that he didn't know about. He was so greedy he would want a share of it even though he had left her penniless. The van parked up and a man about the same age as Ollie climbed out.

'Morning, lad. Took some finding, this place did. It's certainly off the beaten track. No wonder you want some cameras installing.'

'Mark, this is Kate – whose house it is – and yes, we need what you have installing today if possible. It's really important.'

He nodded, looking at the pair of them then he arched one eyebrow at Ollie. Kate felt her cheeks begin to flush and turned to go back inside, leaving them to it. She felt a lot better now. She had no idea what was going on with the banging around or what the hell Martin had wanted, but it could wait. She would go and make some coffee for everyone. She could even have a packet of biscuits still in the cupboard if the lads hadn't already eaten them – her attempt at a peace offering.

She might go for a walk through the woods again, clear her mind. No wonder she was a mess. There was so much going on she didn't know what to start with first. This time she wouldn't be paying Father Joe a visit though, not like yesterday. He'd told her he'd come and see her when he found anything out so she'd have to wait for him. She just hoped he would have some answers for her. Then again, did she really want to know what was happening? After last night was it better to carry on and be oblivious to everything?

Chapter 6

As Father Joe shook hands with the last mourner to file out of the crematorium, he breathed out a sigh of relief. Funerals were his worst nightmare. He hated trying to talk about someone's life – someone who most of the time he'd never met – and make it sound as if he cared. He did care, just not to the extent that he should. How could you? Most people didn't bother with church or religion anymore. Priests no longer received the same respect in communities that they once had and a lot of it had been brought on by their own misconduct.

The family were gathered outside – all hugging, kissing and crying – and he felt like an intruder. He had never met Christopher Phillips and for all he knew the man could have hated religion. Turning around he slipped back into the crematorium so he could leave by the front doors and not have to stand around making small talk with the family. He had promised Kate he'd do some digging around into the history of that house she was renovating, and he had to admit she was a very attractive woman. Not that he was interested in her in that way, but she gave off an air of vulnerability that made him want to help her as much as he could.

He passed the huge, red velvet drapes, which had closed in

front of the coffin for its final goodbye, and he shivered. It was cold in here, yet minutes ago he'd been so warm. Sweat had been forming on his forehead and threatening to drip down into his eyes, blinding him from reading out his passage about the recently deceased. A noise from behind the curtains made him stop in his tracks. Obviously it was one of the crematorium attendants.

He waited to see if it happened again. There was only silence. As he turned to face the curtains, they moved towards him – ever so softly – but it looked as if someone was standing behind them, pushing them forwards. Why would someone be doing that? If they thought they were going to scare him they could sod off. It was hardly the time or the place to play stupid buggers, not when there was a coffin behind there. He didn't care if whoever it was thought it was funny. It wasn't; it was disrespectful.

'Who's back there? What are you doing? It's hardly the right place to be messing around now, is it?'

Silence greeted him and he felt uneasy. There were only windows on one side of the building and they were frosted so no one could see in. It had turned very dark outside as if there was a heavy rain shower on its way.

'Hello, is someone there?'

Still no reply. Joe turned and walked towards the front doors when he heard a distinct giggle and it belonged to a woman. It was far too high-pitched to be a man and it was coming from behind the curtains. His fear turned to anger, and he strode back towards them. Whoever was behind there was disgraceful. There was a coffin with a dead man inside. Why would they want to play tricks on him in a crematorium? It didn't bear thinking about.

He reached the thick, velvet drapes and for a moment he thought about turning around and running as fast as he could out of the doors. It didn't matter if he had to pass the family, he could just smile and keep on walking – only he couldn't. His sense of respect and pride towards the man who was about to be cremated was too strong.

Yanking the curtains to one side he didn't understand because the only thing he could see was the coffin. He inhaled the over-powering smell of fresh lilies and looked around. There was nobody there. It was dark behind the curtains so he tried to push them to one side, but they were heavy and ran on a track, which was remote controlled. The small, dark space was filled with the coffin and floral arrangements and nothing else. He bent down to look underneath the stand holding the coffin in case someone was hiding underneath it.

'Can I help you, Father?'

Joe half screamed in shock at the voice behind him. Whipping around, Joe saw one of the assistants standing there with his hands on his hips, wondering what the vicar was up to.

'Jesus Christ, you gave me a bloody heart attack.'

The bemused man – who was obviously not used to hearing a vicar curse – chuckled. 'Sorry about that. I just wondered what you were doing.'

'I, erm, I thought I heard someone behind here. Behind the curtains, I mean. They were giggling.'

The man walked across to the wall where he pressed a switch and held it in. The curtains began to open again. He didn't stop until they were as wide as they could be. The coffin was once more on display for the public.

'I bloody hope not. I'd hate to think we'd locked someone in here with a coffin on their own. It would be enough to send you round the bend.' He walked behind the coffin and around the sides, then he went to the small door at the side and twisted the handle, which didn't turn as it was locked and he had the key in his hand. He turned to face Joe and shrugged.

'Are you sure it came from in here? It might have been one of the mourners. Sometimes sounds can carry. It's so quiet and eerie in here when it's empty.'

Joe was positive it had come from behind the curtains. Who had made the heavy material move so effortlessly when he'd struggled? 'It must have been – sorry. False alarm. I just didn't want to think someone was messing around in here. Not when there's…' He pointed to the coffin and the man smiled.

'I know what you mean. Honestly there's no one here; maybe it was a ghost. This place is full of them. Well, if you believe in all that mumbo jumbo. I have to say I don't. I've worked here ten years and the scariest thing I've seen is the priest from the other church conduct a whole funeral talking about how missed Janet would be when he was at the wrong one, and it wasn't until he'd finished the end of his sermon when the deceased's daughter stood up and announced that her father had never been called Janet in his whole life. My, how I laughed. It was wrong and terrible, but it was so funny. The poor priest couldn't get out of here quick enough and the poor bloke's brother had to stand at the front and start all over again. Mind you, some of the lads won't come in here on their own through the day and once it starts to get dark they won't come anywhere near, which is a pain in the arse because I always end up doing the late funerals on my own. Good job I'm used to it. They are always saying they can hear things and voices. I can't say they've ever heard anyone giggling though.'

Joe was trying his best not to look horrified and he knew he was failing miserably. If he thought his job was grim it was nothing compared to the poor people who had to work here. 'It probably came from outside; you're right. I didn't sleep much last night. I'm a bit jumpy, that's all. Sorry to have bothered you. I'll let myself out.'

He turned away from the coffin and walked towards the back of the room. He needed to get out of here and get some fresh air. He hadn't imagined it. He'd clearly heard the sound of a woman giggling from behind those curtains, but what the hell did it mean and who was it?

He reached his camper van, which he'd parked as far from the crematorium as possible, and climbed inside, relieved when he started the engine and drove away from the cemetery. He looked at the clock on his dashboard. He was still in time. He'd made an appointment to visit Father Anthony at the retirement home. He was the only priest who once served this area and still lived here. It had been a while since Joe had last visited him, though, and he hoped Father Anthony was still as sharp as he had been last year. As he pressed the buzzer to be let in, he heard the camera as it zoomed in on him. It was sad times when old people's homes needed CCTV systems to keep them safe. He supposed it helped if any of them decided to go for a wander without telling anyone.

The door clicked and he pulled it towards him, stepping inside into the much darker entrance. He walked towards the large reception desk where Julie who he'd gone to school with sat there typing away on the computer. She looked up at him and smiled. Joe smiled back. They'd gone out with each other for about a week when they were 12 years old. They'd even kissed behind the bike shed twice then she'd left him for Stevie Matthews whose dad owned a corner shop, which meant Stevie had a never-ending supply of both sweets and money. He'd been gutted at the time, but he'd got over it, eventually.

'How are you, Joe? It's lovely to see you.'

'I'm good, thanks. Yourself?'

'Oh, you know, pretty much the same.'

He detected a hint of redness creeping up her neck and he wondered if she still had a bit of a thing for him after all this time. He wasn't vain, but he knew he'd turned out slightly better looking than Stevie Matthews who was now married to Julie, plus he still had a full head of hair. He didn't really know what pretty much the same meant, but he did his best to give her his most sympathetic smile.

'I'm here to see Father Anthony; he's expecting me.'

'Yes, I know, he's been here every half an hour or so asking if he'd missed you. Bless him, he's not as sharp as he used to be. He gets a little confused about time, although he's not too bad compared to some of them.'

She stood up to take him but before she could come around from the other side of the desk an elderly man with the thickest shock of grey hair and watery blue eyes appeared.

'Ah, Father Joe, glad you could make it. I've been waiting for you.'

Joe smiled at Julie, then turned to follow Father Anthony back down the long corridor to his bedroom.

'It's very good of you to see me at such short notice, Anthony. I really appreciate it.'

The man laughed so hard he had to stop to catch his breath. When he could finally speak he shook his head. 'Now that's funny. You know it's not as if I'm inundated with visitors. You're the first one I've had for weeks.'

Joe immediately felt bad. How much effort would it take for him to pop in once a week and visit him for ten minutes? He would make sure from now on he did just that, but time flew by so fast sometimes he would find himself standing in front of the congregation on a Sunday morning and wonder where the past week had gone since his last sermon. Anthony opened the door, which led into his bedroom, and Joe was pleasantly surprised that it smelt of lavender air freshener and nothing else. The room was a good size and there was a huge bookcase next to an over-stuffed armchair. Next to it was a small side table piled high with books, a notepad and pen. A half empty bottle of gin and an empty glass filled the last remaining space on the table.

'So what can I do for you, Joe?'

'Do you know anything about the big, empty house that you can get to through the woods at the back of the vicarage?'

Anthony motioned for Joe to sit in his armchair and he sat on the bed opposite him. 'Why do you ask? I haven't thought about that place for a very long time, over forty years to be exact.'

'I was talking to the woman who's bought it and is renovating it.'

'Good God, someone has bought that place? Why? Who in their right mind would buy it? You must have heard the stories.'

Joe shook his head.

'Are they local? This woman – is she married? Does she have a family?'

'To be honest, I don't really know. I only met her yesterday. She came to the vicarage and noticed that both buildings are built in a similar fashion so she wanted to know if there was a connection between them. From what I can gather she's living there on her own.'

Anthony crossed himself. Fiddling with something under his jumper he pulled out a heavy gold chain with a cross on it. He held it to his lips and kissed it. 'I thought that they would have demolished it by now, it's been empty for so long. The last I heard, the church still owned it. I don't understand how they could sell it to a woman of all people.'

Joe was beginning to feel uncomfortable. He hadn't meant to upset the old man in front of him, but he had no idea what he was talking about. 'Anthony, I know nothing about this house or what might have happened. You will have to tell me so I can tell Kate – the woman who has bought it.'

'Yes of course, forgive my rambling. That house – I've never known anything like it. This might sound ridiculous. It's as if it's alive. It knows what scares you. It's like a predator that will prey on your worst nightmares. It feeds off them – off the fear you keep inside of you. It's not like any normal house. It was once a house of God, but not after that terrible night. It changed – they let that woman in and it changed their lives for ever.'

Joe was trying to make sense of what he was hearing. Was it the rambling of an old man or was it true? 'What exactly happened there, Anthony, and how long ago was it?'

'Well now, let me see.' He stood up and began looking through his books until he pulled out a thick, black leather journal. 'This was given to me by Father Patrick. I was taking over the parish and he handed it to me and told me to take good care of it. He left with a stern warning not to go to the convent alone, to make sure it was always boarded up and to warn anyone who might be a potential buyer to think again.'

'The convent – so it was part of the church then?'

'Oh yes, it most certainly was, and it was a very successful convent. I think there were six nuns and a mother superior. It was all going well until some of the nuns got sick and died. This was back in the 1930s.'

He opened the book and began looking around for his glasses, patting his pockets down. Joe pointed to the top of his head where the gold-rimmed spectacles were sitting.

'Yes, it was December 1932 when some of the sisters fell ill and died, and then one fateful night in January 1933, they opened the door to a woman who came knocking in the middle of a snowstorm, asking to be let in. That night one of the nuns died in the most strange and horrific circumstances. It doesn't go into great detail.'

He looked up at Joe. 'Apparently Sister Agnes, who was the mother superior, kept a journal detailing every little thing that happened over the next few days. From all accounts it was horrific, bloody and violent. There was talk at the time of the woman they'd let in. I can't for the life of me remember her name. She was supposed to have been the cause of it all. If you could get your hands on the journal Agnes wrote you would know a lot more than what I can tell you. This is just a record of the people who lived in the house until the day they decided to shut it up for good.'

He handed it to Joe. 'You can keep this if you like. I don't have any need for it now. There was talk about the house being haunted. It was a bit of a local legend in the Fifties when I took over as parish priest. I can't believe the church have sold it, to a woman of all people.'

Joe said, 'I suppose it's like everything else: times are hard. If you don't believe in any of this stuff then it wouldn't bother you, would it? I mean 1933 was a very long time ago. Surely whatever happened back then is over and done with. Do you know where this diary could be, Anthony? Is it still in the house or would the church have hold of it?'

Anthony shrugged. 'As far as I know it's still in the house, although Patrick could have taken it for safekeeping and put it in the vicarage somewhere. I suppose you would have to ask the woman who's living there now what it's like in there. Has she experienced anything out of the ordinary?'

'Yes, she has mentioned some strange goings-on.'

He didn't go into detail – not wanting to upset the elderly man in front of him any more than he already had. He'd felt complete revulsion as he'd driven along the drive towards the house yesterday. It had been so powerful that he'd had to turn his car around and leave. It had been a long time since he'd felt anything so strong. He stood up, feeling guilty that the man in front of him had paled significantly. He'd stirred up long-forgotten memories for him, which he had no right to do. Needing to speak to Kate more than ever, he had a bad feeling inside the pit of his stomach that he should warn her about the history of the house.

'Thank you for your time. I think I'd better get going now. I've kept you long enough.'

'My pleasure, Joe. I wish I could have told you something a little happier. Tell me you are going to speak to this Kate and tell her that house is full of evil. Tell her from me that under no circumstances should she be left alone there.'

'I will. I'll go there now and tell her everything. I think we need to find Agnes's journal. That would be very helpful.'

'Yes you do, but be warned, it's been hidden for a long time, son. There must be some reason for that. You take care and when you go inside that house make sure you surround yourself with God's light and love. Make sure you ask him for protection because to go inside without it would mean whatever it is that lurks inside will be able to get inside of you and you don't want that.'

Joe nodded. He left Anthony staring out of the window onto the front street. He had no idea what he was thinking about; he just hoped he was going to be okay. As he passed Julie she stood up, smiling.

'It was lovely to see you, Joe. Will you be coming back?'

'Yes, of course I will. Thank you, it was nice to see you as well. Take care, Julie. Would you please ask a nurse to check on Anthony in a little while? He may have got a little bit excited talking about the old days.'

'He's such a sweetie. I'll go and check on him myself in a few minutes. Bye.'

'Bye.'

Joe left feeling confused and worried about Kate. What had Anthony meant when he'd said 'that house – it knows what scares you'? How could it? It was a house. Anthony had made it sound as if it was a living, breathing thing. Joe got into his car, determined to drive straight to see Kate and tell her what he'd found out. *And she'll think you're a stark raving lunatic. Do you know how crazy it all sounds?* He did, but if he didn't tell her he'd carry the extra weight of it around on his shoulders until he did.

He looked at his watch; it was almost six. Today had to be the strangest day he'd had in a very long time: first the crematorium and now this. He finally reached the turn-off for her drive and felt the same burning sickness form in the pit of his stomach as he turned onto what should have been hallowed ground. It made his insides churn. His forehead broke out in a cold sweat and his heart felt as if it was going to burst through his chest. He felt as if he was having a full-blown panic attack. As the house came into view, he couldn't help thinking how desolate it looked. There were no cars outside or work vans like yesterday. A pair of ladders leaned against the side of the house underneath what looked like a newly installed video camera. There was no sign of life.

It was getting dusky and the windows were all dark. No matter how hard Joe tried he couldn't shake the image of the house being alive – that it was its own living, breathing entity – and he stopped the camper van because his shaking hands were too hard to control. 'It's just a house, it's just a house,' he kept repeating over and over again as he forced himself to get out of his van and walk towards the front door. The workmen must have all gone home so maybe Kate was in there on her own.

He wanted to turn around and drive away so much, but he knew that he couldn't. She might be all alone, ready to fall prey to whatever it was that she was scared of. That the house knew she was scared of. He wanted to laugh out loud at himself, but he couldn't because right at this very moment every single word that Anthony had told him rang true and he believed him.

He pressed the doorbell but nothing happened. There was no sound of chiming from inside so he lifted his hand, curling it into a fist, and hammered on the old wooden door. The sound echoed around the empty building inside. Stepping away so he could run if he needed to, he waited for the sound of Kate's footsteps to come. There was nothing. He knocked once more then jumped back, his body feeling as if he'd just got an electric shock. A mild sense of relief that there was no one in flooded his body. At least he'd tried.

He turned and walked back to his car. Not once did he turn to look up at the house. He didn't even look at it when he began reversing. For some reason he knew that if he stared up at the windows he was going to see the ghostly figure of a nun or worse. Instead he switched his lights on full beam and drove as fast down the overgrown driveway as he possibly could, hoping that

Kate or one of the builders weren't driving as fast in the opposite direction towards him.

6 January 1933

At some point in the night Agnes woke up. Her throat was so dry she'd begun to cough in her sleep and thought she was choking. As she left the safety of her bedroom to go down to the kitchen she was angry with herself. She should have brought a drink of water upstairs with her. Now she would never get back to sleep. She shivered. The house was cold, too cold, and she pulled her woollen blanket closer around her shoulders. As she got to the bottom of the stairs she jumped to see Lilith standing there, waiting for her in the shadows.

'Sorry, Sister, I didn't want to cross you on the stairs in case it was bad luck.'

The light was terrible, but she could make out the expression on the woman's face. She was wearing that sly smile that she seemed to reserve just for her. 'What are you doing up so late, Lilith?'

'I thought I heard a noise and came down to check the front door was locked. I didn't realise that Father Patrick was asleep in the front room. I only just stopped myself from falling over him, lying there on that sofa.'

Agnes wondered how on earth she'd almost fallen over a man on a sofa when she'd come down to check the front door. The woman made her skin crawl and she got a faint whiff of that terrible smell of rotting flesh once more. She stepped off the bottom step and looked into the huge mirror on the wall opposite – above the mahogany sideboard. The hairs on the back of her neck stood on end; the only reflection in the mirror was hers. Lilith walked slowly up the stairs, her back to Agnes. She should have been able to see the back of the woman's head, but there was only herself staring back.

Agnes turned around to look at the petite woman who was

halfway up. She slowly turned back and stared at Agnes, whose heart was beating so fast she wondered if she was about to have a heart attack and collapse on the spot. Why did she have no reflection? It didn't make sense. It wasn't right and then the burning feeling that had been irritating her underneath her skin for the last couple of days erupted as she realised what she had feared was completely true.

The woman had to be a vampire. There was no rational explanation as to why she smelt of rotten flesh, had the palest of skin, didn't go outside in the daylight and had no reflection. Hadn't Lilith herself thanked her for giving her permission to enter the convent? Vampires needed permission to enter a home before they could feast on the human inhabitants. Agnes forced herself to carry on walking towards the kitchen for her glass of water, her mind a swirling fog of confusion.

She lifted her fingers up to feel the heavy weight of the silver cross that she never took off her neck. If this was true then thank God she had his protection. She switched the kitchen light on and crossed to the sink. She wanted to run and wake Father Patrick up. Oh God what if she'd been down here because she'd seduced him and been feasting on his blood? Agnes turned and hurried towards the lounge where she'd left him earlier. As she opened the door the sound of his gentle snores filled the air and a sigh of relief escaped her lips. *Calm yourself down, Agnes. What on earth is the matter with you? Talking such rubbish. You need to sort yourself out. You're acting like a superstitious old woman.*

As she closed the door, she didn't hear the muffled scream that came from Edith's room, because her own heart was pounding so loud in her ears. Returning to the kitchen, she ran the tap and filled a glass with cold water. While the tap water filled the sink she never heard the sound that emanated from the room at the opposite end of the corridor to hers. Her hands still shaking, she made her way back upstairs and back into her room.

Dragging a chair over, she pushed it underneath the doorknob. Her stomach was churning inside and her hands were shaking. Did vampires exist?

She had been under the impression when she'd read the book that they were all a figment of Bram Stoker's twisted mind. Maybe he'd known all along they were real and that was why his book was so convincing. She would ask Patrick what he thought about it all in the morning. As she climbed back into her bed, she couldn't switch her mind off. Had it been a vampire that had killed Mary? But she had been torn to pieces, literally. Didn't vampires suck blood? If that was the case Lilith would have sucked Mary's blood until she was an empty shell of herself. No, poor Mary had been ripped to bits and there had been blood everywhere – so much of it.

The hammering on Agnes's door woke her from her slumber. It took her a few seconds to focus. She had been in such a deep sleep.

'Agnes, you need to get up and come see. I can't get into Edith's room and I had a terrible nightmare. The door's locked and she's not answering.'

Agnes blinked at the sound of Father Patrick's deep voice. *Please God, not again.* She got out of bed as fast as her weary legs could go. She felt drained, exhausted. What was the matter with her? She pulled a thick grey woollen jumper over her head and caught sight of her reflection in the mirror. She was shocked to see how pale she was. Stepping closer, she turned her head to the side and ran her finger over the two, dark red, crusted puncture marks on it. The blood was dry, but they were there. She wasn't imagining it. How had they got there? It made no sense.

Turning around, she checked if her door was open. The chair was still wedged under the handle. A cold draught ran down the full length of her spine and she shivered. She turned to face the window and gasped. It was open six inches. It had been shut last night, and because it had been such a mad, crazy day yesterday she hadn't even thought to crack it open to let some fresh air in like she usually did.

'Agnes, can you hear me? Are you all right?'

'Yes, Father, I hear you. I'll be out in a minute.'

She stepped away from the mirror, pulling the roll-neck jumper above the two puncture marks. She didn't want Patrick to see them. What did it mean? Was she unclean now? Oh Lord, was she going to turn into a vampire? This was terrible. Unable to concentrate, she dragged the chair away from the door, almost laughing out loud. What a waste of time. It hadn't stopped whatever it had been that had come inside her room one little bit. Patrick was standing outside waiting for her. His face looked almost as pale as hers and she wondered if he'd also had a visit in the night and had two puncture marks on his neck.

'Agnes, why isn't Edith answering? Has she gone out early? Do you know?'

'Father, I have no idea where she is. As far as I know she wasn't planning on going anywhere today.' She dragged her feet along the long corridor to Edith's bedroom.

'Edith, it's Agnes. Are you ill?' Déjà vu filled her head. It was as if yesterday morning was replaying again – only with Edith instead of Mary. Agnes felt her heart hammering inside her chest and her hands trembled. She looked down to see if the key was in the lock like Mary's had been. The lock was empty so she twisted the brass knob, which was freezing cold to her touch. It didn't open. She couldn't think. Where was her spare key? Oh yes, it was attached to the key ring that had been lost. She turned to Patrick.

'Have you looked through the keyhole?'

'No, I have not; it wouldn't be right.'

Agnes supposed the man had a point. She twisted the handle once more and it was definitely locked. 'You're going to have to break it down, now.'

'Shouldn't we call Constable Crosby and let him do it?'

'No, what if she's injured and needs medical attention? Can't you at least try and break it?'

Patrick nodded and stepped back. Agnes moved away. Clasping her hands together, she prayed that Edith had gone out for an early morning walk, locking her door behind her. He ran at it with his shoulder and there was a loud crunch as he slammed into the door and let out a bloodcurdling scream.

'What's the matter?'

'I think I've broken my collarbone.'

Agnes watched in disbelief as he shrunk into himself and backed away from the door. Turning, she went downstairs to phone for the police. Where was Lilith? All the noise they had made and she hadn't put in an appearance yet? Yesterday she had been there on the stairs watching from the sidelines with eyes as wide as saucers. After she relayed her fears to Crosby and told him that Father Patrick had been unsuccessful in his attempts to break the door, she listened to the man on the other end of the phone as he gave his instructions.

'Sister, please step away from the door and don't let the good priest do any more damage to himself. If you could wait downstairs for us to get there we'll be as quick as we can.'

'Thank you, Constable.'

She replaced the receiver and turned around to see Patrick standing at the top of the stairs listening to her.

'We're to wait downstairs for him to arrive and he will take care of it. Come on, let's get something cold to put on your shoulder and see if Sister Edith turns up and wonders what all the fuss is about.' But she knew deep down inside that it was too late for Edith and the poor girl was lying dead in her room behind that heavy, oak door. Agnes didn't want to have to face the mess again like yesterday and her heart didn't know how much it could take. Those girls were the closest things she had to daughters of her own.

If Edith had met a similar fate to Mary she would never forgive herself for not being there to take care of them. Patrick sat down on one of the battered, pine chairs and groaned. Agnes picked up a tea towel from the side and ran it under the cold-water tap. Wringing it out, she told him to undo his shirt so she could place it on his damaged shoulder. Thinking he would object, she was mildly surprised when he didn't and tried to slip his shirt off. She helped him as gently as she could. His shoulder was turning dark purple and blue in front of her very eyes. It was an explosion of colour that seemed to be spreading. She placed the cold cloth on the centre of it and heard him gasp. She looked at his neck. There didn't seem to be any puncture marks on it – unlike hers.

'I'm afraid you've made a bit of a mess of that. I've never seen such bruising appear so fast.'

'I'm sorry, Agnes, but I feel quite faint. My head's spinning.'

'Try and drop your head as low as you can. I'll make you some sweet tea.'

Something very wrong was happening in this house. They should never have let Lilith in. A loud knock on the front door startled her and she went to let Constable Crosby in. She opened it to be greeted by a solemn-faced Crosby and his slightly younger junior constable – if that was what you called him, she wasn't sure.

'Any sign of Edith? Please tell me she was out walking and has come back.'

Agnes shook her head and stepped to the side to let them in. 'Where's Father Patrick?'

'About to faint in the kitchen. I'm afraid it's my fault. I asked him to try and break the door down and he's done some damage to his shoulder. It's a complete mess of bruises and he's not taking it so well.'

Crosby rolled his eyes at the other man. 'You'd better show us which Edith's room is. I have to say I do not really want to look inside in case there's a replay of yesterday.'

'And I am? These girls are under my supervision, Crosby, and up to now I don't seem to be doing a very good job of supervising them.'

She didn't wait for his answer and trudged up the stairs, each one looking steeper and steeper. Her legs were so tired and she felt so drained. She led them to Edith's door, not really wanting them to get it open. Maybe it would better if they all left it alone and ignored the facts. Crosby stepped forward and twisted the handle. It turned and clicked as the door opened. Agnes felt her mouth fall open. How was that even possible?

Before he pushed it wide open, Crosby shouted, 'Sister Edith, it's Constable Crosby. I don't want to come in if you're not decent but we're worried about you.'

The silence that greeted them was so heavy Agnes felt as if it weighed her down even more. He looked at her and she nodded, too afraid to see what was on the other side, yet needing to know.

'Edith, I'm coming in so if you don't want me to you need to tell me right now.'

There was no answer so he opened the door and looked at the sight of the naked, spreadeagled woman on the bed in front of him. A groan escaped his lips. 'Not fucking again. Jesus Christ.' Agnes squeezed past him not wanting to see but needing to. He grabbed her arm.

'Agnes, I don't think you should.'

But she pushed past him and crossed herself. Dear God, what had happened in this sacred house? Edith was tied to the bed by her arms and legs. Her naked body was almost too much to bear. Agnes walked closer, needing to know how she had died. Agnes saw that her arms and feet were bound to the bed with what looked like dirty, off-coloured bandages. Edith's cold, glassy, dead eyes stared at her – sending a shiver down her spine so violent that Crosby reached his hand out and placed it in the small of her back to steady her. There was a dirty strip of bandage wrapped so tight around Edith's neck it was cutting into the soft, fleshy skin. There was a faint smell in the room of herbs and spices mingled with the smell of something damp and foisty – something very old.

'Can you smell that, Constable?'

Crosby tore his eyes away from Edith's body and looked at Agnes. 'Smell what, Sister?'

'I don't know exactly what it is. It smells how something very old, even ancient might smell.'

He shook his head. 'I don't know what you mean. All I can smell is death. Poor Edith. Have you got a sheet to cover her with for now until I've spoken to someone back at the station to see what the hell I should be doing here? Pardon my language.'

Agnes forced herself to walk towards the linen cupboard down the hall for a fresh sheet. There was only her left. What did that mean? She must be next, but why had they kept her until last? It came to her: whatever that woman Lilith had told them was all lies. She was evil, a demon in disguise, and they had let her inside. Of course, no one was ever going to believe her. They would take her away to the local sanatorium for the mentally insane, but it wouldn't matter one little bit where they took her because she was marked. That woman, demon, what-ever she was, had left for now, but she didn't think she was very far away because she would be enjoying this spectacle far too much.

Agnes had to figure out how to stop it because there was no doubt in her mind this was just a game for it, and she was the last piece standing on the board. Unless you counted Father Patrick, but he didn't live here. He hadn't been here the night they had opened the door and willingly invited her in. Agnes took one of the crisp, clean cotton sheets off the shelf. As she closed the door she got a whiff of rotting meat and knew that Lilith was close by.

Lifting her crucifix from around her neck she kissed it and began to pray under her breath. Agnes might be old and weak when it came to her bodily strength, but her faith – which had never let her down all her life – was stronger than ever. As she walked back to Edith's room the smell dissipated. She would fight that thing with whatever strength she could muster. She would not be left for dead in her bedroom – which was her most private sanctuary – for all and sundry to see. She passed the sheet to Crosby who shook it out and threw it across the bed.

'I think it would be best if you were to wait downstairs now, Agnes, and let us get on with our jobs. We need to work out who would want to hurt Edith in such a terrible way and why. I don't want to scare you; there's only you now. I think perhaps when we leave today that you should go too. I don't want you stopping in this house on your own. There's a killer out there somewhere and until we find out who it is and lock them up, we have to consider that you are in grave danger.'

Agnes smiled at Crosby. She felt as if she was losing her mind, shaking her head. 'I can't leave. Whatever has done this to poor Edith and Mary will come looking for me wherever I go. I would rather stay in my home and fight it on my ground because I fear that it will be a fight unlike anything I've ever known.'

The young man standing next to Crosby looked at her then at Crosby as if to say, 'She's mad, maybe we should lock her up.'

'Well, if that's how you feel, Agnes, then I'll be stopping here with you. I'm not leaving you on your own to face a killer. No disrespect to you, but you're not as young as you used to be. If whoever it is comes back, we'll be here, waiting.'

Now the young man looked horrified.

'Thank you, Crosby; however, this isn't your fight and I fear it's not one that can be won with the strength of a young man or two. This is a spiritual fight. There is evil at work in this house of God and I will stand and fight my ground.'

***

Crosby didn't know whether it had all got too much for Agnes and she was losing her mind or whether she had a point. He wasn't a particularly religious man. He'd heard stories about things. He remembered the preaching and sermons from his childhood about God fighting the devil. Did this stuff actually exist or was there some sick individual trying to drive Agnes mad? He took her elbow and led her to the stairs. As they reached the top step, she paused and inhaled.

'You must be able to smell that? There is a stench in this house that was never here before we let that woman in two nights ago. It's as if the house itself is rotting from the inside out. The devil came a calling and we invited her in.'

***

Agnes walked into the kitchen where Father Patrick was sitting, nursing his bruised shoulder. 'I have some bad news for you, Father.'

'I think I already know what it is. Crosby, what happened?'

'I'm not sure a man of your position should know, to be truthful.'

'Well, this man almost broke his shoulder trying to break down that heavy, oak door to check on Edith, yet you arrive and the door is unlocked. It doesn't make sense. Is the key in the other side of the lock? Is there someone hiding somewhere in this house?' Agnes asked.

'I think we need to make a search from top to bottom because Edith's killer isn't too far away in my opinion.' Agnes noted how uncomfortable the policeman looked at Patrick's suggestion. At the same time she felt relief that the priest agreed with her to some degree. He didn't think she was mad. Thank the Lord for that small mercy.

'I'll, erm, I'll go and get Peter. He can help us.'

***

Crosby left them in the kitchen and ran back upstairs to see Peter standing on the landing, his hands tucked into his pockets and facing away from the bedroom. He beckoned him to come inside the room and he watched as Peter forced his feet to walk closer. Once inside the room he pushed the door shut and looked to see the key was indeed in the lock on this side of the door. How had it been locked? Who had opened it? Unless the killer had still been inside when the priest was trying to break the door down?

He crossed the room to check the windows in case they'd left that way. They were closed tight and as he pushed the curtain to one side he could see it was a long drop down to the ground from here. There was a good chance that if someone had jumped from it, they would have broken a leg, if not their neck, and how the heck would they have shut the window behind them? Unless they had a ladder. Yes, that was it. He would go outside and see if there were any signs on the ground of a ladder being there.

'What do you think about this lot, Peter? I know you've never seen anything like it before, but do you think that it could be the priest? Even Agnes, I suppose, could do something like this if she was losing her mind.'

'Are you having me on, Crosby? Why would a priest do something as sick as this? And he wasn't anywhere near here yesterday morning. As for Sister Agnes, I doubt it. She doesn't look as if she could fight her way through a crowd of school children. Why would they want to do something like this anyway? This is pure evil if you ask me.'

'Bloody hell, have you been eavesdropping, Peter? What a load of rubbish – something evil. Yes, I don't doubt for a minute that someone evil has done this. I don't believe in any of that religious crap and I suggest if you want to go far in this job that you don't believe every old wives' tale that you hear.'

'I went to church every Sunday without fail, even when I was ill my grandmother who brought me up would drag me there. I would sit and listen to the priest go on about the flames of hell and eternal damnation. Has it never crossed your mind that there might just be some truth to all of that religious crap that's written in the Bible?'

'Go and look outside and see if there's a ladder propped up anywhere that our killer could have used to make their great escape. If there isn't then we are going to have to search the house because for what it's worth I believe that they are still here, somewhere – hiding – and I think they are listening to us.'

He pointed to the huge oak wardrobe in the corner and nodded his head. He moved towards it and Peter – who placed his hand on his chest as if he thought his heart was going to escape and land on the rug beneath his feet – followed closed behind. Crosby lifted a finger to his lips and reached out a hand to pull the doors open. If there was someone in here, he would beat the shit out of them and then listen to what they had to say. As his hand touched the small brass handle, he wondered if they shouldn't just wait for a couple more men to get here. They hadn't checked the house yesterday. He'd thought that poor Mary had done whatever it was to herself.

He counted to three then yanked the doors open. The wardrobe was empty apart from a selection of robes and a couple of jumpers and skirts that were hanging inside. He pushed them to one side just to be sure. The hairs on the back of his neck began to rise and he felt the skin on his arms form into goose bumps. Someone was watching them. Turning around, he looked but couldn't see anywhere a person could be hiding. He looked up at the ceiling. Unless there was someone hiding up in the attic? Maybe there was a hole in the floor so tiny that you couldn't see it with the naked eye, but whoever was up there was watching and could see everything.

He never said a word but motioned for Peter to follow him out of the room. Closing the wardrobe doors, he walked out to the hall and shut the bedroom door behind him. He didn't speak, but started walking downstairs. Peter followed him, anxious not to be left alone in the house. Once they were outside Crosby whispered.

'Did you feel as if someone was watching you up in that room?'

Peter nodded. 'I did. It didn't bother me until you pointed to the wardrobe and then my heart started to beat so fast I thought I was going to drop dead.'

'I think we need a couple more men. Then we are going to go up in that attic and search every inch of it. You go and wait around by the back door in case they try to escape and I'll wait here until the others arrive. I'll just go inside and use the telephone to ring the station. If you see anyone, shout as loud as you can.'

Crosby watched him trudge around the back and felt a little mean about making him go off on his own, but what choice did he have? He was convinced the killer was hiding inside the house somewhere and they might try to make their escape any minute now. *Or they might kill the nun and the priest whilst you're outside waiting like a scaredy-cat for help to come. What happens if you go back inside and both of them are dead? What then, Mr Policeman? Who will get the blame?*

He swore underneath his breath. What choice did he have? They were together. It was safer in pairs and he would hear them if anything happened. Surely they would shout or scream for help? *Unless one of them is the killer and then they won't, will they?* He shook his head and walked to where the telephone sat on the hall table.

Picking it up he dialled the station and spoke to the inspector. His last words before he hung up were: 'Please hurry.' As he replaced the heavy receiver he still couldn't shake the feeling of being watched. He swung around to look up the stairs, expecting to see either Mary's mutilated, torn body or Edith's limp one staring down at him. There was no one and he sighed a lot louder than he meant to.

Crossing the hall to the front door he thought he heard a

high-pitched laugh behind him. It sounded as if it was distant, possibly from upstairs, but he knew that the only person who should be up there was Edith and she was stone cold dead. So who was that? Once outside, he began to pace up and down, not looking behind him at the convent. He couldn't. He knew he was being stupid, but there was something wrong with that building and although he wouldn't admit it to anyone, he didn't know that a rational explanation could be found for it.

Chapter 7

Kate paid for the tins of paint and box of light bulbs to replace the ones that had blown last night. She didn't want any part of the house not to be lit up should she need to go anywhere inside it. Ollie placed them in the trolley and pushed it towards his van. They loaded it and began the drive back to the house.

'Thanks for taking me there. I didn't want to have nothing to do all night. I get so bored there on my own. Don't get me wrong I love the peace and quiet when all the banging stops, but I miss the company.'

'No problem, anything to help. It's not as if I have much to go home for; in fact, I might come back with you and finish the tiling in the en-suite of bedroom three.'

'Honestly, Ollie, you need a break. You've been here all day.'

'You can't complain about a builder who wants to work longer. Normally they down tools and leave at teatime.'

He winked at her and she smiled. *I'm not complaining but I want you to stay with me – bugger the tiling.*

'What do you think of those cameras? They're pretty good, aren't they? They're infrared as well. I know they're not the cheapest, but I think it's worth it for your own safety.'

'They're brilliant and you're right. I'm going to have a play around with them so I know how to work them.'

The entrance to the drive came into view and for the first time since she'd bought it, Kate found her stomach churning at the thought of spending another night here, alone with whoever it was that had a fetish for crosses and crucifixes. The house came into view and it took her breath away. It truly was an impressive building and she loved it more than she'd ever loved any home she'd lived in.

So no matter what was happening she wasn't packing her bags and leaving just yet. This was going to be her home, her business and the start of her new life. With a bit of luck, the cameras would capture whoever it was that was trying to scare her to death. *And what if they're not human – then what?* She shuddered. Did she believe in ghosts? She didn't really know. It wasn't something she'd ever had time to consider. As much as she wanted to believe that it was because she needed to cut down on the booze or that it was Martin trying to make her life a misery, there was a voice at the back of her head telling her neither of those things had anything to do with it.

It was all a bit like an episode of *Scooby Doo*. She'd loved that programme as a child; in fact, the vicar's camper van looked a bit like the dream machine that they'd all driven around in. She would watch the cameras tomorrow and probably find out it was Martin creeping around in her house, trying to scare her to death. At least then she'd be able to confront him, and everything would be sorted once and for all.

Ollie parked his van around the back so she could take the paint into the kitchen rather than have to carry it through the hallway and down the long corridor. She jumped out and ran to open the door. Her hands were shaking a little. She needed a drink, but she wouldn't drink to excess in front of Ollie because she found it shameful – the fact that she relied on the alcohol to get her through the night. She was trying her best to cut down.

She needed to be clean and sober if there was a chance that she could win her girls back in court, because Martin would use it as a weapon against her if she didn't. He wouldn't hesitate to drag her sordid downfall out for everyone to see and she wanted her girls back so much.

They went into the kitchen where Kate turned the light on. Ollie carried the tins in, putting them on the floor next to the fridge, and she carried the bulbs. He left her standing on her own and went to finish the last few tiles that had been driving him mad this afternoon. Grabbing the small stepladders from the front room she flicked switches in each room, checking if any bulbs needed replacing.

The sooner the electrician came the better, because at this rate she was spending more money on keeping the building lit than she was on paint. The two lads who were helping Ollie and the plumber had left over an hour ago and she'd forgotten about changing the bulbs until she'd realised the sun was setting. She'd had to ask Ollie to nip her to the DIY store. She loved this old house, but until she knew what was going on and every single inch of it enough to feel comfortable in she didn't like being on her own and in the dark, especially not after the nightmare last night.

As she put the ladder underneath the entrance light, she heard the crunch of the heavy Land Rover's tyres on the gravel drive before she saw it coming. She climbed down off the ladder just as the car door slammed shut. Her heart heavy, she wondered what it was Martin wanted. She wasn't about to apologise to him for this afternoon. It had been his own fault. Since he'd discovered she had bought this place he'd not stopped texting her. She knew he wanted to know where the money had come from, but she wasn't about to tell him. If he couldn't work it out for himself it was tough and it was none of his business anyway. And then he was there standing in front of her. He hadn't even knocked and had just walked in. Kate felt the hackles on the back of her neck rise – how bloody dare he?

'I didn't hear you knock?'

'The door was open. How are you, Kate? Have you calmed down?'

She began to laugh and had to force herself to stop when she realised he was being serious.

'How am I? Why would you even want to know? Did you want to know how I was the night of my accident? The night my best friend died and I couldn't get to the hospital to say goodbye to her? Did you ask how I was when you changed the locks on the house and wouldn't let me see my own daughters? No, you didn't. I don't recall you asking once.'

'You mean the night you crashed into the wall near Asda because you were drunk? The night you got arrested for drunk driving and spent in police custody, locked in a cell until you were sober enough to be interviewed? The reason you didn't get to say goodbye to Amy was all your own fault and had nothing to do with me. What was I supposed to do, Kate? You were a complete mess. I didn't want the girls to see you like that or to have to put up with any of the aftermath that was coming. You would have done the same. What did you want me to do?'

She shook her head. She should tell him to get out now, but he'd ripped apart the tiny seam inside her that had been holding everything together all this time.

'I wanted you to hold me, to stand by me. To tell me everything was going to be okay and that you would help me to stop drinking.' She inhaled as her breath caught in the back of her throat. She furiously tried to blink back the tears that were threatening to fall because she had kept them in for so long and this was one conversation they had never had.

'I wanted you to stop going out drinking with your golfing buddies and stay in with me, to come to my first AA meeting with me for some support, but that was never going to happen. I wanted you to stop fucking every girl under the age of 25 who you set your eyes on and that never happened either.'

She could feel her voice rising in anger. He stepped towards her, holding his arms out to her, and she pushed them away. Did he think he could walk back into her life and sweep the whole shitty mess under the table? A tear escaped from her eye and she turned away so he couldn't see it.

***

Ollie had finished the last tile and was just putting his tools down when he heard the loud voices downstairs. He looked out of the window and saw Martin's car outside. He tried not to listen to them, but it was pretty hard when the whole house was silent and their voices carried up the stairs. He had been thinking about Kate a lot – no, more than a lot. If he was honest, she was all he'd been thinking about the past two weeks. Kate was funny, intelligent, she loved to read and it tickled him that every single time she sat down for a break she was on her Kindle. She hadn't worn a scrap of the make-up that she used to plaster herself in, but she did always smell good.

Even underneath the plaster dust or paint splatters she always smelt of Chanel perfume. She was tanned from the warm weather they'd been having and had a sprinkling of freckles on her nose that he thought was so cute. He scolded himself: *man up, this is a business relationship so you'd better keep it that way*. As attractive as he found her, he knew that she also had her demons. He'd watched the bottles she put out in the recycling bin mount up every day and although she never smelt of alcohol through the day he knew once they'd all gone home and she was on her own that she would drink.

He couldn't blame her. She'd had a terrible time, but then so had he and he hadn't turned to drink – although that was more to do with watching his alcoholic dad slowly throw his entire life down the drain. He made his way to the first-floor landing. He would have to go down and face the music unless they went out of the hallway and he could just leave. Thankfully, his van was parked around the back so Martin wouldn't have seen it and he could make a quick getaway without complicating things.

'Just go away, Martin. Why are you here anyway?'

'I just wanted to see how you were. I miss you, Kate. The girls miss you.'

That was the sucker punch right in the stomach. She must have been feeling her heart rip in two. Ollie, who was now standing on the landing listening, wanted to go down and punch Martin for being such a complete and utter bastard.

'I think it's time we talked. I know things went from bad to worse in a matter of days, but you must still love me. You can't have stopped loving me completely.'

Ollie felt his fingers curl into a tight fist. Of all the low-down dirty tricks. He'd heard that Martin was going to divorce Kate. Now he knew about this place he'd be wanting to get as much information from her as possible so he wouldn't have to give her any of his property or wealth. In fact, it wouldn't surprise Ollie if Martin wanted a piece of this place.

***

Martin had crossed to where Kate was standing in the corner, facing away from him. He gently placed his hands on her shoulders, turning her to face him. There were tears running down her cheeks. She was so confused. All she'd ever wanted was to be a good mum and wife, but he'd made it all so difficult. Why did he not get that it was his fault? She tried to pull away from him but he gripped her shoulders and pulled her closer, so close that she could feel his body heat through his tight, white shirt. He smelt of the expensive aftershave she'd bought him for his last birthday.

Her heart was racing. It had been so long since he'd held her, since anyone had held her, and it felt good. She let him wrap his arms around her as he bent down and softly kissed her ear and neck. Just like he used to in the days before the girls came along and they actually liked each other.

***

Ollie wondered why it had gone silent and he looked over the banister. His heart sank. He was angry, partly with Kate for being taken in by Martin, but mostly he was fuming at Martin. He wanted to run downstairs and drag him off her, not stopping until the both of them were outside and he'd punched Martin in the face a few times. He knew then that it was time to leave. He was in way over his head. He made his way to the small staircase that led down to the kitchen from the first floor and he went out of the back door, closing it quietly behind him. He got into his van and drove away so fast the tyres spun on the gravel, spraying it everywhere.

If he'd waited a few more minutes he would have seen what Martin would think of as his greatest seduction fall to pieces in a spectacular fashion, but he hadn't. So angry with the both of them, he drove home, where took a cold bottle of lager out of the fridge, drunk it down in two gulps, then stood under the cold shower to snap out of feeling sorry for himself.

***

Kate led Martin down to the room that was her temporary bedroom and closed the door behind them. He'd continued to kiss and nuzzle her the entire way and for the time being every hurtful, hateful thing he'd ever done to her was forgotten. He kicked the door shut with his foot and began to unbutton his shirt. He did have a nice body, a bit too ripped for her liking, but he always had loved staring into the mirror more than she did.

122

As he unzipped his trousers, his phone started to ring in his pocket. He pulled it out, along with a small, black velvet box which fell to the floor. As he answered his phone she bent down and picked it up. She opened it and the word Tiffany that was stamped on the inside screamed inside her head. Resting on the black silk cushion inside was the most beautiful heart-shaped diamond ring that she'd ever seen. He turned to see her staring at the ring and ended his phone call, holding out his hand for the box.

'Sorry, did I drop that?'

'This is an engagement ring.'

He didn't even blush or look embarrassed. 'Yes, it is. Can I have it back?'

'But why would you have an engagement ring? We're still married so obviously it's not for me.'

'It's for Tamara. I wanted to ask you if you'd have the girls for a couple of weeks whilst I took her away to Mauritius and proposed. Of course, we'll wait until the divorce is finalised before we make any concrete plans, but I think she's the one. Now that you seem to have sorted yourself out I think I can trust you with the girls.'

Kate tried her best not to lash out, but the anger that exploded simultaneously inside her head and chest made it very hard to think like a rational human being. She picked up the first thing to hand, which was her only bottle of perfume, and threw it at him. It caught his ear then smashed against the wall. The strong smell of Chanel Mademoiselle filled the air. He lifted his hand to his head.

'You fucking maniac. What are you doing? You could have killed me.'

She took great pleasure in the shade of deep red his face had turned and didn't care. She looked for another object to throw and picked up one of her work boots, which she then launched through the air. It hit him square in the chest with the most satisfying thud she'd ever heard. He turned and ran down the passage and she followed him screaming.

'Get the fuck out of my house, you smarmy bastard, and don't you ever come back. How dare you think you could get me into bed for one last shag before you got the divorce papers through and then propose to that slut who is young enough to be your daughter?'

He ran along the hall towards the front door, not even stopping to grab his shirt off the floor. Semi-naked, he made it to his car and opened the door to shield himself before she launched something else at him. She stood on the doorstep and aimed the small, black box at his head. It hit the driver's door window and then fell to the ground.

Not being able to look at him for a minute longer, she slammed the front door shut and left him scrabbling around in the dark looking for his expensive ring. She leant against the door. Her hands were shaking she was so furious with him. He must have found the ring because his car door slammed and the engine started. Good, let him go and explain to Tamara why he had no shirt on. She had a good mind to sign up to that bloody Facebook and send her a message to tell her what he'd been up to.

The house was silent, too quiet. Then she remembered that Ollie had stayed behind to get the tiling done. Oh God, the embarrassment. She ran upstairs to see if he was in the room he'd been working on. The door was closed and the light was off. She didn't remember him leaving and wondered if he'd seen her and Martin kissing. Oh, the shame of it. What had she been thinking? Not that it really mattered. What went on was between her and Martin. It had nothing to do with Ollie, but she couldn't push away the nagging feeling that it did matter what he thought; it mattered very much.

She began to cry then. She couldn't hold it in. Martin had once again reduced her to a snivelling wreck. There was a coldness around her that chilled her to the bone. The air was several degrees cooler up here than downstairs. Making her way back down to the kitchen and the fridge for a drink, she thought that it was no wonder she was the way she was. It was all his fault and after a few years she wouldn't be surprised if perfect Tamara left him or turned into a raging alcoholic as well. Perhaps the pair of them would end up best friends at the AA meetings, both sitting and reminiscing about how he took their lives and shredded them to pieces.

She grabbed the bottle of wine and unscrewed it. Not even bothering to get a glass, she just sat at the kitchen table and drank from the bottle. Big, long gulps of wine – the faster the better. If she got drunk, she might just be able to blot the last thirty minutes out. He'd never let her have the girls now, not after she'd assaulted him twice in one day, and she had worked so hard to make sure she did nothing wrong that would stop her. *You've completely screwed up big time, Kate. Now what?*

The wine took hold and the familiar feeling of warmth spread up inside of her chest, but she needed something else – something stronger. She wanted to go to sleep and forget about it for a while, blot it all out. If she drank enough there would be no bad dreams either, just an all-consuming blackness.

There was a bottle of Jack Daniel's on her bedside table, out of sight of the workmen but more so out of sight of Ollie. She didn't want him judging her. As she went to her room to retrieve it, she heard the footsteps again on the floor above her. They were light, but there was no mistaking that someone was up there. She pulled her phone out of her pocket and thought about phoning the police. That was a definite no. Martin might have already phoned them for all she knew; in fact, they were probably on their way to arrest her right now.

There was Ollie – nice, kind Ollie – only he would see she'd been drinking. She grabbed the bottle of whisky and went back to the kitchen, sitting down at the table. There was nothing of value upstairs. It was still a building site. Whoever it was could crack on with whatever they were doing and besides, if those cameras worked they would be on them anyway. In front of her on the table was one of the sharp knives from out of the kitchen drawer. She didn't remember putting it there. She opened the whisky and swigged from the bottle.

The acrid smell from earlier filled the room and Kate watched as she exhaled and her breath came out as a white, smoky cloud. She shivered. The temperature had dropped and she hadn't even noticed. The light bulb above the kitchen table crackled and fizzed as it blinked on and off. She felt the hairs on the back of her neck stand on end as the overwhelming feeling that there was somebody behind her filled her with fear.

Not sure she could turn around and face whatever it was, she felt the hot, salty tears begin to fall down her cheeks. The fear inside her was too great to ignore. She slowly began to turn her head to see what was in the room with her. The whole time she couldn't help wondering if she'd be better off dead than living this sad, scared existence. There was no one behind her and she let out a huge sigh. She could see how dark it was out in the hallway though. Light had filled the house moments earlier but now it was shrouded in shadows. It looked as if there was something standing out there waiting to come into the kitchen. Kate's hands were shaking. She looked at the back door. She could run outside and escape, but would it let her go and where was she going to escape to?

A woman's voice spoke in her ear, as clear as if someone was standing next to her. She whipped her head around to see who was behind her, but there was no one there. 'What are you waiting for, Kate? You know you want to. You've lost it all and you're never going to see your kids again. You might as well end it now. It won't hurt – not if you slice deep enough into your arm. I won't tell anyone. It will be our secret.'

The voice was calm, soothing – almost sing-song – and

reminded her of someone she'd known a very long time ago when she'd been little.

'Come on, Kate, it won't hurt and all of this will be over. Amy will be waiting for you. Have you not heard her calling out for you? She is wandering the halls of this house hoping you'll join her. She's just as lonely as you are. You could be together again. Just pick up the knife and slice.'

Kate let out a huge sob. She was going mad, but the voice was right. She could be with Amy again and she had nothing worth living for. She'd been scared of killing herself with her reckless lust for life when she was younger – the fast cars driven by bad boys, the even faster motorbikes – living her life on the edge as if daring God to take her, but he hadn't. He'd let her live. Now with her drinking, it was only a matter of time before she choked on her own vomit or her liver packed in. So why couldn't she stop?

It was as if she had some internal switch that was hell-bent on self-destruction that she couldn't turn off. The whole point of this house had been to provide an income and a nice family home for her girls, which was never going to happen after tonight. Martin would see to that. She picked up the smooth, blue, plastic-handled knife and held it in one hand. In the other she lifted the whisky to her lips and drank, hoping that if she drunk enough of the stuff it would numb the pain.

Chapter 8

Oliver had the television on even though he wasn't watching it. His mind wouldn't shut off enough to enjoy the programme. All he could think about was Kate and how easily she had let Martin seduce her after everything he'd done to her. He felt so attracted to her that the hurt inside his chest was an actual physical pain. Kate's world had also been turned upside down and she'd lost everything in the space of a week. They'd both been through such a lot. He'd been hoping that they could make a go of it as a couple. He'd finally plucked up the courage to ask her out and then tonight had happened.

He had watched Ellen the last five years of her life fade away until there was nothing left and he'd sworn to her there wouldn't be anyone else. But Ellen had scolded him and told him that he was far too young to spend the rest of his life a lonely widower. She'd wanted him to meet someone else and be happy. Now he was in turmoil because he hadn't realised just how much working with Kate and being with her all day almost every day was having an effect on him.

Martin had cheated on her numerous times and when she'd needed him the most, he'd thrown her out of the family home and taken away everything: her children, her job, her life. No wonder she was keeping herself cocooned up in her own little world. She probably felt much safer there. He wondered what the prick had wanted tonight. Why had he come around? He also wondered if Kate was okay. Why would she let him come back into her life on a whim like that?

Ollie slammed his fist against the cushion on the sofa. Despite everything he couldn't shake the feeling that something was wrong. He needed to go and see if she was all right. It was completely ridiculous, but he knew he wouldn't settle if he didn't. The more he thought about it the more he felt as if she needed his help. After pulling on his trainers, he grabbed his car keys and ran outside. He needed speed so he jumped into his VW Golf and drove off.

Praying tonight wasn't the night he was about to be pulled over by the police, he felt as if something was telling him that Kate needed him. He didn't understand what it was about but he trusted his instinct too much to ignore it.

When he finally reached the drive to her house he sped up it, relieved to see that Martin's car had gone. It had been less than an hour since he'd left so maybe it hadn't gone as well as Martin had hoped. Ollie hoped to God that Kate had thrown him out and seen sense. The house was in darkness. He parked out front and ran up the steps to the front door where he hammered on it. There was no sign of life from inside, which made his stomach flip.

What if she'd gone back to his house with him? He felt in his pocket for the spare key and swore. It was in his van back at home. Running around the side to her bedroom window, he felt better to see the glow from the lamp shining through the crack in the curtains. Cupping his hands, he peered through. The room was empty. There was no sign of her. He ran around to the back of the house and the kitchen, where the lights were blazing brightly. He hoped to God she was in here. As he peered through the glass in the door, he felt his legs begin to shake. She was slumped on the floor in front of the fridge and lying in a pool of bright red blood.

'No.'

He rattled the door but it was locked so he pulled his hooded jacket off, wrapped it around his fist and punched the glass as hard as he could. He knocked the shards out of the frame so he could get his hand inside to unlock it. The door opened and he ran towards her, his heart threatening to jump from his chest it was beating so fast. He bent down and pressed two fingers against her neck. She had a pulse, but she'd lost a lot of blood. He could see the two, incredibly deep four-inch cuts in each of her forearms and he felt sick.

Why had she done this? He was going to fucking kill Martin Parker if it was the last thing he ever did. Grabbing two tea towels from the rack he tenderly wrapped each arm up as tightly as he could, the whole time talking to her. He didn't have time to wait for an ambulance. There was a good chance it would get lost or not find the house in time.

'Kate, can you hear me? It's Ollie. Everything's going to be okay, I promise. I'm taking you to the hospital now, please hold on.'

Scooping her up into his arms he ran with her through the house to the front door and his waiting car. She was only a slight thing, but she was a dead weight. The whisky fumes that permeated from her were overpowering as they mixed with the strong smell of copper from all the blood. He felt as if he was going to throw up. He was relieved he hadn't come in his van. He didn't know if he'd have been able to lift her high enough into the cab on his own, but he managed to bundle her into the passenger seat and clicked her seat belt into place.

He ran around to the other side and drove off even faster than he'd driven to get here. They reached the hospital in no time at all and he talked to her constantly, telling her everything was going to be just fine. In reality, he didn't know if it was. She'd lost an awful lot of blood. They might not be able to do anything. This thought hit him hard. He didn't want to lose her even though she probably wanted nothing to do with him. He was falling in love with her. They shared the same sense of humour and he found her so easy to talk to about almost everything. He wanted more than anything to help her get her life back together.

He parked on the double yellow lines outside the double doors of the accident and emergency department. He managed to carry her in, abandoning his car. He was relieved when a nurse came running towards him with a trolley to lay Kate on. They pushed her through the double doors – pointing at the reception desk for him to book her in. As he did, his hands were shaking and when he spoke, his voice trembled with the shock of the last fifteen minutes. All he could tell them was her name, age, address and telephone number. He knew very little about her otherwise.

He left to go and move the car in case an ambulance needed to park out the front. He felt ill. He walked back in and took a seat on one of the hard plastic chairs. The receptionist came over and asked him who her next of kin was, and he didn't know. He doubted that she wanted Martin to know about this so he shrugged and said, 'Me'. He then rhymed off his address and mobile number for the woman.

The waiting room was fairly busy and he could feel every single person staring at him. They had probably already labelled him a wife beater or a bad husband, thinking that he was the reason she was in this state, when that couldn't be further from the truth. He'd never once lifted his hand to Ellen in their eighteen years of marriage. Yes, they'd argued and she had been feisty at times but it had never ended in violence. After what felt like for ever, a doctor dressed in blue scrubs called his name and he crossed towards him.

'How is she?'

'She's opened her eyes a couple of times, but has gone back

to sleep. We've stopped the bleeding and one of the nurses is currently in the process of stitching the wounds back together. Does she drink a lot, or do you know how much she's drunk tonight?'

He debated on lying to protect Kate from embarrassment and then wondered if he did whether it would it hamper them giving her the help she so desperately needed.

'When I found her there was an empty bottle of Jack Daniel's next to her and yes, she likes to drink – most nights, I think. I'm just a good friend. She's got an ex-husband. He's been around her house tonight and this has to be something to do with him because when I left, she was fine.'

The doctor nodded.

'Just as well she had you to go and check on her because there's no doubt about it: she was serious about dying. Those cuts on her arms were deep enough that she would have eventually bled out and the alcohol wouldn't have helped. It thins the blood so she'd have bled faster. We'll refer her to our mental health team and they won't release her until she's been assessed, but she isn't going anywhere tonight. I'm trying to get her a bed in the mental health unit so they can assess her quicker.'

Ollie felt like shit. Kate would probably be angry with him for interfering, but she couldn't go on like this. If he hadn't gone back – it didn't bear thinking about. He'd rather her be angry with him and alive than dead. The doctor pointed to the cubicle where a nurse was in the process of sewing up the large wounds. Kate's face was so pale and she looked tiny lying on the bed. The nurse looked up and smiled at him, pity in his eyes, and he had to force himself to smile back.

He crossed towards Kate and bent down to kiss her cheek. She was so cold. He lifted a hand and stroked the side of her face. Her eyes opened and it took her a minute to register what was happening. She smiled at him and then looked down to see the nurse bent over her. Ollie watched as her eyes filled with tears.

She tried to talk but her voice came out as a whisper. 'What did I do?'

It was the nurse who answered. 'You did a bloody good job of slitting your wrists, Kate, that's what you did.'

She gasped. 'When? How? I don't remember.'

Oliver shrugged. 'I left you with Martin and everything seemed to be going well, only I couldn't settle when I got home so I came back to see if you were okay, and I found you in the kitchen unconscious and lying in a big pool of blood.'

Her eyes filled with tears and she looked at the nurse then Oliver.

'I'm so sorry. I don't know what happened or why I did it. I remember throwing Martin out because he'd come around to see if he could get me into bed one last time before he proposed to that slut of his. I don't remember the rest except for the woman. I heard a woman telling me to do it, to kill myself. How could I not remember this?' Kate looked down at her arms.

Oliver flinched. So he'd tried to get her to sleep with him but thank God she'd realised what was happening. Neither of them spoke until the nurse had finished patching her arms back together and bandaged them up.

'What woman, Kate? Was there someone in the house with you?'

She shook her head. 'No, I don't know. I didn't see her. I just heard a voice behind me and turned around, but there wasn't anyone there except for the shadows.'

He sat down next to her and held her hand, watching her as she turned her head and cried silent tears. A nurse popped his head through the gap in the curtains. 'You must have someone from above looking out for you tonight, my love. They have a bed on the ward already so we're going to get you moved across as soon as the porter comes. Normally you'd be stuck here for hours on end. Count your lucky stars that you don't have to stop here and listen to all the drunks coming in and puking everywhere.'

And then he was gone, only to return three minutes later with the porter. Ollie bent down and kissed Kate's cheek.

'Ring me if you need me, Kate. This time I mean it. I'll keep my phone on and I'll come and see you tomorrow. Try and get some sleep.'

He turned before he had to watch them wheel her away and before she saw the tears that were filling his eyes.

***

When Kate opened her eyes, the sun was streaming through the small, reinforced windows and it took her a minute to remember where she was. Then she tried to turn her head and the familiar pain of a hangover kicked in. Lifting her arm to hold her head she gasped to see the white bandage that went from her wrist to elbow. It all came tumbling back in a wave of pain and embarrassment. She lifted the other arm and remembered waking up in the accident and emergency department last night with Ollie by her side. Oh God, what had she done? Why had she tried to kill herself? Everything she'd been through and not once had she considered suicide – so why last night?

As a child, her biggest fear had been of dying. This didn't make any sense. She looked around and felt her heart sink. She was in a hospital and judging by the metal grills over the window she wasn't on a normal ward. She'd been locked up in the part where they put the nutters, but she wasn't crazy. She didn't even know why she'd done it. Then again, maybe that was a sign of madness, trying to kill yourself and not even knowing why.

A doctor walked in and smiled at her, introducing himself as a psychiatrist. She wanted to scream at him to leave her the fuck alone. They'd never let her go home if she did. So instead she took the glass of water he offered her and the paracetamol. Then she began to answer the very long list of questions he asked. After what seemed like for ever, the doctor stood up.

'You have a visitor. I couldn't let him in until I'd assessed you. I think he will cheer you up. I don't see any need to keep you here any longer. You've confirmed that you've never been suicidal before and you don't have any thoughts of suicide at this moment in time. Is that right?'

'Yes absolutely. I'm mortified that I did what I did last night. I didn't even realise how down I was feeling. It must have been the alcohol and the argument with my ex-husband. I'm so sorry to have been a complete nuisance.'

The doctor smiled at her. 'Good, I'll go and sort out your discharge paperwork. You'll get a follow-up referral to the mental health team, which I strongly advise you to attend, Mrs Parker. I'll tell your visitor he can come in. He's been waiting patiently.'

Immediately, she knew that it couldn't be Martin because he'd have pushed his way in demanding to see her and gloating at the mess she was in. Ollie stepped into the room. He had a balloon in one hand; his other was tucked into his pocket. She wanted to curl up under the bed sheet and die, but she would have to face him sooner or later so it might as well be now.

'I wasn't allowed to bring in flowers. What's that about? The nurse told me I had to take them back to the car so I bought this at the shop.'

He held his hand out to pass her the cow-shaped balloon and automatically she reached out to take it from him. She started laughing until she spotted the white bandage that ran the full length of her forearm and she snatched her hand back.

'Thank you, that's very kind of you but you shouldn't have. Is the cow symbolic of something?' She winked at him, wondering if this was his way of calling her a stupid cow without actually saying it.

'Not really; it was a choice of the cow or "it's a boy" so I figured the cow was the best option.'

They both laughed and he crossed the room. As he neared her bed he bent down and kissed her pale cheek. Then he flopped down onto the plastic chair next to her.

'So have they said you can go home or do you need to stop in for a bit and get some rest?'

Neither of them acknowledged the fact that she'd almost killed herself – Kate because she was mortified and Ollie probably because he figured it really wasn't any of his business. He was here because she had no one else.

'I can go home, thankfully. They've been great, but I need to get out of here. I hate hospitals.'

'I can take you if you like. I've left the lads replacing the window in that bedroom above yours. That should stop any strange draughts. Kate, can I ask you – did you put those crosses back up on the wall yesterday?'

She shook her head. 'No, you know I don't like them. Why?'

'Well, this morning there were more of them. Three in that room, also three in all the other bedrooms and they were placed periodically along the wall of the first floor landing. There were loads of them.'

Her head started swimming. How had they got there and more importantly who was putting them up? She vaguely remembered hearing faint footsteps last night and the feeling of being watched. It was all a bit fuzzy still, but she didn't hear any banging. Surely, she would have heard them being hammered into the wall. Then again, how was she supposed to hear anything when she was lying bleeding to death? He was going to think she was nuts at this rate.

'No I didn't, I definitely didn't.'

'Then we need to re-evaluate just how secure the house is because someone is coming in and putting them up. It's a good job we got those cameras put up yesterday. I'll check them and see if they captured anything because normal people don't break into houses and put crosses everywhere. Why would they?'

She didn't remember cutting herself either. What if someone had done it to her when she was passed out stone cold drunk at the kitchen table? And how had she got on the floor? Her drink could have been spiked for all she knew. As scary as the thought was of someone prowling around her house and trying to kill her, at least it meant that she wasn't mad. And then she remembered how the light was fizzing, the woman's voice in her ear, the shadows out in the hall and how terrified she'd been last night.

'I don't know, Kate, I'm worried.'

'Ollie, I know you must already think that I've lost the plot, but I'm scared. I heard my name being called, there's been scratching on the bedroom wall and last night I heard a woman telling me to kill myself because there was no point in living. I'm scared the house is haunted by something evil and I don't know what to do.'

He stared at her face, which was deadly serious. Kate thought he probably wanted to tell her she was being ridiculous, but instead he seemed to believe her. Her house was haunted; it had to be.

A cold chill settled over her. The house was so big she didn't go into every room once the workmen had gone home. She didn't check them. She just finished whatever she was doing then went downstairs and had a drink or two.

The door opened and a nurse came in with an envelope. 'Doctor said this is for you. It's a copy of your discharge notice and you're free to go now. If you feel down again, you're to ring the ward or a friend. Talk to someone. He's referred you for some counselling. Is that okay?'

'Yes, thank you so much. You've all been amazing. I'm sorry to have caused so much trouble.'

The nurse smiled, then turned and left.

'I'll take you home.'

'Thank you.'

She stood up and crossed to the small cupboard, opening it to see what clothes she had. A cold shiver ran across her spine and she realised that she was flashing her almost naked back at Oliver. She pulled the gown across and looked back at him. He was pretending to stare out of the window, but his cheeks were slightly flushed as if she'd caught him peeping. Smiling to herself, she turned back.

'Sorry, I didn't mean to flash you. I completely forgot I was almost naked.'

'It's fine; I wasn't looking – well, I tried my best not to.'

She pulled her jeans out and held them up. They had a large dried bloodstain across both thighs. Her T-shirt looked like a tie-dyed mess of blood and cotton, more blood than anything. Her legs began to quake and she had to sit down on a chair. Oliver jumped up to take hold of her arm and helped her down.

'Oh my, I had no idea I'd bled so much. What a mess. I'm so sorry to have you caused you all this trouble. What must you think of me?'

'I think that you need a friend, Kate, that's what – and if I can help you in any way then I want you to know that I will. Why don't you slip your shoes on and you can have my sweatshirt.'

He was already pulling it off and she caught a glimpse of his tanned, toned abdomen as his T-shirt rose up with it. She looked away, not wanting him to think it was her turn to gawp at him, but he had a very nice body. Not overly huge like Martin's body. It was sleeker and so much sexier. Damn, it made her like him even more. He passed his sweatshirt across and she took that and the bloodstained jeans into the bathroom.

As she pulled them on she winced at the smell and the feel. They were stiff and horrible. As soon as she got home, they would be going into the bin. Taking off the hospital gown she pulled on his too big sweatshirt that was warm and smelt so good, which made up for the horrendous smell coming from her legs. She stepped outside and was grateful that his baggy top covered most of the bloodstains. He grinned at her.

'Not quite the designer look that you're used to, but not bad. You carry it off quite well.'

She laughed. 'I look a complete state and I smell like something out of an abattoir. Are you sure you want me to sit in your truck looking and smelling like this?'

'Absolutely. I hate hospitals with a passion so I'd rather take you and your cow balloon home, if that's okay with you?'

'That would be wonderful, thank you.'

Slipping on her shoes, she was relieved to be going back to the wreck that was her home, even if there was something strange going on with it. At least he would be there with her for the rest of the day. She might have to check herself into a hotel for a couple of nights or at least until they got to the bottom of what was going on.

Neither of them spoke on the way home. As they rounded the bend and the house came into view, Kate let out a sigh. No matter what was happening this was her home. Completely hers and she loved it. She had fallen in love with it the minute she set her eyes on it, so there was no way she was going to be scared out of it – whether it was really haunted or whether someone living was trying to scare her away. She wouldn't put it past Martin to pay someone to come in and try to scare her to death, but would he stoop so low as to try and kill her? She didn't think he had the balls, although if he found out that she'd stolen this place from right under his nose he would be pissed off with her big time.

As Oliver parked his truck outside the front door, she sensed movement from the attic and looked up. Her heart skipped a beat. Someone was looking down at them, watching. They wore a black hooded cape or gown with a flash of white across the chest. It was such a fleeting glance that Kate hadn't even seen their face. She didn't know if it was a man or a woman. She would hazard a guess at a woman. Those footsteps she heard most nights were light and sounded like those of a woman. She grabbed Ollie's arm, her fingers clamping into his skin to stop him from getting out of the car.

'What's wrong?'

She pointed to the attic window. There was no one there.

139

'Someone was watching us from the attic. They were dressed all in black. I couldn't see their face.'

'It might have been Ethan or Jack. I left them here. It can't be anyone else unless…'

'Unless what?'

He took a deep breath. 'Unless this house is haunted like you said. I've been thinking about it all the way home and it would make a lot of sense. No matter how hard I try and figure it out I can't understand about the crosses though. It's as if someone is trying to protect you.'

'Well, I'm not ungrateful or anything if they are, but they're not doing such a great job of it, are they?'

She held up her arm.

'Wait here. I'll go and see.'

Kate wanted to say no; instead, she nodded her head. She watched Ollie get out of the truck and run towards the house. She looked up again then scanned the rest of the windows. She couldn't see anyone except for Ethan. He was hanging out of the first-floor bathroom window trying to paint the frame and looking like he was going to fall and break his neck, then he was gone. Ollie must have found him. She didn't know what to do with herself. Her hands were trembling at the thought of her house being haunted. It was creepy. Who the hell was it and what were they doing?

Ollie came out of the front door and ran down the steps towards her.

'Anything?'

'No, Jack said he's been painting the landing and no one has gone past him and they would have to if they wanted to gain access to the attic. Should we go inside so you can get changed and then we'll take a look at the camera footage together? Your house might be haunted, but we need to rule out that there's no one of the human variety coming in and messing around as well.'

She nodded and he pulled her door open, holding his hand

out for her to steady herself. Her legs felt like jelly and her head hurt so much. She was never drinking whisky again. In fact, the way she felt right now she wasn't drinking again full stop – that was until the itch started in the back of her throat and it would only soothe with alcohol.

***

'I haven't told the lads anything. I said you'd slipped and cut yourself last night and they'd kept you in to make sure you were okay. I also came and cleaned the blood up this morning before they started so you wouldn't have to come home and look at it.' He put his head down. 'If I'm interfering then please tell me to mind my own business. I'll completely understand.'

She reached out for his arm and squeezed it. 'No, you're not interfering at all. I owe you my life. If you hadn't come back last night…' The sob took them both by surprise. 'I'm sorry, Ollie, if you don't mind I think I need to lie down. I feel like shit, I smell like shit and I know that I look like crap.'

He nodded. He wanted to kiss her then. Pull her close and wrap her up in his arms, tell her he'd keep her safe, but for all he knew she might not like that kind of corny, tough-guy behaviour. She walked towards her bedroom and he stood there watching her, his heart tearing in two. He couldn't leave her alone in this house. He could ask her to stop with him, but he didn't know if he'd be able to cope. Taking another woman into their house, which was filled with pictures and memories that he and Ellen had created.

'Ollie, I've been shouting to you, mate. What are we doing about these bloody crosses? They are freaking us both out. Who the fuck keeps putting them up and why?'

He jumped, turning round to see Ethan leaning over the banister above him.

'I don't know, seriously if we take them down they get put

141

back up. Until we can figure out who the hell is doing it you might as well just leave them for now. Listen, Kate's not feeling too well so no banging around or shouting. Crack on with painting the hallway or something that isn't going to disturb her.'

'What are you going to be doing – keeping her bed warm?' Jack appeared next to Ethan with a huge grin on his face.

'Shh, have some respect, will you. Did you hear what I just told Ethan?'

'Yes, boss, we'll get on with the painting.'

'Good, I'm going to check the camera footage from last night. See if it captured anything.'

He turned and walked towards the room next to Kate's where they'd installed the monitors and hard drive. He wasn't very good with technology, but he didn't think he could go wrong. They'd only started recording from around six last night, so there wouldn't be hours of footage to go through. He sat down on the small stool and began to press the buttons on the hard drive.

Eventually he got it to the part where Martin had come to visit. He didn't want to pry, but he was interested to see how it had ended. He watched it slightly speeded up until it came to the point where a shirtless Martin had run for his car, and then he played it in real time. The grin that spread across Ollie's face as Kate threw something at Martin was huge. He didn't know what it was. The man spent a few minutes scrabbling around in the dark, searching for it. He must have found it because he stood up and got inside his car, driving off at speed.

Ollie switched to the internal camera and felt his heart break in two to see Kate in a heap on the floor, crying. The anger that filled his chest was so hot and intense he thought that he was going to kill Martin with his bare hands. He was glad that the sound wasn't working because he didn't want to hear her sobbing, all alone. Her heartbreak was so raw it unsettled him. She was so much like him it was scary.

This was wrong. He was prying on her most private moments,

but he needed to see if there was anyone in the house with her – so it was for her own safety. A dark shadow passed the camera on the landing and he switched to that one. It was hard to see what it had been because it had happened so fast. He rewound it again and again but couldn't make much out apart from a black shape moving fast. He couldn't say it was an actual person. What it did look like wasn't human. It was see-through like a dark cloud or shadow – that much he could tell. He continued watching. It had to be Kate's ghost.

The camera below in the front hallway showed Kate walking towards the kitchen. He lost sight of her as she pushed the door open and stepped inside. They hadn't put a camera in there, which was both a relief and also a pain because as much as he didn't want to watch a live replay of the woman he was falling madly in love with trying to kill herself, he would have liked to have made sure that no one had waited to do it to her once she was drunk enough. A short time later she came out of the kitchen, crossing the hall to her room. She didn't look drunk or too upset. After a minute she appeared again with the bottle of whisky and went back into the kitchen.

'Fuck my fucking life. What the fuck?'

The shout was so loud that Ollie almost fell off the stool he was perched on. He ran towards the front door where Ethan and Jack were standing, looking horrified at something in the wall.

'What the hell's the matter with you? I told you to be quiet.'

'Boss, you are not going to believe what we've just found. Take a look for yourself – it's fucking gross. It can't be real. Who the hell put it there and why?'

He crossed the hall towards them and looked at the oak-panelled wall that Jack was pointing to. There was a panel missing. Somehow, they had triggered a secret opening. As he stared down into the dark space he couldn't register what it was he was looking at. He looked at both men then back at the life-sized, shrivelled, mummified head of a nun with a crucifix wrapped around the frayed off-white band of what was once a headpiece.

'You fucking tossers. I don't know which one of you thinks this is joke, but take that thing and get it out of here now. It's not even remotely funny.'

'We didn't put it there. We didn't even know about it until Ethan pressed something behind that panel and it opened. Where would we get something like that from?'

'I mean it, I don't think it's at all funny and I told you to be quiet. Pick it up and take it out of here now before Kate comes to see what's happening.'

'No offence, Ollie, and I know you're the boss man, but you can piss off. I'm not touching that for a million quid. What if it's a real head? It bloody well looks real; I think you'd better call the cops.'

Ollie looked at them. They were both staring in horror at their find and he felt a wave of sickness move through his body. It hadn't been them. They would have started to laugh by now.

'Go get me a torch from the kitchen drawer, please.'

Ethan ran to the kitchen. Seconds later he was passing a torch to Ollie. Ollie bent down, switching it on. The head looked even more horrific with the light shining on it. The skin was wrinkled and leathery. It looked like one of those Halloween masks you could buy in the fancy dress shop. The mouth was open and the eyes were staring in horror at something. Ollie was glad he couldn't see what.

'It looks real. Jesus why would someone chop off a nun's head and stick it there? That is seriously fucked up.'

'I don't know. I'd better go and get Kate and see what she wants us to do.'

'I think you'd better phone the police, Ollie. You can't just sweep that into a bin bag and chuck in the skip. And where's the rest of the body? What if that's still in here somewhere? This place is freaking me out.'

Ollie couldn't think straight. Jack was right. Something was wrong and they would need to ring the police.

'You two go and get your dinner. There's nothing we can do now until the police arrive.'

'Cheers, as if we feel like eating after looking at that. I feel sick. My hands are shaking like I was out on the lash last night. No thanks, we'll wait out in the van for you. I need a smoke.'

Ethan, who had recovered from his shock slightly better than Jack, had his phone out and was now taking photos of their grotesque find to show his mates later.

'Don't show anyone those until the police have been. No Snapchatting your mates or whatever it is you do.'

They both walked towards the front door, leaving Ollie standing there not wanting to have to break the bad news to Kate and not quite believing what it was he was looking at in the first place. He walked towards her room and was about to knock when the door opened. A bleary-eyed Kate looked at him.

'Is something wrong?'

'I don't know how to say this, but yes. Something is terribly wrong. You need to take a look at what the lads have found in a secret cupboard in the hallway.'

His eyes slid down to the small white vest and shorter than short pyjama pants she was wearing and he looked away. The burning sensation in his cheeks made him feel like some dirty old man. He snapped his head up but didn't miss the amusement on her face as she turned to pull some clothes on. Dressed in a baggy sweatshirt and pyjama pants, she still looked sexy to him.

'So what is it that's so bad you can't tell me?'

Ollie led her down the corridor. 'I honestly don't know how to describe it. You have to see it for yourself.'

He stopped in front of the space and pointed. Kate looked down at the mummified head and gasped. 'Jesus, what the hell is that thing?'

'It's not a joke; well, it's not one that any of us thought was

145

funny enough to play. Judging by the state of that head, if it's a real one it's been there a lot of years.'

He held the torch out and she took it from him. Squatting down, she surprised him once more by being the bravest out of all four of them. He'd been expecting her to start screaming. She was in front of it, shining the torch at it. He watched as a violent shudder made her entire body tremble; still, she didn't scream. She turned to look at him and her face was even paler than before. She leant in to pick something up and he flinched, wondering what on earth it could be. She turned to him again with a small, dusty, black leather-bound Bible in her fingers. It had a gold crucifix on the front of it and it smelt musty. She blew some of the thick dust from it before opening it.

***

Inside, in small, neat handwriting it said the name Sister Agnes Nicholas. She felt a strange sensation inside her chest and head as the name rang a bell. She thought again of her great-great-aunt called Agnes Nicholas. The only photograph she'd ever seen of her had been in her nun's habit. No one really talked about her. She knew that the woman had been a nun a long time ago. Could this be her? She didn't even know how she'd died. What if Agnes was her relation and she was the one who was haunting the house? It would make a lot of sense. If that were the case, if they'd found her head, she'd be able to move on and not have to haunt here anymore.

Kate's mind was swimming with so many possibilities and she had no one she could ask because her mum had Alzheimer's and she didn't get on with her dad. She wondered if she should tell Ollie this – only she didn't want him thinking she was completely mad because it sounded mad to her. What if there was a reason she had been compelled to buy this house? She'd fallen in love with it at first sight. Maybe Agnes had wanted her to be the one to buy it and find her head? There were so many questions that needed answers and she had no idea how she was going to find them. She stood up.

'I think we'd better phone the police. I can't say for sure, but I think that's actually someone's head. The teeth don't look rubbery; they look real and whoever it is was a nun. A religious woman. Who would want to keep her head hidden behind this panel for years – and where's the rest of her body?'

'That's what Jack said. I don't know why it's there and yes, we should call the police, but I wanted to make sure that was okay with you.'

Kate took a step back so she was standing next to Ollie. She reached her fingers out for his and he clasped them. She was so cold and worn out. Standing on her tiptoes, she whispered in his ear – not wanting the house or anyone who might be listening to hear.

'I'm scared. I don't know what to do anymore.'

'I know you are.'

He wound his arms around her, pulling her towards him. He hugged her close. She paused for a moment then her arms wrapped around his waist and she hugged him back. After a minute, she went back to her room and tucked the Bible into the bedside drawer next to the diary she had been too afraid to finish reading. A Sister Agnes had written the diary, so they must both belong to the same woman. Kate knew that she had no choice now. She would have to finish reading the diary to find out what had happened in this house. She wanted to read it herself before she showed it to anyone else. Then she picked up her phone. It was time to ring the police.

6 January 1933

Agnes and Patrick sat at the kitchen table whilst the house was being searched from top to bottom by the police. Neither of them could speak. The horror was too much to think about. Agnes was aware that the police could be thinking that Father Patrick might have something to do with it all, but she knew that was rubbish. Yes, he'd been here tonight, but he wasn't the sort of man who would want to tie a naked woman to a bed and strangle her. He was a good man. They might even think that she was responsible and if she had been younger they definitely would, but at her age that was ridiculous.

And where was Lilith? The woman was nowhere to be seen and as far as Agnes was concerned that proved her to be guilty. The only problem with that was the fact that Lilith was such a petite woman. She wasn't big and certainly didn't look like a strong woman, but somehow this was all linked to her. She hoped Crosby would find her hiding away in the attic and take her away from here so they could return to normal – as normal as things could be after these traumatic events.

Agnes knew that she'd never picture Sisters Edith or Mary the same way ever again. Instead of the warm, happy, smiling faces all she could see was the blood, depravity and horror of their deaths. They could hear the thunder of feet running up and down the stairs. Doors were opened then slammed shut. Agnes had told them to check every dark corner of the attic and the cellars.

She didn't know if Lilith was afraid of the dark. Somehow, she very much doubted that she was afraid of anything. Didn't vampires live in cold, damp, dark cellars? Wasn't that why they hated the light and came out at night? Agnes wanted to tell her fears to Crosby and to Patrick – only she was afraid they would think she was mad and take her away to Hellshall Mental Asylum, which was in the next town. A breathless Crosby came into the kitchen and sat down opposite her.

'The house is empty, apart from us. We've searched every room, nook and cranny. The attic, cellars, cupboards, wardrobes, underneath beds, behind curtains. I just don't know what to say, Agnes.'

'Did you not find the woman?'

'What woman?'

148

'Lilith Ardat. She has something to do with all of this – you mark my words – and if she's left then surely that is a sign of her guilt. It has to be. And you know what woman. She was here yesterday when you found poor Mary.'

Crosby looked confused. Agnes realised that he didn't remember her, or maybe she had somehow cast a spell so that he wouldn't. She wouldn't put it past Lilith at all. If she was a vampire she would be able to come and go as she pleased, with no one being any the wiser. She wanted to tell herself to stop being ridiculous, but how could she? The proof was there for everyone to see. She had the marks on her neck.

'Crosby, what I'm going to tell you will make you think I'm mad, but I'm not. I may be old and my bones ache an awful lot more than they used to, but my mind is still as fresh today as it was when I was twenty. Patrick, you too, this involves us all. I don't know if she has her sights set on you yet. She certainly has a thing for the women in this house.'

***

Patrick nodded. He had been questioning himself for the last thirty minutes about whether or not the door had been locked. He knew that it had been. Agnes had tried the handle; he'd rattled and twisted it several times and it hadn't moved.

'Agnes, I'm listening. I'm sitting here in agony from trying to break that door down. Yet when he tried, it opened straight away. Forgive me if I'm wrong, but how long has Edith been dead? Could she have opened the door and then killed herself?'

Crosby shook his head.

'That would be impossible, Father. She has signs of rigor mortis setting in and she's cold to the touch. If she had only just died her body would still be warm. It takes a while for it to cool down once the heart has stopped pumping the blood around the body.'

'So we have to consider that whatever Agnes is going to tell us might be the truth – no matter how hard we find it to believe.'

'I suppose we do.'

Both men looked at Agnes. Her face was pale and her hands were clasped together as if she'd been praying.

'I don't know how or why or if this is even possible. I've done nothing except think about it since yesterday after we found Mary. We let Lilith Ardat into the house two nights ago. It was late, dark and snow was falling, yet she wasn't dressed for the weather and didn't even seem cold. She told us that she'd escaped from her violent husband, who had crashed his car, and she'd left him unconscious, as it was her chance to get away from him before he killed her. Crosby, have you ever heard of her or her husband? I don't know what his first name was but Ardat isn't a common name around here.'

Crosby closed his eyes as if trying to reach deep down into the dark depths of his mind. 'I have to say it's not a name I've ever come across. If he was a violent man, I'm sure the police would have some prior knowledge of him.'

Patrick pushed his chair back, standing up. 'Wait a moment, that name is familiar. Ever since I heard it, I knew that it was something I'd read about a long time ago. Off the top of my head – and this might not be accurate – but from what I remember reading in scripture class there is a female demon called Ardat Lili. According to the book, she is a night demon who can arrive in a storm. She likes to wed men and wreak havoc, but there's nothing to say that she wouldn't get any less pleasure from terrorising women. Lilith means spirit of the night, so this could be who we're dealing with.'

***

Agnes felt as if her heart was about to burst from her chest it was racing so hard. Crosby seemed to be trying his best to let what he'd heard sink in.

150

'So you think that this woman – Lilith – who you let in, isn't a woman but a demon in disguise? You think that she's the one who has killed Mary and Edith and now she's disappeared? If that's so, how come you haven't been touched, Agnes?'

Crosby was probably thinking that he'd just walked through the doors of the insane asylum and not a house of God. Agnes knew there was no way on this earth he would accept what they were saying to him.

'Well, that's the thing; I have been. I woke up in the night and saw her downstairs around three. When I looked into the mirror she had no reflection. Whenever I get too close to her I can smell something like spoiled, rotting meat. It's very unpleasant and turns my stomach. I went back to bed last night and fell into a deep sleep. This morning I felt so tired. More tired than I've ever been in my life, and when I looked in the mirror I had two puncture marks on my neck, which were crusted with dried blood. Are you familiar with the story *Dracula*?'

'So last night this demon turned into a vampire and sucked your blood before killing Edith and now we can't find her anywhere. Is that what you're telling me?'

Agnes looked at Patrick to see if he thought she was mad. He was listening to her and nodded at her to continue.

'Yes, I believe that she did.'

'I can't believe I'm hearing this with my own ears. If you two weren't such respected members of the church I'd be carting you off to Hellshall. Why would she do any of this?'

'I think that she knew I was scared of vampires, just like she knew that Mary had been reading *Frankenstein* and it was scaring her – so somehow she turned into Frankenstein's monster and ripped her to pieces. I also know that Edith and Mary had recently been into town to the picture house and watched *The Mummy*. They came home and Mary thought it was highly amusing that Edith was scared by a dead man wrapped in bandages. I haven't been to the picture house with them, but I did read Bram Stoker's

Dracula a long time ago and I'm not afraid to say that it scared me beyond belief. I have no comprehension how she could do this. I think she somehow knows what our worst fears are. She played on them and turned them against us. What I don't know is why. Why would she pick on three nuns who live out in the middle of nowhere and keep to ourselves?'

'I think I can answer that, Agnes,' Father Patrick said. 'It was for that exact reason. Three women, living in this huge house in the middle of nowhere – it's a perfect hunting ground for a force of darkness. You are easy pickings for her. If this is true, she is playing with you and I'm afraid that she hasn't finished playing with you yet.'

'Why do you say that, Father?' But Crosby seemed to know the answer before he'd asked the question.

'Because, Agnes, you're still alive. I think that she'll be back tonight to finish what she started.'

'In that case we'd better be ready and waiting for her. Wouldn't you agree?'

Agnes, who had been feeling sick all morning, felt a calmness spread over her entire body. She played with the crucifix around her neck and thanked God for sending her a sign that she was strong enough to do this.

'What are we going to do? Wouldn't it be better to leave this house, board it up and move somewhere else?'

'No, Father, I don't believe that it would. If we were to leave it wouldn't make any difference. She isn't here now. The police have searched it from top to bottom. If I left, I think she'd follow me wherever I went. It's far better to face her here, and besides, this is my home. It has been for over twenty years and I love it here. I will not be chased out of my home by some evil, demonic entity that thinks it has the right to come into a house of God and kill his children. I would rather die fighting than run away.'

'Those are very strong words, Agnes, but how do we fight something like that?'

'How do we fight evil, Crosby? By asking God to help us in our hour of need. If we are prepared then we can fight her, it, whatever. With God's help we should be able to send her back to wherever she's come from. Isn't that right, Father?'

'Yes, yes we should.'

***

Crosby didn't want to upset either of them. The good priest didn't sound quite as enthusiastic about it as Agnes. He'd give it to her, she was a feisty woman; he didn't know what to go back and tell the inspector though. If he started spouting rubbish about the murderer being a woman who was actually a demon that thrived on turning into people's worst nightmares to kill them, the inspector would not only have him sent to Hellshall but also the nun and the priest. He rubbed his head and wished that today had been his day off work. Why was it him who was up to his neck in it?

Chapter 9

The police car arrived fifteen minutes after Kate had phoned them. Her stomach was churning. The only experience she'd had with the police had been the night she'd got arrested for drunk driving and they hadn't been what she'd expected. They had been pretty nice to her considering what she'd done; still, the shame of it all filled her with embarrassment. She opened the door to see two policemen, one around her age and one much younger. They both smiled at her and she felt some of her worry melt away.

'I'm really sorry about this. I didn't know what to do. One of the builders found it and it looks real. Then again, you can get some good masks now off the internet so I thought I'd better leave it to the experts.'

'Well, you did the right thing, although I can't say I'm an expert on severed, mummified heads. I'm Simon and this youngster is Josh.'

'I'm Kate and this is Ollie – one of my builders. The lads who found it are outside in the van.'

She led them to the opening in the wall and heard Josh say, 'Fuck me,' which made her smile. It was highly inappropriate and she was glad he'd had the same reaction as her, almost. Simon

154

took out a black torch and shone it inside. Standing up, he pulled on some blue rubber gloves.

'It looks real, but I can't say for definite. What a thing to find. Most people find family heirlooms.'

'Tell me about it.'

'What do you think, Josh? Should we bag it up and take it with us or do you think we should call out CSI and CID?'

'Urgh, I'm not sitting holding that on my knee all the way back to the station.'

'Good. Glad you've been listening to me whilst I've been training you. We need to call out one of the detective constables and forensics. If it's a mask or some kind of joke then we'll never hear the end of it; however, I'd rather be safe than sorry. If this is really someone's head then they deserve to be treated with the utmost respect.'

Kate liked the older man. He seemed to know what he was doing and he hadn't talked down to her once. He walked away from them so he could speak on his radio in private. When he turned back he had a pair of blue gloves in his hand, which he passed to Josh.

'Put these on, Josh. Kate, I'm afraid I'm going to have to ask you to leave this area now. Until we know more this is going to be treated as a crime scene.'

'Should we wait in the kitchen? It's at the far end of the house.'

'Well, technically we should clear the house but I suppose you can. This place has been empty for years so whoever it is has been in there an awful long time. Once the DS gets here you might have to leave and find somewhere else to stay for the night until the scene has been processed. They'll be able to tell you more than me. I'm a humble response officer and this is not my field of expertise. Do you have anywhere you can stop?'

She was about to say no when Ollie spoke up, 'Yes she can stop with me.'

'That's great; hopefully they'll be here soon. It hasn't been that busy today.'

Kate and Ollie walked back to the kitchen. She didn't know what was going on, but she couldn't stop shivering. She was cold, felt like shit and needed a drink – though she could still taste the stale whisky in her mouth despite brushing her teeth and mouth-washing several times since she'd got back from the hospital. The painkillers had started to wear off now and her arms were aching where she'd sliced them open. She was a mess; there was no doubt about it.

If she stopped with Ollie, she wouldn't be able to drink. She didn't want him thinking she had no self-control what-soever. She didn't want to be in the house on her own either, although at least if she was, she could lock herself in her room, turn the heater up, wrap herself in a duvet and feel sorry for herself.

She sat down and Ollie switched the kettle on. He went out of the room and Kate wished that she'd never hired him. She wished that she'd got someone ugly and smelly to come and do the work so her heart wouldn't break in two every time he left her on her own. He was so kind and caring, the complete oppo-site of Martin. She knew she had fallen for him big time despite telling herself after Martin she would rather be single. He came back in with the soft, pale pink blanket off her bed and wrapped it around her shoulders.

'Kate, I don't know what to say. It's a complete mess and I'm worried about you. Don't you think we should tell the police about the footsteps you keep hearing and the crosses – just in case?'

'No. Definitely not. They'll think I'm some lunatic. They're not going to listen to me if I tell them I think the house is haunted. I'm fine, or I'll be fine. It's just a bit of a rough patch. God knows I go through them often enough. It will be okay; I'll be okay. I just feel like crap tonight. I want to go to sleep and not wake up

156

until tomorrow afternoon, although that doesn't look like a possibility.'

'I'll feel better if you come and stop at my house. I don't want to say this, but it would be good for you to meet my dad. He, erm, he runs the local AA meetings. He was an alcoholic for thirty years. You would really like him. He gets it and he might be able to help you.'

Kate felt her face burn. The shame was so heavy she thought her head would begin to crush her body. She looked at him. What could she say to that? He was practically telling her to sort her life out. Well, she didn't need him or his bloody dad. She'd got herself into this mess and she would get herself out of it, somehow.

'My life is none of your business. How dare you stick your nose in? I don't need advice from him. I'm having a bad day, that's all.'

'I'm sorry. I can't watch you do this to yourself. It breaks my heart. You have so much to live for yet the answer to everything seems to be inside a bottle of alcohol. It will kill you and I can't watch a perfectly healthy woman do that. You're throwing your life away.'

Kate stood up and hissed at him, 'Well then, why don't you go home and mind your own business? I don't need you telling me what to do. This is my shitty mess, my shitty life, so go back to your perfect life and stop worrying about me. I'm your employer – not your responsibility.'

She walked out of the kitchen feeling so ashamed of herself. Yes, she wanted Ollie's help, but to admit it was admitting defeat. She'd worked so hard to build the walls around herself over the years of being married to Martin. The hurt he'd caused her had ruined her and she didn't want anyone else to see what a mess she was. It was pretty obvious Ollie could see through the brave face that she wore like a mask. He could see her for the scared drunk that she was. Realising how ashamed she felt strengthened her resolve to stop drinking for good. She realised that the two policemen who were standing at the front door talking to Jack and Ethan would have heard everything. *Fuck me, could my life get any worse?*

'I'll be in my bedroom. When you need me, knock on the door. I can't go anywhere tonight. I'll have to stay here, so you can tell whoever it is that's coming they'll have to work around me. I won't get in the way.'

She walked inside and slammed the door. Her legs were shaking and she only just managed to throw herself onto the bed before they gave way. Rolling herself up in the duvet, she cried as quietly to herself as possible. She didn't need anyone. He should have left her last night. Why had he come back and stuck his nose in? If she was dead then none of this would matter.

***

Ollie was so mad at himself he wanted to punch the wall, the door, anything. She was right. None of this was anything to do with him. So now what? He stood clenching the sink so tight his knuckles were white. She didn't know the details about how he'd watched Ellen die such a horrible, slow death. She didn't know anything about his life either so they were equal. He was angry with himself for interfering, but she'd almost died last night and looked terrible today.

Then they'd found that monstrosity in the hall and the police were outside, yet he'd decided that it was the right time to patronise her about her drinking when it was the last thing she needed. He turned around and walked past her bedroom door. God, he wanted to go in there and hold her, tell her how sorry he was, that he shouldn't stick his nose in, but he couldn't. Jake and Ethan were standing staring at him along with the two coppers. It was Ethan who approached him first.

'We can't do anything else today, boss, until they've finished. Should we go home?'

Ollie nodded. 'Yes, no point in you hanging around.'

'Is everything okay, Ollie? You know with…' Ethan didn't say her name, but nodded in the direction of her bedroom.

Ollie nodded again. 'See you both tomorrow.'

They said goodbye and he waited until they'd left then turned to the policemen and rhymed off his contact details in case they wanted him.

'I'm a bit worried about Kate. She's not too well. Will there be someone here for a while?'

'Yes, I would say so. The DI has been called out to come and take a look as well as a doctor. It all depends on whether this is a real head or not. In my opinion it is, but it's not down to me. There could be officers here for hours yet and they might want to do a search of the house and gardens, although that could probably wait until the morning. It's not as if it's just happened.'

'Good. Could I ask you a favour? When everyone is ready to leave, could someone contact me and let me know? It's just I don't want her to be on her own at the moment – but I need to go home for a bit. I'm only going to be in your way.'

'I'll ask whoever turns up. I can't promise though because most of the time they can't remember to tie their own shoelaces, if you get what I mean.'

He winked at Ollie who smiled back, then he walked past them and out to his car. Ollie was tired. After he'd left the hospital last night he couldn't sleep when he got home. He kept replaying it over and over again. The sight of Kate lying in a pool of blood had really upset him. He didn't want to lose her although he'd done a pretty good job of pissing her off. He wanted to help her. Maybe when they'd both had some sleep and she was feeling better they could sit down and discuss how they felt about each other.

Before he knew it, he was home and parked on his drive. His house looked tiny compared to Kate's even though it wasn't. It was a decent-sized detached house with a garage and conservatory, not that he ever used it because that had been Ellen's favourite room. She had a large, soft leather sofa in there and a bookcase full of books that she would read. God. he missed her, but he missed having a life as well. He felt about Kate the way he'd felt about Ellen all those years ago, and if he didn't know any better he'd say that somewhere along the line Ellen had stepped in, throwing them together. Knowing that he was lonely and Kate needed someone to help her, love her and stand by her.

As he walked through the front door and kicked off his boots, he didn't bother making something to eat. He went upstairs for a quick shower and then got into bed. Leaving his mobile on full volume in case the police or Kate rang, he thought sleep would never come. It did, hard and fast. Before he knew it, he was in a different time. A time where his wife was still alive and in their kitchen cooking dinner. She had coloured her hair and he'd been so glad to see her standing there. He couldn't remember the exact date that she'd last cooked a meal for him. It had been a couple of years ago. He made some remark and she laughed, turning to look at him.

Only it wasn't Ellen; it was Kate and he heard Ellen's voice whisper in his ear: *It's okay, Oliver, she needs you, but you need her even more. I want you to be happy. You should know that there is something very wrong with that house. Evil walks through it when it thinks no one is looking, but the nun will help you to make it all right.* The phone he'd tucked under his pillow began to ring, jolting him from his sleep. The dirty, grey light of dawn filtered through the blinds. He had no idea what time it was. After pulling his phone out, he answered it to a voice he didn't recognise.

'Mr Nealee?'

'Yes, speaking.'

'I'm Detective Constable Dan Sullivan. I'm currently at the house – Kate Parker's house, I'm not sure what it's called. One of the officers passed me your details and said to give you a ring when we've finished.'

'Oh, that's good. Have you sorted it out then?'

'Well, not so much sorted it out. We've removed the head and it will be taken up to the mortuary. Because it's so old it's very doubtful there will be much we can do with it.'

'Oh, it's a real one then?'

'Yes, it's definitely real and both yourself and Miss Parker will be relieved to know that we actually know whose it is. I don't have the exact details to hand. There's a bit of a story to it as it happens. Way back in 1933 when the house was a convent, they found the body of one of the nuns upstairs. She was minus a head. I guess for whatever reason it was hidden there. At least we know who she was. We've done the basics and taken whatever forensics we can, but it's so long ago I doubt that the perpetrator is still alive.'

'Have you told all this to Kate?'

'I haven't, my colleague has. I think Miss Parker could do with a friendly face. It's not every day you find the mummified head of a murder victim from the 1930s in your house. Thank God.'

'Yes, I'll be there soon. Thank you for ringing me, I really appreciate it.'

'Oh, just one more thing. This could possibly bring the press to the door. You know what they're like; if they think there may be a good story they'll be snooping around.'

'Thank you, I'll keep an eye out for them.'

The line went dead and Ollie rubbed his eyes then peered at the clock. It was 5 a.m. Jesus. He got out of bed. Within five minutes he was dressed and had cleaned his teeth. He didn't care how angry Kate was with him, he wasn't leaving her on her own. She was far too vulnerable at the moment. If she wouldn't let him in, he'd sit outside in his van, but he didn't want to leave her inside that house all alone.

***

161

Kate watched as the police packed up the last of their stuff and drove away. She shut the door behind them and tried her best not to look into the dark space where the poor woman's head had been put all those years ago. A violent shiver ran down her spine. It was horrific. This place had been a convent in 1933, with lovely, peaceful nuns living here. So who in their right mind would decapitate an elderly nun and stuff her head behind a secret panel that no one knew about?

How she wished she hadn't turned on Ollie earlier – the one person in a very long time who had stood by her. He had saved her bloody life, for Christ's sake. He was her only friend and she had thrown him out because he'd offered to help her. The fact that he'd dared to speak the truth to her had filled her with embarrassment. She'd got all defensive – just like she would when Martin used to come in to find her slumped over the chair.

His hurtful words rang in her ears, 'Get a fucking grip, Kate. When are you going to realise the world doesn't revolve around you? You're a complete embarrassment. Do you think the girls want a drunken slut for a mother? Marrying you was the biggest mistake of my life.' And on and on it would go. Not once had he offered to help her, unlike Ollie.

She found herself back in the kitchen. The house was cold because the front door had been open for the last eight hours as the police had gone in and out. There was no milk left because she'd made them all numerous mugs of tea and coffee. She was so thirsty. She should get a glass of water, but her mouth was dry and itching.

She knew her mind was telling her what would quench her thirst, and she opened the fridge. She was almost out of alcohol. There was a solitary bottle of wine in the fridge. The taste of sour bourbon filled her mouth when she looked at it. How was she supposed to sleep here, on her own, after everything that had happened? She slammed the fridge door shut. Her bloody arms were smarting and throbbing. She turned around and jumped to see Ollie standing there, concern etched across his face.

'The police rang. I'm sorry about earlier, Kate. You're right, your life is none of my business and I had no right sticking my nose in. I was so worried about you. I just want to help, in any way that I can.'

'You have nothing to be sorry about. I'm such a bitch when I'm faced with the truth. I've never been very good at admitting I can't manage. I spend each day pretending how I'm fine, coping with life.'

She lifted her arms up, holding them out, the sleeves of her dressing gown revealing the white bandages wrapped around them. 'Well, I'm not fine and I'm definitely not coping. I've been on my own for so long, even when I was married I was lonely. Martin never cared about anything I did. He didn't care about me and I guess I'm not used to it. I'm sorry for being so nasty to you. Thank you for coming back.'

He leant against the door frame. Kate thought he looked as if he was trying to support himself.

'I didn't count on getting to know you so well. I really, really like you, Kate. I know you have your problems – don't we all – but I think if you had the right support you could turn your life around. I'd like to be the one to help you, but if you think I'm talking rubbish and you're still mad at me then I'll leave and I promise not to bother you. I have a friend who can take over the rest of the building work and finish the house for you.'

Her eyes sparkled with tears for this kind, gorgeous, too good to be true man. She blinked them back and crossed the room, wrapping her arms around his waist as she pulled him towards her. 'Oh, Ollie, I'm so sorry.'

'Thank you. I've been struggling with my feelings because I loved Ellen so much. I was devastated when she died – I still am – but she's gone and I know that she wanted me to live my life to the full. She made me promise I would before she died, but I couldn't. I was just going through the motions until the day I came here to speak to you about the renovations. For the first time in a long time you gave me a reason to get up and come to work each day and look forward to it.' He pulled her closer, leaning down. Her lips met with his and the kiss that followed was one of the most explosive kisses that either of them had ever had.

**

Ollie pulled away, breathless. 'Where did you learn to kiss like that?' He winked at her and she laughed.

'To be honest I thought it was you who was the expert kisser. Maybe we just make a perfect kissing couple.'

He laughed. 'So, Kate, what happens now? I mean I would like nothing more than to pick you up and carry you to your bed where I could show you just how good my kissing skills really are, but I don't want to rush things. I value your friendship far too much. I don't want a quick leg-over and that's it. I've never been a one-night stand kind of guy.'

'Well, I'd very much like you to kiss me again – just to prove to me it wasn't a one-off because kissing is something I like, a lot. So it's one of the key stipulations of any relationship that we might have.'

He pulled her close again, this time not wanting to stop. He scooped her into his arms and carried her towards her bedroom where he used his foot to kick the door open. It slammed against the wall so hard the sound echoed around the room. Kicking it shut, he walked across to the bed and laid her down. She wouldn't let go of his neck and pulled him down onto the bed with her where he lay next to her.

They both lay staring at each other. Kate lifted her fingers and traced the outline of his cheek down to his jaw. He kissed her fingers, which then found his hair. She tugged his head towards her and she reached up and kissed him with even more passion than before.

6 January 1933

Father Patrick hadn't spoken much to either Agnes or Crosby. He stood up. 'I need to go to the church. I need to speak to the bishop about all of this. What you're talking about is out of my hands. It needs an experienced priest. If this woman is indeed a demon, she will need more than I can give to get rid of her. I've never done anything like it in my life.'

Crosby stood up too. 'In the meantime, I'm going to get two of my officers to make some enquiries around the town to see if anyone knows Lilith Ardat. I suggest we meet back here at four o'clock before it gets dark, if that's all right with you, Agnes. What are you going to do with yourself? Would you not be better to leave this house with the good Father and come back later?'

Agnes knew that Crosby and Patrick were right. They did need expert advice and she shouldn't be here on her own, but she felt as if she was attached to the house herself. Poor Mary and Edith's souls were still here. They had died so horribly there was no way they would have crossed into the light. If she walked out and left now the house would fill with darkness before she came back, and that was what Lilith wanted.

Agnes knew that for whatever reason the woman wanted this house of God to turn into a house of evil. She had already done a very good job of achieving that, but Agnes would stop her. Her faith in God and the light would help her to fight. She would send the demon back to wherever it was that it came from. Vampires slept throughout the day. They couldn't go out in the sunlight. So if Lilith was appearing as a vampire to scare her then she should be able to track her down and put a stake through her heart. She would play her at her own game.

'I'll be fine while it's daylight. She doesn't like to do her work unless it's in the black of night. Just make sure you are both back here before the light fades. As stubborn as I am, I don't want to be here on my own when it gets dark.'

Both men nodded and stood up to leave. The quicker they did what they had to the quicker they would be back. She watched them walk out of the front door and prayed that she was right about Lilith only showing her true colours at night. After putting her crucifix back around her neck, she picked up her prayer book and walked to Edith's bedroom where she stood outside the door and prayed for Edith's soul. She had a small bottle of holy water, which she'd tucked in her pocket. She took it out, sprinkled some onto her fingers and made the sign of the cross on the door. The wood smouldered as steam rose from the surface. Agnes didn't let that put her off.

Lilith might have turned these two rooms into shrines to the devil himself, but Agnes wouldn't be scared. As she crossed the hall towards Mary's room, she heard a low, deep, guttural growl come from inside. It struck the fear of God into her, turning the blood running through her veins into iced water. It was so animalistic.

She threw the water at Mary's door and began to pray to God to protect her from evil. This door did exactly the same thing. The smell of smouldering wood and something much darker infiltrated her nostrils. Terrified to open it, but having no choice, she threw it back until it slammed against the plaster. Inside, it was very dark and empty. She felt relief wash over her body, even though the essence of evil was everywhere. It felt as if it was seeping from the very walls, with the master of evil hiding out of sight. Of this Agnes was one hundred per cent sure.

They needed to find Lilith, and Agnes knew that she wouldn't be too far away. The woman, beast, abomination had sensed the three of them living here on their own in a house that belonged to God and had taken it upon itself to claim the house for its own. This whole thing was probably no more than a game to it.

Was this how demons sought their pleasure? Picking off innocent souls and claiming them for their own?

Agnes felt her whole body shudder with revulsion at the very thought of who Lilith really was. Even though the police had searched the house from top to bottom, it was big – with plenty of hiding spaces they could easily have missed. She would start to search it herself and make her way down. In the book, Dracula had spent his days confined to a coffin in the cellar of the castle. So it was common sense that Lilith would be hiding in the cellars of the convent.

This idea felt so right Agnes wondered if she should just go straight down there and get the confrontation over with, because there was no doubt in Agnes's mind that this was going to end in a fight – one that she might not win. She just hoped that surely God wouldn't abandon her like he had the others. Wouldn't he want to protect his own? She was the last one left to fight this battle for him.

She continued to bless every door along the hallway; the others didn't react to the holy water until she got to the door to her bedroom. Scared to bless it, she had to lift her trembling fingers to shake the water out of the bottle. Before her finger touched the door, she smelt that terrible, earthy, rotting-meat smell and knew that Lilith or whatever it was that pretended to be Lilith was nearby, taunting her like some complicated game of cat and mouse.

As Agnes's fingers touched the wood, it smouldered and the heat was far more intense. She felt it burning the fleshy tip of her finger and carried on despite the searing pain. Afraid to open her door, she knew that somehow the monster was waiting inside for her. She stopped her fingers from reaching out for the door-knob and turned away. She would be damned if she was going to make this too easy for it.

She walked as fast as her arthritic knees would go. She was going down to the kitchen for some garlic cloves and she needed a wooden stake – something to stab Lilith through the chest with. Agnes's heart pounded in her ears as she reached the ground floor. She ignored the sound of her bedroom door as it creaked the way it did each morning when she opened it. *What are you doing, woman? You're too old for this. Get out of here now. Get to the church. Who in their right mind would want to fight monsters at your age?*

She silenced the terrified voice in her head and carried on. She was almost at the kitchen. The warm glow from the lights she'd left on were like a beacon, telling her she was almost home. She hadn't realised just how dark the rest of the convent was until she saw the light. As she stepped through the door she felt better. It was the light. There was no doubt about it.

She could hear noises out in the hallway, but she didn't turn to see what or who was making them. There was a string of garlic cloves hanging from one of the kitchen door handles and she grabbed it, putting it around her neck. She tipped holy water from the bottle and splashed it around her neck, rubbing it all over. As she touched the two crusted puncture wounds, they began to smart and burn as if she had rubbed pure alcohol onto them. The pain in her neck was intense, but for the first time that day she felt clean, as if the goodness in the water had washed out the dirty, unclean germs.

She looked around but couldn't see anything she could use as a wooden stake. Pulling each drawer open then slamming them shut, the only thing wooden was the heavy rolling pin, which would only be any use if she wanted to bash its brains in. There was a wooden spoon, but that also had a blunt, rounded end. If she were to try and stake someone's heart with that, she was going to need a lot of help from God himself.

She turned around expecting to see the vampire standing behind her with a smirk on its face, but there was no one around. She caught sight of her reflection in the kitchen window and wondered if she was going insane. What did she look like standing there – her face white with a garland of garlic for a necklace – and what would happen if Crosby came back with Father Patrick and saw her like this? They'd think it was her who had killed Mary and Edith. That poor Sister Agnes who had spent her entire life doing good deeds and worshipping God had lost her mind. They might even blame it on her age.

Tucking the wooden spoon into her trouser waistband, she looked around for something sharper. They could think what they wanted. She knew the truth. She knew that she wasn't mad and that was all that mattered. The sharp butcher's knife on the chopping board caught her eye. It was big and sharp enough to stab through anyone's heart. She reached out for it, her fingers wrapping around the wooden handle, and picked it up. It felt heavy and right. It might not be wooden, but it should do the job. Just to make sure, she sprinkled some holy water onto it and said a prayer.

Looking up at the kitchen clock, she saw she had an hour before Crosby and Patrick returned. The sky was already turning inky grey as the sun faded. This wouldn't take an hour. As soon as her shaky legs were ready to continue, she was going down into the cellar to confront the beast. If she had luck on her side it would still be asleep and she could end it all now. If it was waiting for her then so be it. God would help her to fight her best. This was out of her hands now and in the good Lord's, and she had the advantage because Edith and Mary had been caught by surprise. But not her – oh no, she knew what its game was and she would be the one to stop it.

The cellar door was situated outside the kitchen door. She couldn't see it from where she was standing, but a cold draught enveloped her ankles and she knew that it was ajar. Someone had opened it. Less than a minute ago she had passed it and it had been shut. It was as if it knew what she was thinking and pre-empting every move. Then Agnes realised that yes, it did know exactly what she was thinking because it was feeding off her fear. It had fed off all their fears and now there was only her left.

She began walking towards the open door. She tugged it so it was wide open. The smell of rotting flesh reached her nostrils. It was much stronger down there. She nodded her head, praying to God to give her the strength to overcome the evil waiting down in the darkness for her. She tugged on the cord. The single bulb illuminated the steep steps that led down into the cellar. Her legs felt like lead weights, but she forced them to move, taking one step at a time. She hated coming down here at the best of times when she didn't think there was some evil, demonic entity waiting to kill her and take her soul to hell. The knuckles on her right hand were white, the knife secure inside them. She could smell the garlic as well as the earthy, rotting stench, and her stomach was churning.

She had never in her entire life envisaged dying this way; her left hand clasped the silver crucifix to her chest as she began to pray. As her feet stepped onto the damp, earthen floor she listened for some sign of where the monster could be. It was a huge cellar with single bulbs periodically spread along it, not giving off enough light to see the sides, which were cloaked in blackness. There was no silk-lined coffin in the middle of the room as she'd expected and for a second, she wondered if she had gone mad. Then from the far end of the cellar she heard a scratching sound, like nails on a chalkboard, and an image of those long, red talons on the end of slender, white fingers made her shiver.

'Who's there? This is a house of God; you have no right to be inside here. By the power of the Lord I'm commanding you to leave.'

Her words, which had felt so bold as she spoke them, fell flat in the huge room.

'I know you're there, hiding in the shadows like the coward that you are. Step into the light and show yourself, demon. I'll not be scared out of my home by the likes of you. I won't let you – and God certainly won't let you.'

Movement somewhere in front of her made her step forward. Her only exit from the cavernous room was up the stairs. There was another door that led straight out into the garden, which she'd instructed Mary to put a lock and chain on for the winter, to keep the wind from blowing it open in stormy weather and letting every animal known to man from making beds down there. For all she knew it could be rats scratching and moving around.

As she was about to turn around and go back upstairs, she felt a dark shadow fall over her and she muttered: '*You sneaky little bastard.*' As she turned around to face it, the smell was so repugnant it made her eyes water. When she saw what was standing on the bottom step of the cellar, she took a step backwards. Instead of the monster she had been imagining there was a man in a crisp white shirt and black tuxedo. He was almost as tall as the door frame and was stooped a little to fit in. His body blocked out what light there had been filtering down. He moved towards her and his black, satin cloak billowed out behind him. Agnes couldn't draw her eyes away from his face. He was very attractive. His eyes fixed on hers and he smiled, holding his hand out for hers. She tried her best to look away, but it was impossible. She couldn't break his gaze.

'Agnes, you can make this as easy or as hard as you want. This is your decision – whether to succumb to me like you want to or whether to stand your ground and fight. Tell me: where is your God now, Sister? Because I'm looking around and it seems to me he's let you down.'

She clenched the knife and tried to clear her mind of impure thoughts, but she was struggling. It was hard to think of anything except the man in front of her.

'I can see it's a bit of a dilemma for you, Agnes. Are you really happy now that you're here on your own? You didn't mind me last night when I was up close to you, caressing your neck. You were quite happy for me to drink your blood. You murmured in your sleep with pleasure.'

As he spoke. he pulled back his lips so his long, white, razor-sharp incisors glinted in what little light there was.

'I mean, let us be honest with each other – we're certainly both old enough. What has spending your life a lonely spinster done for you? Has God rewarded you for your lifetime of servitude?'

He stepped closer, bridging the gap.

'Mary and Edith gave themselves to me willingly. You can be reunited with them. All three of you will have eternal life and be rewarded for your sacrifice. There is something so sweet about the blood of a woman who has never been tainted by a man.'

He ran his tongue over his lips and Agnes couldn't stop staring into his eyes. They were so big and hypnotic. What he was saying made sense; she wasn't getting any younger. She could be with her two friends again. They could all be together. Then she heard Mary's voice scream inside her mind. It was so loud that it broke her trance. '*Agnes, don't listen. It wants your soul. You'll spend the rest of eternity in hell; it's torture. Every minute I'm dying the same horrible death over and over. Kill it and release us.*'

The vampire in front of her smiled, holding out his arms for her to step into them, and she did step towards him, but at the same time she lifted the knife. She was determined she was going to sink it straight through its heart and kill the monster. It didn't realise she was holding the knife in her hand because she had kept it tucked behind her back the whole time. As she stepped into its embrace, she brought the knife around and thrust it with every piece of strength she could muster into its chest. The vampire gasped, stumbling backwards, and then it let out a roar so loud that she lifted her hands to cover her ears.

The ground rumbled underneath her feet and the stench of decay became so overpowering she found her eyes starting to water. She stepped away from the quivering, shaking thing in front of her. It looked at her with blood-red eyes as it began to change its shape in front of her. Her heart started racing and she knew that she was going to die. She hoped it was of natural causes and not some bloodthirsty, agonising death at the hands of one of Satan's henchmen.

She felt herself being lifted off the ground and thrown. As she collapsed in a heap, she heard the bone in her ankle snap. The noise was as clear as if a twig had been snapped in half. The pain filled her mind as she looked out of the corner of her eye to see the mountainous shape in front of her. It was half woman, half winged beast. It no longer had a handsome face and big, mesmerising eyes. Now it had terrifying eyes that were watching her.

She prayed over and over again as it gathered strength and the shape that had been hard to see through became solid. There were two huge horns that stood on the top of its head but the face was that of the woman who had been the start of all of this. Lilith peered at Agnes, her red eyes glowing, and her top lip curled up in a snarl. There was blood pulsing from a gaping wound in her chest where the knife had been plunged deep inside.

'You should have let me kill you, old woman, just like the others did.'

Her voice filled the entire cellar; Agnes lifted her hands to cover her ears. She wanted to run, but there was nowhere to go. She couldn't, walk let alone run. Instead she closed her eyes, placed her palms together, and prayed to God to forgive her and take her soul before Lilith could.

Chapter 10

When Kate opened her eyes she couldn't believe it was morning. She had slept right through without so much as a drop of alcohol and no bad dreams. Her mouth was dry with the familiar thirst that no amount of water would quench. She stretched out her arm to see if Ollie was still there – too afraid to turn around and look in case he'd decided it had all been a horrible mistake and crept out hours ago. She felt his warm arm and ran her fingers across his naked chest.

Smiling to herself, she turned around. He was fast asleep and she lay there watching him. She had never been a selfish person, not until wine became her best friend. If Martin hadn't slept around and made her feel like crap, she wouldn't have got herself into this state – she knew that. It had started off being an escape for her. One glass of wine used to make her feel warm and fuzzy inside. Two glasses she'd be giggling at everything, even Martin's terrible jokes. Three and she was gone, falling asleep in the chair.

How things had changed. Now it was more like three bottles. She was glad that she'd made a conscious decision to cut down when she'd moved into the house, even though she hadn't always stuck to her plan. She climbed out of the bed trying to make as little noise as possible. She wanted to phone the doctor's and see if there were any appointments. She wanted to stop drinking – now, today. Not next week. She grabbed her mobile off the bedside table and crept out into the hall. There was a draught coming from somewhere and she walked up towards the front door to check it was shut. The open panel with the blackness inside made her shudder. Shit, she'd almost forgotten all about the head.

Walking across to the panel, she could feel the cold air that was blowing through it and wondered where it was coming from. She wanted to go inside and look at just how big it was, but something told her not to. She felt along the wall for the hidden button, which had been accidentally activated after all this time. She just wanted to close it for now and forget all about that poor woman's head. It was so damn scary to think someone decapitated her and stuffed her head in a secret cupboard for years. Why would they want to do that? And what if it turned out to be her distant relation – then what? What had she ever done to anyone that would warrant that kind of death? It didn't make any sense.

Kate wondered what the priest would find out for her. She should really give him a ring and let him know what had happened. The doctor's receptionist told her she would get the duty doctor to ring her back sometime to speak to her. She put the phone down and punched the air. For the first time in a long time she felt in control, that she could make the right choices for once.

She went to the kitchen and pulled the eggs, bacon, sausages, tomatoes and mushrooms from the fridge. She was starving. She couldn't remember the last time she had woken up feeling as if she could eat a substantial breakfast instead of the obligatory slice of burnt toast and jam. She even rooted through the cupboards until she found the box with the unused Christmas gift set that Amy had bought her containing a cafetière, a bag of ground coffee and two Starbucks mugs.

Kate checked the date on the coffee was still okay. She didn't want to poison Ollie. It was good until the end of the month, so it was just as well she was going to use it. She busied herself making breakfast. It felt so good to be useful again after all this time. She was a very good cook. There just hadn't been much point when there was only her to feed. She heard the sound of the toilet flush just as she was setting two plates of cooked breakfast down onto the table. Perfect timing. Ollie walked in and groaned.

'How did you know I was starving?'

'I didn't. I knew that I was, so I just hoped you would be as well.'

She sat down and he followed suit. Ollie stuffed everything on his plate between two slices of toast, making her smile. Amy used to do the same. Every time they went out for breakfast she would cram everything between the bread then try and eat it, usually dribbling tomato or bean juice down her chin. God, she missed her so much. Kate had never realised just how much she loved her friend until it had been too late. She stopped herself from thinking too much about it, or she would feel herself sink down into the blackness that swirled around in her brain like a vortex.

'Are you okay this morning? I was a bit scared you'd have woken up and wondered what the hell you'd got yourself into last night.'

She laughed. 'I've never been better, thank you. Last night was amazing and perfect; you are amazing.'

Kate looked up from her plate, pleased to see the redness that was creeping up his neck towards his face. It was nice that he wasn't big-headed like Martin. Ollie didn't think he was God's gift to women – unlike her ex-husband.

'And so are you, Kate.'

It was her turn to blush. She tucked into her breakfast. There was a loud knock on the front door and she put her fork down and stood up. It was Saturday and far too early for the lads to appear. She walked through the house to the front door and shivered. It was so cold out here. Opening the door, she squealed to see her two daughters standing there. She wasn't so happy to see Martin, but he'd brought them to visit. Kate opened her arms and both girls ran towards her. She hugged them close.

'Can we come in?'

Kate looked up at him, desperate to mouth the words *Go get fucked* to him, but she knew he'd take the girls away and she needed this. She nodded and stepped back. 'Girls, why don't you go down to the kitchen and see if there's any biscuits in the tin by the kettle.' They let go of her and raced through the hall towards the kitchen and Ollie.

'What do you want, Martin?'

'Well, thanks to you Tamara thinks I'm having an affair.'

Kate laughed. She couldn't help herself. It was so bloody ironic. Why should she care what bloody stupid, immature Tamara thought and why would Martin think she'd be bothered?

'You have no one but yourself to blame. What were you thinking trying to get me into bed? If you loved Tamara you'd keep your dick in your trousers.'

'I don't know, Kate. I do love her; I want to marry her. So I've come to ask if you'll have the girls for a few days while we go away for the weekend to try and smooth things over.'

'Of course I'll have the girls. You have no idea how much I miss them. Not that you'd care, but I do. Oh, and for your information, Martin, I don't care about you and Tamara; I care about my daughters, so don't think I'm doing this for you because I'm not. I'm doing it for me and for them. They need their mother not some 22-year-old whore.'

She winced as the words left her mouth in case he saw his arse again and stormed off, but he didn't. He nodded.

'Thank you. Should I go get their stuff from the car?'

'Yes.'

Kate had no idea where they were going to sleep, but she was sure Ollie would take her to buy some beds and help her build them. Martin carried two small cases from the car to the front door, putting them down by her feet.

'I'll be back late Monday afternoon if that's okay. Autumn has my phone number in her new phone so if you need me she'll ring me.'

She nodded. He turned and walked back to his car and for once he didn't seem so full of bullshit. Maybe he really did love this Tamara. She shut the door and walked back to the kitchen. The sight of her two daughters sitting at the table and chatting away to Ollie took her breath away and she had to blink back the tears that welled in her eyes. God, what if he didn't like kids? He turned to face her and grinned.

'Autumn wants to know if I'm your boyfriend. I wasn't sure what to say.'

'Ollie is my friend and he's the man who is going to help me get you two a bedroom ready, or so I hope.'

She looked at him to see if he thought she was taking it too far, but he nodded.

'Of course I will. Which room do you think you girls would like to sleep in and what's your favourite colour?'

They both chorused green and he looked at Kate. He'd been expecting them to say pink. She smiled. They'd always been different to the other kids in their classes at school.

'Why don't you go and see which room you like, then we'll have to go shopping for some supplies, because I haven't got much food in and we need some duvets, curtains and teddies for your bedroom.'

Both girls ran over and kissed Kate, then they raced off to go and look upstairs.

'I'm sorry, I had no idea he was going to turn up out of the blue and let them stop.'

Ollie stood up and took both plates over to the sink. 'Don't be sorry. They seem like good kids despite having Martin for a dad. Should we get dressed and go pay a visit to IKEA? At least you'll be able to buy everything you need and not spend a fortune.'

'Is that okay with you? That would be amazing.'

'Yes, I'll go home for a shower then I'll be back in thirty minutes. We could stop off somewhere for lunch, then on the way home we can go food shopping. If it's okay with you – until we know what is going on with the house, I think I should stop here to make sure you're all safe.'

He walked across to where she was standing and pulled her close, kissing her. She kissed him back. The sound of thunderous footsteps coming down the stairs made them pull apart. He left through the back door and jogged around to his van. Kate watched him, her heart beating faster at the thought of his soft lips on hers. Today was a good day. She'd gone from being an unhappy, scared, suicidal, alcoholic wreck to a happy family again in the space of twenty-four hours and she loved it. This was how her life was supposed to be. She deserved some happiness.

Chapter 11

Joe felt terrible. He'd been so busy he still hadn't made it back to visit Kate and he wasn't sure if it was because he was actually scared to go back there. He looked through the old books in the huge bookcase in the drawing room, just in case there was something about the convent in one of them. The house was silent as usual and it didn't normally bother him, but today he was jumpy. He kept seeing dark shadows out of the corner of his eye, then he'd turn and there was nothing there.

Before he'd become a priest he'd had some experiences with the paranormal, which he didn't usually talk about to anyone. His gran had told him he had the gift when he was a kid, only he didn't consider it a gift because who wanted to wake up in the middle of the night to see some long-dead relation they'd never met sitting on the end of their bed freaking them out? Not him. She'd had to take him to visit a friend of hers with purple curly hair and the biggest silver hooped earrings he'd ever seen to make it stop.

The woman had sat with him and taught him how to block them out so he didn't get scared. Even though she'd smelt like those small purple sweets he used to buy at the corner shop, she had been kind and funny. She also knew what she was talking about because after he started to do what she'd told him to, his ghostly visitors had stopped appearing. Apart from the odd one, but they had to be really strong to get through the blocks he'd put in place.

That was why he'd been so upset at the crematorium. He also knew there was something bad up at the convent. Kate seemed like a nice woman. How she was living up there on her own he didn't know. He didn't think he would be brave enough to. He walked into the drawing room and shivered. It was so cold in here he could see his breath. Joe walked across to check the radiator. He reached out to touch it then withdrew his hand. It was red hot.

Trying not to let his mind fill with the images that were floating around the edges, he turned and opened the glass door, which the books were kept behind. He loved reading. He'd not had much time since he'd moved here. For a small town it was very busy. Most of the books were classics: Dickens, Shakespeare, Brontë, and Austen. As he made his way down the shelves, he stopped at the bottom row. He was drawn to a thick, heavy Bible and he tugged it out. It was very old and dusty. He didn't think it had been touched for years.

A loud bang from upstairs made his blood run cold. It had been raining when he left so he knew for a fact that he hadn't left any windows open for a draught to come through. Footsteps moved across the ceiling, along with a heavy dragging sound. Putting the Bible back he shut the glass door and crossed the room to listen from behind the doorway. Could someone have broken in?

He felt in his pocket for his phone and tugged it out. When his finger was poised ready to press 999, the sound stopped as if whoever it was knew that he was listening. The hairs on the back of his neck stood on end and he felt his skin begin to prickle, just like it used to when he was a kid and there was a visitor from the other side. There was no more sound from upstairs and he knew he should go up and check it out, but he was afraid that he'd get up there and not find anyone. He'd rather take his chances with a burglar than a ghost.

The most precious things he owned were his iPad and Xbox; apart from those he wouldn't say he had many material possessions. He didn't wear designer clothes or shoes; his hobby was his camper van, which seemed to take up most of his money. He supposed some of the stuff that the church had lying around – like the heavy crucifixes and religious statues – might be of some value to someone, but they'd have to be desperate to want to steal that stuff. He knew he should ring the police. But if they came and there was no one upstairs he'd look like a fool. Taking a deep breath, he stepped into the hall. 'Hello, is anyone up there? I'll give you to the count of five before I ring the police.' He counted as loud as he could. No reply.

'Right, I'm phoning them. I don't care what you were doing up there as long as you come down right now.'

If Joe was honest, he didn't know what he'd do if a man came downstairs at this very minute in time. What else was he supposed to say? Feeling braver, he walked to the stairs and put his foot on the bottom step. Another door slammed and the sound of heavy footsteps coming towards the landing made him turn around and run straight out of the front door. Out of breath, he rang 999 and asked for the police; then he went and sat in his camper van. If anyone came out, he could either run them over or drive away. He felt safer inside his little haven.

Before long he heard sirens in the distance. Thank God they were on their way. A police van screeched into the narrow drive and came to a stop next to his camper van. The policewoman driving it turned the sirens off. He could still hear faint ones in the background. He jumped out feeling a bit embarrassed that he was hiding behind his steering wheel like some numpty when a woman who was talking on her radio was about to go into the vicarage on her own and see if there was a burglar.

'I'll come in with you. Should I?'

'No, it's best if you wait out here, Father. I'll go and do an initial check of the building. My backup will be here soon and they'll follow me in. Where do you think the intruder is?'

'Upstairs.'

She jogged off towards the front door and he felt terrible. What if something happened to her? What would he do then? He'd look great standing outside like a big wuss. She'd already disappeared through the door and he shook his head, striding across the gravel to follow her. A police car turned into the drive and he felt relieved to see two much bigger, very hairy men jump out and run towards the house.

One went inside and the other ran around the back. Joe didn't know what to do so he waited at the front door. He could hear them shouting, 'Police!' as they checked out each room in the house. He had a terrible feeling that whatever it had been, it wasn't a burglar. If that was the case, though, what was it and what had it been dragging? He couldn't exactly tell them he'd been frightened by a ghost. Today was not a good one for him. He just hoped it wasn't going to get any worse. The small policewoman came out followed by the big hairy men and Joe knew what they were going to say.

'We've checked the entire house: every cupboard, wardrobe and under every bed. There's no one inside, Father.'

Joe shook his head. 'I was afraid that was what you would say. I'm sorry for wasting your time, but thank you so much for coming and so fast as well. It's very kind of you.'

'What made you think there was someone inside your house?'

'There's only me that lives here. I came home from visiting an old friend and heard a loud bang upstairs followed by heavy footsteps. I should have gone up and taken a look around before calling you out. I'm so sorry.'

'No, don't be sorry; you did the right thing. You can never be too careful. If there was someone they managed to leave before we got here. I suggest you make sure all the windows and doors are secure and if you think they've come back please don't hesitate to call us. That's what we're here for.'

He thanked them and watched them go back to their vans where the lights were still flashing, illuminating the dusky sky. He looked up at the landing window and crossed himself. He turned to wave as the officers got ready to go to the next emergency, then he strode into the house whilst he was feeling brave. He went into every room and checked the windows were secure. The house was empty just like it always was. Nothing was out of place, so what had the dragging sound been? He shivered, not wanting to think too much about it.

Satisfied there was no one of the mortal kind in the house, he went back downstairs to the drawing room and the book he'd been about to take a look at. This time he walked in and the room felt warm. It was no longer freezing cold; in fact, he felt hot under his starched, white collar and he had to unclip it to let his skin breathe. He crossed to the cabinet and opened the door, but the heavy black leather book was no longer there. He ran his finger along every single book to double check. When he got to the bottom row there was no mistaking it – the book had been removed. He looked down onto the floor in case he'd dropped it in his hurry to get out of the house. It wasn't anywhere to be seen and he'd checked every room apart from this and knew it wasn't in any of them.

He lifted his hand and rubbed his head. What was happening? He didn't understand it. How could a book so old and heavy disappear into thin air? Somebody or something hadn't wanted him to look at it and had drawn his attention away from it. Puzzled, Joe decided it was time to make something to eat and have a drink. Maybe he was tired and needed to give himself a rest. He locked the front door and went into the kitchen. He was going to warm up a pizza and get a bottle of ice-cold Grolsch from the fridge, then go upstairs with his pizza and lager to play on his Xbox until he fell asleep. Tomorrow morning, nice and early, he would go and visit Kate to tell her about the convent and its tragic history. The woman had lived there without serious incident up to now; one more night wouldn't hurt.

***

It was almost dark by the time Ollie pulled up outside Kate's house. The girls were fast asleep in the back seat cuddling their new dinosaur teddies. Kate looked in the mirror and smiled. She'd never felt such an overwhelming rush of love for her children, who looked so angelic whilst they were asleep. Autumn was the serious one and loved to read as much as Kate did. Summer was more giggly and fun-loving. They were both very individual and she loved them more than anything. Ollie whispered in her ear, 'You should be very proud. They are great kids. They didn't ask for much and were so well-behaved. It was a pleasure to take them.'

'Thank you so much for today; I don't know what I'd have done without you. It's pretty late now though and you must be tired. Why don't we take everything inside and order a Chinese. We can leave all the boxes in the hall and put the mattresses on the floor in my room for tonight. They can sleep there.'

'Yes to the takeaway. I love any kind of Chinese food. And it's okay if that's what you want, but I don't mind putting the beds up. They shouldn't take too long. As long as you feed and water me I can work all night, boss.'

He laughed and she nudged his side. 'Am I really a slave driver?'

'No, I'm joking. I love being with you, Kate. I also have an ulterior motive. If I don't build the beds the girls will be sleeping in your room and I'll have to go home and sleep on my own. I know it's very selfish of me, but being in bed next to you last night gave me the best night's sleep in months and if I'm honest, I don't want to leave you girls here on your own.'

'I want you to stop too. Let's get everything inside, then you can crack on whilst I order the food.'

'Yes, my lady; right away, my lady.'

He jumped out of the car before she could elbow him harder this time. She got out and went to unlock the front door. The house smelt of fresh paint. Ollie had left Jack and Ethan finishing painting the room the girls had picked out to be their bedroom. It was the first one at the top of the stairs, so it was close enough that Kate would hear them if they needed her in the night.

They left the sleeping girls whilst they unpacked the car, dumping all the boxes in the hall. They'd bought beds, chests of drawers, bedside tables, lamps, rugs and the cutest dinosaur bedding Kate had ever seen. Ollie had pointed out the girls' section of bedding, but both girls had shaken their heads in disgust and picked out the dinosaur duvets and matching pillowcases. As they put the last boxes down, the doors on the van slammed shut and both girls climbed out. They wandered inside rubbing their eyes.

'Are you hungry?'

They nodded in unison. 'Good, what do you fancy to eat? Ollie and I are going to get a Chinese, but you can have pizza or whatever you fancy.'

'Chicken chow mien, no bean sprouts, prawn crackers and salt and pepper chips, please.'

Autumn nodded at her sister's choice. 'I'll share with her, if that's okay.'

'Of course; I'll order it now.'

'Do you have a television, Mum?'

'I don't. I always prefer to read. We can go and get one tomorrow although I haven't got Sky TV.'

'It's okay. Have you got internet?'

Kate nodded, wondering when her girls had turned into miniature tech geeks. They sounded so grown up.

'That's okay then, you don't need a television. We can watch Netflix on our iPads.'

'Why don't you go and lie on my bed? You can watch your iPads in there whilst me and Ollie go and sort your room out.'

They grinned and ran off towards her bedroom. She turned to Ollie.

'Wow, they've grown up so much since I last saw them.'

'They certainly know their stuff. What the hell is Netflix?'

They picked up one end of a long box each and carried it up the stairs. Kate went first and as she reached the top step a cold draught surrounded her, making her shiver. Then as if someone had walked through her she felt her insides turn to ice water and her heart froze. She let out a gasp.

'Kate, what's the matter? You've gone white.'

She heard Ollie's voice, but she couldn't speak. Her mouth felt as if it was full of cotton wool and her tongue was too big.

He put his end of the box down, worried about her. She had frozen to the top step, disorientated. Panic filled her chest as she tried to breathe and couldn't. Something had hold of her heart. It felt as if there was a pair of icy hands wrapped around, squeezing it. She looked at Ollie and he must have seen the look of fear in her eyes. Pushing the box to one side he ran up and grabbed hold of her, shaking her shoulders.

'Kate, what's wrong?'

She let out a loud gasp as if she'd been holding her breath whilst whatever it was that had stepped inside her body stepped back out.

'I don't know. I couldn't breathe; it was so cold.'

He pulled her close. Her body temperature had dropped so drastically in seconds. She was shivering so much her teeth were chattering. With shaking arms, she held on to him. She had no idea what had just happened. She wondered if it was alcohol withdrawal, but she didn't really believe it was. It was as if someone had stepped inside her body, taking over it, but that was impossible.

'I don't feel well.'

187

Pain shot through her arms where she'd cut herself. She looked down at them to see Ollie's white T-shirt now turning blood red where her arms were wrapped around him. Pushing away from him she stifled the scream that welled inside her, not wanting to scare the girls or let them see what was happening.

Ollie looked down to see the blood dripping through the long-sleeved shirt she was wearing. Kate, who'd never been good with blood, felt the room begin to swim as her ears turned fuzzy. As if he could read her mind, he scooped her up into his arms and carried her to the en-suite bathroom in the bedroom a couple of doors down from the room the girls were going to be sleeping in. He tried not to get blood on the freshly painted walls, which would scare the girls. Ollie looked terrified. Neither of them understood what was happening. First of all, Kate had almost choked on nothing, and now she was bleeding again, badly. Ollie sat her down on the toilet. Holding her hands he lifted them into the air.

'Kate, did something attack you? Try not to look at the blood; put your head down. I'll try and stem the bleeding. What happened?'

She nodded, unable to speak. He rolled back one of her sleeves to inspect the now blood-soaked bandage. 'Keep your arm up whilst I take a look at this one.' She did as she was told even though it was hard to concentrate. As he unwrapped the bandages she winced in pain. The blood was dripping down her arm; he turned it around, inspecting the cut. The wound had opened up. How had that happened? Ollie pulled his T-shirt over his head. It was ruined now anyway. He wrapped it around to try and stem the flow of blood. He looked at the other arm; thankfully it wasn't bleeding as much.

'I think we need to get you back to the hospital. Carrying those boxes must have opened up the wounds in your arms.'

She shook her head. 'No, no hospital. Not when the girls are here. I don't want them to know I'm a complete fuck-up. Please,

Ollie, can you get the first aid kit from under the sink in the kitchen? I have some bandages in there. I'll put some dressings on and a clean top. Sorry about your T-shirt.'

'If you think that's best.'

'Ollie, I felt as if someone stepped inside my body. It was so cold and they were squeezing my insides so hard that I couldn't breathe.'

'Has it gone?'

'Yes.'

He ran off and she leant back, the cool tiles behind her head clearing the fog in her brain. She had no idea if that was even possible, but something strange had just happened, whether she wanted to believe it or not. Ollie's footsteps as he raced back up the stairs sounded comforting. He came back in with the green box tucked underneath his arm.

'It's okay, the girls are both in your room laughing at something they're watching. Sounded like *Little Britain*. They have good taste.'

'Thank you, I owe you again.'

He stroked her cheek.

'You owe me nothing. I'm here because I want to be and if I can be of some use whilst I'm here then that's even better. I'm worried about your arms though, Kate. Are you sure we shouldn't take you back to A&E to get them checked out?'

'Not bloody likely. Did you see the way they all looked at me with pity when I was there? I don't need anyone looking down on me. Today has been the best day in for ever; I'm not ending it sitting in the hospital for hours when I could be with my daughters and you.'

He smiled and bent down to kiss her cheek. 'My, you're tough, Ms Parker, and I'll do my best to wrap them back up. Do you think we should try and find some paranormal group or a priest to try and help us figure out what's going on?'

She watched as he kneeled on the floor in front of her. He

opened the green plastic box and took out an assortment of dressings and bandages. Within minutes he had pads on both arms and had bandaged them up almost as well as the nurse had done. They were tight and so far, so good; the blood wasn't seeping through them. When he'd finished, he took hold of her hands, holding them above her head.

'Just for a couple of minutes to make sure.'

Kate nodded. 'Thank you, and I've already spoken to a priest. The other day when I went for a walk, I ended up at a vicarage. He is supposed to be looking into the history of the house for me.'

'Good. Let's hope he can find something out that can help us then.'

He leant down and kissed her lips. She kissed him back with so much passion she thought her heart was about to explode from her chest. A loud knock on the door startled them apart. Ollie let go of her arms.

'Keep them up; it will be the food. I'll go.'

'You're semi-naked.'

'Oh yes, I forgot about that. I'll answer the door then run to the truck and get my sweatshirt before I take it into the kitchen.'

Kate leaned back against the cool wall to try and stop the burning sensation inside her head. There was something about him that made her act like she was desperate for a man. She needed to calm herself down. She was too old for this. Or was she? Just because Martin had made her feel like an old maid it didn't actually mean that she was. Maybe she should start wiping her time with Martin from her mind; she'd dwelled on those miserable twelve years of her life for too long. It was time to move on.

The thought of Martin reminded her that she hadn't had a drink for over twenty-four hours. The thirst was like nothing she'd ever known. Her hands trembled and she lowered them to inspect the bandages. They were still crisp and clean, no sign of any blood. Good, she didn't want to upset the girls. How was she going to get into her bedroom for a clean top with them in there? The front door slammed and she heard Ollie run down to the kitchen. He shouted to the kids as he went past her room and she heard the sound of them chattering as they went into the hall and made their way down to where she could hear the sound of plates and cutlery being banged around as Ollie began to dish up the food. Good.

She stood up on legs that felt as if they didn't belong to her. Something was going on in this house and she was too scared to think too hard about it. She got to the top of the stairs, her heart racing in case there was a replay of the incident of less than twenty minutes ago. Gripping on to the banister, she walked down each step, careful not to fall over her own feet. She reached her bedroom without incident and wondered if she'd imagined it all before. Was she hallucinating because of the alcohol withdrawal? Yes, she decided there was a good chance she was.

Slipping into her bedroom she opened the drawer and pulled out a black, long-sleeved top just as she heard Summer call, 'Mum, the food's here.' Taking a second to look at herself in the mirror she had to do a double take. The face staring back at her was much older with grey hair. She blinked and her own face was watching her. She really needed to get a grip of herself. She'd known the withdrawal from the wine would be bad, but she hadn't realised it would be like this. She walked into the kitchen and smiled at the sight of Ollie and Summer dishing food onto plates, whilst Autumn watched from her perch on the kitchen table, nibbling at the prawn crackers and making sure she got just as many noodles as her sister.

If Kate was honest, she didn't feel as hungry as she had earlier. Ollie turned around, passing a plate to Autumn, who took it from him, grinning. He smiled to see Kate and passed her the next one; Summer had already taken hers and was tucking in. Kate sat down in between her girls and wanted to pinch herself. Was this even real?

She reached out, letting her fingers brush along Summer's arm, then smiled; yes, it was real and a bloody miracle. Summer looked at her and smiled, her expression one of someone much older and wiser than an 11-year-old girl. They ate amongst the giggling from the girls as Ollie tried his best to use the chopsticks that had come with the food. He spilt more of it down his top and gave up, going back to using a fork. After they'd eaten the girls asked if they could go back to watching their iPads and Kate nodded.

'Yes, of course you can; we still need to build your beds.'

Ollie groaned. 'Bugger, I'd forgotten about that. I don't think I can bend down I've eaten that much chicken chow mien.'

Autumn laughed. 'Why don't we sleep on our mattresses tonight and you can build the beds tomorrow? It is quite late and I don't want you puking all over my new bed because you're too stuffed to bend down and screw it all together.'

'Wise words from that kid over there, Kate. Very wise.'

'Is that okay with you as well, Summer?'

Summer nodded. 'Yep, I don't care what I sleep on as long as it's comfy and I have my dinosaur bedding.'

Kate stood up. 'Well then, if you girls would scrape the plates and put them in the sink to soak we'll go up and make up your beds.'

Ollie, who was now leaning back in his chair, held out his hand. 'You'll have to prise me off this chair. I don't think I can move.'

She held out her hand and he grabbed it. She tugged him much harder than he expected and he stumbled towards her. He turned to look at the girls.

'Hey, she's much stronger than she looks. Remind me not to get in her bad books. She'll probably chase me down the drive with a frying pan in her hands.'

The girls giggled and ran off back to Kate's comfy bed and their tablets.

'Sorry, you don't have to help. Tell me if I'm being bossy, won't you?'

'I love it and you're not being bossy. It's nice to have someone telling me what to do again. I've missed it. I always did enjoy being henpecked.'

He winked at her and ran off towards the stairs. Kate took off after him, giggling like a teenager. This time as she reached the top of the stairs nothing happened and she breathed a sigh of relief. Within thirty minutes Ollie had put the lampshade up and assembled the lights, whilst Kate had taken the plastic off the mattresses and duvets and made the beds up.

It was a big room with its own bathroom. What she would have given for a room this size when she'd been growing up. Her parents had lived in a tiny two-up two-down, terraced house. Her bedroom hadn't even been big enough to hold a wardrobe, but she'd loved it there. It was small, but the house was always spotless and smelt of homemade baking or cooking. They may not have had much money, but her mum made sure they never went hungry. They always had cakes and biscuits she'd freshly bake twice a week; her friends had always loved playing at her house because there were always fairy cakes or shortbread biscuits for them to eat.

Kate missed her mum, who was now in a home because her Alzheimer's had got so bad that she was a danger to herself. She missed her dad too. He still lived in the house on his own – or so she'd thought until she'd gone around one day for a visit and found him snuggled up on the sofa with her mum's best friend Joan. Kate had left, mortified that her dad would do that to her mum. She hadn't spoken to him since. Not that she didn't want to – it was more the fact that her life had turned to shit and she was embarrassed to face him. She'd been so quick to judge him when really it had been none of her business. Why should he spend the rest of his life alone and mourning for the woman who didn't even remember his name?

Then Kate had got arrested for drunk driving and the shame had made her unable to face him. She'd taken the moral high ground with him for what? When she'd managed to lose everything in the space of a week. She made up her mind to go and visit both her mum and dad. She knew her mum wouldn't remember her, but she owed it to her. She also hoped her dad would forgive her for being such a selfish cow.

***

Ollie nudged her in the side. 'Hello, earth to planet Kate. Is anybody in there?'

She looked at him, blushing. 'Sorry, memories. It's funny how they come flooding back at the most random moments, when you're not expecting them.'

'I know how that feels – tell me about it. I'll be fixing a broken roof tile and remember snippets from the days before Ellen got so poorly. It's like watching someone else's life play out before my own eyes. Then I'll snap out of it feeling like my heart's been wrenched from my chest and cursing God for taking her away.'

He stopped talking, worrying he'd upset Kate, but she crossed the room towards him and hugged him. He hugged her back and heard Ellen's voice whisper in his ear: *She needs you, but you need her more.* Ollie turned, convinced his wife was standing right behind him. The empty space made his heart ache and he wondered for the hundredth time if he was doing the right thing. Was he getting too involved with Kate?

'Are you okay?'

He turned to face her. The concern etched across her face erased the doubts. He did need her; he didn't want to be lonely for the rest of his life.

'Yes, I'm fine. Sorry I thought I heard something. I guess I'm getting as jumpy as you are.'

He winked and he didn't miss the blush which crept up her neck.

'Should I go home tonight and let you and the girls have some time together? You have some catching up to do.'

Horror filled her eyes.

'I'd rather you didn't. I wouldn't be able to settle. Today's been amazing and both girls seem to have accepted you with no questions asked. I'd really like it if you stayed, but if you need a bit of space I also understand. It can be a bit overwhelming having to listen to three females chattering nonstop.' She lowered her voice. 'I can't stop thinking about that woman's head. It gives me the creeps – the thought of it being hidden away behind that panel since the 1930s. Do you think the girls will be safe up there on their own?'

Ollie knew what she meant. It had been in the back of his mind all day. Whenever there was a lull in the conversation he kept replaying the image of the withered, mummified head. He wanted to know what had happened to her and who had put it there. Tomorrow he would see if he could do some digging and get some answers, starting with the police. They said they thought they knew who she was. Or the priest Kate had mentioned might have some local knowledge or records.

'I can think of nothing more I'd like than to stay in this gorgeous house with three beautiful ladies. As long as you don't snore. You wore me out last night so I wouldn't have heard you if you had. And yes, I think they'll be safe. They're not too far away. We can leave the door open so we can hear them – and that is about the only room that hasn't been furnished with crosses.'

'I hope you're right. I'd never forgive myself if anything happened to scare the girls. Come on, you, our work is done here. Anyway, you could build the beds for me in the morning and then they're sorted out. I'd really appreciate it.'

He groaned, but smiled and led her by the hand towards the stairs. They went downstairs. Ollie headed into the kitchen to clear up the mess and wash up, whilst Kate went in to get her daughters.

'Right then, should we take your overnight bags upstairs and you can have a look at your room? See if it meets your approval. Ollie said he'll put the bed frames up tomorrow so you'll be more comfy.'

Summer and Autumn both climbed off the bed. Grabbing their cases, they followed Kate upstairs. Both of them shouted, 'Goodnight, Ollie!' in unison and he yelled back, 'Night!' He came to the kitchen door and smiled at Kate. Despite having Martin for a dad they were good kids.

***

Kate led them upstairs, her heart beating too fast. She was worried in case there were any more strange incidents, but they reached the girls' room without so much as a breeze passing by them. Both girls squealed at the sight of their makeshift beds, running and jumping on them.

'Thanks, Mum, it's great. I can't believe we have our own toilet as well.'

Autumn ran over and threw her arms around Kate's waist, squeezing tight. She ran back to her bed. Summer ran over and did exactly the same thing, hugging her mum tight, then jumped back onto her bed.

'I'll leave you to get undressed and clean your teeth. If you need anything shout. I think I'll hear you from here. Leave the lamp on if it's all a bit strange. Sometimes it feels weird sleeping in another house and room, but I'm not far away. I'll come and tuck you in soon.'

She left them with a huge smile on her face and for the second time that day blinked back tears. This time they were tears of joy.

She'd missed them so much it had been a physical pain inside her chest. She didn't know what she would do when Martin came to collect them. The house would feel so empty. At least she had Ollie now though to keep her company.

There was a dull ache in her arms, which was accompanied by a burning sensation. As soon as she got to the bottom of the stairs, she rolled a sleeve back to check they weren't bleeding again. The bandages were still white, thank God. She wanted them to start healing up. The kitchen was sparkling, all the pots were put away and the worktops were wiped clean.

'You are pretty perfect for a man. Do you have any faults?'

'Nope, it's true – I am indeed a perfect specimen of the male species. Well, if you discount the love of rugby, lager and James Bond films.'

'I like rugby and James Bond – not too keen on lager although a couple of days ago I would have drunk it if there was nothing else.'

'Ah sorry, Kate, I didn't think. How are you doing on that front?'

'I'm okay, I think. My hands are a bit shaky. I'm also scared I might be imagining things. Not to mention the thirst I have in the back of my throat that I don't think a cold glass of water could satisfy, but I'm managing, just. Thank you.'

'In that case you are a pretty amazing specimen of a woman as well. I'm very proud of you.'

She sat down. 'The girls love their room. I can't believe they're here, in this house, and to think that a couple of days ago I apparently wanted to end it all. Thank you for coming back to check on me. If it wasn't for you I could be lying in a mortuary fridge right now instead of being here. I can never repay you, Ollie.'

He crossed the room and bent down to kiss her. 'You don't need to repay me; I'm just glad that I did come back. I think that you and I make a pretty good team. Are you going to ring that detective tomorrow and see if they have any news for you? I can't stop thinking about that poor woman. It's barbaric to think someone could murder a nun and do that to her. It makes you wonder what happened, doesn't it?'

Kate shuddered. 'It makes my skin crawl thinking about it, but yes I will call.' A thought slammed into her mind. What if it was the nun who was walking around at night and putting the crosses back on the wall? That made perfect sense. Why was she obsessed with the crosses? Did she think her killer was still lurking around? If they hadn't stopped whoever it was the first time around, it didn't seem like there was much point in still putting them up. Or was she trying to protect Kate? She shivered as a cold chill ran down her spine. Trying to protect her from what?

Trust her to buy the house of her dreams along with its resident ghosts and murder victims. She wondered once more if her daughters would be safe upstairs alone. She couldn't really tell them she'd changed her mind and they had to sleep with her and Ollie. Surely they would be okay if the house was haunted by the nun, who could possibly be some relation to Kate. She had been a woman of God – a good person. She wouldn't want to harm anyone, especially children; she might have been wandering around up there looking for her head. Oh God! The thought of a headless nun wandering around her house freaked her out even more.

***

Ollie, who was busy making two mugs of coffee, turned around to pass her one and paused. She looked terrified.

'Kate, what's the matter? This is the third time today you've gone all quiet and the colour has drained from your face. Something's wrong. Is it me?'

She shook her head. 'No, don't be daft. I can't help thinking. Oh God, this is going to sound nuts, but I promise I'm not. I've been putting it down to not having any alcohol; it's not that though. Yes, I'm dying for a cold glass of wine, but having my family and you around is worth more than that.'

'What is it then?'

'Do you really believe in ghosts?'

It hadn't been what he'd expected her to say at all. He didn't know what to say. He'd like to say no and laugh it off. He thought back to last night and just before when he'd heard Ellen's voice whispering in his ear, as clear as if she'd been standing right next to him.

'I, erm, I don't know to be honest. It's not something I've ever considered before I met you and began working in this house. So much has happened that I find hard to brush off. Do you?'

'Yes, I believe I do. It's not something I've ever given much thought to either, if I'm honest. There's definitely something going on with this house though. Those footsteps I've heard when I've been on my own; they weren't heavy thudding steps. They were light as if it was a woman moving around up there. And what about the crosses? I can't count how many times I've taken them down or got Ethan to take them down yet they still keep appearing. Then there's the voices and strange smells, the scratching. What if the woman whose head they found yesterday is still here, looking for her head?'

Ollie felt every hair on the back of his neck stand on end. He didn't know what to say. He felt as if the atmosphere in the kitchen had changed. Kate turned around as if she was expecting to see one of the girls standing behind her. There was no one there. He looked down to see the skin on his arms had broken out in goose bumps. The air felt electric.

She turned back to him and whispered, 'Can you feel it? There's someone in here with us. I'm sure of it.'

A loud bang from upstairs startled them both and Kate took off running, closely followed by Ollie. They took the stairs two at a time and she threw the girls' bedroom door open. Both of them were lying on the mattresses they had pushed together, earphones in and watching a film on their tablets. Autumn looked up and smiled. Kate didn't want to scare her. Ollie went to check the en-suite then turned, sticking his thumb up at Kate.

'What's up, Mum?'

'Nothing. I heard a bang and thought one of you had fallen over. I was just checking you were both okay.'

'Well, it wasn't us and yes we're fine.'

'Good, that's good. Right then, I'll leave you to it.' She crossed the room, bending down and kissing them both on the forehead.

'Night. Don't forget: if you need me shout.'

Autumn already had her earphones back in. She looked at them both and stuck her thumb up. Ollie backed out of the room and Kate followed him.

***

'Where did that come from?' Kate asked.

'I don't know. I don't really want to go looking either. My heart's beating that bloody fast I think I'm having a cardiac arrest.'

Kate giggled. 'My hero, you're supposed to be the tough one and you're a quivering wreck.'

'Why don't we check the cameras?'

'I forgot all about those. Yes, that's a good idea – sort of. I'm not sure if I want to see what it was.'

'It could have been a draught. This house is still not fully airtight. Why don't we go downstairs and think about it? What I really want to do is get into your bed and hide under the duvet.'

Tears rolled down her face. As worried as she was about the banging and footsteps, she couldn't get the image of him hiding under the duvet out of her mind.

'Do you think the girls are really okay up here on their own? I don't want to leave them if something is wandering around up here.'

200

'They don't seem remotely bothered. You could leave your bedroom door open so we can hear them if they shout out for you in the night.'

She nodded. 'Come on, I think you're right. We're letting our imaginations run away with us. All this talk of spooky stuff is enough to make anyone jumpy.'

She went back downstairs with Ollie close behind her. They both went to check the front and back doors were locked. Satisfied, Kate led the way back into the kitchen.

'Now what? Do we watch the camera footage or just go to bed and watch a film on your iPad?'

There was no hesitation from Ollie. 'Go to bed and watch a film. We know the house is secure and if we watched the footage and saw a headless nun wandering around I think it might just kill me off.'

She agreed with him. Whatever it was she didn't think she wanted to find out. As long as it didn't scare her girls or her too much she could live and let live.

6 January 1933

Crosby and Father Patrick both arrived back at the convent within minutes of each other. The first thing they noticed was how black it was inside. There were no lights shining out into the darkness from the house. They looked at each other and said, 'Agnes.' Crosby felt his heart sink. He was never going to forgive himself if he went into that building and found her lifeless body. Shit on a stick, what had they been thinking? Leaving her all alone in there when there was a murderer picking off nuns and killing them in the most horrific ways known to man. Patrick looked uncomfortable.

Crosby nodded. 'Whatever has happened inside I need to use the telephone to call for more officers to come and assist me. Now it's up to you, Father, but I get the distinct impression something horrible may have happened to Sister Agnes in our absence. The question is: do we go inside to see if she needs our help or do we turn around and go back to the village to get some backup?'

Patrick shrugged. He knew the answer, but he just didn't want to speak the words out loud. Instead he whispered, 'What if she needs our help? We can't turn our backs on her now.'

Crosby nodded, cursing under his breath. He was glad the vicar had some backbone, but at the same time he had wanted him to insist on going back to the village to get some more officers. He looked at the vicar, who was clutching a bottle of holy water in one hand and a Bible in the other, then he walked up the steps to the house hoping that Patrick wasn't about to run out on him. He heard Patrick's footsteps behind him. He knew the front door would be open. Whoever or whatever it was wanted them to come into the house and find Agnes.

Pulling out his wooden truncheon because it gave him some measure of comfort, he pushed the heavy oak door with it. The creak it gave sounded ominous even to him who didn't believe in any of this hocus-pocus stuff. Well, he hadn't until today and now he wasn't so sure. The first thing he noticed when he stepped inside the darkened house was the smell. It was so strong it made him gag. It smelt like rotting meat tinged with the coppery smell of blood. His stomach lurched and he heard the vicar whisper, *'Dear God almighty, what is that stench? Oh Lord, protect us from whatever it is we are about to encounter.'* The fear made the vicar's voice tremble.

A voice inside Crosby's own head was telling him to turn around and leave right this minute. It was too late and there was nothing he could do. *'Save yourself,'* a woman's voice whispered in his ear, and he could have sworn it was Agnes. He turned to the right to see if she was standing there, but it was just him and Patrick – who had his Bible clenched to his chest, his lips moving in silent prayer. Crosby prayed that God was listening to him.

The house was so bloody big he didn't know where to start.

He stretched out his fingers, feeling along the wall for a light switch. They had no other means of seeing where they were going. He just hoped the lights were working. Finally, his fingers brushed the freezing metal switch and he flicked it down, bathing the hall in light. Everything looked the same as it had less than an hour ago. He nodded at the priest who gave him a half smile. His fingers gripping the wooden handle of his truncheon as tightly as they could he shouted, 'Agnes, are you okay? Where are you?'

Silence greeted him. There wasn't even a murmur. Up to now all the murders had occurred upstairs and this was where his feet were trying to lead his reluctant body. He let them lead the way. Patrick stuck close behind him, so close he could feel the heat from his body as they climbed the stairs, their hearts heavy. 'Agnes, where are you?' He didn't need to ask because he knew where she would be. Just like the others, she was in her bedroom. As they reached the top of the staircase the smell was that bad it made him retch. So did the priest. The air was so cold up here that he could see his laboured breath in front of his face. A hand grabbed his arm and he turned around to see Patrick stepping up then making his way past him.

'I fear this battle is bigger than you or I, but it's time for God to step in now and do his work. It's been nice knowing you, Crosby; you are a good man. I understand if you decide to leave and go and get help, but I can't. I have to stay and do this for the sake of Mary, Edith and Agnes. I never realised it before, but I no longer feel afraid. I feel ready to step up and do what must be done – something I should have done sooner.'

Crosby couldn't speak. The man who had been a trembling wreck looked as if he'd grown at least two foot taller, he was standing so straight. He opened the Bible and recited a passage as he led the way to Agnes's closed bedroom door. The man flicked holy water around the walls and floor, then he flicked it at the door and watched as the door sizzled. Patrick reached out to twist the doorknob. 'Agnes, I know you're in there and I'm coming. If you're still with us, hold on.'

The door didn't move. Crosby pushed Patrick to the side and gripped the knob with his hand, twisting it sharply. It moved this time, but it was locked. Patrick flicked more of his water on it and nodded at him to try again. This time it opened. The room was in darkness, but this was where the stench was emanating from. It assaulted their nostrils. As Crosby's eyes adjusted he saw Agnes's frail body. She was kneeling on the floor. He tilted his head to one side because there was something wrong with the picture in front of him.

Patrick flicked the light on and both men gasped at the same time, because Sister Agnes's body was headless. The bloodied stump of her neck contrasted starkly with the white collar of her nun's habit. Crosby couldn't understand why the woman was still upright. She was on her knees, her hands clasped together in prayer. It was a sight like he'd never seen before and one he hoped to God he wouldn't see again.

'Where's her head, Crosby? Where's her fucking head?'

Crosby had never heard a man of the cloth use such bad language and it snapped him out of the trance he was in. He looked around the room. There was no sign of it. Blood was splattered everywhere, mingling with the foul smell of rotting meat. He sidestepped around her body to see if her head had rolled to the other side of the bed, out of their view. It wasn't there. He stepped closer to the bed, lifting the white sheet up with the end of his truncheon in case it had rolled underneath. It wasn't there either. He turned and shrugged at Patrick, who was staring at the elderly nun's body.

'Father, I think that we should probably leave now. There is nothing we can do for her now and whoever did this may still be here.'

His voice fell on deaf ears. The priest was so horrified yet enthralled by the sight of the headless corpse in front of him.

Crosby, who had a very bad feeling that someone was coming for them, moved fast. Grabbing Patrick's cassock, he tugged him until he was looking at his face instead of Agnes's body.

'We need to leave now. Can you feel it? The air is getting thicker, heavier. Something is coming.'

He pulled Patrick's arm. As he left the bedroom the light in the hall exploded, making both men yell in fear and bathing them in complete darkness. The atmosphere was so fraught with tension it was uncomfortable. Crosby blinked his eyes, trying to get them to adjust to the darkness so he could get his bearings. Patrick had clutched hold of the man's jacket and wasn't letting go.

'What's happening? Shouldn't we get out of here?' Patrick whispered into Crosby's ear. He shook his head as the priest's cold breath tickled the tiny hairs inside of his ear.

'Do you remember what Agnes said? That woman thrives off your fear and somehow manages to turn into whatever it is you're scared of. What are you scared of, Father?'

'Nothing much. I suppose I've never liked the dark. I don't read any scary novels or watch scary films, if that's what you mean. How about you, Crosby? What are you scared of?'

Crosby felt stupid for what he was about to admit, but wasn't that part of a priest's job – listening to people confess their guilty sins?

'I watched a film last year at the picture house with Vera. We only went because she has a bit of a thing for that film star Guinn Williams and normally I don't mind, because he usually makes Westerns, but this one was different. It was one of them horror films called *The Phantom* about a killer who escaped death row to carry out his revenge on the man who sent him to prison. He stalks a group of people in a mansion wearing a mask. I suppose you could say that film scared me a lot. I kept thinking about how doing my job – you never know who you come into contact with and…'

A loud thud from the attic made both men jump. It was

followed by a heavy dragging noise and loud footsteps. Crosby's heart was racing so fast he thought it might just kill him. He should really be going up there to apprehend whoever it was for Agnes's murder, but the thought that it could be the masked crazy man from that film filled his entire being with fear.

Patrick tugged on Crosby's jacket. 'Come on, we can't do anything in the dark. We need to get out of here.' Crosby forced himself to turn towards the stairs. Patrick led the way this time, all the time praying under his breath for God to save them both. It was hard to see. The darkness in the house was so dense, unlike his own home when the lights went out and the fuse needed fixing. He knew every piece of furniture, nook and cranny back home so it never felt scary. This darkness was so all-consuming he couldn't even make out his own hand in front of his face.

This time it was Crosby who clutched onto the back of Patrick's robes, hoping the priest had better night vision than he did. They almost made it to the bottom of the stairs when a loud cackle filled the air. It sounded as if it was coming from downstairs and behind them all at the same time. Crosby felt the hairs on the back of his neck stand on end. He didn't want to die here, in this big house of death. Killed by a figment of his own bloody imagination. How did that work?

Patrick stumbled over something, falling forwards, and Crosby just managed to catch himself from landing on top of him and winding him. The air was filled with the smell of fear and he knew it was from him. *Stop it, man, you're sounding like one of the inmates from Hellshall. Monsters from your dreams don't come to life and kill you. Take control. Get yourself and the priest out of the house and it will all go away.* He recited the Lord's Prayer. Although he went to church every Sunday – his work permitting – he couldn't say that he was a religious man. It was something he did out of duty to his wife. He tried to block all thoughts of Vera from his mind. He loved her dearly and he didn't want whatever evil it was that was lurking in this house to know about her.

***

Patrick pulled himself onto his knees, fumbling in the dark for his Bible and bottle of holy water, which had flown from his hands when he'd fallen. Panic was beginning to fill his chest. He'd lost his security blanket. The water and Bible had been his tools against whatever evil force was at work here. He had no doubt that Agnes had been telling the truth. Evil had taken over this house of God and was threatening to take over him. He could feel its long tendrils of darkness reaching out and probing him. He had to believe that God would help them both. He didn't need the Bible or the water. What he needed was his faith in God and in the power of good over evil to overcome whatever demon it was that had decided to make the convent its home.

He stood up straight, knowing what he had to do. He had to pray for this house, for Mary, Edith, Agnes, Crosby and himself. If the thing showed itself he would be ready. He filled his mind with the warmth of God's love, wiping out all thoughts of darkness and fear.

***

Crosby felt a slight shift in the air around them. He realised that he could see the priest's black outline in front of him when moments ago it had been impossible.

'Show yourself, demon. I have no time for your tricks. I'm asking in the name of God that you come forth and show me who you really are. God commands you.'

Crosby thought that Patrick had lost his mind. He grabbed hold of him and tried to drag him towards the direction of the front door. Patrick pushed his hand away.

'We will not run; we will stand here, our faith in God and the light protecting us from your darkness. Now I command you to show yourself.'

Patrick's voice filled the entire hallway. It sounded as if it had been amplified, but at the same time it sounded stronger than any voice Crosby had ever heard. A white light filled the hallway, making it easier to see. Crosby wasn't sure if he wanted to see what was going on or not.

Patrick turned to him. 'You need to pray to God, harder than you've ever prayed in your life. Through his love and forgiveness, we can send this demon back to where it came from.'

Crosby began reciting the only prayer he knew from start to finish. 'Our Lord who art in heaven, give us this day our...'

A figure appeared in front of them. Crosby shut his eyes, afraid to look, but his survival instinct kicked in and he opened them again. He couldn't fight what he couldn't see. He was shocked to see the petite woman standing in front of them. She was beautiful, with long, silky, raven hair. Her face was so pale it looked white. She pouted her blood-red lips at them. She took a fighter's stance, crossing her arms, and he couldn't miss the long, red talons on the ends of her slender fingers. She looked like some Hollywood film star.

***

'What do you want, priest? I'm busy.'

'I want you to leave this house of God and go back to the hell that you came from.'

She laughed. 'Oh, you are a funny man, but I think you'll find this is no longer God's house. It's all mine.'

'This was built to be a house of God and will continue to be a house of God long after you've taken your filthy being out of it.'

'Then you're going to have to make me leave. How will you do that now you've lost your Bible and holy water?'

Patrick didn't answer her. It was taking all his strength to face her. He knew this was one of the demon's many faces, but he'd been surprised to find out that she was in fact a female. She'd reverted to her human form to throw them off guard and it had for a second.

***

Crosby looked past her to see the huge dark shadow forming on the wall behind her. It was growing by the second and he didn't want to hang around to see what it turned into. He whispered in Patrick's ear, 'Why don't we just leave? There's nothing we can do, is there?'

The woman tilted her head, trying to listen to what he was whispering. Patrick shook his head in defiance at Crosby's suggestion.

'Tell me your name, demon.'

'You know my name, priessst.'

'By the power invested in me by God, tell me your name.'

'Are you sure you want to know my name? What good will it do you?'

'Your name now, your God demands it.'

'He's not my God, neither are you my priest.'

Patrick began walking towards her, lifting the heavy silver cross from around his neck. He held it out towards her and Crosby watched as the woman stepped back from him.

'Your name, demon.'

A loud growl filled the air around them, but it didn't seem as if it had come from the woman standing in front of them.

'Lilith Ardat.'

'Your real name or I swear to God I'll push this cross down your throat and make you choke on it.'

Patrick was standing directly in front of the woman who Crosby thought looked as if she had shrunk since she'd first appeared.

'I told you, priest, my name is Lilith. I am the princess of hell.' She laughed, a cold, high-pitched sound that hurt both men's ears.

'I have no idea why you killed these women of God, but God now commands you to leave this house for good – and don't come back. You are banished back to where you came from. Now get out.'

He shouted the last words, which were lost in the howling wind that was filling the hall. Crosby reached out and grabbed hold of the banister to keep himself upright. Patrick stood with his arms outstretched, praying, only Crosby couldn't hear a word of it for the howling wind. The woman stumbled backwards towards the shadow on the wall and he watched in horror as it seemed to swallow her up. Then the shadow folded in on itself until it disappeared. The wind dropped as fast as it had appeared, returning the house to normal. Crosby looked at Patrick, who had fallen to his knees and was praying his thanks to God. He clasped his hands together.

'Dear God, I have no idea what just happened, but thank you for helping the priest to get rid of that bitch. Amen to that.'

Patrick turned around and for the first time in hours he laughed. It was such a loud, happy sound Crosby couldn't help but join in. The pair of them were laughing as if it was the funniest thing ever. Eventually Patrick pulled himself up. He stopped laughing.

'I don't know if you want to put any of what just happened down in your police report – or is this just between the pair of us?'

Crosby wiped his eyes. 'If it's okay with you we'll keep this between ourselves. If I write any of this on a report they'll have me taken away to Hellshall and locked up. To be honest, I'm not quite sure what just happened, but can I just say that you were amazing? Has she gone for good?'

'I agree with you about the report, but I can't answer that

question. I feel as if the house is different now. The atmosphere doesn't feel as heavy as before. I hope that it's gone back to wherever it came from.'

'I don't understand though. How did it get in and why did it kill the good sisters?'

'I think that it was looking for somewhere to reside and the sisters invited it into this house, with the best intentions of course. They had no idea that it was a demon in disguise, but they paid the price with their lives. What are you going to tell your inspector?'

'I'm going to tell him that we gave chase to someone who managed to get away from us and that they won't be coming back, but we'll keep them on high alert as our most wanted. Of course, he will never believe that the beautiful Lilith Ardat had anything to do with these deaths.'

'This house needs to be closed up for the foreseeable future. We can't let anybody move in until we know that it's safe. Once you've removed Agnes's body, I'll speak to the bishop and arrange for it to be boarded up.'

'Can you stay here with us until we've finished?'

As if on cue there was a knock on the front door and the sound of multiple voices carried through to them. Crosby opened the door to his inspector and a couple of constables. He told them about Agnes's body and then gave them directions to search every inch of the house from top to bottom to see if they could find Agnes's head. After an hour every room, closet, drawer and inch of space had been searched, but to no avail. There was no sign of it and the sky was getting darker by the minute. The grounds would have to be searched tomorrow.

An ambulance arrived to take Agnes's body to the hospital mortuary. As she was carried out of the house on a stretcher, her headless corpse covered with a blanket, all the men bowed their heads in respect. As the ambulance drove away, Crosby gave the order for everyone to leave the house. He asked the two constables to wait on Bill Mosson – the local builder and handyman – to come and board the windows and doors up. The younger of them had looked at Crosby in wonder.

'What… You want us to wait up here in the cold? For Bill to come and board this huge place up? Can't it wait until tomorrow and we'll just lock the doors for now?'

'No, it can't wait until tomorrow. Three women have been murdered in this house in cold blood. I don't want anyone else going inside. We've searched the place from top to bottom. If we leave it unsecure now the killer could come back and hide in there. I want it boarding up tonight and if it's too cold for you to wait around, tough. You can cry to your mammy when you go home.'

'Yes, Crosby.'

***

Patrick nodded his agreement with what Crosby had just said. Although he believed that Lilith Ardat had gone for now, he couldn't be sure it had been a permanent banishment. He'd done his best, but he wasn't a trained exorcist. Once the house was boarded up, he would come back with the archbishop and bless every entrance to the building, sealing it up for good. Crosby got into the car, motioning for Patrick to get in.

'Come on, Father, I'll drop you off before I go to the hospital. I think it would be fitting under these circumstances to have a wee nip of whisky and drink to our winning the battle.'

'I think you're right; however, I can't shake the feeling that it was too easy to get rid of her. I thought she would have put up a much bigger fight than she did. I think I'm going to spend the rest of my life looking over my shoulder, waiting for her to come back.'

'Maybe you should have some faith in yourself, Father, and not just in God. You did it. You stood up to whatever she was and sent her back. For that I'm truly grateful. I'm just sorry we couldn't have done it before poor Agnes was killed. Where do you think her head is? We can't bury her without it.'

'I don't know. I expected it to be in the house somewhere. Maybe it's in the grounds. I hope that when you search them tomorrow you find it.'

'So do I, Father, so do I.'

Chapter 12

The cool air blowing on Autumn's face woke her from her sleep. She opened one eye, wondering where she was, and remembered she was at her mum's big old house. Summer was curled up next to her, her duvet tucked around her so she looked like a sausage roll. There was a faint glow from the night light that her mum had insisted they buy because the house was new to them and she didn't want them waking up wondering where they were. Which was exactly what had just happened to her – yay for her mum being a mind reader.

Where was that draught coming from? She sat up, rubbing her eyes, and pulling the earphones from her ears. She heard fast, scurrying footsteps as someone passed by their bedroom door, which was ajar. It must be her mum going to the bathroom. It sounded like her. She was sure Ollie would make far more noise. She whispered, 'Mum,' and was greeted by silence. This time she said it louder, but not loud enough to disturb her sister who could sleep through a hurricane. 'Mum.' Still no reply.

The footsteps, which seemed to be going from room to room, stopped and Autumn felt the hairs on the back of her neck stand on end. Her mum would have answered her. Who was scurrying around the landing? Part of her wanted to get up, turn the light on and see what was happening. The other part of her wanted to scream for her mum and hide under the duvet.

A picture of the clown from that awful film her dad had been watching with Tamara one night when she'd gone to bed and woken up for a drink flashed in front of her mind. It had been a horrible stuffed toy, really tall and freaky with a white painted face, huge red eyes and lips. Her dad had shouted at her for creeping around. She knew he was mad because she'd made them both jump, scaring them so much Tamara had screamed and thrown the bowl of popcorn she'd been nursing all over the carpet. It had made Autumn giggle until she'd gone back to bed and had to turn the light off; then she couldn't get the picture of the horrible toy clown out of her head.

What if it was the clown from that film? She told herself she was being stupid. Her mum didn't have a clown in the house. At least she didn't think she did, but could she be sure? She hadn't been into the attic because it was too dark up there. What if there had been an old rocking chair up there with a clown doll sitting on it, rocking back and forth? Then what?

Her stomach churned as her arms broke out in goose bumps. Making herself lie back down, she pulled her duvet up around her, tucking it under herself like her sister. If she put her earphones back in she wouldn't hear any stupid noises out on the landing. She was being silly. She lay down facing the back of her sister's head, not wanting to turn and face the window. In her mind she started to sing her favourite Pink song, anything to stop the scary thoughts about killer clowns.

Her eyes beginning to grow heavy, she felt herself drifting off to sleep and was almost there when she heard the scurrying, shuffling sound, which was now much louder, coming towards their open bedroom door. Her eyes opened wide as terror filled her entire body. She opened her mouth to shout to her mum, but no noise came out. Shaking her sister, she swore under her breath when she didn't move. This time she shook her as hard as she could. Summer turned around. 'What's wrong with you? It's the middle of the night.'

'There's someone shuffling around on the landing. I'm scared.'

Summer, who was a year older than her, rolled her eyes. 'It's probably Mum or Ollie.'

'I shouted for mum, it's not her. What if it's a...' She didn't know what to say. Her sister would tease her for the rest of her life if she said she thought there was a killer clown shuffling around on the landing. 'A burglar.'

'Then they'd have to be pretty stupid. This house is empty. There's nothing in it to steal and I'm sure Ollie would chase them off. Go to sleep, Autumn.'

Summer flopped back down, closing her eyes. There was no mistaking the shuffling, scurrying sound on the landing outside. She sat up and stared at her sister. Autumn was hugging her knees and feeling terrified.

'Who's out there? Mum, Ollie?'

There was no reply. Autumn felt the tears build up in the backs of her eyes and she needed to wee. She'd never been so scared. Summer stood up. She lifted her finger to her lips to shush Autumn before she spoke. She crossed the room to where the light switch was and flicked it, looking relieved when the room was bathed in bright, white light. Autumn stood up. She was terrified, but she wouldn't not stand by her sister. If someone was out there, they would have to fight the both of them.

The light from their room flooded through the crack in the door, filtering some of the light out onto the landing, enough so that Summer could reach out and switch on the landing light. She flicked that switch down as well then threw the bedroom door open so hard it thumped against the wall with a loud thud. The landing was empty. A small childlike giggle echoed around the stairs, making Autumn scream.

***

216

Autumn's scream was so loud that Kate's eyes flew open and she jumped from her bed, running for the stairs to see what was wrong. She was shocked to see both girls standing there, holding hands and shivering.

'What's the matter? Are you all right?'

Ollie was close behind her. He bounded up the stairs. 'What's wrong?'

'Autumn heard someone walking around, then we both heard a child giggling.'

Autumn shook her head. 'They weren't walking, they were shuffling, well, actually more like scurrying around from room to room. I thought it was you, but I called out and there was no answer.'

Kate looked at Ollie and he couldn't miss the horror in her eyes.

Kate pulled both girls close, wrapping her arms around them. She was torn. She didn't want him to check the bedrooms on his own, but she couldn't leave her daughters standing there shivering. He made his way along the landing, opening each bedroom door and reaching inside for the lights, looking relieved when he found that every room was empty. The attic was bolted shut from this side so even if somebody had been up there they wouldn't have been able to get through the door.

'It's clear up here. Should we all go down?'

Kate nodded. Ollie led the way downstairs and they followed. She glanced at the clock in the hall and noticed it was twenty past three. Didn't they say that 3 a.m. was the haunting hour? She shuddered, leading the girls into the kitchen.

'Who wants a hot chocolate? And then we can all go and snuggle up in my bed. Ollie will sleep on the sofa, won't you?'

He nodded emphatically even though his eyes betrayed what he really felt. He no more wanted to sleep alone on the sofa than she did. He left them to go and check the rest of the house. The cellar door was bolted shut from this side so again if someone had gone down there they wouldn't have been able to lock themselves in. Kate didn't expect him to down there in the dark on his own to check.

Kate busied herself pouring milk into mugs and microwaving each one. She spooned the chocolate powder into each one and stirred it, turning and passing one to each of them.

'I wasn't making it up, Mum. I swear I heard someone moving around and we both heard that laugh.'

'Of course you weren't. I know you wouldn't do that. I don't know what to say, sweetie. I believe you, but I don't have any answers for you. I don't know what it could be.'

She couldn't tell them that she'd heard the footsteps herself or that they'd found the shrivelled up, long-dead head of a woman behind a panel in the hall. God, they'd have nightmares for the rest of their lives and never want to come here ever again. Ollie took his hot chocolate from her and patted her hand.

'This is a big, old, empty house. I'm not saying that you didn't hear those noises because there's no doubt in my mind that you did. However, sometimes when you're in a strange place the wind and the noises the house makes can sound very scary. I kept thinking I could hear footsteps the other day and it drove me mad. I finally realised that the wind blowing through one of the bedroom windows and the cold air was making the wooden floorboards where there was no carpets contract, and they kept creaking. Not to mention the doors that wobble in the wind.'

Both girls were staring at him with eyes wide. Their heads were nodding in unison and Kate hoped that their tired minds were accepting Ollie's explanation.

'Your mum has been living here for ages on her own and isn't scared. Isn't that right, Kate?'

Kate nodded. That wasn't technically true, but if it made her daughters feel better she'd agree to being the Queen of England. Both girls began to sip their hot drinks. They looked tired and Summer's eyelids were getting too heavy for her to keep open.

'Come on, why don't I tuck you into my bed? I'll just go and make a bed for Ollie and I'll be straight in.'

The girls stood up, following their mum to her room. Kate tucked them in once more. She would sleep on the chair if it meant they felt safe. 'I won't be long.' Summer's head hit the pillow and her eyes closed.

Autumn smiled. 'Sorry, Mum, for being a nuisance.'

Kate bent down and kissed her forehead. 'Don't be silly, you're not a nuisance. You have no idea how much I've missed you both.'

'Dad said you were a drunk living on Benefit Street and you couldn't look after us.'

Kate flinched. She'd been expecting this, but hadn't expected it to hurt quite so much. Martin was such an idiot. What else had he been telling their children?

'Your dad and me, well, we don't really get on anymore. I was drinking a lot, but I was never a drunk – not the sort that he meant. When Amy died it broke my heart. She was my best friend and I got poorly. I'm much better now and I don't live on Benefit Street. I live in this beautiful old house, which one day will be a bed and breakfast with paying guests.'

'I know, Mum. He can be mean sometimes. He wouldn't let us come and see you even when we begged and cried. I don't think I'll ever forgive him for that.'

Kate felt another strip being torn from her heart as she blinked back the tears once more. She was turning into an emotional wreck. She looked down at Autumn, who was drifting off to sleep, and she wished she could turn back the clock and put things right. How had her daughter got so wise? She turned around to see Ollie standing outside the bedroom door with his arms wide open. She fell into them and began to cry. He pulled her close and let her cry, rubbing her back.

'I've never wanted to hit another man as much as I've wanted to hit Martin these last few days. The more I hear about him the worse the anger inside me gets. Has he no shred of decency inside him?'

She shook her head as he continued. 'Well, wait until I get him on my own. I'll be telling him a few home truths and if he doesn't listen I'll be using my fist to drive them home.'

'He's really not worth it. I'm just glad the girls know he was being unreasonable and a fucking bastard.'

Hearing Kate swear made Ollie laugh. She pulled away from him then started laughing herself. 'Sorry, but he really is.'

'Yes, he is. So what should we do? Stay up or curl up on the sofa together? I'm going to be man enough to tell you that I'm feeling pretty freaked out by all this. I have no idea how you've managed to live here on your own for so long.'

'I can tell you why, because the last two days I've been stone cold sober. Before then when you and the lads left I'd hit the bottle and be comatose by ten. I need to get hold of the priest and see if he managed to find anything out. Do you think I should ask him to bless the house for me?'

'I can't see that it would hurt. Anything has to be better than living in fear of ghostly footsteps.'

She looked at his face to see if he was being sarcastic. He wasn't and that made her fall in love with him even more.

'I'm tired, but I don't want to leave them alone again until we find out what's going on.'

'Why don't we bring the sofa in here? It's not that big and then if we fall asleep at least we're nearby.'

She nodded. 'You're full of good ideas.'

Between them they managed to carry it through without making too much noise. Neither girl stirred – they were in such a deep sleep.

'Who's going upstairs for the spare duvets?' Ollie winked as he said it, but he meant it.

'I think we should both go. I'll run in and get them and you wait at the top of the stairs for me. That way you can hear the girls if they start to scream – and me too.' said Kate.

His face turned an even whiter shade than it already was. She hadn't realised how scared he was. She was scared, but she didn't want to show her fear because this was her house and she wasn't going to be run out of it by some mischievous ghost or whatever it was that was residing in here. If she'd known then exactly what it was she might have changed her mind and gone straight to Ollie's house until the priest had come to do a blessing, but she didn't know or have any concept of how bad things were about to become.

9 June 1940
Crosby was writing up his last report of the day before going home when his office door burst open.

'Have you heard what they're doing? It's madness, I've told them so, but they told me that it had already been decided and I was to shut up and help out as much as I could. I can't. I don't want anything to do with it. It will bring nothing but trouble, mark my words.'

'Good afternoon, Father. Now seeing as how I have no idea what you're talking about, would you be so kind as to start from the beginning so I might be able to understand?'

'That God-forsaken convent – that's what I'm talking about. The government or those do-gooders who have nothing better to do with their time have suggested that with all the evacuations due to take place from the cities, it was a sin to leave a huge, empty house unattended when it could be opened up to rehouse so many of the children who are to be evacuated.'

Crosby felt a ball of lead form in the pit of his stomach. Why would anyone want to put children into that house of death? Surely not. 'Is this a rumour or is it official?'

'It's official. What are we going to do?' Patrick pulled a

crumpled letter from his pocket, throwing it in the direction of Crosby's desk.

Crosby picked it up and read, the colour draining from his already pale face. 'It's been empty since that night. It can't be habitable. Surely it will be cold and damp?'

'Unbeknown to me they've already opened it up and had builders in the last two days, sweeping the chimneys and fixing any problems. The women's union are going in tomorrow to clean the place from top to bottom. The children are due to arrive on the eighteenth.'

Crosby shook his head. 'Who gave this the go-ahead without speaking to you or me beforehand? We need to go up there now and see who's in charge.'

'I'm sorry, Crosby, but there's nothing we can do.'

'There must be. We can't let children go into that house. Who is going to be looking after them?'

'Some nuns from Windermere are coming through to run it. They're arriving on the fifteenth to make sure everything is ready.' He flopped down into the chair opposite Crosby, running a hand through his mane of now silver hair. 'I don't know what we can do. It seems that the archbishop has already given consent.'

'He must know the history of the house – what happened there. Surely it's a topic they haven't brushed under the rug and forgotten all about.'

'He's new, only been in post six months and very young. If you ask me, he's far too young. He will have been told about what happened, but do you think he'll believe it? If I hadn't been a part of it myself I would probably think it was an old wives' tale to scare anyone away. He will only be thinking of the good the church is doing for those poor children. He won't even have any idea that the church is more than likely sending them to a far worse fate than Hitler's bombs.'

Crosby stood up. 'We need to go up there now even if it's only to warn the builders or whoever is working on the house. The last thing I want is for bodies to start stacking up again with cause of death "unexplained". Maybe we can speak to whoever is in charge and tell them what happened seven years ago.'

'I can't. I've been forbidden by the church to talk about it to anyone.'

'What, are they mad?'

'I'm afraid the answer to your question is quite possibly yes.'

'Well, you can keep quiet then. I'll do all the talking. Patrick, we can't let innocent people back into that house. Did you ever go back and finish?'

He realised why the good Father was in such a flap – of course he hadn't. The convent had been boarded up and left to rot. As far as they were concerned no one was going to use it ever again and judging by the look on Patrick's face he wasn't convinced that the house was safe enough to be lived in.

Patrick lifted his head and stared Crosby in the eyes. 'You know the answer to that without me telling you. I was too afraid; the church didn't want any bad publicity or to lose any more of the congregation. I'm so ashamed of my cowardliness. If I was half the priest I should be, I would have gone back in there and if needed into battle with no concern for my own safety, but I didn't. I hoped that it would get bored of waiting around in that empty, dark, desolate house and move on of its own accord.'

'Wouldn't that empty, dark house be the perfect place for a demon to hide?'

Patrick nodded.

'Then what do you suggest we do, Father? I thought that you'd sent it back to hell that night?'

'So did I, but you have no idea how powerful these things are. I have such terrible dreams about that house and I'm afraid it's still there, lurking and waiting for the perfect opportunity. Do you think that because they are innocent children and there will be a lot of them that it won't be interested? After all, there was only Agnes, Mary and Edith living there when it happened. Maybe

223

the fact that there's too much going on will deter it from rearing its head.'

'I think that could be wishful thinking. Wouldn't a house full of innocent children be like a dream come true for a monster?'

Patrick's whole body seemed to crumple in front of Crosby's eyes. It literally looked as if the weight of the whole world was balanced on his shoulders, and his skin had now turned a grey colour.

'Let's go and visit the builders, Father. You can wait in the car and I'll go and speak to them – try and find out if anything has happened whilst they've been inside. Then we'll decide what to do.'

Crosby watched as the priest had to force himself up off the chair. All the fight and anger from when he'd burst into his office had dissipated, leaving him looking much older than he was. He felt the same, as if he'd aged another ten years in ten minutes. His entire body felt sluggish. Crosby had never been a coward. He didn't mind brawling with the best of them, but the thought of that woman who had turned into the scariest thing he'd ever seen in his entire life terrified him.

Patrick followed Crosby through into the main office of the police station where two of his constables were sitting pretending to be busy. He thought about making them come with him, but then he'd have to explain to them what was happening and he didn't want to be a laughing stock. No one was going to believe him. It sounded like one of those stupid horror films they showed down at the picture house once a month – not a real-life situation.

'You two listen out for me. If I shout for help you make sure you get off your lazy backsides and hotfoot it up to the old convent. Do you understand?'

'Yes, Sarge.' Both of them nodded.

'Good, because if I have to wait ages for you to come because you are sitting here talking about what you're eating for your tea or picking your noses, I'll make sure you work the back shift for the next six months.'

The blue sky, which hadn't had a cloud in sight all day, grew increasingly dark as huge thunderclouds filled it. A low rumble made Crosby and Patrick look up at the same time. The air was heavy with ozone and fear, which was emanating from both men. Neither of them spoke. They didn't have to because it was as if both their minds were in tune with each other. They knew this oppressive atmosphere had something to do with the pair of them returning to the convent.

A loud crack made them both jump and run for the cover of the one police car that belonged to the station. If he needed help, they would have to use the pedal cycles to come and save his backside. It was just as well it was the two youngest recruits, who were a lot fitter than Malcolm and Peter who had gone home an hour ago. They made it into the safety of the car before the first huge drops of rain began to fall, splattering the windscreen. As he turned the engine a flash of lightning illuminated the now black sky. Patrick looked at him, his eyes wide with fear.

'Is this a sign from God, Father, or is it the devil at work? I'm really hoping for the first because I'm not afraid to tell you I'm terrified.'

Crosby drove towards the road, which would lead them to the convent. As he squinted through the windscreen – because the wipers didn't move fast enough to clear the rain – he stole a glance at the priest who was sitting next to him trembling, his hands clasped together in prayer and his eyes shut. The heavy feeling in the pit of Crosby's stomach had now moved up to his chest and he wondered if the shock of this was going to be the end of him.

Another loud crack of thunder made the pair of them jump. The storm was going to be bad. There were already rivers of water streaming along the narrow, bumpy roads, making him drive slower than he normally would. He had the car's headlights on, but it was still dark. He hoped he wouldn't meet any other road users because it was so bad they probably wouldn't see each other until they'd met each other head to head.

It took for ever to reach the entrance gates to the convent, but he finally saw them and turned into it. The sickness that filled his insides was so strong he wanted to pull over and vomit. He had to start taking deep breaths in through his nose to try and force down the hot liquid that was threatening to spew from his mouth all over his shiny, new police car. The rain was bouncing off the car now and the sky was so dark that if anyone had taken a guess, they would have said it was after midnight, not a quarter to six.

As the outline of the convent came into view, Patrick let out a loud gasp. They couldn't see it properly because of the rain; however, they could feel it. They didn't have to say anything to know that it was as if the house was alive – a living, breathing entity in its own right. Crosby drove as close to the front steps as possible and turned the engine off.

'Father, you stay here and pray for us both because I can feel it. Can you?'

Patrick looked as if he was about to cry. 'I can't for the love of God leave you to go in there on your own. Let's do this before we change our minds.'

Patrick threw his door open, got out of the car and ran towards the front steps before Crosby had even opened his door. Crosby followed suit. He had to give it to the man, he'd have bet a week's wages that he wouldn't have got out of the car. He was wrong and he would be the first to admit it if asked by anyone. He got out of the car, bracing himself against the torrential rain. As he reached the front door he could see it was open and a light was burning inside. Before he could say anything to Patrick, the priest had stepped inside. He followed suit again. The house looked exactly as it had that fateful night seven years ago. It smelt damp and musty, but it was dry inside. It didn't look as if it was in such a bad state.

'Hello, is anyone here? It's the police.'

Crosby's voice echoed around the empty hallway. He waited to see if anyone answered. The house didn't feel as bad as he'd expected; maybe their fear of the place had worsened because of the refusal by both men to go back and face it all this time. Feeling braver, Crosby walked further inside, leaving the priest hovering by the front door.

'Hello, it's the police.'

A loud bang from somewhere upstairs made them both jump. Crosby turned to look at Patrick, who didn't look at all well.

'I think I'll go upstairs and see if there's anyone up there. Someone must be here because they wouldn't leave the lights on and the front door open if they'd gone home.'

Patrick nodded. He couldn't look Crosby in the eye and he wondered if the priest was too scared of what he might see reflected in the black of his pupils. Forcing his feet to move, he climbed the stairs with a heavy heart. They'd never found Sister Agnes's head, much to his distress. The grounds had been searched twice over, inch by inch, by a search team of constables and some volunteers from the village. He'd watched Agnes's coffin lowered into the ground and sworn to her he would find her head, but he hadn't.

Once the second search of the gardens had been conducted, he'd given strict orders for the house to be completely sealed up once more and under no circumstances to be opened back up. What if one of the young kids sent here found her skull somewhere? The poor kid would have nightmares for the rest of their life and he'd never forgive himself, although if he was honest, he didn't know what he could do about it apart from try and scare the builders off – maybe get them to say the house was unsafe to live in. He reached the top landing and paused for a minute. The bloodied images of Edith, Mary and Agnes filled his mind and he couldn't see anything but the crime scenes he'd been the first to encounter behind their bedroom doors.

'Can I help you, officer?' a voice shouted from the far end of the landing and the attic stairs. Crosby nearly fell backwards down the stairs and had to grab hold of the banister to stop himself.

'Jesus Christ, I've been shouting. Did you not hear me?'

'I did, but I was on a ladder trying to stop the water pouring through the hole in the roof before it soaked the entire attic.'

'Ah, yes sorry. That is some storm. Haven't seen rain like that for a long time.'

As if to prove how bad the storm was a huge crack of thunder rumbled around the house.

'Me either, but I'm sure you didn't come to discuss the weather. How can I help you?'

'Is there just you here?'

'At the moment – I sent my lads to go and get some stuff to fix the leak.'

'Have you had any problems whilst you've been working in here at all?'

'None whatsoever – well, apart from the leaking roof. Why do you ask?'

Crosby didn't know what to say. He didn't want to sound as if he'd escaped from the mental asylum and no matter how he said it he would. 'I just wondered. There were some very sad, sudden deaths here a few years ago and the house has been empty ever since. I, erm, didn't know if you were aware of the house's history.'

'Aye, terrible they were, by all accounts. I'm not local, but I've heard all about it. Have you come to ask me if I've seen any ghosts?'

The man who had stepped out of the attic laughed at his own joke and Crosby didn't know whether he wanted the ground to open up and swallow him or whether he wanted to strangle the man in front of him.

'No, not at all. I was just wondering how you were getting on and if there were any reasons the house wouldn't be suitable for those evacuees.'

'If we fix the leak and get the place warmed through to air it out, then there's no reason it can't be used. It's one hell of a fine house – such a shame it's been left empty all this time, but at least it's going to be put to good use. Hitler wouldn't be able to find this place to drop any bombs, I'm sure of it. I couldn't bloody find it with a map and I'm very good at map reading.'

'It's true; it is off the beaten track. Oh well, I'd better let you get on with it. I don't want to hold you up. If you have any problems then don't hesitate to call the station or get one of your lads to come down. There's always someone around.'

With that he turned and walked away, his cheeks redder than the hall carpet. This place was fine. Being empty all these years must have got rid of whatever evil it was that had decided to make its home here. The man shouted after him, 'Thank you, officer; don't worry, I will.' If Crosby had turned around one last time he would have caught the red glow in the man's eyes and the grin that had spread across his face, but he didn't.

He was glad to be leaving and hopefully never coming back. He almost ran down the stairs and out of the front door back to the safety of the brand new black shiny Wolseley motor car that was his pride and joy even though technically it wasn't his. Father Patrick followed him out and once they were both inside the car Crosby looked at him. 'It seems fine. The house smelt cold, but it didn't feel anything other than desolate and damp. What did you think?'

'No sign of…?'

'Nothing. I think that everything is going to be all right. It's been a long time, Patrick; maybe we've been living this nightmare for more years than we should have. It's time to put it behind us and move on with our lives.'

Patrick reached out and grabbed his arm. 'You're sure about that?'

'As sure as I can be. I've told him to report anything unusual – other than that there's little I can do. He knows the background of the place and didn't seem bothered, so I suggest we let them get on with it and hope for the best.'

'I hope you're right, Sergeant Crosby. I really do.'

Chapter 13

Joe woke up, relieved to see daylight streaming through the blinds he'd forgotten to close last night. His neck was stiff because he must have dozed off whilst sitting up playing his game. His head felt heavy and he looked across at the bedside table to see how many bottles of lager he'd drunk. There were four empties. Normally he'd only have one or two. This was going to be a long day with a banging head and stiff neck.

The front door slammed and he flinched. 'Morning, Father, sorry I'm late.' Mrs Walker then proceeded to bang around as loudly as she could downstairs. He smiled to himself. At least she was human and he wasn't going to be on his own for a couple of hours. He swung his legs out of bed and stood up, his head thudding even louder as the blood rushed to it. He didn't think about not being dressed as he made his way to the bathroom and walked straight into Mrs Walker, who let out a screech and covered her eyes. He looked down and realised that she'd probably never seen a priest in his boxer shorts before and blushed.

'Sorry, I forgot I wasn't dressed.' His cheeks burning, he rushed into the bathroom and slammed the door shut. He couldn't help smiling.

'I'm sorry, Father, I'll make myself busy downstairs until you're more decent.'

He heard her footsteps as she hurried down the stairs and he burst out laughing. When he looked into the mirror above the sink to see what the damage was he almost let out a screech himself. He looked as if he was in his forties not early thirties. He stepped closer. Surely not. He'd only drunk four bottles of lager. Why on earth was he looking so rough? There were small lines around his eyes and a couple of deep furrows on his forehead that he'd never noticed before. Turning his head to one side the light caught the wisps of grey hair on his temples that yesterday had been dark brown. He checked the other side and it was the same. Was that possible? Could you age overnight?

Splashing cold water all over his face, he patted it dry with a towel, wondering what was happening to him. He took the bath sheet off the towel rail and wrapped it around his waist so as not to upset Mrs Walker. He needn't have worried. When he opened the door he heard the hoover being turned on downstairs as she began her twice-weekly cleaning spree. He went into his bedroom and dressed a bit more casually than he had yesterday – although if he was to pluck up the courage to go and visit Kate he would need to put on his dog collar and crucifix. But first, he needed breakfast and some paracetamol.

He made both himself and Mrs Walker a mug of tea and a huge plate of doorstep slices of toast. He was starving. He hadn't eaten much yesterday; maybe that was why he was feeling so crap today. As the elderly woman, who walked with more spring in her step than he ever would, entered the kitchen to get her tea and toast she smiled.

'Glad to see you're wearing some clothes now. It's been a few years since I've seen an almost naked man.'

'Sorry about that, I forgot. Can I ask you something, Mrs Walker?'

'Dorothy. I wish you'd call me that, or Dottie. You make me feel ancient calling me Mrs all the time.'

'Really, I had no idea. Sorry, Dorothy. How long have you been the housekeeper for the vicarage?'

'Ooh let me see, I started when I was eighteen in 1950. Before that it was my mum who was the housekeeper. She got crippled with arthritis, though, and I used to come and help her out. Until she couldn't do it anymore and then I took over. The pay wasn't bad either for the time. Why do you want to know?'

'I just wondered if you knew about the history of the place. Have you ever been to the big old house through the woods? It used to be a convent until they shut it down.'

She shuddered. 'That place gives me the creeps. It's a proper scary house. I've heard all sorts of tales about that building and the goings-on up there. If I was you I'd stay well clear. It's a bad place.'

'How can a house be bad? I don't understand it.'

'It happens. Look at that film they made back in the Seventies about that house in America. I can't remember the name now, but one of the kids killed an entire family and they were okay until they moved into that house.'

'This house was a convent though; nuns lived there.'

'Yes they did, and died there in horrific circumstances. *Amityville* – that was the film. Apparently one of them nuns was found without her head – cut clean off it was, and they never found the head. Poor woman had to be buried without it. What sort of person could do that to a woman who was nothing but pure of soul?'

'What happened after that?'

'They shut it down, boarded it up and didn't let anyone go in it for years. Until the war started and they had to evacuate all the kids from the cities out to the country. Someone – I don't know who – decided that the convent was a perfect place to rehome a trainload of young kids with nuns and volunteers to help run the place.'

233

Joe felt his blood run cold. The thought of children who had to leave their families being housed there was too horrifying to contemplate. His stomach churned and he wasn't sure he wanted to know what happened.

'Well, it would have been a fabulous house and perfect too, out in the sticks away from the cities and that bastard Hitler. The nuns weren't local and I don't think they'd been told about what happened to the last lot of nuns that had lived there either, because if they had they wouldn't have wanted to live there.'

'Did anyone die?' Joe said this with a heavy heart.

'Another nun and I think a little boy. It was such a long time ago my memory's not as good as it used to be.'

'What happened?'

'The nun killed herself; I'm not sure about the little boy. He could have died of natural causes.'

'Did you know there's a woman who has bought the convent and is in the process of renovating it to open it as a bed and breakfast?'

She crossed herself. 'Sweet Jesus, why would she want to do that?'

'Because she has no idea about its history. What should I do? What would you do?'

'Get round there as fast as you can and warn her before something bad happens to her. How long has she been there? I can't believe they would sell it to anyone let alone a woman. Is she on her own?'

'You're not the first person to have said that. I think she's living there on her own as well.'

'You need to go and tell her. She needs to go and speak with Beatrice Hayton. She knows everything there is to know about every gossip and scandal that ever happened in this village.'

'Beatrice from the post office?'

'Yes, and Father, you should make sure you protect yourself when you go up there. I don't know if after all this time there would be anything bad in that house, but you don't want to take any chances, do you?'

If Joe had felt ill when he woke up it was nothing compared to how he was feeling right now. No wonder that house made him feel scared. Something was wrong with it, but surely after being empty for all these years whatever it was would have moved on? Then again, if you were dead or an evil entity, time would have no meaning whatsoever. What felt like a lifetime to him might only be days to something like that. This was something he'd never experienced. Ghostly visitors who wanted to pass on messages to their loved ones, yes, he'd met plenty of them – but a full-blown evil house full of only God knows what, he definitely had not.

Chapter 14

Kate woke up first, surprised to see everyone else still fast asleep. She managed to extract herself from between Ollie's legs and creep out of the bedroom to go to the bathroom. It was a bright, sunny morning and the house took on a completely different atmosphere in the daylight. She had no idea what was going on. It didn't matter. She loved this old house so much she would find a way to deal with it. For some bizarre reason she felt more at home here than she had anywhere in her entire life. She wondered if in a past life she'd lived here once and had found her way back. There was a thought. What if she'd been reincarnated and had been destined to find the house all along? Maybe her destiny had been written for her before she'd even been born.

Ollie walked into the bathroom, making her jump and bang her head on the mirror she'd been staring into whilst brushing her teeth.

'Oh shit, sorry, Kate. I didn't mean to scare you. Have you hurt yourself?'

She spat her toothpaste into the sink and started laughing. 'Jesus, Ollie, no – for a change I haven't.' She ignored the slight raised bump on her forehead. She was turning into a walking disaster zone.

'What's the plan for today? Do you want to do something with the girls? Take them out for the day while I get cracking? I'd love to spend time with you, but this house won't finish itself and I wasted a day yesterday. No sorry, I didn't waste a day at all. I had a great day with you all. What I meant was I lost working hours.'

'It's okay, I know what you meant. Would you mind? I'd like to take them out somewhere and spend some time with them if that's okay?'

'Of course it's okay, you should. Before Dickhead comes back and puts the boot in to spoil everything.'

She wiped her mouth and kissed him on the cheek. 'You, Oliver Nealee, are the best thing that's ever happened to me.' Kate put a long-sleeved top on and then went into the kitchen and began making breakfast. Despite the heat that was already starting to build, she didn't want her daughters to see the bandages on her arms and question her about how she'd hurt herself. She still couldn't believe that she'd actually slit her wrists; it wasn't her. After everything she'd been through, why would she try to kill herself now? Why couldn't she remember cutting her wrists so deep that she almost bled to death all over the kitchen floor?

Surely that would have hurt. They'd been smarting like a bitch ever since it had happened. Alcohol numbed pain – she knew that. How did she do it though? She had to have been awake. A cold shiver ran down her back. What if something had tried to kill her when she'd drunk herself unconscious and tried to make it look like suicide? She knew she'd had cameras installed then but did she want to watch her sad, pathetic self-trying to end it all? Probably not. Still, the feeling that it hadn't been her doing was hard to shake. Ollie walked in just as she'd squirted brown sauce all over his bacon and egg sandwich. She passed him a plate.

'You do know the way to a builder's heart is through a bacon and egg sandwich, don't you?'

She giggled, then smiled at the sight of her two girls who had

237

just trudged through the kitchen door with hair sticking up all over the place.

'Did you both sleep better in my bed?'

Both of them nodded. They'd never been morning people and now they were getting older she supposed the art of conversation would eventually dry up. They sat down and she put plates in front of them. Autumn wrinkled up her nose then pushed hers away. 'I'm vegetarian.'

Summer burst out laughing. 'You weren't yesterday when you ate that huge box of chicken nuggets from McDonald's.'

Autumn glared at her sister. 'Well, I am now. I don't eat bacon.'

Kate smiled at Summer, at the same time swiping the plate away from Autumn.

'That's no problem. Ollie will eat it, won't you?'

He nodded his head and stuck up his thumb.

'I have some cereal. Would you like a bowl of that?'

Autumn shook her head. 'Can I have some toast? Please?'

Kate turned away before she started laughing at the girl who had a sullen face and was giving her sister evil eyes.

'You're so funny, Autumn. Honestly, who are you following on Instagram now? Some model who thinks eating meat is animal cruelty? Or are you just being a goon?'

Luckily for Summer, she saw her sister's hand draw back to slap her face and moved away from her with millimetres to spare.

'Autumn, stop that now and Summer, stop teasing your sister. It's not very nice.'

Autumn glared at them both, scraped her chair back and stomped off in the direction of the upstairs bathroom. Kate didn't know what to say. They'd both grown up so much since she'd seen them. At least Autumn wasn't afraid to go upstairs now it was daylight. She wondered if Summer would be as blasé about what happened last night. She didn't want to bring it up and remind them if they'd both forgotten about it and brushed it off as a bad dream. Summer finished her sandwich. 'Don't worry about her, she's always moody. I'm surprised she lasted this long really. What should we do today, Mum?'

Ollie stood up. Taking his plate to the sink he rinsed it then grabbed his mug of coffee and left them to it.

'I'll see you later. I'm going to go and make a start on the bedroom.'

Kate blew him a kiss, which Summer groaned at. All the same, she smiled at them both.

'I don't know, sweetie. Whatever it is, promise you won't upset your sister. I only have you both until your dad comes to pick you up at six and I want to enjoy every moment that I can. Is that a deal?'

'Sorry, yes it is. I'll just tease her when we get home then and drive Dad mad if that's okay?'

Kate laughed. 'The teasing is not okay. You should be kind to your sister. However, the being naughty for your father is okay because he deserves it.'

She winked at Summer who smiled back.

***

Ollie waited until he heard the front door slam and the sound of Kate and the girls' voices drifting off as they walked along the drive to the main road and the nearest bus stop. He hadn't mentioned anything in front of them. He didn't want to scare them, but he needed to know what had happened last night. He felt a lot braver now it was full daylight. As soon as the lads turned up and he'd given them a list of what they had to do, he was going to go through the CCTV system and check every camera there was.

He was trying to figure out how to use it when he heard the voices of Ethan and Jack as they were laughing at something while walking through the front door. He was amazed they'd come back. He leant over the banister, about to shout to them,

239

when he felt a pair of hands give a sharp shove into his lower back. He let out a loud shout, but when he turned around there was no one there. Luckily for him he wasn't leaning right over or he could have fallen.

'Everything okay, boss?'

His knees had turned to jelly. There was no one behind him yet something had just pushed him, wanting to do him some harm. Kate was right, there was something of the supernatural kind going on and he wasn't afraid to admit he was scared.

'Yep, sorry I nearly fell over. Can you two come up here?'

He took a couple of deep breaths. He couldn't tell them what had just happened because they'd turn around and run for their lives. Ethan reached the top first and looked at Ollie.

'Are you sure you're okay? You're pale. Are you coming down with something? Because if you are, keep away. I've got a big night planned tonight. I don't want to be ill.'

Jack laughed. 'A big night – you're taking Emily Woods to the pub for a game of darts, pint of lager and a packet of crisps.'

Ethan gave him the finger. 'Fuck off, I'm taking her for a meal at the new Italian.'

Jack laughed even harder. 'You mean Pizza Hut?' He looked at Ollie. 'He means Pizza Hut.'

'It sells pizza and pasta. Isn't that Italian? You're such an arse.'

Ollie couldn't help but smile. 'I'm fine, just tripped over and gave myself a fright. Listen, can you two go and check the attic out – every box that's up there? Can you go through the ones you didn't have a nosey through last time? I want to see if there is anything about the history of the house up there for Kate.'

That wiped the smile off Jack's face. 'Really? We only checked it the other day.'

'I know we did, but please, as a favour for me can you do it again?'

Ethan looked uncomfortable. 'Well, if you really need us to. I have to be honest with you though, boss, I don't like it up there.

I'd rather go down in the cellar. It's damp and cold down there, but it doesn't feel like the attic does.'

'What do you mean, Ethan?'

It was Jack who answered. 'I know what he means; it doesn't feel right up there. When we were up there it felt as if someone was standing behind us, watching us the whole time. It was creepy.'

'It does.' Ethan agreed. 'Have you been up there lately?'

Ollie shook his head.

'We'll go up if you come as well. It will be quicker if all three of us go up there and check it anyway. You might see what we mean; it's scary up there.'

He ran his hand through his hair, not sure what to say. He'd wanted to get on with checking the cameras, but he couldn't really force them to go if he wasn't willing to. Before he chickened out, he strode towards the far end of the hallway and the small door that led up to the attic.

***

They finally reached the bus stop and Summer sighed. 'I'm tired already. Where are we going?'

'I thought we could go into town, have a look around the shops and then go have lunch.'

Autumn sat down on the edge of the kerb. 'I wish you still had a car. How are you going to manage living all the way out here without one? It's so far from everywhere.'

Kate couldn't tell her that she had no choice, that the police had taken her licence away from her for crashing her car when she was drunk. She did the maths. Another nine months and then she would be able to drive if she had any money left over to buy a car after the house was finished.

'I have a bike – I like riding around on it. It's great exercise and doesn't cost any money. I know, why don't we go and buy you each a bike? Then you can ride it around the grounds of the house and go for bike rides when you're stopping with me. I used to love going for bike rides when I was your age. My mum would make me sandwiches, put a packet of crisps and a can of pop in a bag, and I'd be off.'

Summer began jumping up and down. 'Yes please. Really? I'd love a bike. I haven't had one since before you left us. Dad threw them out when he cleared out the garage so Tamara could fit her car in when she stopped.'

Kate smiled, even though inside her heart was breaking in two. *I never left you; he made me. He threw me out and changed the locks so I couldn't get back in.* 'What do you think, Autumn? Do you fancy a new bike?'

Her beautiful daughter looked up at her and smiled. All the blackness that seemed to have been clouding behind her eyes cleared and she looked more like her old self.

'Can you afford to buy us each a bike? They're not cheap.'

'Yes, I can afford two bikes and helmets. It's much cheaper than a car.'

She winked at Autumn, whose cheeks began to turn a very faint red. A loud sound in the distance like a tank echoed around the quiet road and Kate wondered what on earth was heading their way when the pale blue VW camper van that belonged to Father Joe rounded the bend. It began chugging its way along the road towards them and she lifted her hand to wave at him. He started waving back, then realising who it was did an emergency stop – almost losing his nodding dog through the windscreen. He got out of the car and came running around.

'Kate, I'm so glad I've seen you. I was just going to check on Father Anthony and then I was coming to see you. I need to have a chat with you about some things?'

Kate looked at her daughters, and then looked at him. She didn't want them hearing anything that might scare them to stay at her house. Joe realised what she was trying to tell him and nodded his head.

'Anyway, it can wait. I'll speak to you later. When would be a good time for you?'

'The girls are going back to their dad's at six, so any time after will be fine. We're off into town to buy some bicycles, aren't we?'

Both girls nodded, amazed that their mum was having a conversation with a priest. They'd never really seen one in the flesh. The closest they got to one was watching *The Vicar of Dibley* on UK Gold.

'Good, that's good, I'll come around then. Forgive me, can I offer you a lift somewhere?'

'Well, seeing as how the bus doesn't look as if it's going to be here any time soon, that would be wonderful, thank you.'

He smiled and slid open the rear door for the girls to climb inside. Once they were in, he shut it. Kate reached out with her fingers to grab the door handle, when he grabbed her arm.

'I've been speaking to some of the locals about the house. My cleaner suggested that you talk to Beatrice Hayton who runs the village post office. She's a bit of a local historian and knows everything about everyone around here. I'll come and see you after the girls have left, but I think you really should go and speak with her if you can.'

'Thanks, I will. I take it there's a lot of history to my house that I should know about.'

He nodded his head. 'Kate, don't be alone up there anymore. Maybe stop in a hotel or B&B, but whatever you do don't stop in that house on your own any longer. It's not a good place for a single woman.'

'Thank you, Joe, but I can't. I'm not really in a position to waste money like that. I need every penny to get the house finished – even if I'm terrified of my own shadow at the moment.'

He nodded his head. 'Look the vicarage is huge, too big for a single man and his Xbox. You could move in for a while until things have settled down.'

'That's really kind of you and if I don't get things sorted out soon, I might take you up on that offer, but for now please don't mention anything in front of my daughters. I don't want them to be too scared to come here.'

Letting go of her arm, he walked around to his side to get back in the van. Both girls were chattering about what colour bikes they wanted. He started the engine and Kate smiled at him. Lowering her voice, she said, 'They're all I have. I'll go and visit Beatrice this afternoon.'

'Good, that's a very good idea.'

Joe stopped the van outside the one and only bike shop in the small town. The girls clambered out and rushed to the window to look at the limited selection of bikes on display.

'Thank you.'

'You're more than welcome. Be careful, Kate.'

She shut the door and waved at him as he drove away.

'Was he an actual vicar?'

Kate looked down at Summer. 'Yes, he was. He's nice, isn't he?'

'I suppose so. He drives a funny car for a vicar and isn't he a bit young?'

'I don't really know. I don't think there's an age limit on choosing to spend your life devoting it to God.'

'Well, it's a waste if you ask me, he's quite nice.'

Summer turned her attention back to the bikes and Kate felt a wave of relief. She wasn't qualified to answer questions on God, the priesthood or how good-looking Joe was. She opened the door to the shop and smiled as the old-fashioned bell rang to signal there were customers. Autumn ran straight over to a luminous green mountain bike, which made Kate's eyes water it was so bright. Summer looked at the fluorescent yellow one next to it and beamed at her. *That was easy. Let's just hope the prices aren't as eye-watering as the colours.* The middle-aged man who was repairing a puncture looked up at them and grinned.

'Well now, haven't you two got good taste? But wouldn't you

like to look at the selection of girls' pink and lilac bikes over here?'

Kate felt her cheeks flush red as both girls gagged, pretending to be sick.

'I guess not.' He wiped his hands on his trousers and came over to them. 'So you're not into all that pink dribble then?'

Both girls shook their heads.

'Good, because I've been staring at those two bikes for far too long. They make my eyes go fuzzy and water they're so bright.'

Kate turned the price tag over on the green bike that Autumn was clinging on to: a hundred and eighty-five quid. She didn't know if she could afford that much with all the money she needed for the house. She'd been hoping to get some for a lot less.

'I can do you a deal if you're wanting to buy both of them. Three hundred for them both and I'll throw in the helmets if only to give my eyes a rest.'

Kate laughed. She looked at her daughters, who were silently pleading with her, and she didn't have the heart to say no. 'Two helmets and you'll make sure they can ride them out of here?'

He stuck out his hand. 'Deal.'

'I guess we'll take them then.'

The girls whooped with delight and Kate followed him to the counter at the back of the shop.

'Birthdays, is it?'

'No, we live quite a long way from civilisation and I promised them a bike each if only to stop them driving me mad.'

'Well, that's as good an excuse as any.'

He rung up the sale and she took out her debit card. Her girls deserved a treat. She hadn't been able to buy them anything for months. If it meant she had to buy cheaper taps for the bathrooms it was a trade she was willing to make.

***

245

Ethan and Jack stood back to let Ollie go up into the attic first. He could feel his palms begin to sweat and his heart was racing at the thought of going up there. He couldn't let them see how scared he was because they'd never let him live it down. Sliding the bolts back on the door, he pulled it towards him. When he turned around he couldn't help but see the looks of fear that passed between the two 20-year-olds standing behind him.

There was a light switch on the inside wall, and he leant forward and flicked it down. The watery light wasn't very bright. He needed to see if Kate wanted the fitments all replacing with either fluorescents or spotlights. It was far too dark for such a big space and if you needed to see in all the corners this crappy lighting was never going to do. He climbed the creaking stairs. That was a plus sign. He'd never heard them creaking at all last night so there definitely hadn't been anyone of the human variety walking up or down them.

Then he realised that meant only one thing and he didn't want to even contemplate what else it could have been that could move silently. The fear that was taking over him was completely irrational, but his feet didn't want to get any closer to the top than they were now. He thought about Kate yesterday when she'd got to the top of the stairs on the first floor and felt something rush through her. He'd brushed it off. What if it happened to him – what would he do then? He stepped into the darkness at the top and gave his eyes a couple of seconds to adjust to the gloom. The light up here was a simple pull-string one, but he wanted to see if there was anyone hiding in the shadows before he turned it on. The attic space was too big and too gloomy.

'Turn the fucking light on, boss. How the hell are we supposed to see where we're going?'

He lifted his hand to pull the string and didn't realise just how much they were shaking until it took him three attempts to grab hold of it. Tugging the light as hard as he could, the single bulb came into life. It wasn't much brighter than when it had been

246

off. He stepped forward, scanning everywhere as fast as he could. He couldn't see anything and he felt Ethan standing behind him. Jack lost his footing and managed to trip and fall into the back of Ethan, who then fell forwards and knocked into Ollie.

'Jack, you stupid fucker, watch what you're doing.'

'Sorry, I could have sworn someone pushed me and made me lose my balance.'

Ollie felt his blood run cold. Hadn't someone or something tried to push him over the banister not long ago? He turned around to see if there was anyone standing behind Jack. There wasn't.

'Come on, you two, let's do a quick search and then we can get the hell out of here. I hate it up here and I have no idea why.'

Ethan muttered something in agreement. Ollie went in one direction where there was a pile of boxes and the other two, who wouldn't leave each other's sides, went in the other. Normally they would have been laughing and joking, taking the piss out of each other. Ollie had never heard the pair of them so quiet. The atmosphere up here was so heavy. It made him feel tired just thinking about all the work that needed to be done up here. Maybe he could convince Kate to leave the attic alone for the time being.

The roof was sound and didn't leak because the first thing they'd done had been to repair all the holes – in the early days before things started to get weird. If she wanted to renovate up here she could get another team of builders in because he didn't think for one moment that he would be able to work up here without being scared of his own shadow the whole time. Changing his mind about checking the boxes, he walked back towards the stairs.

'Come on, thanks for coming up with me. We've wasted enough time. Let's get on with what we're getting paid to do.' He reached the bottom step and let out a huge breath. He hadn't realised he'd been holding it in. Ethan was behind him and Jack thundered down the narrow staircase. He shot out of the door and slammed it shut.

'I bloody hate it up there. Don't make me go back up again, Ollie. Let's just bolt it, put a padlock on it and forget about it.'

Ethan began to laugh. 'Woo-hooo, you're such a wuss. You'd never survive on *Scooby Doo*. That red-haired girl had more bottle than you'll ever have.'

'Scooby fucking Doo is a cartoon and that red-haired bint wasn't real.'

Ollie couldn't help grinning, but he agreed with Jack that putting a padlock on was a good idea. As far as he knew none of them had any reason to be going back up there. He had a new one in the van, a heavy-duty one he'd bought a while ago for the garage at his house and never got around to using.

'You two get cracking on that last bedroom. I'm going to stick a padlock on here then I'll come and help you.'

Both lads walked off to the opposite end of the hallway, relieved to be working well away from the attic space. Before long The Bay radio was blaring out and it almost felt like any other normal working day. Ollie ran down to the van, got what he needed then ran straight back up. He'd never fit a hasp so fast in his entire life. The sense of relief as he snapped the lock shut was huge.

There was no denying there was something wrong with this house. How could a grown man be pushed by nothing? How on earth did you deal with a problem that you knew was there, hovering in the background, but that didn't how itself enough for you to know what it actually was?

The girls would be going home at teatime. He would try and convince Kate to go home with him for a couple of nights. He didn't know if she would because she was so stubborn and independent. It made him a little uneasy, the thought of letting another woman sleep in his marital bed – although once Ellen had become too ill to get around he'd made her a bed downstairs, converting the front room into everything she could need. She'd died in his

248

arms in that room and he no longer went in there. At first he'd slept in her bed, wanting to be close to her, until the local authority had turned up out of the blue one day to remove it and every other piece of medical equipment that they had loaned them.

He was sure that Ellen would want him to be happy again. Hadn't she spoken to him and told him to help Kate? Or had that been wishful thinking on his part? He didn't know, but Ellen had been such a kind, amazing woman, she would want Ollie to help Kate. In fact, he thought that Ellen and Kate would have made great friends had circumstances allowed. He shook himself from his daydream and lost himself in his work, concentrating on the job in front of him so much that he didn't have time to think about anything else.

***

When Summer's bike was given the good to go she screeched in delight. Autumn was already riding up and down the quiet main street, having a practice. Kate thanked the man once more and stepped outside to watch her daughters wobble along on the bumpy road and try not to crash into each other. They were grinning and seemed so much happier than they had when Martin had dropped them off yesterday. She didn't want them to go. The house would feel so empty without them. She would feel empty without them, but surely he would let her start to have regular contact with them now she was trying to sort her life out.

She wondered what Ollie was doing and her heart skipped a beat. It had been a long time since she'd felt so much as a flutter of excitement. Amy would approve one hundred per cent. She knew that Amy would be so happy to see her in a relationship with the cowboy and being able to see her girls again. At one point after the court case Kate had gone back to that crappy council flat and drunk so much vodka that she'd passed out in the tiny bathroom without even making it to the bed. She never wanted to be like that ever again.

No matter what was wrong with the house, she would sort it out. She wanted to go and see this Beatrice woman as Joe had suggested. If they made their way back to the village, they should be there in half an hour. It was going to be painful having to walk and try to keep up with the girls on their bikes. Her phone vibrated in her pocket and she took it out, smiling at Ollie's message.

'*Hey pretty lady, I hope you're having fun? Xxx*'

She began typing then gave up and rang him instead. He answered on the fourth ring.

'Hello, handsome, I was wondering if you could do me a massive favour?'

'For you, anything.'

'I've ended up buying the most horrendous mountain bikes I've ever seen for the girls, but they love them. I thought it might keep them out of trouble and out of our hair for a bit; however, I didn't factor in how we would get them home.'

'I'll be there in fifteen mins. Where are you?'

'Ulverston, on the main street near the bike shop.'

'See you soon.'

He ended the call and she smiled to herself – just enough time to get something from the butcher's for tea and get an ice cream for the girls.

27 June 1940

Sister Isabella waited outside the vicarage for the priest to come outside. She knew he was inside because she'd followed him here, from a distance of course, from the church. As the other sisters and volunteers had ushered the children back through the woods to the convent, she had told Sister Maria that she needed to speak with the priest urgently, then she had turned and followed him. She had tried to knock on the door, but for some reason her shaking hand had been unable to actually touch the wood of the door. She felt as if she wasn't good enough to be knocking on a priest's front door, which was completely ridiculous. It was ever since she'd moved into that house that she felt like this. It may have been built for the purpose of being a convent, but never in her life had she been somewhere that seemed to be a mockery of the word 'religion' in such a way that the house made her feel.

It scared her; the nightmares came every single night. Always the same, always of her causing harm to one of the children. She would wake up just as she'd looked down at her bloodstained fingers. Her eyes would fly open and she'd feel her heart racing and the cold sweat pouring down the back of her neck. What was wrong with her? She loved children – loved God even more. She could no more hurt a child than she could abandon the sweet Lord.

She knew she was ill. She felt so tired all the time, her skin felt clammy and she had lost her appetite. All she wanted to do was to sleep, yet when she did she had the same dream and it scared her because what if it was a premonition of something that was about to happen? Was she losing her mind enough that she'd hurt an innocent child? She knew the answer to this was no. She'd kill herself before taking the life of someone else. She was going to go insane if someone didn't help her. She stopped and tried to knock on the front door once more. This time it opened before her hand reached it.

'Hello, Sister, can I help you?'

She wanted to say yes but instead she cried. Not just a few tears. Oh no, she sobbed so loud her whole body shook with the intensity.

***

Father Patrick was taken aback; he had no idea what to do with a hysterical nun. He had no idea what to do with a hysterical woman full stop. Reaching out he patted her back, trying his best to comfort her. He stepped out of the house and into the bright sunlight. The young woman, who was no older than 25, seemed to lose the ability to stand upright and she slid to the floor in a heap of tears. He sat down next to her and began to pat her head as if she was a dog. He felt in his pockets and passed her his handkerchief. She took it from him and gave him the most beautiful smile he'd ever seen. It lit up her whole face. She was a very pretty woman and he wondered why she had chosen to become a nun when she could probably have the whole world at her fingertips. She was so beautiful she could have become one of those Hollywood actresses or a model.

'Thank you, Father; I'm so sorry,' she said in between sniffles and blowing her nose.

'You're welcome, Sister. Now would you like to tell me what on earth it is that has upset you so?'

She nodded her head. Her face was full of misery. 'I don't know what's wrong with me. I'm staying in the convent helping to look after the evacuees and I love it, I really do. I love looking after children. They are so innocent and beautiful.'

Patrick felt as if cold fingers had reached out and grabbed hold of his neck. He shivered, trying to shake the feeling, but instead he felt as if the cold was seeping through his skin and into his bloodstream, replacing the warm blood with iced water. The sun, which had been shining brightly, was now obscured by a huge dark cloud. He stood up. Leaning down he grabbed hold of her arm and pulled her up.

'Let us go and talk in the church; I was on my way there. We can talk inside.'

She nodded as if she knew what he was thinking – about how scared he was and how much he didn't want to hear what she was about to tell him. They walked together, the elderly priest and the pretty young nun. They made a compelling picture of grace and beauty. Patrick's heart was racing and it wasn't until he opened the church door that he realised just how out of breath he was.

Isabella followed him inside, immediately bowing her head in prayer. Once more he was struck by what a beauty she was. If they needed a picture of the perfect woman then she was definitely the most beautiful specimen he'd ever seen. She lifted her head, her dark brown fringe covering the huge, chocolate brown eyes that were hidden behind thick, black lashes. She smiled at him. 'Thank you, Father, I love being inside church. It makes me feel so much nearer to God.'

'Me too, Sister. I didn't catch your name before.'

'Isabella – my mother is Italian.'

'What a beautiful name, it's perfect for you.' Patrick wanted to kick himself. He sounded like some creepy old man. 'How can I help you, Isabella? I'm not used to seeing anyone so upset. You gave me quite a shock back there. Are you feeling better?'

She nodded. 'I always feel better in the house of God, thank you. I'm so very sorry. I didn't mean to scare you. I just don't know what to do or what's wrong with me.'

'Why don't you tell me and let me be the judge of that. Does it have anything to do with the convent?' Patrick didn't want her to answer him. He wanted her to laugh, shake her head and tell him she was in love with someone or pregnant. He could cope with either of those problems. He couldn't cope if she was about to tell him some horror tale about that godforsaken house in which there were lots of children living.

'Before I went to that house I never used to have bad dreams, well, only on the rare occasion and not enough that I'd remember them when I'd wake up.' She sobbed as tears filled her eyes and threatened to fall once more.

'You're having bad dreams all the time now, every night?'

She nodded.

'It's been a big upheaval for the children and yourselves, not to mention the worry of the war. You must be under a lot of stress, having to take care of so many youngsters.'

'I'm not worried about the war – no more than I was before I moved here. I keep dreaming the same dream every night. I'm not an angry or violent person, Father. In fact, I'm the opposite. I'd get teased at school because of my looks and name all the time. I never retaliated or got too upset by it all because I knew that God was watching out for me and he would make sure the teasing would stop before it got too bad – and it did.'

Patrick imagined how jealous the girls in her class would have been of the girl in front of him. He nodded.

'Well, the very first night we moved into that house I had this dream. I woke up in a cold sweat with tears falling down my face and I was so scared because it felt so real. I've had the same dream every single night since. I'm so tired. I wake up feeling exhausted and I have to go and check on all the children to make sure that I haven't hurt any of them in the night. What if I started to sleepwalk and did something unforgivable?'

'I know what it's like to have bad dreams, Sister, but a dream is exactly that. It's nothing more than your overactive imagination not being able to switch off when the rest of your body is resting.'

'Father, every night I dream I kill a child. I wake up and can feel the warm, sticky blood on my fingers. I can smell the awful, metallic smell that blood leaves. It feels as if my fingers are coated in so much blood that the smell has seeped into my skin and I can't wash it away.'

'Is it the same child or different children?'

'I don't know, I think it's the same one – a little boy who is as cute as a button and has the biggest blue eyes and gives the best hugs. He is a very special boy and I'm terrified that I'm going to wake up one day and actually have his blood on my hands. What if I hurt him in my sleep? I could never forgive myself and neither would God. I think I need to leave the house and get away from there before I do something bad.'

'Sister, you would no more harm a child than you would forsake God. That house has a history to it and I think when bad things have happened somewhere the memories can imprint themselves into the surroundings, which is probably all that is happening.'

A voice inside his mind whispered, *What a load of rubbish you're talking, Patrick. Tell her about the house then tell her to get the hell out of there before something bad happens. You know it's going to; give the girl a fighting chance while you can.* He wanted to tell her, tried to, but the words wouldn't come out of his mouth. What came out was a load of slurred, jumbled-up rubbish. He felt as if his mouth wasn't connected to his brain. Sister Isabella looked at him. The last thing he saw before everything went black was her concerned face coming closer to him.

He collapsed to the floor with a loud thud and she let out such a piercing scream, the passing family who had come to lay flowers on their recently departed grandfather's grave came running into the church to see what was happening. The man, who also happened to be the local doctor, took over, issuing orders to his shocked wife and to Isabella. He sent his son to find Crosby and to get an ambulance to the church as soon as possible.

***

Crosby came running in with the young lad. He took one look at the sister whom he recognised from the convent and nodded. Patrick looked as if he was already dead. His face was so grey and his lips were hanging apart. There was a line of spittle dribbling from them and Crosby's first thought was that it was starting all over again.

When the ambulance finally arrived and Father Patrick was driven away, Crosby took one look at the panic-stricken nun and felt his blood run cold. He was scared to ask her what was wrong

255

and why she'd come to visit Patrick. He hated that he wasn't man enough to say it out loud. He didn't need her to tell him something was happening up at the convent. The very fact that she was here and Patrick looked on death's door was answer enough.

'Sister, would you like a lift back up to the convent?'

He regretted the words as soon as they'd left his mouth, but he was a policeman and reckoned that up to now he'd been a pretty good one. He didn't want to turn into the ignorant man his old sergeant had become before he retired.

'If it's not too much trouble, although I really don't want to go back there.'

Don't ask, don't ask, don't… 'Why would you not want to go back, Sister?' *You stupid bugger, now you've done it. You're almost as dead as Patrick – should have kept your mouth shut.* He shook his head to try and get rid of the voice in his head. He didn't need some smug inner self telling him he'd just sealed his own fate. He showed her to the car, opening the door for her, and set off feeling as if someone had lodged ice down his spine.

'My name is Isabella – I don't think I told you earlier. I don't want to go back to the house because I don't like it. There's something wrong with that house. It gives me bad dreams.'

He couldn't answer because he didn't know what to say, so he continued driving. 'What happened with Father Patrick?'

'We were talking about the convent and he was trying to tell me something, but he couldn't speak. His words were coming out all jumbled as if he had something in his mouth. He'd been fine moments earlier.'

He stole a glance at her. She was staring out of the window. Her delicate fingers were twisting the crucifix around her neck so tight that the gold chain was starting to mark her skin. The drive to the house came into view and he saw the young woman physically shrink back into the seat as if she was trying to protect herself. She didn't speak. He turned onto the gravel drive, all the time berating himself for being so selfish. As the house came into view so did a group of children who were all playing a game and running around screaming and shouting.

'Blimey, they're noisy. Are they always like this?'

'Yes, they are. They're very well-behaved though and always do as we tell them; they seem to know that when they are inside the house they have to be quiet, so as soon as they go outside they let off steam. I love watching them play – such innocence.'

Crosby nodded. He stopped the car and watched as a young boy no older than 10 ran towards the car, waving at the sister whose name he hadn't even wanted to ask for fear of getting dragged into whatever it was that was happening. The nun waved back. 'Thank you for bringing me back, Sergeant. I hope Father Patrick will be all right.'

'It was my pleasure and I'm sure he'll be fine. I'll go to the hospital and speak with him now. See what he thinks he was doing giving us all a fright. Take care, Sister, and if you need any help you know where to find me.'

He regretted the words as soon as they left his lips. He didn't want to help unless he had to. She got out of the car and the young boy wrapped his arms around her. She bent down and hugged him back. Crosby would never forget the look of sadness on her face; it would haunt him for the rest of his days.

He drove straight to the hospital where he was told to come back later. Father Patrick was resting after having a stroke. There was nothing he could do at the moment except to bring him some things up later on. He left, not sure what to do. He could go back to the convent and ask to speak with the nun. He *should* go back and speak to her, but the fear that lodged in his heart each time he thought about that place was getting worse. Instead he went back to the station where he spent the next hour locked in his office twiddling his thumbs.

***

Sister Isabella walked back into the convent with a heaviness inside her heart, which was worse than ever. She didn't want to be here. She didn't think that anyone should be here really. Those dreams were distressing her too much. She'd never hurt a child – it wasn't in her. She couldn't even watch a chicken being plucked – it made her skin crawl – so why did she dream each night of taking Albert by the hand up to the attic and then slicing open his throat with her own hands?

It was making her feel sick. Each night the dream was getting more vivid. Last night she had heard the bone in his neck crack under the pressure of the knife because she'd pressed down so hard. She'd woken up and had to run to the toilet to throw up.

The house was unusually silent, which was a rare moment indeed. All the children were outside being supervised by the other nuns. She had no idea where the mother superior was. Isabella trudged up the stairs to her room. Taking the clean sheet from the bottom of the bed that she'd put there before going to visit the priest, she began to fashion a clumsy noose from it. She had no idea what she was doing and if she had been able to she would have given herself a good shaking, but her mind felt detached from her body. She wasn't thinking straight at all.

Going out onto the landing, she stood in the middle by the banisters and looked down. There wasn't anyone around. The house had never been this quiet since the day she'd arrived, and Isabella knew that the house had something to do with how she was feeling and why it was empty. It wanted her to do it; it was waiting on the sidelines for her to throw herself from the banister. This house was a living, breathing entity – of that she was sure.

Fastening the sheet around her neck as tight as she could with shaking hands, she wanted to run away, but her legs wouldn't let her. She then tied the other end to the smooth oak railing and climbed over it. Balancing on top like a circus performer, she thought about how she'd always loved watching the trapeze artists when she was a girl. Happy thoughts of her childhood ran through her mind and she blinked as if she was waking up from a trance.

Realising she was standing on the banister about to throw herself off, she tried to lean backwards – better to fall onto the landing floor behind her than forwards to her death. She heard Albert scream her name and tried to launch herself backwards, but she couldn't. An invisible pair of hands shoved her from behind. Instead of landing on her back on the landing floor, she fell to her death. The sound of Albert's screaming rang in her ears as her neck snapped.

***

Mother Superior Maria Wilkes ran in to see what the cause of all the commotion was and screeched as she crossed herself. She pulled Albert into her so he no longer had to look at the grotesque marionette dangling from the first floor landing. The other nuns came inside and she screamed at them to keep the children out. Passing Albert to Florence, she watched as the woman ushered the hysterical child out of the house, closing the door behind her. Maria ran as fast as she could upstairs where she tried her best to pull Isabella back towards the safety of the first-floor landing, but she couldn't move her. The girl was dangling there, obviously dead, and Maria screamed in frustration.

Why, why would she do this? It doesn't make any sense whatsoever. Dear God, please take Isabella into your loving arms. She devoted her short life to you. Please don't let her down when she needs you the most. Tears fell from her cheeks at the helplessness of the situation.

***

Crosby was staring out of the window when Tony came charging through the office door as if the building was burning.

'Need us now, up at the convent. Sudden death.'

Crosby felt the blood drain from his face as he turned cold. It had begun despite him not offering the lovely Isabella any support. The heavy feeling in his stomach made it hard to move fast.

'Who is it?'

'Don't know – one of the nuns. They've only gone and chucked themselves off the first-floor banister.'

Crosby felt his skin crawl. He knew that when they got there sad, beautiful Isabella would be the person they would find. He'd let her down. He could have warned her and he didn't. He passed the keys to his beloved Wolseley to Tony who did a double take.

'Are you sure, Sarge? You never let me drive.'

Nodding his head was about the limit of communication that Crosby could provide at this moment in time.

'Bloody hell, you've gone a funny colour. Is everything okay?'

'No, it's not and it never will be. Shut up and get me up to that God-forsaken house as fast as you can without killing us both, will you.'

Tony knew better than to argue with him and did as he was told, driving towards the convent as fast as possible.

Chapter 15

Ollie saw Kate smile as his van rounded the bend. She had come over tired and didn't have enough energy to keep up with the girls on their bikes. Both girls waved frantically at him as they stood next to her, holding their bikes up. He grinned at the sight of the three of them waiting for him. Parking up he got out and ran around to lift the bikes into the back.

Once they were safely stowed and the girls were inside the van he whispered into Kate's ear. 'I've got a headache just looking at those bikes. They're awful.'

She laughed and pushed his arm. 'You're telling me. I can't concentrate on anything. I feel as if my eyeballs have been tortured. They wouldn't go for the lovely pastel pink and lilac bikes most other girls would.'

'They're cute kids, almost as cute as their mum.' He bent towards her and stole a kiss before walking around to get back in. He didn't know if she wanted to go public about their relationship yet although she had no reason to hide it. Kate climbed in and sighed.

'Thank you for this. I wanted to go into the village before the post office shuts. If you take me home I can get my bike and we'll ride there.'

'Are you sure? Would you not like me to just drive you there and wait for you?'

'No thanks, I don't know how long I'm going to be. Father Joe suggested I go and speak to Beatrice Hayton to see what she can tell me about the house. I could be some time if she's free. The girls can ride around the village whilst I'm chatting with her.'

'No problem. Is that the nosy old bird who runs the post office then?'

'I think so, yes it must be.'

***

Before long Ollie pulled up outside the front of the house, which looked beautiful in all its glory in the daylight. It was only when the sun set and the sky turned black that it took on a sinister appearance – well, to Kate it did. Ethan and Jack were sitting on the front steps and waved at them as Ollie parked up.

'Dinnertime already?'

Ollie waited until both girls had got out. 'Sort of, well more like a coffee break. They won't stay inside the house on their own. The pair of them have been jumpy all morning. They've driven me mad.'

Kate didn't know what to think. She didn't want this house – her house – to be haunted. She wanted people to come here and stay for a holiday, not be afraid to come anywhere near it.

'What am I going to do? Everyone is getting scared to be inside it.'

'Ah, you've picked up on that?'

'It's pretty hard not to. I'm a little bit afraid myself. It's only the fact that I've invested every single penny I have into it that is making me determined not to be as scared as the rest of you.'

'If you can get the priest to come and bless the house, surely

262

that will make a difference? I really don't understand how a house of God can be so…' He paused as if not wanting to say it out loud, but for want of a better word said: 'haunted.'

'You think it is then?'

Ollie shrugged, indicating that he had no idea what to think. They got out of the car. Kate went to retrieve her bike from the shed and Ollie went back inside, closely followed by Jack and Ethan. Kate shouted to the girls to follow her and they set off, all three of them in a line.

***

Ollie watched from the upstairs landing window and he smiled, putting his fears about the house to the back of his mind. He was going to get his old mountain bike out of the garage when he went home and give it a service. He could leave it here and then when the work was done they could all go for bike rides. In the space of a month he'd gone from lonely widower to a family man and he loved it. He thought the girls were funny and very much like their mum, and he knew he was going to enjoy spending time with them.

***

Before long they arrived at the village. The post office was the biggest shop in the square and Kate headed straight for it. 'If you girls wait outside I'll buy you some sweets and pop.'

Both of them nodded. She went inside the shop, which was gloomy compared to the bright day outside. An older man was at the counter collecting his pension and by luck the lady serving him was who Kate assumed was Beatrice. Kate picked up some ice-cold bottles of cola from the fridge and filled two bags with an assortment of sweets, then stood in line to pay. She normally wouldn't fill the girls with so much sugar, but they were going

263

home and it would serve Martin right if they were hyper and drove him mad. The man turned to leave and smiled at her. She smiled back.

'Just these, please.'

'Hello, you must be the lady the whole village is talking about.'

Kate felt her cheeks start to burn. How did they all know about her? She kept herself to herself and only Ollie knew about her past. She wondered if he'd told the lads who might have told their mums or girlfriends all about her sordid life.

'Well, I'm Kate, but I don't know if I'm the one everyone is talking about or not.'

The grey-haired woman with the warmest smile she'd ever seen lifted her hand to her mouth.

'Oh, forgive me, that sounded awful. What am I like? Forever getting my words mixed up and saying the complete opposite to what I meant. I should have said: are you the lady who has bought The Convent, which the whole village is talking about? I'm sorry.'

Kate felt her shoulders relax and she laughed. 'Phew, that's a relief. I thought you were going to tell me some awful gossip about myself. Yes I am. Is that what it's officially called – The Convent?'

'Yes, it's always been called that, probably because it was, you know, back in the 1930s. How are you getting on? It's been empty for an awful long time.'

'Considering that it has – not too bad at all really. It's quite a solid house. Do you know anything about its history? I know some bits and pieces, but I'd really like to find out more about the place.'

Both women were skirting around the obvious facts. Kate didn't want to blurt out that she thought it was haunted and Beatrice didn't want to upset this woman she barely knew who might turn into a good customer.

'I do know pretty much everything. It's quite a long story. How long have you got?'

Kate looked back over her shoulder at the girls who were mid-argument and bored of waiting around for her.

'Not very long I'm afraid, judging by those two outside. It's only a matter of minutes before there's a full-scale blowout.'

'Kids, they don't half test your patience at times, but we wouldn't swap them for the world.'

She gave Kate a knowing wink and she smiled back.

'Would you like to come up to the house, see what I've done with it and we could have a coffee and a chat? The girls are going home around six so any time after then would be great. I've also asked Father Joe if he could call around that time. It would be really nice to have some female company though. I'm stuck in the middle of a small army of men at the moment.'

'Lucky you – that builder is a bit of eye candy, isn't he? Such a shame his wife died so young.'

Kate nodded, wishing she'd come here sooner. She liked Beatrice even if she was a gossip.

'I would really love to come for coffee and have a look around. I won't be able to stop for long. I don't go anywhere near that place once it starts to get dark. I can't believe you've been living there on your own. You're very brave.'

'So people keep telling me. I haven't had any major problems.' She wondered why she'd just lied. Beatrice probably already knew about the head and God knows whatever else was happening up there.

'I'll be there around six because I don't close up here until five-thirty if that's okay with you.'

'Brilliant, thank you.'

Kate paid and turned to leave, but not before she caught sight of the friendly woman behind the counter crossing herself. She felt as if she'd been immersed in an ice-cold bucket of water. Her dream home had turned into a house of horror and she felt as if she was living her worst nightmare. The girls were now standing apart from each other, clutching on to their bikes. Feeling flustered, she went back outside.

'What's the matter with you two?'

Summer pointed at Autumn. 'She started it.' Autumn stuck her tongue out at her sister. Kate passed them their drinks and sweets.

'Come on, let's go and sit on the bench over there and have ten minutes. We've had a busy morning and I don't know about you two, but I'm tired.'

The girls followed her over and they lay their bikes onto the grass and sat either side of her.

'Do we have to go back with Dad?'

It was Autumn who'd asked and Kate wanted to say no. She didn't want them to go back, but she didn't have custody of them and Martin was a bastard. If she tried to argue with him he'd never let them come back.

'As much as I want you both to stay with me, I'm afraid that you do. It's not my decision to make. Once the house is sorted then I'll try my best to see what I can do.'

'Why though? We've lived with him for ages. I hate him and I hate Tamara even more. All she cares about is what handbag to use and if her lip fillers need a top-up.'

Summer looked at her sister. 'Don't be a brat, he's done his best. It wasn't his fault Mum went off the rails.'

Kate felt her eyes fill with hot, salty tears. This was what they'd been arguing about whilst she'd been in the shop. Their divided loyalty to her and Martin, and the fact that she'd let them down when they needed her. Never had she felt so ashamed in all of her life. Her arms smarted as if to remind her of her failed suicide attempt, and she knew then that there was no going back. She'd never touch a drop of alcohol again. It hadn't helped anything; in fact, it had ruined her life.

'Look, please don't argue. You need to go back with your dad today because if you don't, Autumn, he won't let you come back to see me and I'd hate that. I love you both so much it breaks my heart having to let you go.'

She looked at Summer. 'I did go off the rails, but there were a lot of reasons for that. Your dad wasn't a very good husband to me and then Amy found out that she was dying and I just couldn't cope with it all. One day when you're old enough to understand I'll tell you everything. For now, I need you to do what your dad tells you and hopefully between the two of us we'll be able to work things out.'

'What do you mean – you'll get back together with him and we can all live back at home like we used to?'

'No, Summer, I don't think I could ever get back with your dad. I don't want to. We don't really like each other anymore. Sometimes even though you're married you grow apart – and we've done that. Maybe we could be friends again. That would be okay, wouldn't it?'

Summer nodded her head and Kate knew she would rather befriend Peter Sutcliffe than become friends with Martin again, but the girls didn't need to know that and for their sakes she would pretend to get along with him.

Autumn pouted. 'So we can't live with you?'

'Not at the moment, I'm sorry.'

'But we can come and see you and go for bike rides and eat sweets?'

She laughed. 'Of course you can, whenever your dad allows you to.'

'Okay.'

Kate stood up. All of sudden she felt exhausted. She needed to go home and have a strong cup of coffee. Her hands were beginning to tremble and her mouth felt parched. An ice-cold glass of wine would make all this real-life stuff not seem so hard to deal with, but the thought of Ollie waiting for her and the fact that she wanted to see her girls again would hopefully be enough to stop the thirst.

'Come on, girls. Let's go home and get something to eat. I'm starving.'

Chapter 16

Kate was nervous. She didn't want to say goodbye to her girls and she definitely didn't want to see Martin, but for now she had to do both and put on a brave face. Ollie had been busy all day, stopping briefly for a bacon sandwich then getting straight back to work. She knew he was letting her spend as much time with Summer and Autumn before she had to say goodbye to them and for that she was grateful. Martin's car approached the house. At least once the girls had gone home, she had a visit from Father Joe and Beatrice to look forward to.

Kate walked the girls to the front door. Summer ran off to hug Martin as he got out of the car. Autumn hung back, clinging on to Kate's hand. She whispered, 'I don't want to leave you.'

Kate bent down and whispered back, 'I don't want you to either, but remember what I said. It won't be long before you'll be back. I promise.'

Martin held out his arms for Autumn, who reluctantly let go of Kate and walked towards him.

'Did you miss me, baby girl?'

Autumn nodded her head, the whole time watching Kate who smiled at her.

'Say goodbye to your mother then get in the car. I just want a quick chat with her.'

Both girls ran back to hug and kiss Kate. Kate didn't think she'd ever wash her cheeks again. Summer grabbed her sister's hand, dragging her back towards the car where they climbed in. Tamara was watching from the passenger seat, looking as if she was bored already. Martin walked as close to Kate as he could get and sniffed.

'Well, well, you don't even smell like a drunk. I can actually smell your perfume instead of eau de chardonnay.'

Ollie, who was standing at the top of the stairs listening, clenched his fists.

'No, I don't. I haven't had a drink for days. I'm afraid that you, Martin, still smell of eau de bullshit though.'

He laughed. 'I quite like this new feisty Kate; in fact, I think it makes you look sexy as hell when you're mad at me. What do you say I come back later on when I've dropped the girls off for old time's sake – finish what we started the other night?'

Ollie ran down the stairs in time to hear Kate reply. 'I say that you go and take your girlfriend and give me a break. You and me have been over since you changed the locks so don't try and pretend any different. I want to start having regular visits with my daughters and I'm going to a solicitor to make sure that it happens. In the meantime, a thank you would be nice.'

Ollie appeared at the door. He stood next to Kate, his face a mask of anger. Martin backed away with the palms of his hands in the air.

'Only kidding. No need to go to the solicitor's just yet. I'm quite happy for the girls to come and spend time with you now that you're capable of taking care of them. I'll leave it up to them to arrange it with you.'

He turned and walked quickly back to the car in case Ollie ran after him. Kate could feel the warmth of Ollie's arm, which was snaked around her waist, gently clenched against her side to stop her from running after Martin and hitting him with a brick. He got in and began reversing. She waved and blew kisses at the girls, forcing herself to stand there until all she could see were the tail lights of his car. Once they were out of sight she felt herself slump and if it wasn't for Ollie she would have fallen to the floor and had the biggest screaming tantrum of her life. He pulled her close, holding her head up so she was looking in his eyes.

'That man is a wanker and you were amazing. Don't listen to a word he said. You're a wonderful mother and as sexy as hell. I'm falling in love with you, Kate Parker. Those big blue eyes get me every time you smile.'

He pulled her close enough that his lips pressed against hers and she kissed him back with more passion than she'd ever had in her entire life. She had no idea how this wonderful man had come into her life, but she was eternally grateful that he had. They stayed that way, locked in a passionate embrace until Ethan came up behind them.

'Urgh get a room; that's disgusting at your age.'

Kate pulled away, her cheeks burning, and Ollie burst out laughing.

'Jealousy will get you nowhere, mate. You have no idea how to treat a lady. I bet you don't get a kiss like that after taking your girlfriend to the Italian tonight.'

Jack started laughing. 'Haha, I bet he won't. See you tomorrow. Are you guys going to be okay here on your own tonight?'

Ollie winked at him. 'I guess so.'

Kate nudged him in the side and walked back into the house, but Martin's words were stuck in her head like the blade of a dagger and she couldn't get them out. All she wanted was an easy life for a change.

The front door slammed as Ollie closed it after the lads. He wandered into the kitchen where she was standing, gripping the sink and staring out into the back garden. He walked behind her and wrapped his arms around her. 'Your girls are amazing, just like you.'

The tears that she'd tried so hard to contain all day ran down her cheeks and she whispered, 'Thank you.' He held her close, feeling her frail body trembling as she cried silent tears. She finally turned to look at him. He kissed her again and held her tight.

'You look exhausted. Should I take you to bed for a rest?'

Lifting her sleeve, she wiped her cheeks and blotted her eyes. 'There is nothing more that I'd like right now than to go to bed with you to keep me company, but Father Joe and Beatrice from the post office – who thinks you're rather handsome – are coming soon, so I'd better go and sort myself out.'

He kissed her forehead. 'Does she now? The dark horse. Well, I suppose I'd better contain my lust and behave myself. At least until she's left. Why are they both coming?'

'They're not coming together; I just ended up inviting them both. Beatrice is going to fill me in on the sordid history of this place, although I'm not sure I really want to know the more I think about it. She said that she doesn't want to be here when it gets dark though and that scared me even more.'

'What about the vicar?'

'He said he needed to speak with me about it as well. The more I hear the more I feel sick. Surely after all this time it's okay? I mean I love this place. It's looking so much better with all the work you've been doing. It's my dream home. I never thought I'd be able to live in a place like this so I don't want to sell it or abandon it. I want to make it a good place to be. If it was a convent it must have been a good place once upon a time.'

'We'll see what they say and take it from there. It is a fabulous house and you deserve to live in a wonderful home because you've had a crap time. I thought my life was bad, but at least Ellen died knowing that we still loved each other completely. Martin is the meanest person I've ever met. He comes across as one of the lads and a good bloke, but you don't treat women the way he treats you. It's so wrong and he makes me feel so violent.'

Kate laughed. 'He's not worth it. He never was and never has been. He thinks because he's got money he can treat everyone like that. I'd hate you to get into trouble because of him.'

'Trust me, I've never been in trouble, but it's something I'm willing to take a chance on – and besides I'm not stupid. I'd drag him down a dark alley where there's no cameras.'

A knock on the door echoed throughout the house and Kate looked at Ollie. He reached out to squeeze her hand. 'Whatever it is we can deal with it. I'm here to help you now. I won't leave you on your own.'

She stood up. 'Thank you.'

***

He watched her walking away and hoped that they could deal with whatever it was that was happening, because he'd never experienced anything like it. He heard the loud chatty voice of the woman from the post office whose name he'd never taken much notice of until Kate had mentioned it. Kate led her into the kitchen where he was filling the kettle.

'Hello, I'm Ollie. I'll leave you ladies to it, should I?'

Kate shook her head. 'I'd rather you stayed. This involves you, Ollie.'

'If you're sure?'

'I'm sure.'

He walked over and kissed the top of her head and watched Beatrice's eyes fly wide open in surprise. 'Now would you like tea or coffee?'

'Coffee would be nice, thank you. I didn't realise that you two were… well, I don't know why I would. It's none of my business, is it? I have a reputation as a nosy old crow, but it's just my nature. I'm naturally inquisitive and there isn't anything you don't

273

find out when you work in the busiest shop in the village. You know I think you two make a lovely couple and I'm glad that you've found each other. It's your love that will see you through this mess and you do love each other. I can see it in your eyes.'

She stared at Ollie. 'Ellen said that you have her blessing. She thinks you both make a great couple as well.'

The mug he had been holding crashed to the floor, breaking into many pieces. He turned around, his mouth open, and looked at Beatrice to see if she was playing some kind of sick joke, but the woman looked embarrassed.

'Oh dear, I'm sorry. Sometimes it just happens and the words come out before I can think about the consequences. I didn't mean to upset you. She's here with us right now though and she said that Kate needs your help, but you need hers as well. I'm not sure what that means. Do you understand any of it?'

Ollie sat down, his mouth open. He couldn't stop staring at Beatrice. 'Yes, sort of. I thought I heard Ellen whisper that in my ear a few days ago when I was at home, but how do you know that?'

Her cheeks had flushed pink. 'Believe it or not this isn't common knowledge. I'm a medium – and no jokes about how am I sure that I'm not a large, please.'

Kate looked at Ollie. Reaching her hand out, she held on to his. 'You're a psychic medium?'

'Yes, since I was a girl. I don't always listen to what the spirits have to say. They can get a bit noisy. Ellen is standing right behind you, Ollie. Her left hand is on your shoulder and she's relieved to see you happy. She said it feels as if a weight's been lifted from her shoulders.'

His fingers lifted up and he touched his shoulder.

'Ellen wants you to know that you were a wonderful husband and she loved you dearly, but she couldn't stand to see you alone and in your own little world. She said you deserve to be happy and she's glad she had a helping hand in getting you and Kate together. She also wants you to know that there is something bad in this house. She doesn't know what exactly. It hides out of sight most of the time because it needs inviting in again, but the nun is nice and she's trying to help Kate.'

The shock had made his normally tanned face drain of every bit of colour. Kate, who couldn't stop staring behind Ollie, didn't seem to know what to do.

'Is she pain-free and happy?'

Beatrice nodded. 'Yes, very. It was a bit of a shock at first, but finding that she could flit between this world and theirs has been a huge help. You're to get on with your life, look after Kate like she deserves and be very careful. What was that, dear? Oh yes, and she said that seeing you with Kate's daughters made her very happy. You would make an amazing dad.'

Ollie turned around hoping to see Ellen, but there was nothing there.

'She's gone, said that it's time to let you get on with your life. She will be around if you ever need her though. I'm sorry if I've upset you. I didn't mean to.'

He looked at Kate, who shrugged. Then he turned to Beatrice.

'No, well I'm upset, but not because of that. I've been feeling guilty that I was betraying Ellen by being so happy and falling in love with Kate. Thank you.'

Beatrice grinned. 'Glad to be of some use. Now let me get on and tell you what I came here for. Although I have a sneaky feeling Ellen engineered this meeting so she could tell you herself. She is a very determined lady.'

Ollie laughed. 'Yes, she is and always was. I can't believe it. I never even imagined this stuff happened for real.'

He clenched Kate's hand, feeling as if the worry about letting Ellen down had finally been lifted. She liked Kate and wanted him to be happy. What more could he ask for?

'Beatrice, this house – did you know about the severed head the lads working for Ollie found a few days ago?'

'Not officially. I heard there was a bit of a commotion up here the other night. That would make sense. Have they reunited it with her body yet?'

'I think so. The detective who phoned yesterday said they would be doing it today.'

'That's good. The nun who we are talking about was the mother superior for this convent and by all accounts she was a very good woman. The only way this thing can be fought is if they bury her head in its rightful place. It will give her the strength to fight the darkness in this house for good and banish it.'

Beatrice looked around the kitchen, which was full of light and was safe for now. When the lights went out though it was a different matter.

'Kate, I'm a very strong believer that things happen for a reason. There is a reason you were led to this house and why you are the owner. I think that Agnes believes that too. I can't hear her properly, but I can see that she wants you to be the one to banish the evil that hides inside here for good.'

***

A sharp pain in Kate's head made her feel faint. She felt the flow of blood running down her arms and stood up, turning quickly so Beatrice wouldn't see the bright red stream of warm liquid that was seeping through the sleeve of her top. She could hear Ollie's voice behind her, but it sounded fuzzy. Her legs gave way and she collapsed to the floor.

'Kate.'

She couldn't speak because she had realised herself all along there had been a reason she'd discovered this house. The evil inside it knew that and wanted to hurt her. It was afraid of her and what she might be able to do. It wanted her dead and she knew that it wanted to take over her completely.

***

Ollie jumped up and ran to her. Kneeling, he lifted her head into his lap.

'What's happening? I don't understand.'

He took out his phone and rang for an ambulance. Kate was unconscious. Beatrice began searching through the cupboards until she found a bottle of brandy tucked away at the back. She ran across to Ollie and passed him the bottle.

'Give her some of that; it might bring her round.'

He passed the bottle back. 'I can't, she's a recovering alcoholic. I don't want her to get the taste of it again when she's doing so well.'

Beatrice straightened up, freezing as she looked in the direction of the stairs. She whispered, 'You need to get Kate out of here. Whatever it is knows everything about her and is trying its very best to sabotage her. It won't stop. It thrives off making people's worst nightmares come true and it's doing its very best to take control of Kate.'

The light in the room began to fade and Ollie looked up to see a huge, black mass forming at the bottom of the stairs, blocking the front door. Panic filled his chest and he was about to scoop Kate up into his arms and run out of the back door with her when a brilliant white light filled the kitchen. It blocked out the darkness, stopping it from spreading. Both Ollie and Beatrice had to squeeze their eyes shut. A loud, guttural growl filled the air, making Ollie's heart skip a beat. The atmosphere, which had been unbearable moments ago, felt much lighter. The room felt peaceful. Standing on the other side of the kitchen door was Joe, who had his crucifix and Bible clutched to his chest.

'Holy mother of God, what is happening in here? It's like a bad day at the house of horrors.'

It was Beatrice who spoke. 'I can't say exactly. What I do think is happening is the evil in the house has just been sent back to its hiding place for now by Agnes and Ellen – and because of your appearance, Joe. However, it's getting stronger and they won't be able to keep it at bay for much longer.'

Kate groaned and Ollie gently patted her cheek. Her eyes flickered open. 'What happened?'

Father Joe stepped forward. 'I have a feeling that the battle has commenced. There is a demon that lives in this house. It wants you, Kate. We need to get you out of here and somewhere safe until we can decide what to do about it.'

Ollie nodded his head. He scooped Kate up into his arms. 'I'm taking her to the hospital, then we're going to my house. I'll phone you both when we're home and she's feeling better. Thank you. I don't understand what's going on, but as soon as Kate is feeling better, I need you to tell me everything.'

'No hospital, please, Ollie. Take me to yours.'

'Beatrice, can you phone and cancel the ambulance? Tell them she fainted, please, and we don't need them. I live in the black and white Tudor house on the corner of Hollybrook Lane, if you want to follow us there, you're more than welcome. I think we need your help – both of you.'

She nodded her head. Father Joe went first, followed by Ollie carrying Kate and Beatrice followed behind. They left the house to get into their cars. All four of them were terrified of what was happening and feeling helpless because they were involved whether they wanted to be or not. There was nothing they could do about it. Ollie managed to get Kate into his car for a second time.

'I'm so sorry; I don't even know what happened. I saw the blood and everything went fuzzy.'

'You don't need to be sorry. I think we have a much bigger problem with the house than either of us could ever have antic- ipated. Can you believe that Beatrice could see Ellen? It's all so strange.' He didn't want to upset Kate by talking about Ellen too much. She was a big part of his life though and if they were to make a go of it he wanted to be able to mention her name. Kate reached out and grabbed his arm.

'I really do believe the things she said. Ellen sounds like she was a lovely lady and I feel very privileged that she thinks I'm good enough for you. It's so sweet that she wants you to be happy.'

'She was amazing – and thank you for saying that. Who'd imagine my dead wife would turn into a matchmaker from the other side?' He chuckled to himself.

***

Kate sighed. She wished she knew what to do about the darkness inside her house. As she leant back against the leather car seat she felt the sharp corner of the diary that she'd put into her jeans pocket to show Beatrice.

27 June 1940
As Tony swung the car into the drive up to the convent, the sun was shining so brightly through the trees both men had to lift their hands to shield their eyes. As the car approached the house nothing looked out of the ordinary. The front gardens were filled with children and nuns. The laughter, shouts and screams were so loud you would never know the tragedy waiting behind the closed front door. The only sign anything was wrong was an older nun standing guard, wringing her hands and crying silent tears. The children, who were oblivious to them, carried on with their game of chase. Crosby got out of the car and hurried across to the distraught woman. Tony, who had no idea what was happening, followed him.

'Thank you for coming so soon. I don't know what to do. I can't let the children go back inside the house because none of us are able to lift her down. Why would such a lovely young girl with her whole life ahead of her choose to end it so suddenly, without warning?'

Isabella's voice whispered in Crosby's ear, *'I did warn you though, didn't I? But you were too scared to do anything and now you've had to come back to the house anyway and look at my cold, dead body.'* He shuddered.

'I'm sorry for your loss. If you show me where she is, Constable Price will assist me in getting her down. I've asked for the local undertaker to come as soon as possible. Did Sister Isabella have any family?'

The nun looked at him, her pale blue, watery eyes staring straight into the depths of his soul. 'How did you know it was Isabella?'

Crosby felt his skin burn and his starched white collar felt far too tight for his generous neck. He also saw Tony watching him closely from the corner of his eye. *That's right, how are you going to explain this one without letting the world know what a complete selfish, heartless bastard you are?*

'I, erm, I spoke to her earlier. She called at the church to speak to Father Patrick.' As much as he didn't want to tell them he had no choice.

'What did she want, Sergeant?'

'She came to ask about this place.' He said it with such disgust it came out as a hiss. 'Sister, this place should never be lived in. It's not a good place to be. Things have happened here in the past – bad things – and we need to see about getting these children moved somewhere far more suitable before anything else happens.'

'I'm not too sure what you mean. Are you saying that we're all in danger?'

Tony, whose mouth had dropped so far open he could catch flies, looked from his boss to the old woman, not believing what he was hearing.

'Yes, Sister, I think you all are. We need to find suitable accommodation. I'll tell the church this house is a crime scene and until we've investigated Isabella's death thoroughly no one can live here. Now, let us go and pay our respects and make her more comfortable. Do you want to contact whoever it is you need to speak to? If needs be, we can move you all to the village hall for now.'

She nodded. 'I'll try. I'm not so sure they'll agree, but I'll try my very best. You know I've been having nightmares for the last few nights. I wake up in a cold sweat and my heart is racing, yet I can't remember what they're about.'

Crosby felt his heart go out to this frail woman who reminded him of Agnes.

'You don't have to believe me, but I have no reason to lie. I've been to more deaths in this house than I have the entire village. Please make sure you leave as soon as you can.'

He reached out and patted her shoulder, then turned and walked inside the much darker hall. It took a minute for his eyes to adjust to the gloom. Inhaling sharply when he saw the dangling figure of the beautiful Isabella, a pain shot through his heart. This was his fault, all his fault.

'Jesus Christ Almighty, what a waste. Should we check to see if she's still alive?'

Crosby turned to look at Tony.

'Really? If I thought she was alive I'd have run up there and dragged her back over single-handedly. Do you think she looks as if she's alive?'

Her eyes were half open, her mouth slack with her tongue protruding from between her soft, full lips. Her beauty had been stripped away from her and she would forever be remembered as a grotesque marionette. Crosby walked up the stairs, his heart heavy. He felt so bad that he wanted to join her. His life was over now. What was there to live for? The guilt he felt over Isabella's death would never leave him. A movement from the direction of the attic doorway caught his eye and for a split second he thought that Lilith was standing there watching them, having the last laugh. He wouldn't be surprised if she was. He knew then that they hadn't banished her, it, whatever it was for good, because it had been too easy.

'Come on, stop gawping and give me a hand to pull her over. It's not right. She looks…'

'She looks scary; I'll be having bad dreams about this for ever.'

Crosby glared at him. 'Will you have some respect? Less than two hours ago she was the most beautiful young lady I'd ever had the pleasure to meet.'

The two men tugged on the sheet, trying to pull her back over. Although she was only little, she was a dead weight. The sweat was pouring from Crosby's brow.

'I can't do it. We're going to have to wait for the funeral director and see what he suggests. Probably need a big ladder and a strapping, muscular bloke to cut her down and give her a fireman's lift. Actually, that's not a bad idea. Ask if you can use the phone and ring the fire brigade. They might be able to help.'

Twenty minutes later the undertakers arrived followed by the fire engine. The commotion outside of excited children signalled its arrival. Crosby, who was sitting on the top stair feeling ill, signalled for Tony to go and meet them. Minutes later the hall was filled with the sound of male voices. Once they realised the nun was still hanging there the silence was louder than the noise. Between them they managed to get her body down in as dignified a manner as they could.

The undertakers had a coffin ready to put her in. Crosby, who couldn't breathe properly, watched, unable to help. The nuns who were now aware of poor Isabella's demise had ushered the children around to the back of the house so they wouldn't have to watch her being carried out and put into the waiting hearse. The mother superior had come back inside and reached out for Crosby's arm. He turned and she whispered, 'They won't let us leave until tomorrow. What are we to do?'

'They have to. You can't be here any longer. It's not safe for anyone. Look at all these innocent children who they're putting at risk. You need to get what supplies you have and we'll go to the village hall. I'll get Tony to go and open up, warm the place up a bit. I'll see if I can get a bus up here to move everyone. Leave it with me. If we get the children away from this place first, you can send some of the nuns back up with me and some more of my constables to gather the supplies.'

A piercing scream made Crosby freeze to the spot. Afraid to turn around and see what had happened, he forced himself to move. He ran to the front door and stared out into the gardens. Under the huge oak tree in the distance was a group of children and nuns. One of them was on the ground cradling a child. Crosby ran towards them as fast as his bulky frame would let him. As he got nearer, he had to push his way through the crowd to see the lifeless figure of a boy, no older than ten, being rocked back and forth by one of the nuns. He shook his head.

'Come on now, you all need to move away and let me have some space.'

Tony appeared.

'Go get everyone from the station now. Call me an ambulance and tell the undertakers to come back. And get these kids away from here now.'

30 June 1940

Crosby, Tony and the mother superior stood outside the convent watching. They had already been inside to check nothing of importance was left behind. It had been the quickest walk-through of a property Crosby had ever conducted. The joiners had turned up in force, huge sheets of wood for every door and window. After some heated conversations between the archbishop and Crosby, it had eventually been agreed that the house would be emptied, boarded up, left secure and never inhabited again. Well, not as long as Crosby was alive it wouldn't. He would personally make sure of that.

If anyone had told him that a house could harbour so much evil and kill such beautiful innocent people he would have laughed and told them they were nuts. He'd seen it though – more times than he wanted to remember. That house or that woman, demon, whatever she was had taken more lives than he wanted to believe could be possible. It was a house of death, a house of horrors and for some reason even God would not set foot inside it.

The best thing would be to have it demolished, but the church wouldn't agree to it. They said it was unethical. He'd argued that so was letting innocent people live inside there and die horrific deaths, but that hadn't worked. The house would stay as it was, boarded up, and hopefully whatever evil lurked inside would eventually move on, get bored, and go find another house to overtake. He didn't care as long as it wasn't in this area. He was done with the convent. It had aged him and ruined his life.

Chapter 17

Never had Ollie's house looked so welcoming. All the way there he kept stealing glances at Kate who had sat with her head pressed against the glass, staring out of the window. He was at a loss. He didn't know what to do about the situation. It wasn't as if he could go into her house and tell whatever it was to get the hell out before he called the cops.

All these years he'd watched horror films with Ellen, scoffing at how ridiculous they were and here he was in an actual situation like the ones he'd laughed at. It didn't make any sense. He had no idea if Beatrice or the priest would follow him here. As much as he wanted to forget any of it had ever happened, he was worried about Kate. She looked dreadful. Her arms needed dressing. He could smell the strong, coppery smell of the blood, which had seeped through her clothes, and it was making his stomach churn. As he parked outside, he reached out and shook Kate's arm.

'Hey, how do you feel?'

She shrugged. 'Tired.'

He got out and walked around to her side. He opened the door and helped her down, having to catch her as she lost her footing and almost made them both fall to the floor. One arm around her waist, he supported her as they walked to his front door. Once they were inside, he took her to the kitchen where he then proceeded to turn on every light in the house. He ran upstairs to the bathroom to get the first aid kit, hoping he could patch her arms up once more. He also got one of his spare T-shirts for her to wear; he couldn't stand to look at the dried, bloody mess that covered the one she had on. He went downstairs to find her slumped across the table.

'Kate, please can I call the doctor to come and check you over? I'm worried about you.'

'No, Ollie, I'm okay. I just need to sleep. I'm so tired and my arms are fucking smarting like a bitch. I don't need anyone, okay? Just leave me alone.'

Shocked by her change in behaviour, he turned away. He was worried. This wasn't the woman who he'd got to know and love over the last couple of months. He'd never heard her speak like this, not even when she was in the hospital or after that argument with Martin. She was always so upbeat, so determined not to let anything get her down. Yet here she was either sinking into a deep depression or there was something else wrong with her and he didn't know what he should do.

'Well, at least let me clean up your arms and put some new dressings on; you can't leave them like that.'

She lifted her head so he could look at her arms. Ollie thought she looked different. Her eyes seemed much darker and the way she was watching him made him feel uncomfortable. He gently tugged off her top and she let him. The bandages on her arms were covered with now drying blood. After filling the washing bowl up with warm water he carried it over and bathed the blood around the wounds. When he'd finished, he patted it dry and took two fresh bandages and began to wrap her arms up once more. When he'd finished he slipped his sweatshirt over her head. Her skin was so cold to the touch it shocked him.

'Come on, Kate, why don't you come upstairs and get in my

bed? Snuggle up under the duvet and have a sleep. You might feel a lot better when you wake up.'

He pressed two paracetamols out of a blister pack and handed them to her. 'Take these. They should take away the smarting pain in your arms.' He filled a glass with water and watched as she swallowed the tablets, along with a huge gulp of water.

'Thank you, I don't know what's wrong with me, Ollie. I don't feel right; I feel funny.'

He wanted to tell her that she looked funny, but didn't want to upset her any more than she already was.

'You've had a busy few days – well, few months. You've never stopped working since you bought the house. You've stopped drinking, which on its own makes anyone feel like shit. You're amazing. A couple of hours and you'll be right as rain.'

She nodded. He reached out for her hand and lead her upstairs to his bedroom.

'Are you coming to bed, Ollie?'

He shook his head. 'Nope, you need some undisturbed sleep. I might start snoring and then you'll wake up and not be able to get back off. I'll come up in a few hours though if that's okay.'

'I'd like that.'

He pulled back the duvet and he watched, feeling helpless and scared as she climbed in. Tucking her in, he bent down to kiss her forehead.

'Sweet dreams.'

She murmured, 'I'm scared.' Then closed her eyes.

Ollie whispered, 'I'm scared too.'

He went back downstairs and saw two figures standing at his front door. He let Joe and Beatrice inside. Lifting one finger to his lips, he pointed upstairs and they both nodded. He led them into his kitchen at the far end of the house, waited until they were inside and then shut the door to muffle out the sound of their voices.

'Kate's gone for a lie-down. She doesn't feel well and if I'm being honest, she doesn't look well. She looks different. Her face doesn't look as soft as it did. Her features look... God this sounds stupid, but they seem much harder. I sound as if I'm mental. I wish I knew what was going on and what I could do about it.'

He breathed out as he finished speaking; it had come out without him stopping for air. Joe reached out and patted his arm.

Beatrice spoke first. 'We have no choice. That house is possessing Kate. I've never in my entire life come across a situation like this. I normally tell people their nearest and dearest loved them – even though they'd fallen out ten years ago. I've never been caught up in anything so intense and I'm not going to lie to you, I'm scared and not sure of the best way to go. This isn't going to be straightforward. We need to exorcise the house.'

A creeping sensation made Ollie shiver, but what if she was right? What if this was the only way to get rid of the evil in Kate's house? It was taking over Kate. If they didn't stop it, she could die and he didn't want to even think about losing her when he'd only just found her. Beatrice walked over and placed her hands onto Joe's shoulders.

'Why don't you ask Agnes yourself? Don't bother saying you can't because I know that you can communicate with the dead. You just don't want to. If you ask her, she'll tell you what you should do. She said that she's already been to your house, but you were too afraid to stand your ground and ask her what she wanted. It's not right to let the lovely Kate become so possessed that the house will kill her – and you know it will. It's already had several attempts. Whatever is in that house is growing stronger and if we don't stop it now then I think that to put it bluntly we're all fucked. It won't let any of us escape. It's too late because whether we wanted to be or not, we're involved. So grow a pair of balls and act the hero. I don't want to die just yet and I'm pretty sure neither do Kate or Ollie. What about you, Father? Are you ready to throw it all in and go to an early grave?'

He looked at her. 'No, I'm not. There must be another way to sort this out. There are three stages of possession. Stage one is infestation, where the demon attaches itself to an object or a person. In this case this demon has attached itself to the convent. I don't know why it has chosen to.'

Kate walked in, rubbing her eyes. 'I do. I've been reading the diary that I found and it details quite clearly what happened in 1933. In fact, it's horrifying. Those poor women died the most brutal, awful deaths imaginable and it all started when a woman called Lilith Ardat knocked on the door one cold winter's night looking for sanctuary.'

Beatrice nodded her head encouraging Kate to continue.

'She asked if she could come in and the nuns, being kind, compassionate women, invited her inside. The house was the perfect place for a demon to hide and it took over it completely, taking whatever it was that scared each woman and killing them in that way. Sister Agnes, whose head we found, believed that this woman was evil and thought she was a vampire.'

Beatrice looked at Joe who continued, 'The second stage is oppression. This is where the victim becomes depressed, filled with anxiety and despair. Does any of this ring a bell with you, Kate?'

'Yes, it does. I've had a terrible time these last twelve months yet a few nights ago – just as I was thinking my life was getting better – Ollie found me unconscious, lying in a pool of my own blood because I'd slit my wrists.'

Beatrice looked horrified and Joe nodded. 'So it's already tried with you, Kate?'

He turned to look at the others. 'Do you know how dangerous the thing we're dealing with is? This isn't some friendly grand-parent wanting to say a final goodbye. It's a full-on demon with more power than you or I could begin to imagine. It's killed people. It will carry on killing people and do you know why? Because it likes it; it gets its kicks playing with people's lives.'

'And that is exactly why we must put an end to it, Father. We can do this with your faith, my belief and Kate's inner strength. We can gain control and send it back to hell. Don't get me wrong, I'm not saying that it's going to be easy, but I can't see that we have any other choice. Do you?'

Joe looked at Kate. 'The third stage is possession, where the demon takes over you completely. Ollie said you were acting a little strange before, Kate. How do you feel now?'

'I'm tired – so tired – and I felt odd, but I feel okay now that I'm here and away from the house.'

'Good, that's good. I think we may have got you out of there before it managed to take over you. If it had you'd require a full-blown exorcism. We have to keep Kate away from the house. It's not safe up there for her now. Things have gone too far. It was only a matter of time before it completely took over.'

Ollie nodded. That wouldn't be a problem because until this was all sorted out, he didn't think he'd be able to set foot in there anyway. He was terrified and he certainly wasn't letting Kate go back in.

'What we need to do is go in and completely cleanse the house. I don't think it will be easy. In fact, I think we are in for a huge battle of good against evil. It can be done though. I think this demon thrives on terrorising women. I don't think it is as brave against men. I have a gut feeling that if I can fight this off and bless the entire house we might be able to get rid of it. If Sister Agnes's spirit is still in the house and trying her best to protect Kate then the demon hasn't gathered its full strength. At some point in the past, I think one of the priests has done a pretty good job of cleansing the house. We just need to finish it off and banish it for good.'

Kate smiled at him then turned around and went back upstairs to lie down. She clearly didn't feel good. Ollie watched her go, wondering what on earth they had got caught up in. Beatrice stood up.

'I need to go now and get ready. I think it needs the both of us to go into battle tomorrow. I can communicate with Agnes and the others whilst you fight the demon.'

'Thank you, I'm sorry about all of this.'

She took hold of his hand. 'Oliver, this is no one's fault. That house is a portal to hell, and this was going to happen one day sooner or later. The church should have torn it down, brick by brick, and consecrated the land beneath it. Greed is the reason they didn't and now the church owes it to Kate to put things right. I just hope that we can do it before it's too late for any of us.'

She left, got into her car and drove off without so much as a backward glance or wave of her hand. She was so absorbed in her own thoughts about what was going on. Ollie went back into the house. Joe was still sitting with his head in his hands. Ollie took the emergency bottle of Jack Daniel's out of the fridge and poured them both a generous shot.

'Sorry, I haven't got any ice.'

Joe took it from him and clinked his glass against Ollie's. 'Cheers, that's all right. To us – the village idiots on God's crusade.'

Ollie, who had almost swallowed the amber liquid in one mouthful, coughed and spluttered. When he regained control, he grinned at Joe. 'Yes, to the village idiots. Let us be so naïve that we don't question what the hell it is we're doing tomorrow, but more than that let us pray that it works and we get rid of the problem once and for all.'

***

Joe stopped himself from saying it wasn't his problem. It was. He'd been hearing things and things had been happening to him even before he knew any of this. Tomorrow he would be having an interesting telephone conversation with his superiors. Technically he needed to request an exorcism. That could take months and it meant a clerical psychologist being sent out to assess the situation; however, time was not on their side. Kate was in danger and they needed to stop this Lilith now, as soon as possible.

'Right, I'd best be going. Thanks for the drink; I'll speak to you tomorrow. We'll discuss the fine details in the morning; I'll come here around eleven.'

He stood up and walked towards the front door. His legs felt like jelly and his head was thumping as if he had the world's biggest hangover about to kick in.

***

Ollie followed him, locking the front door behind him. He didn't know if wanted to sleep in the same bed as Kate – especially if it wasn't technically Kate and she'd been possessed – but then he remembered what Ellen had said. Kate needed him, but more importantly he needed her. She had seemed a little better when she'd come back down before. He turned off the lights and made his way upstairs to his bed, where he was going to lie with his arms around Kate to protect her from whatever it was that wanted her just as much as he did.

Chapter 18

Kate woke up feeling much better than she had last night. Her head wasn't muzzy and her arms were no longer throbbing. She felt Ollie's arm, which was wrapped around her waist, and she smiled. She tried to remove his arm without waking him up. He murmured, 'Morning, beautiful.'

She grinned. 'Morning, handsome, I didn't hear you come to bed.'

'Good. I didn't want to disturb you. I tried my best not to. Should we get up and have some breakfast? I'm starving.'

'It's funny you should say that – so am I.'

***

She got out of bed first and he studied her. She looked like she always did. She didn't look strange like she had last night and she seemed a lot happier. He knew why. She'd had a full night's sleep away from the house – time away to refresh her body and soul, no scary ghosts or demons. Then it hit him. Were they really going to try and exorcise the house? He'd let her have something to eat and drink first. She needed her energy before he knocked the stuffing back out of her.

293

It had crossed his mind to not even tell her what they had been talking about last night, but this directly involved her. The house belonged to Kate. It was her dream – her money that she'd invested in it – and it was her body and soul that whatever it was that dwelled in the house wanted. He had to tell her. There was no choice in the matter. She would never forgive him if something went wrong.

After following her downstairs, he watched as she filled the kettle. He could have kicked himself when he realised he'd left the whisky bottle and two glasses on the kitchen table in full view. He picked it up, carried it out of the kitchen and took it into the living room. He shoved it into a cupboard that he never used so it was out of her sight. As he went back into the kitchen, she was rinsing the two glasses under the hot water tap.

'You didn't need to do that, but thank you. I don't expect that because I'm an alcoholic who can't control her thirst that you can't ever have another drink or have alcohol in your own house. That would be incredibly selfish and unfair of me, but until I'm sure I can handle it I really do appreciate it.'

'I'm so sorry, Kate. Father Joe was a little bit upset so I offered him a drink. I didn't even think. I'm so used to being on my own and not cleaning up after myself.'

She laughed. 'It's your house, Ollie, and you're entitled to do whatever you want here.'

'Yes, but I want you to feel as if you can be safe here and not have to worry.' He looked at her and wondered if now was a good time to break the news to her.

'So Joe, Beatrice and I kind of came up with a plan last night. Well, it was more Beatrice if I'm truthful. Joe wasn't so keen to agree to it.'

'Really? Are you going to tell me what it is then or do I have to guess?'

'I'm not too sure you're going to want to hear it. I couldn't get my head around it last night. It sounds so ridiculous – like a plot from a scary movie, not something that would happen in real life.'

A loud knock on the door made Ollie jump.

'Are you all right, Ollie? You look like you've seen a ghost.'

He shook his head. 'I'm fine. Just a bit on edge. I'll just get the door.'

He came back in followed by Father Joe.

'Morning, Kate, how are you feeling today?'

'Better, thank you.'

'Good, that's good. Has Ollie told you our plan?'

'He was just about to when you knocked.'

Ollie shrugged. The priest looked like crap. Ollie hadn't looked much better when he'd cleaned his teeth earlier.

'Why don't you sit down and we can discuss it with you whilst we're waiting for Beatrice to arrive? I feel it's only right we tell you what we know,' said Joe. He looked at Ollie as if to call him a wimp and he completely agreed with the man. He'd never been one to shy away from a challenge, but what they were asking this poor bloke to do just because Beatrice had a hunch was insane.

Joe continued, 'Well, Beatrice thinks that Sister Agnes has been trying her best to protect you from whatever dark force is growing in strength in your house. The demon is getting stronger. We are going to go to the convent and do a full-blown exorcism. I've asked for help from the archbishop only it won't be today – or for a long time come to think of it – and I'm afraid time is a luxury that we can't afford.'

Ollie stole a look at Kate whose mouth had dropped. Her eyes were wide open with shock. She turned to look at Ollie who nodded as if to confirm everything that Joe had just said was completely normal.

She finally found her voice. 'Are you sure you can do this?'

Both men nodded. There was another knock on the door and Ollie got up to let Beatrice inside. She came into the kitchen dressed from head to foot in black, looking like some geriatric ninja. Looking at Kate's face, she sat down.

'Ah, I see you've told her then.'

Joe nodded. 'Well, we've told her some of it, not all of it.'

'This is insane. Do you realise what you are saying or what could happen?'

Beatrice took hold of her hand. 'Kate, we haven't got any choice. It was a mistake to remove Agnes's head from the house. We didn't realise it was her who was trying to protect you. Of course her head should be reunited with her body. But whilst it was inside the walls of that house her spirit remained strong and she kept the demon from taking over. I'm sorry, there is no way we can sugar-coat it and make it sound better. The evil entity that lives and breathes life into that house is gathering strength now Agnes's bond to the place has been broken. You might not believe in any of this, but I do and Joe should. The Bible is full of tales of battles between God and Satan. Just because we don't see them every day doesn't mean they don't exist.'

'So the crosses and footsteps – they were Agnes?'

'Yes, I very much think so. She was trying to protect you from the horror that lives inside that house. It will stop at nothing until you're dead.'

'I took them all down. I hid them outside in the barns because they freaked me out and she was only trying to help me. Oh God I'm so sorry. Why didn't she tell me this?'

'I think she was trying to in her own way. Some of us—' Beatrice pointed to Joe '—well some of us have a gift, a sixth sense. Maybe if we'd been the ones living there we would have figured that out. I double checked what you said last night about the nuns dying so horrifically and it was all true.'

'So what are we going to do? I can't lose that house. It means everything to me.'

'I know and you are in grave danger now. Whatever it is will only get stronger the longer we leave it there.'

'As morbid as this sounds, Beatrice is right. I can't go on living like this: scared to be in my own house and feeling so ill all the time.'

'Right then, what are we waiting for? Let's go do this,' said Joe.

***

Joe had decided if he wanted to look the part he'd go the full monty, as his mum would say. He was starting to sweat underneath the heavy, black cassock. Ollie smiled at him, obviously noticing how uncomfortable he looked.

'Thank you, Joe, I'll take you in my car along with Kate. Beatrice, you go in yours – just in case we need two cars.'

'Please can we call at the church first? I want to pray with Sister Agnes.'

All three of them got into the car and Ollie drove them to the church. Beatrice followed behind, parking next to Ollie.

They all got out and Joe led the way to the grave where Agnes was buried. 'Sister Agnes, I don't know if you can hear me. I hope that you're happy your head has been found and will be back with you very soon. I know it's been a very long time. We also know that you've been trying to help Kate up at the convent, but whatever it is that dwells inside the house is gathering strength. We are asking for your help. If you're able to, can you help us to fight it and send it back to where it belongs so Kate and her family can fill the house with love and light? Amen.'

Everyone else muttered, 'Amen'.

Ollie turned to Kate. 'I think it's time we went back to the house, don't you? Let's see what we can do. Joe, are you ready?'

All eyes were on him, waiting for his reply.

Beatrice spoke first. 'Yes, I think we should too.' She smiled at Joe.

Joe wanted to tell them all to *fuck off and leave me alone,* but he couldn't. For whatever reason, he'd been dragged into this, so

297

there was no going back. Technically blessing Kate's house should be a piece of piss. He silently thanked Agnes for giving her life to the church and asked her again if she would help him up at the house. A warm feeling filled his heart as if someone had rubbed deep heat onto it. He felt as if somehow she was trying to fill him with hope and comfort. He was the last one to leave her small graveside, but he whispered, 'Thank you,' to her as he walked away.

He felt much calmer. The churning in his stomach and indigestion in his chest had gone. He had one last job to do here and then his work was done. He wasn't sure if this was a sign from God that he was doing the right thing or whether he was plain delusional. He knew that he was going to try his best to free that house of the evil that had been lurking inside it for over eighty years. He just hoped that he could do it without any of them being hurt or mentally scarred in any way. Maybe this had been why he had felt such a strong pull to become a priest.

This moment in time could have been his destiny from the very beginning. As he walked through the graveyard he was greeted by wonderful silence and the warmth of the sun shining down on his face, which he took as another sign from God that he was doing the right thing. They went to their cars and agreed to meet up outside the convent. None of them were to go in until all of them were present.

1955

Crosby had been retired from the police force for three months. His beloved wife had died the week after his retirement and he was missing her more than ever. His house, their house, was like an empty shell. There was no life in it anymore. As he sat in the chair she used to sit and do her knitting every night, he closed his eyes. He was so tired of it all. Tired of being sad, tired of being lonely, but the thing he was most tired about was the fact that earlier today he'd had a visit from Tony, who was now the sergeant in charge of the small police station. Crosby had known the minute he saw the police car pull up outside his house what the visit was about. He'd opened the door before Tony had to knock on it.

'You'd better come in, lad. Congratulations by the way. I don't think I've seen you since you got your promotion.'

'Thanks. How are you keeping? It must be lonely around here without Vera.'

Crosby nodded, turning his head away so Tony couldn't see the tears that filled his eyes and were threatening to fall. He lifted his sleeve and brushed his eyes with it. Then he coughed to clear his throat.

'Aye, you're not wrong. It's miserable is what it is. I never knew what a boring job it was making the tea until I had to do it myself every day the week after she passed. Poor lass had been doing it for forty-four years and never complained once.'

'That's because Vera enjoyed it, you daft bugger. She made the best beef stew and dumplings I've ever tasted in my life. She was a lovely woman and I'm sorry that she's gone.'

Crosby nodded. 'She was. So what brings me the pleasure of a visit from you?' He didn't really want to know, because he already had a sneaking feeling what it was.

'The church have decided to open the convent; it's going to be an orphanage.'

The words hung in the air. Crosby inhaled sharply. His throat constricted and he felt as if he couldn't breathe.

'Sarge, you've gone grey. Are you all right? Come on, let's get you sat down.'

Tony took his arm and directed him to the chair he'd been sitting in; then he went in search of a bottle of whisky. He knew that Crosby was partial to a drink so didn't have to look very far. He came back into the sitting room with a half empty bottle and a glass. Crosby watched as he poured out a large measure and handed him the glass.

'Here, drink this. I'm sorry, I didn't want to bother you with this. I know you have enough on your plate, but I couldn't not tell you. I didn't want you to find out at the post office or the pub. I think you have a right to know and I have to tell you, boss, I'm terrified. I don't know what to do; I've spoken to the priest who's taken over from Father Patrick. I've phoned the archbishop. None of them are interested because none of them ever set foot in that house. They never saw the horrors we saw or dealt with the aftermath, and now they're going to fill it with kids who have no families, no one to love them. They're sending them to their deaths. All those innocent souls are going to get dragged into whatever dark place that exists in there and I don't know how to stop it.'

Crosby swallowed the amber liquid in one mouthful. 'They can't. Don't they realise what they're dealing with?'

'Obviously not – they don't care because they weren't here when it happened. What should I do?'

'Burn the fucking place to the ground. I'm sorry, Tony, but I can't see any other way around it. If it's burnt down they can't open it up as an orphanage, can they?'

'I can't do that. I'd end up getting arrested and lose my job. I'd go to prison. I have too much to lose.'

Crosby nodded. 'I suppose not. Well then, Tony, I don't know what to suggest. I do know that whatever the price you can't let innocent children live there. It doesn't bear thinking about. I'll phone the church tomorrow and speak to the priest. I don't really know him that well, although he seems a decent enough chap. He came to see me after Vera died and he's been a couple of times since. Maybe it's time to fill him in on the history of the convent. If he's got any conscience he will agree with us and do his best to put a stop to it.'

Tony nodded.

'That would be great, thank you. I'm sorry I had to bother you with this, but I didn't know who to turn to. You were there

– you know how bad that house is. What would you do if you were me?'

'I've told you, son, burn it down until there's nothing but ashes left.'

'I wish I could. If there was some way possible, believe me I would.'

Tony had left with the promise to come back and let him know if they'd managed to stop the convent being opened up again, but Crosby knew. He knew fine well that the powers that be had decided and they wouldn't change their minds. Hell, he wouldn't believe it if he hadn't witnessed firsthand the brutal deaths that house had caused.

He looked at the bottle of whisky, then picked it up and took a long gulp from the bottle. He stood up. He knew what he had to do and he was going to do it. Screwing the cap back on the bottle, he carried it to the garage where he kept the box of cleaning rags that Vera no longer had use for. He took the heavy metal can he kept full of petrol and put it into the boot of his car along with the rags, then he put a crowbar and sledgehammer inside.

It was time to end this before anyone else died. He should have done it years ago. He opened the garage door then got into his car, half expecting it not to start as if the house would know what he was going to do and try to stop him. He looked at his watch. It was almost eight o'clock. With any luck he'd be home before anyone realised the house was on fire. He'd go to bed and lock the door in case the police came to speak to him. Hopefully it would be Tony. Even though he would know it was him, he would realise he'd done it for the right reason and decide not to come and arrest him. If he did arrest him then so be it. At least he'd have some company in prison.

He never passed a single soul on the way to the convent; the roads were deserted – so far so good. As he approached the drive his head, which had been slightly muzzy, cleared. All traces of the alcohol disappeared from his system. He wished he was still drunk and looked at the whisky bottle on the seat next to him. He turned into the drive. He could turn around; it wasn't too late. He could forget about it, but he was here for the right reason. It was the perfect time. There was no one living in that house. As the car rounded the bend, the headlights illuminated the house. Crosby's heart skipped a beat.

It loomed against the backdrop of the inky sky like some giant beast, but he forced himself to keep on driving towards it despite the cold shard of fear that had lodged inside his chest. There was no going back. This had to end now, tonight. He stopped in front of the house and grabbed the bottle of whisky. He unscrewed the cap and took an extra-long gulp, then he took one of the rags from the boot of the car and pushed it inside until it was soaking up the alcohol.

He lifted the heavy can of petrol out of the boot and began dragging it towards the front door. After fumbling with the cap, he managed to unscrew it and poured it around the front door, then along the perimeter of the house as far as he could go until he'd emptied the can. As he ran back to the car he took out the box of matches he kept in the glove compartment. With hands that were trembling, he tried to strike one to light the rag in the whisky bottle. It blew straight out. He struck another and this one snapped in half.

Praying for God to give him a break and at least help him halfway he struck one more, which lit. He held it to the alcohol-soaked rag and grinned, then he stumbled towards the house and launched it at the puddle of petrol he'd left by the front doors. As the glass bottle smashed there was a loud whooshing sound and the flames rose. They licked at the heavy oak doors. Movement from the upstairs window made him look up. He was horrified to see Vera watching him from up there. She was banging on the glass for him to get her out.

'Vera, oh my God. I'm so sorry. I'm coming. I'll get you out, love.'

It never crossed his mind that Vera was dead and even if the house burnt to the ground it couldn't hurt her. Shouting her name, he ran towards the front steps to get to the front door. He stepped in a puddle of petrol and it soaked the bottom of his trouser hems, which he'd been meaning to take up and had never got around to it. As he carried on shouting her name and trying to get through the flames to rescue her, his trousers caught alight and within seconds he was fully ablaze.

Crosby stumbled back, falling down the stone steps. His body burned as the flames engulfed him. As he fell to the floor and looked up, he could no longer see Vera. In her place was the young woman with the darkest hair and the reddest lips he'd ever seen. He gasped. *Lilith.* As the flames began to burn the flesh from his bones, he realised he'd been tricked and he prayed for death to come quick. The house had won yet again and this time he was the victim.

***

Tony couldn't settle. He kept thinking about what Crosby had said and he wondered if he was right. Maybe they should burn the house to the ground. The telephone on his desk rang and he picked it up. 'What now? Christ, have you called the fire brigade? Right, I'm on my way.'

It didn't take a genius to work out that Crosby had decided to finally do something about the convent and had taken the matter into his own hands. He ran from his office and slapped Jed around the head. Jed was in his chair, eyes shut and snoring loudly. Jed jumped up.

'Sorry, boss, what's the matter?'

'The convent is on fire. Come on.'

'What's the rush? It's empty and you were complaining about it earlier. Aren't you glad to see it burning down?'

Tony never answered him as he dashed towards the car. Both

men got in and he drove as fast as he could through the narrow, winding roads to get to the house. Although he wanted the house to burn to the ground, he wanted to make sure Crosby wasn't in any trouble.

As they approached the house, they could smell the acrid smell of smouldering wood and something else. Tony knew before he even got out of the car what he was going to find and his heart felt heavy. *Crosby, you old fool, what have you done?* He stopped the car next to Crosby's and climbed out. The only thing alight was the body lying at the foot of the steps to the convent entrance. It was almost out, but the stench was horrendous. Tony covered his nose and mouth as he heard Jed gag next to him.

'Is that...? Oh my God that's a person! Oh shit, I'm going to...'

He didn't have time to finish his sentence as he stumbled away and was violently sick all over his own boots. Tony stepped as close as he could. He couldn't recognise his old boss and friend, but he knew it was him without a shadow of a doubt. Crosby's car was there.

Tony looked up to see if the house was burning down. The flames had all extinguished themselves. There was some smoke damage to the brickwork and the front door had black singe marks running up it, but apart from that there was no real damage. Tony knew why. There was no way the evil in that house was ready to give up without a fight. Crosby had died for nothing; the house didn't even look as if it needed anything more than a hose down and the door needed a lick of paint. Movement from the upstairs window caught his eye, but instead of looking up like Crosby had, Tony chose to ignore it.

'Boss, boss, there's someone inside. Upstairs. I just saw them.'

'No, you didn't. It was the curtain blowing in the wind. That front room is draughty; it always looks like that. I need you to get something out of the car to cover him over with. I can't bear to look at him like this.'

'But I swear...'

'And I'm telling you, Jed, if you know what's good for you, go and get a blanket. There is no one in that house. It's been empty for years.'

Chapter 19

Ollie and Kate arrived first, closely followed by Beatrice and Joe. Ollie took hold of Kate's hand. 'I have no idea what's going to happen – or if anything will – but I want you to know that I'm falling in love with you more and more each day. If we can't sort this thing out and it's too dangerous for you to live here, then I'd like you to move in with me. You can sell the house. It should get a good price with the amount of renovations that have been done and you can find somewhere else.'

'I love you too, Oliver, and thank you. I also love this house and I don't know why I feel so strongly about it, I just do. Today I'm going to fight all I can to reclaim it. Do you believe in reincarnation? From the very first moment I set eyes on this place I felt as if I was finally home, as if I'd been away a very long time. I know I was destined to buy it and turn it back into a house filled with light and love. That's what I intend to do. Whatever evil is lurking inside there isn't going to scare me off. I'm reclaiming my home and it can bloody well go and fuck off back to wherever it came from.'

Despite the graveness of the situation he laughed. 'Maybe you're right. I wonder if you were one of the original nuns who lived here. Before it all went horribly wrong and turned bad this would have been an amazing place to be. Well, if you stay and fight I'll be right by your side.'

'Thank you, but if you need to leave then you must go. If you are in any danger then you get out as fast as you can and don't worry about me.'

'What about you? What if you're in danger?'

'I have a feeling that Agnes and the other sisters might help me to find the courage to fight my corner. I truly believe that this was meant to happen, that things happen for a reason. My whole reason for buying this place was to come here and stand up to whatever it is that's been lurking in there for far too long. I think that God wants me to reclaim his house of worship.'

Oliver didn't know if she was delusional, coming down with some kind of fever or being plain brave. He wished he felt as confident as she did. Kate jumped out. Ollie followed along with Joe. Beatrice, who had been having an animated conversation on her phone, also got out of her car. They stood in a circle as Joe blessed them all, asking God to protect them with his love and light.

Ollie thought he was about to throw up everything he'd ever eaten in his entire life, his stomach was churning so much. Beatrice's cheeks had lost every ounce of colour that had been there moments ago and Joe looked ashen. They were scared, but if they didn't try and do something more lives would be lost. Only Kate seemed to be glowing. Her skin looked fresh and her normally blue eyes were shining brightly. There was an aura of calm spreading out from her, which the others could feel through their fingertips, making them feel slightly better about the whole about-to-go-into-battle-with-the-devil thing. The clouds filtered over the sun, blocking out the bright light and making it gloomy.

Joe broke the circle. 'I'll lead and begin to bless the house. Where should we begin?'

***

Kate thought about it for a split second.

'I think whatever it is likes to hide up in the attic, so should we bless the rest of the house so it can't escape? We could corner it up there.'

Joe nodded. His voice came out as a whisper. 'Sounds like a plan to me.'

She let go of Ollie's and Beatrice's hands and led the way to the front door. It opened before she could even put the key into the lock.

Ollie caught Beatrice's arm. 'Wait, what if the house has been burgled and there's someone still inside?'

'Ollie, I don't think any burglar in their right mind would break into this house. It's always had a stigma to it, a bit of an urban legend sort of thing. That's why I was so surprised when I found out the church had sold it to a woman, a single woman. But now I think I understand. I think Kate's right. Her whole life has been engineered to lead up to this very moment. I believe in her one hundred per cent. I think she's been sent by God to put this right – to make up for the past – and I believe that he thinks she's strong enough to do his work.

'Forgive me, Joe, but I don't think this is about you. I don't think you blessing the house is enough to make it leave. It hasn't worked in the past. I do think that Kate's love for this place and her belief that it can be the family home she's always dreamt of is the key to this. With her connection to the house's past through Agnes, I think that Kate will be the one strong enough to rid the house of the demon once and for all. Although don't get me wrong, I'm not saying you shouldn't try anyway. We need all the help we can get – no offence.'

'None taken, Beatrice; let's hope the pair of you are right. I feel like I'm some pawn in a game of chess that's being played between God and the Devil. So it's our move. Let's hope we can make it to checkmate before the dark side does.'

Kate smiled at them both. 'You're making it sound as if it's the next instalment in the *Star Wars* series. Come on, let's do this so I can reclaim my home and life.'

She pushed the front door as wide open as it would go. The minute she stepped inside she could feel the drop in the temperature. As she breathed out, a thick cloud of fog filled the air in front of her face. Ollie stepped in behind her and did the same. They hadn't turned the heating off yesterday before they'd left so there was no way it should have been this cold inside. Joe and Beatrice followed them. Immediately Joe prayed, asking God to bless the house.

***

As they went from room to room downstairs the light outside faded fast. Beatrice looked at her watch. It was only one. There was no way it should be so dark. The curtains were all open and the darkness cast shadows in the rooms. She thought she saw the shadowy figures of three nuns standing in the hall at the bottom of the staircase and tugged Kate's sleeve to get her attention, but when she turned back they had disappeared. She leant towards Kate's ear. 'They're here. I've just seen three nuns standing by the stairs.'

'Good, that's good. I'll take all the help we can get.'

'So will I.'

As each room was blessed there were no incidents – nothing to scare them and make them turn and flee. Joe got louder with each incident-free blessing.

***

Ollie, who stood behind them, thought that maybe they'd got it all wrong. That they'd made a big drama out of a few unexplained occurrences. They'd be sitting around the kitchen table in ten minutes laughing at themselves. As they climbed the stairs to the first floor he heard the footsteps – the same light ones as they flitted from room to room. Beatrice nodded at Kate. They'd heard them too.

Ollie looked at Joe. He was so engrossed in his prayers he clearly hadn't heard anything. They blessed three of the five bedrooms and were about to enter the one Kate's daughters had claimed as their own, when there was a loud crack above their heads. It sounded like a thunderclap, but it wasn't thunder. The weather was far too cold for it. Footsteps began to cross the attic floor above their heads. They were so loud that the floor started to vibrate. Ollie whispered, 'We need to get out and ring the cops.'

Kate shook her head. 'No, there's nothing they can do. Joe was right. Whatever it is has been hiding up there hoping we'll leave it alone. It knows we're getting nearer and it's trying to scare us away. Well, fuck it. I'm not going anywhere.'

Ollie thought that at this very moment in time Kate had finally succumbed to a nervous breakdown, that she was mad. His hands were shaking and he was so scared that his feet didn't want to move. He couldn't move forwards or backwards. He was literally frozen to the spot. Kate pointed at the ceiling and Joe nodded. He continued praying and Ollie couldn't miss how the Bible, which had moments ago been held steady in his hands, was now trembling from side to side. Joe's voice was barely a whisper.

Beatrice closed her eyes. She nodded her head. 'Yes, I hear you. I know you're here. Thank you.'

She looked at Kate.

'Sisters Mary and Edith are here. They want you to know that you're doing the right thing and should carry on.'

'Where's Sister Agnes?'

Beatrice closed her eyes. 'I don't know, Kate. I can't get a hold of her. It's either blocking me or her. I can't say for sure that she's here, Kate. Are you sure you want to continue if Agnes isn't here with us?'

Before Kate could answer the walls and floor began to pound as if someone was hammering on them with huge fists.

'I don't think we have a choice, Beatrice. We have to finish it. I don't care who or what you are, we're coming up. This is my house now and you need to get out.' Kate screamed the words at the top of her voice and the banging stopped. 'See, we just need to let it know who the boss is.' She giggled and Ollie looked at her in disbelief. Her face didn't look the same as it had outside. Once again it had taken on the distorted, misshapen look it had borne last night. He looked at Beatrice who was also studying Kate's face. She took hold of Kate's hand.

'Are you sure you want to continue, Kate? You're so cold.'

Kate threw back her head and laughed; only it wasn't the normal, quite high-pitched laugh she usually had. This was a deep, gravelly sound.

'Of course I want to continue, you stupid fucking cow. If you're going to talk such rubbish get out of my house.'

'Kate, whatever is trying to get inside you stop it. Block it. Say the Lord's Prayer, sing your favourite song, but don't let it get inside your mind. You can do it.'

Kate's head flew around to stare at Beatrice, and Ollie took a step back. Her lips were peeled back in a sneer and there were drops of spittle on her lips. Beatrice managed to keep hold of her arm.

'Get out of her now. You're not welcome inside Kate or this house. Come to mention it, take your filthy self and get out. I command you by the power invested in me by God.'

At the mention of God, Kate snatched her arm away from Beatrice.

'Go and die, you interfering old woman.'

Beatrice shook her head. 'Not today.'

Joe, who had been watching the scene before him play out, looked on in horror. He stepped forward and pressed his cross against Kate's head.

'Get out of her, beast. You have no right to be in there.'

She looked in his eyes and smiled. 'Why, would you rather I came into your head, Father?' Kate's voice was light and mocking. 'Would you like to see some graphic images of what your God won't ever show you? I can show you how good hell is and I can change your life if you want me to, priest.'

***

Kate, who could hear the voice she didn't recognise coming from her throat, closed her eyes and summoned up the picture she had in her head of Agnes. A loud growl erupted from her throat and her hands flew up to her face as if to try and block the image of the elderly nun out.

Joe continued to pray, then said, 'Tell me your name, demon. I want to know your name.'

Kate didn't want to lose the image of Agnes. She kept her eyes closed. The elderly nun was tiny, but she was surrounded by a halo of pure, white light and she was smiling at Kate and nodding her head. A voice whispered in her ear, 'Keep fighting, Kate. It's scared of you. That's why it's trying to get inside your head. Don't let it.'

She shook her head, trying to free it of the blackness that was threatening to take over. 'Get the fuck out of my head, demon.' There was a loud thud from upstairs and suddenly she could think clearly again. She opened her eyes and stared straight into Joe's.

'It's scared; it's hiding upstairs. We need to carry on and chase it out while we have the strength. Agnes is here, but she's struggling to keep up. She's still quite weak,' Joe told her.

Ollie was as white as Beatrice. Kate knew he wanted to leave and drag her with him.

***

312

Joe could see the darkness had left Kate's face for the time being and she looked as if she was full of light and determination.

'Come on, I'm claiming my house back once and for all. I don't intend to spend the rest of my life looking over my shoulder playing cat and mouse with some evil bitch from hell. It's a woman. I can't believe it. I always thought that demons were male, not female.'

Joe shrugged. 'They can take on whatever form they wish. You're right. We should go and finish this.'

He could have slapped his own forehead as the words left his lips, but Kate was right. It was time to send this demon back to where it came from. He would finish what Father Patrick and Sergeant Crosby had tried to do and failed. He didn't want to live the rest of his life in fear of this house. He went first, closely followed by Kate.

Beatrice tugged Ollie's hand and whispered in his ear. 'If it's too much you can wait downstairs. This isn't going to be pretty and it's dangerous.'

He looked at her and hissed, 'I'm scared fucking stiff, but I'm not about to leave those two alone to fight the Stay Puft Marshmallow Man or whatever ghoul it is that is waiting in the attic for them. I need to see it with my own eyes or I'll spend the rest of my life locked up in a mental institution, rocking backwards and forwards, scared of going to the toilet on my own.'

'Good, because Kate needs you.'

They followed them along the corridor to the attic. Joe blessed the doorway to the attic. He anointed it with holy water but snatched his hand back as steam rose from the wooden door, burning his fingertips.

***

Kate, who was fired up and angry that it had been inside her mind, threw the door open and turned on the light.

'Coming up, ready or not, you mother fucker. You are getting out of my house whether you want to or not. I command you, God commands you and the lovely Sisters Mary, Edith and Agnes command you.'

The growl was so loud it deafened them. Kate had never felt such anger in her life at being violated. She ran towards it.

***

Ollie thought that she was mad and was probably going to need antipsychotic drugs to calm her down. Still, he followed her because he wasn't going to let her fight this on her own. As he reached the top step he almost fell back into Joe. Kate was standing in the middle of the attic and in front of her was a huge, black winged beast with the reddest eyes that pierced through the dark.

Both of them were locked in some form of battle. Kate didn't utter a word and Ollie wondered if it was because she had just scared herself catatonic, because he didn't know if he'd ever be able to hold a normal conversation after this ever again.

Joe stepped in behind him and whispered, 'Oh fuck.' Ollie tried to walk towards Kate to stand with her, but he couldn't move his feet. The three of them were stuck. There was an invisible force holding them back. The stench of rotting meat and burnt flesh filled the room, making Ollie gag.

Beatrice began to recite her favourite prayer over and over again in a whisper as if her voice wasn't working properly. Maybe that was frozen as well.

***

Kate couldn't speak. The multitude of voices crying out for help inside her mind was deafening, and the thing in front of her was grinning at her.

'Get out of my head. I'm telling you now to leave me alone. Get out of my house and go back to hell.'

The laughter was so loud it made her brain hurt as it filled her mind.

'You're a strange one, I'll give you that. Such strength for a woman so weak-willed. Where does it come from?'

The voice that spoke next didn't belong to Kate. It was much older and slightly hoarse. 'It comes from God, demon, and you should know that. You might have reigned supreme for a little while down here, but know your place. God is claiming his house back to fill with light, so you can go back to hell and get out of here.'

The figure in front of her wavered a little and looked a little lighter.

'We cast you out of this house. I revoke your invitation to come inside. You're no longer welcome to be here. This house belongs to God and Kate. You have no place here, so leave now and don't you dare come back.'

'And who is going to make me? You, old woman? You didn't manage it the first time. What makes you think you can manage it now?'

Kate felt the room fill with brilliant white light and she turned her head to see Agnes holding hands with two other nuns to her left. As she turned to her right she saw Ellen, who was holding hands with another nun, a small child and a big man. Both Ellen and Agnes reached out for Kate's hands. Joe had stepped forward and was holding on to the young boy and the other nun, all of them standing in a row.

'By the power of God, I command you to leave this house now. Your invitation to enter has been well and truly revoked, motherfucker, so get out now so God can fill it with his love.' Kate screamed at the black figure, which was shrinking in size before her eyes. The light coming from them was blinding. All of them raised their hands, pushing the light forwards until it completely consumed the black beast in front of them.

A scream of fury filled the room. It was so loud Ollie thought he was going to wet himself. He couldn't believe what he was seeing. Beatrice clasped his hand and they stood hand in hand behind Kate and the heavenly row of angels next to her. Later on, when Ollie would have time to think about it, he would realise that was the only way to describe the sight in front of his own eyes. Ellen was standing in front of him, clasping Kate's hand, and he wondered for a second if he was dreaming it all. It was so outrageous to see his dead wife standing shoulder to shoulder with his girlfriend to fight a demon.

He'd lost his mind. Any minute now he was going to wake up on a hospital bed and find out he'd had a mental breakdown and this had all been one bad trip. The entire attic was now filled with so much light. He noticed something else: the atmosphere up here no longer felt menacing. It felt warm and embracing. Ellen turned around to face him.

'I love you, Oliver, but I'm tired now. I need to go and rest. Agnes is going to take me to the light. Look after yourself and Kate. I will see you again, just not for a very long time.'

One by one the figures in front of him shone brighter and brighter, and then they were gone. It was Joe who caught Kate as her legs gave way underneath her. Ollie was still staring up at the roof to see where they'd gone. Joe turned and made his way with Kate in his arms down the narrow staircase.

'I think she's dead. Phone an ambulance now.'

The panic that filled Ollie's chest was so painful it crushed his heart. 'No!' he screamed at the top of his voice. 'She can't be.'

He followed Joe down the narrow staircase. Kate was like a rag doll in his arms. Joe kicked the door to the nearest room open and lay her down on the bed. Ollie was trying to phone 999 but couldn't get a signal. He ran across and felt for a pulse. Beatrice pushed him to one side. 'Heavens above, she's not dead;

she's fainted. Get some water. The poor lass – it's been too much for her. Kate, Kate, can you hear me, love? It's over. You can open your eyes; you did it. You sent it back and set them all free.'

Kate's eyelids fluttered and Ollie ended the phone call. The last thing they needed right now was the police turning up to see what they'd all been doing. Kate looked around the room. She saw Joe who smiled at her, and Beatrice who mouthed 'thank God', and then she saw Ollie who bent down and kissed her softly on the lips.

'Phew, we thought you were a goner.'

She pushed herself up on her elbows. Tears filled her eyes.

'Did you see them all? It was amazing. They all came to help. Do you think we did it? Did we send it back?'

Beatrice nodded. 'Yes, you did, you all did. I've never seen anything like it. What a beautiful band of angels. You set them all free, Kate; they're no longer tied to this house. They've all gone to the light.'

Kate looked at Ollie. 'Are you okay? Did you see Ellen?'

It was his turn to brush away the tears. 'I did. I can't believe it. I'm just glad she's at peace now. It's all I ever wanted for her.'

Joe shook his head. 'If I hadn't just witnessed that with my very own two eyes, I would be thinking you were all stark raving bonkers. Seriously, Kate, well done; what a team we all make.'

Kate laughed. 'Thank you, Joe; however, I'd rather this was a one-off and we didn't have to repeat any of this ever again.'

'Oh, I wouldn't worry about that, Kate, I can't see any demon in their right mind wanting to pick a fight with you in a hurry.'

'I bloody well hope you're right.'

Ollie helped her to sit up. 'Come on, I know you've done a better job than Bill Murray or Dan Aykroyd ever could, but for tonight can we please just go back to my house?'

She wrapped her arm around his neck. 'Of course we can. I feel so tired – as if my energy's been depleted.'

He helped her up. Taking her hand, he led her downstairs.

317

Beatrice and Joe followed. As they got to the front door Beatrice turned to look around. 'The house feels completely different.'

Joe nodded at her. 'It's gone, no doubt about it. It feels so much lighter in here. This is going to be a splendid home for your family, Kate. And one day when you feel up to it, perhaps you could research the history and document exactly what happened. Who knows, you could have a number one bestseller on your hands.'

Six weeks later

The house was almost finished. Kate's bedroom was now a dining room. She and Ollie had moved into the room that once belonged to the gentle nun called Agnes. Each room now had a cross above the door and Kate thought that Agnes would approve. The living room had a big, open fire, which Ollie was currently stoking. The girls had finished decorating the huge, real pine tree that they had picked out from the Christmas tree farm two days ago. The fairy lights twinkled brightly, reflecting against the gold and silver balls that adorned its branches.

Autumn and Summer had just set up the Monopoly board and they were about to start playing when there was a knock on the door. Kate looked at the clock on the mantel. It was six o'clock and they weren't expecting any visitors. Ollie stood up.

'I'll get it.'

He went to answer the door. As he peered through the peep-hole he felt his blood run cold. Standing on the other side were two of the detectives who had come the night Ethan had found the head. God, it all seemed so long ago. Both Ollie and Kate had tried their best to forget about what had happened and the fact that Agnes's head had been found.

He opened the door and smiled at them. 'Good evening, detectives, what brings you out here on a cold, snowy night? Is everything okay?'

He stepped to one side to let them come in.

318

'There's been an incident at the hospital and we need to speak to you. Is now a good time?'

Ollie shrugged, trying his best not to look like a major criminal. 'I suppose it's as good as any.'

'Is Ms Parker around? We need to speak to the both of you.'

'Why don't you take a seat in the kitchen? I'll go and get her for you.' He led them to the kitchen and pointed to the chairs. As he turned Kate appeared. Her face was ashen and he shook his head and lifted his finger to his lips. They both went, and sat down at the table.

'Hello, detectives, is everything all right?'

'Good evening, Ms Parker. Not really, we have a bit of a problem. You remember that head one of the builders found and we took to the hospital?'

Both of them nodded.

'Of course you would. It's not every day you find a shrivelled up head in the hall, is it? Well, when the pathologist went to look at it a few days ago, there was a bit of a problem. It wasn't there.'

Ollie spoke. 'What do you mean it wasn't there? Where was it then?'

'That's the million-dollar question; we'd all like to know where it is so we were wondering if you knew.'

'Why would we know where it is? We phoned you to take it away in the first place.'

'Well, that's exactly what I said, but we just thought we'd better check with you.'

Kate shook her head. 'I have no idea where it could be.'

Ollie ran his fingers through his hair. 'You think that we have something to do with the missing head?'

'No, I'm not sure. I can't prove who has taken it and I have no idea why anyone would want to steal back the mummified head of a nun who was murdered in 1933. So I'm here for you to tell me – if you wanted to confess?'

Ollie sat back and smiled. 'We have no idea what you're talking about. The last we heard, it was being buried in Sister Agnes's grave.' Ollie thought he was doing a great job of not sounding like he was about to crack up and confess to it, even when he didn't know where it could be.

'Now that's a shame because I have to say I'm intrigued to say the least. We were supposed to do that, but it got delayed and now we have permission to do it we've discovered that it's missing. I don't know how or why someone would take it. Unfortunately for me there's no evidence and if I'm being totally honest whoever it is has done us a bit of a favour. The bosses have issued a media blackout, as have the hospital. No one wants the bad press or to have to confess to losing that poor nun's head and I suppose technically – seeing as how it was found in your house – it could be seen as belonging to you. Now I've ruled out devil worship and I've checked your eBay accounts to make sure you haven't flogged it, but I'm completely stumped. Did you bring it back and put it where you found it, Ms Parker?'

Kate shook her head. 'No, I did not.'

'Well, in that case then you won't mind showing us that panel and hidey hole again, will you?'

'Of course not; you can search the entire house.'

Ollie stood up. 'Yes you can, but you'd better come back with a warrant because I've never heard anything so preposterous in my life. What would we want with her head?'

'That is what we're trying to find out.'

Kate led them to the panel in the hall and felt along the top until she found the raised edge. She pressed it down and it slid open to reveal a black, empty space. Both men took out torches from their pockets and bent down to have a look around. Satisfied it was empty, they turned off their lights and nodded.

'Thank you, I didn't really think you'd have put it back there to be honest, but you just never know. When you've been in the job as long as I have you don't take anything for granted. You know we've been to the church and checked the grave for Sister

Agnes and that hasn't been tampered with. Whatever they've done with it they must have had a good reason. It's a strange one.'

Kate folded her arms across her chest. 'I'm really sorry, detective, but I have no idea what you're talking about. As my partner said you're welcome to come back and search the house, but it won't be tonight and not without a warrant.'

'That won't be necessary, Ms Parker. We have no further reason to search your house. Thank you for your time; we'll let you get on now. If we hear anything we'll be in touch.'

Oliver opened the door for them and watched as they stepped out into the cold. Snow had begun to fall again and the ground was a blanket of white. He shut the door behind them and Kate fell into his arms.

'Oh my God, do you think they're going to come back?'

He shook his head. 'I don't think so. Like he said they have no proof or motive for us to have taken it. He was just fishing, but I wonder who took it? Come on, I'm going to thrash you at Monopoly and show you just how much of a brilliant businessman I am.'

Kate couldn't help laughing and followed him down the corridor to the lounge where her daughters were arguing over who was going to be the top hat.

**

The petite woman stood staring up at the house, the house she'd owned like no other. She saw the car's bright headlights coming towards her and stepped back into the darkness so the driver couldn't see her. Pushing her long, black hair behind her ears she let her tongue run over her blood-red lips. The thin dress and cardigan she was wearing didn't offer much protection from the biting cold and the snow that was falling all around her.

Once the car left the drive, she walked towards the house. It had been a very long time since she'd first set her sights on this house. She reached the front door, oblivious to the biting cold that was cooling her skin and lifted the dragonfly knocker.

***

The sound as it hit the heavy oak door echoed around the hall. Kate looked across at Ollie who was sitting opposite her.

'There is no way the police have got a warrant in the space of ten minutes. They said themselves they have no grounds. Just ignore it. We aren't expecting any visitors, are we?'

Kate shook her head. 'If it's that important they can come back tomorrow. Anyone else can wait. I want to spend time with my family.'

Ollie reached over for the remote control and turned up the television so they couldn't hear anyone knocking. No one was getting invited into this house tonight.

***

Lilith peeled back her lips, revealing her sharp, white teeth. She turned and walked back down the steps. She may have been cast out for now, but there was something so very special to her about The Convent. As she walked down the drive, leaving her delicate footprints in the snow, she looked back over her shoulder and smiled.

Acknowledgements

I would like to thank my fabulous editor Victoria Oundjian for her patience and guidance; also huge thanks to the rest of the team for making this book what it is.

A big thank you to the lovely Jan Johnson for answering my strange questions without raising an eyebrow.

I'd like to thank my husband Steve for making me write on the days I didn't want to.

My kids for cooking their own meals – trust me, it's much safer that you feed yourselves. I'd like to thank Jerusha for looking after Jaimea so that I can escape to my office and work. You're a little star. I'd also like to say a big thank you to all my writing friends, who are always there with support and guidance.

Thank you to Sam and Tina who are always there when I'm in need of coffee and to talk about real life. I don't know what I'd do without you.

Finally, a huge thank you to my gorgeous Mam and Dad for being the best, most supportive parents a girl could ever wish for. I love you both for ever and always.

If you loved *The Good Sisters* turn the page for an extract
from *The Girls in the Woods*, the fifth Annie Graham thriller

HELEN PHIFER

the
girls
in the
woods

Prologue

Summer 1895

The smell was always the big giveaway – no matter how many fresh flowers were placed around a room, the stench of decomposition would always seep through the cracks. Maybe not at first because the sweet scent from the roses or sweet peas, dependent upon the season, would infiltrate your nostrils with their heady fragrance, but after a few minutes you would realise that the underlying, more cloying scent wasn't such a fragrant one after all. In fact you would more than likely wonder which flower it was that was giving off the almost too sweet, sickly smell. The black cloth covering the large ornamental mirror above the fireplace confirmed what you already knew. That this was a house of death. Upon further investigation as you looked around the room at the waiting subjects one would always stand out just that little bit more than the others; it was always the hands that would give them away. Those petite hands that had once been ivory coloured were now mottled purple and black. The rest of the body, underneath the layers of petticoats, pinafore dresses and thick tights, was probably turning the same colours – but the face you could disguise, if you worked your magic with the thick, heavy, cosmetic face powder.

The three girls were all dressed in identical long white nightgowns; the only flesh showing was their hands, necks and faces. He smiled at the two that were hovering to the side of their dead sister looking uncomfortable; he wouldn't want to have to stand next to a dead person and smile for the camera even if it was his brother. The dead girl was on her own, standing tall in the middle of the room. He tilted his head to see if the heavy, black stand that was holding her decaying body upright could be seen but it was well hidden underneath her nightgown. Although her eyelids were closed someone had drawn open eyes on her lids so she looked as if she was still watching everyone. A life-sized, human doll that would probably be the cause of many years of nightmares for her siblings. Her mother was in the opposite corner being comforted by a much older woman. Both of them dressed all in black. He cleared his throat.

'Should we begin?'

The girls stared at each other, both of them holding hands. It was the older woman who nodded her head. He set his tripod up and placed the heavy camera onto it; a couple of photographs and he would be done. There was a certain beauty about death that he found very attractive but he had never told anyone this; it wouldn't be the right thing to do or say. His wife would be mortified at the thought of him enjoying photographing corpses; she hated that he did it for a living anyway, but if she knew he enjoyed it she would make him stop.

'Mabel, Flora, go and stand either side of your sister.'

He felt a little sorry for the girls, who both looked as if they were about to burst into tears. They were looking at each other and still holding hands.

'Now, please. If you continue to fuss about it the longer it will take – what on earth is wrong with you both?'

Mabel looked the oldest out of the three of them; she implored

Flora with her eyes. He folded his arms across his chest and watched them. Mabel stepped forward pulling the younger girl, who let out a sob.

'Please don't make me touch her; she's cold and she smells. I'm scared – I don't want to stand next to her. Why do we have to do this?'

Her mother looked up from her crumpled handkerchief, surprised by her daughter's outburst of insolence. She didn't need to speak because the girl's grandmother walked across and slapped Flora across the face.

'Stop that at once, child – that is your sister, not some stranger from the street. It is the very last chance your parents have to get a photograph of you all together. Now you will stand next to your sister and smile for the camera before she is taken away and buried.'

The girl stopped speaking but her hand came up and began to rub at the red finger marks that had appeared on her pale, perfect skin. She let Mabel take hold of her shoulders and position her next to the dead girl, then Mabel took her position on the other side. Neither of them looked at their sister. He put his head underneath the cover to take the picture but it was no good. Those red marks on her cheek would stand out on the still when it was developed and it wasn't as if he could arrange to come back and do this all over again; he only had this one chance to get it right. He lifted his head up and walked across the room, taking hold of Flora's shoulders.

'I'm sorry but the mark on your face is too prominent, I need you to turn and face your sister. I promise I'll be quick and you won't have to stay there for very long.'

He didn't think he'd ever forget the look the young girl gave him then; obviously this was a huge ordeal for her. This must be her first brush with death and an experience that would no doubt stay with her for the rest of her life – but her parents had made it quite clear when they asked him to call around yesterday. They could only afford to pay for two stills so he couldn't make any mistakes; these two pictures needed to be perfect. He gently turned her to face the dead girl and could feel her entire body shaking; he then went to Mabel and turned her in a similar position so they were both staring at their sister with what he hoped would be assumed was loving attention and not abject horror. He then went back to his camera and buried his head back underneath the cloth. Holding up the flash he snapped first one, then another still.

'That's it. Thank you for your patience, girls. You can leave now.'

Flora scurried away from the girl that she had no doubt shared a bedroom with for the last twelve years; they had possibly even shared the same bed. How sad that two such close sisters should now be so torn apart by death. Still it wasn't his place to say anything; his job was done here. He would pack his equipment away and go back to his house so he could develop the films. He would of course keep a copy for his own records; he was getting quite a collection in his brown leather book. People were dying of all sorts of diseases, and more and more families wanted their loved ones photographed before they were buried. When he'd taken up photography as a hobby he'd never envisaged that memento mori photography would prove to be such a lucrative business move. He packed up his stuff and carried it out to the waiting horse and carriage; he lived too far away to carry his equipment around town. The grandmother walked him out to the front door, leaving her sobbing daughter alone with her dead granddaughter. The other two girls had run from the room as fast as they could once they had been dismissed; it was indeed sad to watch such grief day in day out, but it was also providing his family with a way of life they could only ever have dreamed of.

'How long will it be before you can bring the pictures?'

'As soon as they are ready I will personally hand deliver them;

it should only take two days but it depends how busy I am tomorrow.'

'Thank you for your time, Mr Tyson. It is very much appreciated.'

He nodded his head then turned and ran down the last few steps and climbed into the waiting carriage. As it pulled away from the side he looked up to see the two girls watching him from the upstairs window. Flora's face was damp, no doubt with the tears she had finally been able to shed, but Mabel looked as if she was weighing him up. Embarrassed they had been caught staring, Mabel stepped back, pulling her sister with her, and he looked straight ahead, pretending he hadn't noticed either of them.

1995

'Beautiful, really beautiful – that's it, hold that position.' The camera flashed several times. 'Gorgeous, you look stunning. So demure yet so damn sexy. I love it.' Heath Tyson walked towards her and pushed her head to the left, just a touch. 'That's it, don't move, we're almost done. You're going to love these pictures; I swear you've never looked so good.' He snapped a few more shots then let his camera drop around his neck and clapped his hands.

'Bravo, bravo. You have been the best model I've ever had. Thank you so much for your patience.'

He walked away towards his dark room, eager to develop his films and add these very special photographs to his secret album. Left lying on the chaise longue, she didn't move to get up and change out of the long, cool, linen nightgown he'd dressed her in. She would stay there until he came and lifted her onto the makeshift trolley he used to push her to and from the freezer in his garage. When he was happy with his photographs he would undress her and put her back inside the cold blackness of the large freezer he'd bought when the village butcher had been closing down. Slamming the metal door, he would lock her in until he had no further use for her or until her body started to decompose too much, whichever came first. Probably the decomposition because he didn't think he would ever get tired of staring at her. There was something so beautiful about death that was never present in the living. Her hands had already begun to turn black despite the freezing temperatures. He wondered why it was they did that – in his collection of Victorian mourning photographs you could always tell the deceased family member by the discoloration of their hands.

It had fascinated him the first time he'd seen a photograph of three sisters, all no older than 15 – he had been 8 years old when he found that photograph album. Heath had been sent to bed but he could hear his father whispering on the phone; he knew he shouldn't be listening in because he shouldn't be out of bed, but he couldn't sleep. He loved his granddad but today's visit had been playing heavily on his mind; his normally fun-filled granddad had been lying in a bed in the front room of his terraced house in the busy town centre street. The smell had been pretty bad; he didn't know what it was but as soon as he'd walked in he'd had to screw his nose up and try not to breathe through it. His mother, who refused to come into the house because she was 'not going to be there when he croaked', was back at home and for once he wished his father had left him at home with her. His older brother didn't care; he had gone straight into the converted front room which was now a bedroom and stood by the frail old man who was asleep. Heath watched the shallow rise and fall of his chest underneath the covers; the rattling sound of the breaths he was struggling to take would stay with him for ever. They could hear their father in the kitchen banging around; he turned away for a split second and when he turned back his brother, who had just celebrated his eleventh birthday, was stroking the old man's hair. Heath shuddered; this wasn't the happy, funny man he remembered and he wanted it all to stop. Their dad came in, his tear-stained face a mask of grief.

'Right you two, go in the kitchen and get yourselves something to eat. I need to sort your granddad out.'

His brother leant down and kissed the man's forehead and Heath tried to force himself to move towards him to do the same but he couldn't. His legs wouldn't move. As his brother walked past he whispered in his ear '*Scaredy cat*'. His dad came over and placed his hands on his shoulders, then pushed Heath out of the room and shut the door behind him. Finally finding his feet, he went into the kitchen where his brother was sitting eating a packet of crisps.

'He's going to pop his clogs any minute.'

'How do you know that?'

'I just do. You wait and see.'

Sometimes he hated how his brother was such a know-it-all. It made him feel stupid and like a big baby. He got himself a packet of crisps out of the cupboard and they both sat on the high stools near the breakfast bar waiting for their dad to come back in. After what seemed like forever he finally did; his eyes were red and he'd been crying. Heath had never seen his dad cry. He walked over and hugged them close to him.

'Your granddad's gone to heaven now; you can both go in and say goodbye.'

This time it was Heath who wanted to go in first – he desperately wanted to see what you looked like when you were dead – and it was his brother who lingered behind. He jumped off his stool and went to the room where the door was ajar. The first thing he noticed was how peaceful it was now that horrible sound his granddad had been making had stopped. He stepped inside. The sheets were no longer moving and he walked closer to look at the man on the bed. The second thing he noticed was how different he looked; his skin looked yellow but it was no longer scrunched up and wrinkled in pain. It was smooth, his mouth was open and his false teeth had slipped down. He'd expected his eyes to be closed but they were open slightly, staring straight ahead. Heath marvelled at how wonderful his granddad looked now he was dead – how much younger. It was amazing. Did everyone who died look like this? His foot kicked something soft and he looked down to see one of the pillows from the bed there. It puzzled him how it had got there; it wasn't there before when they'd been in the room and his granddad hadn't moved at all. His dad must have taken it from under the old man's head but he didn't understand why. He picked it up and felt a warm patch in the middle; placing it on the chair next to the bed he thought nothing of it. It wasn't until some years later when he replayed that last scene in his head that he realised that the pillow was warm in the middle because that was where his granddad's last breaths had gone. He had known all along that the grief his dad had shown had been filled with guilt – but he hadn't known why until his dad's own dying confession had confirmed the sneaking suspicion he'd always held. His dad had been the one to end his granddad's life that morning all those years ago; he could have gone to prison but he'd decided it was worth the risk. The only regret that Heath had was that he'd had no means to photograph how wonderful his granddad looked, more wonderful than he ever did when he was alive. It was as if his true inner beauty had been revealed and it was something Heath never forgot; in fact he thought about it an awful lot. When most kids his age had been playing with action men or cap guns, he had spent all his time locked in his bedroom wondering how he could see more dead people.

There was a certain beauty in death which could not be achieved at any cost in life, even with the amount of plastic surgeons and cosmetic surgery available. When he was ten years old he knew that he wanted to be a photographer but he did have a backup plan. He would probably one day become a funeral director if his photography didn't take off but his one passion in life was photography. What he really wanted to do was photograph the dead. He didn't really want to have to deal with the grieving families; he just wanted to photograph their loved ones like his great, great grandfather had back in the Victorian days. It had

335

been quite normal back then, but if you told anyone now that you liked photographing the dead they'd lock you up and throw away the key. There were some things you didn't admit to and getting your rocks off over corpses was almost certainly one. He spent hours locked in his room studying the photos in the album they'd found when clearing their granddad's house out. Luckily for him, he'd been on his own in the bedroom when he found the dusty album at the back of the wardrobe, wrapped in faded yellow newspapers. His brother had gone to the tip with his dad and a car boot full of their granddad's belongings. At first he hadn't realised just what it was he was looking at but he knew there was something strange about the pictures in the album. It had *Memento Mori* in gold letters engraved into the soft brown leather cover. He'd had no idea what that meant, but would try and find out. There was no one in the pictures that he knew and they looked as if they were very old. Not wanting his dad to throw it out on his next visit to the local tip, Heath ran downstairs and stuffed it into his backpack. It was his secret, and he wouldn't tell anyone about it – not even his brother. Well, not unless he was going to help him somehow find dead people to take pictures of. That photograph album had started this obsession with death, be it in male or female form – although he much preferred females; they were so much more elegant and prettier than men. His warped obsession with death had now resulted in the dead girl in front of him.

She was his first and quite possibly his last; it was too risky. He'd briefly considered the implications before it all happened but he hadn't realised just how seriously a missing teenager would be taken. He thought they'd assume she'd run away and that would be that – the reality had been far different. The police had been crawling all over the village, surrounding fields and woods looking for the missing girl who had been on her way to visit her friend who lived at the opposite side of the village. It had scared him, seeing the crowds of villagers that had gathered with their dogs and the many police officers who'd been drafted in to search for her. He'd known her since he had moved back to the village he'd lived in as a child and set up his business, taking her first photographs when she had been seven. Then every year since until she was seventeen. Sharon Sale had come to him alone this time, asking him to take some photos she could send off to a modelling agency, only he wasn't to tell her parents because they would freak. She had told him she would pay him but he had shook his head, telling her that he would do it for her if she would do a big favour for him and she'd agreed. Perhaps if she'd known what it was he'd wanted she would have run away as fast as she could and never come back. He knew her by her name, just like he knew all the local children that the parents brought to him for their portraits to be taken.

It had been two weeks now and he deemed it safe enough to take her to the woods behind the cottage and bury her. He had already dug a deep grave in the early hours this morning; it had taken him hours but it had been worth it because the woods had been searched three times now, by police, the villagers (including himself) and then searched again with sniffer dogs. Yesterday they had publicly declared that they thought the girl had left the area. He wished he could keep her for ever but if they did come looking, how would he explain to them that he had a dead girl in the freezer in his garage? It was far too risky; he was a patient man and was happy enough to wait until the fuss died down, even if took a couple of years, before he tried it again. At least now he had started his own collection of photographs of the dead, and it was a work in progress – the best works of art weren't achieved in a day. He would wait until the opportunity arose and it was the right time to do it all over again. He had no doubt that soon enough another girl with big ambitions of becoming a model would turn up at his doorstep and when they did he would be ready.

Chapter 1

Annie Ashworth let out a sigh and turned on her side. The heat from the late afternoon sun was warming her skin and even though she'd tried her best to keep out of the direct sunlight she still had a warm, golden glow. Her husband, Will, had a deep, bronze tan, his normally clean-shaven chin was covered in dark stubble and his dark blond hair had lightened considerably with the sun. He looked the picture of complete health and happiness but she knew different. He was lying on his side with his back to her and her eyes fell on the angry, red scar which ran across his right kidney. It would take a long time for it to fade into oblivion and when it did she hoped the memories would go with it. She was so lucky he was still alive, that they both were.

She shivered at the thought of that man, Henry Smith, and his accomplice, Megan. What she would have given to have watched their bodies being brought up from the cellar of Beckett House in black body bags and wheeled out to the waiting private ambulances. But she'd had to go with Will; he had been so badly injured and she had needed to be by his side. Jake, her best friend and colleague, had stayed along with Cathy and Kav, their inspector and sergeant when they were both stationed back in Barrow, to watch on their behalf. They had brought Megan up first because her body had been the most straightforward to bag up. She'd fallen down the cellar steps from top to bottom at Beckett House and instantly broken her neck. Henry, though, had got what he deserved. That strange man/monster thing had sliced his throat open with its long sharp claws but not before Annie had watched the terror on Henry's face as he had stuck his knife into its strange, grey body. Jake had told her when he came to see her in the hospital that even Matt the pathologist had been horrified to see the mess of blood and limbs. No one had ever seen anything like the strange creature that lived in the drains below Beckett House, and it had been badly injured by Henry because there had been a trail of blood which led to the huge drain in the corner of the cellar – but then it had disappeared. Search teams had been brought in with special infra red and thermal imaging cameras and apart from a trail of blood that stopped suddenly in the sewers there had been no trace of it. Annie suspected that it had gone deep underground to another lair and either died or gone into hibernation. She hoped for Martha Beckett's sake that it had curled up and died. The last time she had spoken with the elderly woman she had arranged to have the drain filled in with concrete and the cellar door permanently sealed shut. She had told Annie about the long letter she had written detailing the history of the house and everything that had happened there. She had given it to her solicitor with strict instructions that when the day came that someone was eager enough to buy Beckett House they would be given a copy of the letter so they were fully aware of the circumstances. It had made Martha feel much better but Annie knew that the house would be snapped up by some property developer who wouldn't be remotely interested in the letter or the history of Beckett House. They would turn it into luxury apartments and move on to the next project. Annie just hoped that history wouldn't repeat itself and no one with small children moved in there. All of this had been kept hush, hush and out of the media for the sake of Martha who had kept the terrible secret of the thing hidden for years. One day they could make a film about what happened at Beckett House; it was that horrific no one would ever believe it was all true.

She picked up her Kindle. It was amazing how Will could lie there for hours and not get bored. Turning to face her he smiled as his hand reached out for hers and she held it tight. His fingers trailed across the baby bump and he let them rest there.

'I thought you were asleep again.'

'What do you mean, again?' He opened one eye and winked at her, 'I'm just making the most of the last day before we have to go back to reality. I've been thinking about it, and you know I'll have to go back to work soon, don't you?'

She nodded, wishing they could stay here – cocooned on this island for ever, away from the madness that seemed to take over their lives on a regular basis.

'I know you do, but are you ready to go back? I mean they couldn't exactly say no if you had a bit longer off, could they? You almost…'

She couldn't say the words because it set her heart racing every time she thought about what had happened at the Lake House where she'd almost lost him.

'I think I'm ready, Annie. As much as I love spending time with you I'm getting a bit fidgety, restless. I need to be doing something a bit more challenging with my life than pottering around pretending everything is okay.'

She knew how he felt – she was on restricted duties because she was six months pregnant and she was bored, bored, bored. Although she was glad to be away from the prying eyes of the public and every weirdo that seemed to be attracted to her, she still liked to do her job.

'If you're ready that's fine; I'm just being completely selfish but I love having you around. Although I suppose you're bound to start getting on my nerves sooner or later.'

She winked at him and he shoved her arm. Jumping up he bent down and kissed her lips then he moved further down and kissed her swollen stomach.

'I thought I was already getting on your nerves; you were a right grump before we came on holiday.'

'Well, maybe just a little; you know I like my own space and I was getting fed up of doing nothing myself. But I've forgiven you because you brought me here.'

'So it was a good choice coming here?'

'Yes, probably the best idea you've ever had apart from marrying me. I'd never even thought about Hawaii until you showed it to me on the internet. It's so perfect, just how I imagined paradise to be. Could you imagine living here? It must be so wonderful.'

He smiled and she knew that he loved to please her and she also knew she was very lucky that both of them were still alive to be here enjoying this perfect holiday.

'Come on, how about we take a dip then go and get ready for tea?'

She held her hand out for him to pull her up, tucking her Kindle under her towel.

'I'm starving.'

Will laughed, 'Funnily enough I thought you might say that; after all it's been, what, two hours since you last ate?'

'You know I'm feeding for two; it's the only time I'll ever have an excuse to eat what I want without worrying.'

'You could eat for three for all I care; as long as you're happy then so am I.'

They walked hand in hand towards the crystal blue ocean which was gently lapping at the sand. She didn't hear her phone which was at the bottom of her beach bag ringing; she'd switched it to silent – in fact she hadn't bothered to look at it for days. She wasn't bothered about telling the whole world on Facebook what she was doing every single second of the day, unlike most of her friends. They walked into the water, which made her yelp at the coldness. Will began to splash around and she sank into the water and began swimming, relishing the sudden change in temperature which cooled her warm skin. Further down she could see the beach was full of people but their hotel had its own private beach which was never busy. Even their ground-floor room had sliding patio doors which looked out onto a lush green lawn, with palm trees towering above to provide shade from the constant heat. It also had the shortest walk to the Pacific Ocean she could imagine. When Will had booked this holiday he had thought about everything, knowing that if it was hot she wouldn't feel like walking far. Her phone kept on ringing in the bottom of her bag but oblivious to it she began to swim towards the floating sundeck not far from the shore, to work up an appetite before they went back to get ready to go out and make the most of their last evening together in paradise.

DIGITAL HQ

If you enjoyed *The Good Sister* then why not try another gripping from HQ Digital?

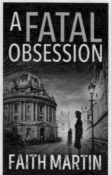